SONG OF REDEMPTION

MALIKA J. STEVELY

MJS PUBLISHING LAB

ISBN: [Ebook] 978-0-578-34393-8
ISBN: [Hardcover] 978-0-578-33653-4
ISBN: [Paperback] 979-8-218-54816-2
ISBN: [Audiobook] 979-8-218-59504-3

For information about special discounts for bulk purchases, contact MJS Publishing Lab at info@mjspublishinglab.com

MJS Publishing Lab can bring authors to your live event. For information or to book an author, contact info@mjspublishinglab.com, or visit www.mjspublishinglab.com.

SONG OF REDEMPTION

To the once-enslaved men and women whose words and songs were silenced. May your stories be kept alive and forever tuned to my heartstrings.

A Note from the Author

Song of Redemption was developed at a time when the torch of Family Historian had been passed to me. As I walked amid the soil of my family tree and into the footsteps of my ancestors who were enslaved, their experiences breathed life more vibrantly into my connection to the protagonist, Danielle, offering a better understanding of the psychology behind the decisions of a teenager in bondage. Just as I began to feel the presence of my ancestors around me as people who were once of flesh and strength rather than single names and ages on slave documents, Danielle too became more than just a description of her demise. I was able to unpeel the things that made her smile, fearful, and passionate, and imagined what she may have wanted out of life. This made me embrace the gifts that I was once guilty of taking for granted, such as the layers of freedom and what sovereignty may have looked like for her compared to what is granted to Black women in today's society.

The creation of this story has been in the works longer than I wish to admit. There were times when I was convinced that I had writer's block and would put the novel aside and allow life and unforeseen circumstances to carry me away to other tasks and responsibilities. I later learned that time was a blessing because I needed to mature, gain certain life experiences, and become a mother before I could fully understand the magnitude surrounding the circumstances of many of the characters and comprehend the choices that many enslaved individuals were forced to make. It was never in my nature to abandon any composition, and I never intended to do so with *Song of Redemption*. Even if I wanted to, something or someone would never allow it and would continue to tug at my daydreams, pleading for me to finish the work.

In a moment of self-reflection, I faced the battle within myself that I did not realize I was fighting. I learned that I was avoiding writing and immortalizing the most painful parts of Danielle's journey (parts that could potentially become triggers for some readers). This meant I would have to visualize and almost feel a sliver of what she experienced. There were even times when I questioned whether there were some incidents Danielle would not want shared. Putting my selfishness aside and revisiting my commitment to tell the story allowed me to be in a state of vulnerability that I had never experienced, and one that overpowered my fears. And it was then that I was able to walk alongside Danielle and other characters in laughter, mourning, or jubilation.

When preparing to write *Song of Redemption*, it was extremely difficult to transport myself into a world where certain words, phrases, and ideas were acceptable. It was especially challenging as a mother, an African American, a woman, and a wife to an African American man, to fathom the concurrence of blatant laws and systems that allowed an elite group to have power over the lives of other human beings and their families. As painful as it was to insert myself into such a time frame that many Americans experienced, it was necessary in order to construct, in this novel, an authentic reflection of what our country used to be.

Numerous outdated and offensive terms and epithets float throughout the book to describe women and Black characters. Historically, words such as colored, wench, Negro, Mulatto, and the "n-word" were often used in casual and formal discussions, periodicals, and advertisements, illustrating the harsh, yet realistic, period in time. Today, some people work hard to lessen the bitter taste of less savory acts in US history. But I imagine it to be difficult to fully accept a nation if I chose to only celebrate its accomplishments and sweep aside its monstrosities, such as systematic slavery and the prohibition of female empowerment. We owe it to younger generations to acknowledge and correct what was to "keep moving forward," as Alphonse Santee says in the book. If we opt to candy-coat or mute the voices of those who lived long ago, then the residue of the past is bound to be inherited by our future.

For as long as I can recall, the definition of Creole has been a general sempiternal debate. I remember sitting in a college literature class discussing stories that featured Creole characters. The footnotes of the book offered its definition as early Louisianans mixed with French and Spanish heritage. The teacher would confirm its truth by proclaiming the definitive meaning of Creole as all the student sponges made black or blue notes of it in their binders. Being the only Black student and one with ties to Louisiana and Creole culture, I executed my normal response in many of my college courses where information was skewed; I raised my hand and verbally questioned the accuracy of the textbook (as I had learned at an early age, who tells your story and how it is told matters).

In actuality, Creole, the people, are the descendants of Louisiana's early French settlers. While the French-speaking settlers distinguished themselves from other whites within Louisiana, they also partitioned themselves from Cajuns, and definitely the Black families with whom were created by Creole men. I would further mention in class that day that not once was there recognition in that textbook, that there were and are, Creoles of color. My paternal grandmother was Creole. In my world, white Creoles were rarely mentioned because while they were our family, they represented former ownership of it. And at the time, there was not enough information about them to warrant a valuable conversation. Therefore, any mention regarding Creoles as a definition was restricted to what we knew best, our family and Prince who some may argue was not Creole.

In *Song of Redemption*, there are subtle displays of the exclusivity of Creoles. But at most, Creoles and Creoles of color are recognized, speaking a gumbo of languages that toggle between English and

French (rather than the Cajun-French that some Creoles spoke within specific regions). The Blacks and Creoles of color within the novel, however, have the advantage of speaking French and English. Some of the Black Creole characters infuse Kouri-Vini into their conversations. Kouri-Vini, also known as Louisiana Creole, is an endangered language typically spoken in specific regions of the Bayou Teche, deeply merging West African and French tongues.

Often, when we read or see films surrounding the topic of slavery, we learn about incidents that took place on the plantation, compounded with brutality and sometimes death. While these occurrences were common, it was not the only experience of all who were enslaved. What about African Americans who were seized by banks, were slaves on college campuses, exploited at circuses? It was important to me that this novel illustrates that the institution of slavery was not only confined to a plantation, or even a single family but expanded into various regions of opportunity where owners and companies saw profit and capitalized off free labor in every aspect of the 19th century.

While it is not often discussed, many Blacks were faced with not knowing or defining their own identity during and after slavery. As slave schedules and other historical documents have illustrated, most people in bondage did not have an official last name. Some gave themselves the surname of their owners or the last owner they had, usually to maintain what family unit they had left. After emancipation, some kept the last names of their previous owners in hopes of reuniting with separated relatives. It also helped to indicate where someone was from or where they may have resided. Others changed their surnames entirely, hoping to disassociate themselves from former slaveholders and/or reclaim their identities. On rare occasions, a slave owner might give his or her surname to his or her property. While this act was usually reserved for a slaveholder acknowledging his lineage to a slave, it was not customary or widely documented, however, it did occur.

My mother is a registered nurse who specialized in home health care for over 25 years. Through her, I have met incredible people who shared phenomenal stories of their lives. Some decided certain chapters were too painful to discuss but kept the tattooed numbers on their arms as reminders.

Many years ago, the story of Danielle was told to me by a patient of my mother's, who has since passed away. It was her father who discovered Danielle's body while working with his construction crew when refurbishing a mansion in Louisiana. The story remained etched in my mind, giving me the overwhelming need to write it down, for fear that it would never be shared with the world, or worse, forgotten. I needed to be the one to share Danielle's story, give it the care it deserved, and help provide the voice she never had.

While this novel is inspired by true events, I intricately interlaced findings based on personal and historical sources of the time and setting. I presumed motives and character backstories for narrative flow. Legislation, especially as it pertained to tightening the limitations of "free" people of color, seemed to shift minute-by-minute, pushing the battered liberties of Blacks closer to the edge of cliffs. What a free man could accomplish in one part of Louisiana, could get him killed in another. And what body of water a Black mariner was allowed to dwell near in one state had its repercussions across other nautical boundaries. While it was extremely important for me to tell this story with fine accuracy, I truly hope that any liberties I have taken with this work of literature are forgiven.

Song of Redemption

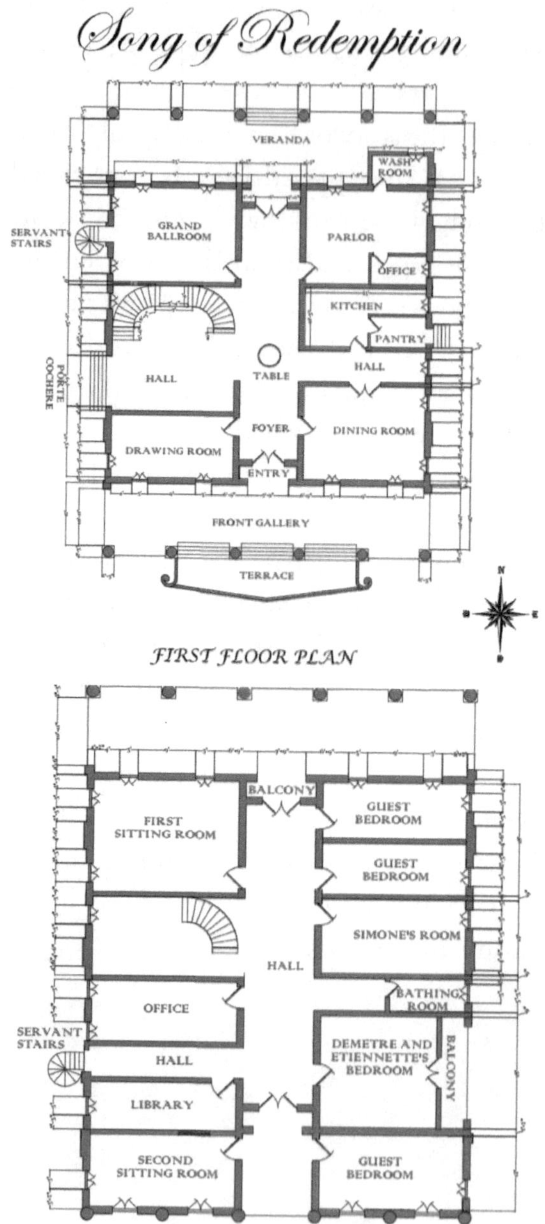

FIRST FLOOR PLAN

SECOND FLOOR PLAN

One

Lafayette, Louisiana
Summer 1932

The dryness of sawdust and plywood in the once-abandoned mansion intertwined with the thick humidity of the summer's morning. Ordinarily, the foul-mouthed employees of Thibodeaux's Construction & Contracting Company would entertain each other with exaggerated stories of loose women and dramatic poker parties. Feeling as if they had cannon-balled into a nearby swamp, the workers continued ripping away dry rot and reviewing floor plans. Within the second-floor sitting room in the east wing of the antebellum mansion, they secretly wished for a radio but settled for the diminishing shouts of paperboys in the distance.

"Looks like another day of rain," Diaz observed, breaking the silence and rearranging his tool belt by the window.

"Yeah, feels like another storm is coming," answered Johnson, removing square nails from a wooden plank on the floor.

"The wind was so strong it almost knocked my drawers off this mornin'," said Collin, resting on the floor against a wall and with a flask in his right hand.

"Too bad it didn't," chuckled Johnson, "it would've given you an excuse to slip a fresh pair on your pale bald ass for once."

"How do you know that his butt is pale?" Stephens joked.

"Or bald?" Diaz laughed.

The men flinched when hearing a crack in the sky followed by the beating of rain. Collin pushed a tin pail toward a corner with his left foot to catch the drops of water from the leaky ceiling. He eyed the area of the room, thinking that it looked slightly different than the sitting room in the west wing. On the floor plan, Collin remembered that the upstairs sitting rooms were designed to be identical. He measured the room a second time to make any necessary changes to the floor plan. He began with the wall behind him, whipping out his measuring tape and lodging his flask in a pocket of his tool belt.

He measured a corner of the wall that protruded like a tall, rectangular box that was smoothed with the rest of the wall. Collin thought that it was too narrow to have been a closet in its earlier years. He would have concluded that the wall-covered pipes or electrical wires added by the mansion's owners a little after the turn of the century had he not seen strands of hair coming out of the wall's corner. He reached for his flask and took a swig while tugging at the hair, only to discover that some of the strands were getting longer. He picked away at the many layers of faded paint with his nails before finally reaching a plaster-type substance that someone had covered over wooden slabs that had since rotted. The longer he chipped away at the paint, the more strands he discovered—now a crumpled ball of curly locks in his palm.

"Somebody, come over here and take a look! Hurry!" Collin shouted, dropping his flask in fear. The men raced to his side, eager to see his findings. They stared at the wall, afraid to say what was on their minds, but somehow knowing what the other was thinking.

"I'm knockin' it down," said Stephens, grabbing a sledgehammer. "Stand back now!" He took a swing at the wall, trying to avoid damaging whatever might be behind it. Little by little, pieces of the wall crumpled as if the sound was a response to the shutters slamming back and forth, surrendering to the violent wind. Pieces of a deteriorated hand-carved door lapsed behind the plaster with its once intact side bolt flipping near one of the men's feet.

When every bit of the wall had fallen—when all of the dust had cleared—when the men shielded their mouths and noses from the heavy tart smell, the workers felt as if their hearts had stopped beating for an instant. It was then that they saw the remains of a small woman sitting in a roundabout chair whose hands and feet had been bound with rope, and her mouth, covered with what used to be a handkerchief. Her hair had grown, even in death, straggling down to the floor and curling up again, like ivy around the gate of a forgotten residence. There were small mountains of dust surrounding her, and her long fingernails had yellowed. Along with the rope and handkerchief, her clothes, engorged with rotten bodily fluid, were rugged and torn but seemed to be garments of a servant who lived many decades ago.

"There's something around her neck," Diaz said lightly, swallowing after his statement. Johnson stepped closer to the corpse than any of the men had cared to, before coughing and covering his nose and mouth with his shirt. He discovered that the diamond-shaped object around her neck was not a necklace as he had thought, but a badge. He cleaned away the dust and other particles on the flat piece of metal with his thumb before the words appeared before him:

Lafayette Paroisse, Louisiane 1859
Esclave Domestique, Plantation Soileau
(Lafayette Parish, Louisiana 1859
House Slave, Soileau Plantation)

Cold ripples slid down the spines of some of the men as the shutters banged heavily against the windows and the rain rapped aggressively on the roof. "What sick bastard would do this?" asked Collin over the bellowing wind.

Within hours, journalists and a few photographers from northern gazettes, weeklies, and quarterlies learned of the contractors down south who discovered the corpse of a woman who had been severely punished in a heartless manner. What she had done to receive such punishment remained a mystery. Before they could dig up unsolved cases of missing women, in Louisiana, reporters learned that she was a "Coloured" slave, and soon, for some, sympathy shifted. But as word spread through newspapers and people with ties to the parish, to one 81-year-old woman, the discovery was a distressed blessing that she waited years to confront.

* * *

The old woman sat anxiously in the passenger seat of the 1930 A-Model Ford. Her nervousness ceased when looking out of the window and recognizing areas of her former home that now contained stores, restaurants, and a bakery rather than the wooded areas she remembered. She smiled a little when seeing the large burgundy movie theater sign with a marquee promoting an Our Gang short and a Laurel and Hardy film. This reminded her that she still wanted to see the talkie, The Girl from Chicago. She stared at the theater until her neck could no longer withstand the strain, for she marveled at the modern technology and the moving picture shows used to entertain and inform an audience. She blinked twice when seeing a pretty, white woman in a large hat who resembled Mademoiselle Simone. She stood fanning herself as she looked in the window of a clothing store. When the young lady turned to walk on, the senior realized she was mistaken and quickly looked away to avoid eye contact.

"Grandma Lettie?" said the young man driving the vehicle, covered in sweat. "You mind if I roll down the windows? I think we just entered the devil's armpit."

Lettie chuckled, "That'll be fine, Charles," she said as she looked up at the sky. "But you will have to roll them up soon, rain is coming." Her face became serious as the earthy aroma of a nearby river became stronger. A wave of memories crashed her thoughts, forcing her to recall quivering with fear as a child on that same body of water. To distract herself, she slid over a copy of The Negro Traveler's Green Book that sat in the seat next to her and grabbed one of the many newspapers beneath it and began to read.

Most newspapers shared comparable stories related to the effects of the stock market crash, and many fought to uncover a "refreshing change" in subject to boost sales and the curiosity of its readers. "A Real-Life Story of *The Cask of Amontillado*," read one of the headlines. Others tried to force an unsuccessful link between the occurrence of Delphine LaLaurie and her craving for the torture of her slaves. Some periodicals apathetically offered readers five dollars for anyone who could create the best essay that might explain the reasoning behind the slaves' fate. Some state residents urged the media to "go about their business," claiming that findings such as this, slave graveyards, and even spirit sightings often attracted the wrong type of tourists who disregarded the heart and history of Louisiana. A civil rights organization criticized local Parish officials who allowed the remains of a human being to be displayed like a freak show on the opening day of a circus for financial gain from incoming travelers.

It began to rain as Lettie and Charles drove past polished Confederate monuments crafted with care and funded upkeep. The statues triumphed in nostalgic glory in nearby counties surrounding the debris-covered slave cemeteries in various towns. However, as preparations were being made to place the nameless slave in an unmarked tomb among others deemed forgotten, many locals visited the secured mansion, hoping to get a glimpse of the small woman. Lettie frowned at the line of people waiting to get inside on the final day of the exhibition and despised those who allowed them in.

Charles parked under a large oak tree away from other cars and helped his grandmother out of the vehicle, holding an umbrella over her. She looked around at the plantation, able to see the field and hear the refinery, now a dilapidated building and home for wildlife. She scanned for her old cabin when the slave graveyard left her transfixed.

"Mrs. Dubois?" said a man approaching wearing a suit of light material, removing his hat. Lettie turned and nodded at him. "I'm Nelson Athens from the historic commission," he said, offering a handshake to Charles and shaking Lettie's gloved hand. "A couple of the state archeological officials are inside studying the home. When you said in your telegram that you were one of the last survivors of the Soileau Plantation, I immediately wanted to meet you. I must admit, I don't know much about this land. The previous owners did a good job hiding any information about it." Lettie looked away as if searching for someone or something. Nelson continued, "I believe your telegram said that you had something to show me?"

Charles responded for Lettie. "Yes, she does. Show him, Grand-mommy," he said, softly placing his hand on her arm. From her tooled leather handbag, Lettie retrieved an exact match of the old slave badge worn around the deceased woman's neck.

Nelson's eyes widened. "Well," he said. "Right this way. We have all been expecting you." He escorted the family toward the house, where onlookers whispered to one another. Lettie motioned toward the back entrance of the mansion. "No ma'am," said Nelson, "you're going to enter through the front with me."

The senior clutched her purse and the arm of her grandson, who held tight to her arm and wet sweater as Nelson and an officer escorted them up the grand staircase. She gazed around the house, remembering a bright home full of life and extravagant possessions—a home smelling of fresh fruit year-round, and several guests filling the spaces in the rooms with laughter. She could still see Madame Etiennette admiring the locked mahogany cabinet filled with her inherited collection of muskets and other firearms that she sneakily used for sport when her husband was away on "business."

The old woman almost felt, once again, the sweaty gust of Monsieur Demetre's bruised and bloodied nephew storming through the servant's entrance after raping a male slave, Rubar, in the barn one evening. With graying irises, the old woman peered around the house once more, noticing the decayed, stained burgundy wallpaper covered with faded blue flowers. How the mansion withstood hurricanes and floods years before served as a testament to the skill possessed by the slaves she knew by name. The air tasted warm, bitter, and musty. Indeed, the house was dead, and the old lady almost delighted in its demise until a blink of lightning startled her. "Watch your step Grandmommy," said her grandson.

"I used to run up and down these stairs with ease, now look at me," she told the men. They paused when they heard a roll of thunder but pressed on.

Before turning the corner to enter the sitting room, the elderly woman took a deep breath but could not contain the shivers in her body. "You don't have to do this," said her grandson. "We can go back home to Chicago—"

"No, Charles," she exclaimed, removing her white gloves. She released his arm and turned the corner, where she first saw a guard, two men from the state archeological office, and three reporters taking notes and blocking the woman's view of the corpse. Charles quickly galloped to her side and caught hold of her arm. The reporters noticed the old woman approaching slowly and stepped aside, watching her closely. She stood before the remains longer than any of the tourists had previously, with an expression absent of fear or disgust as others illustrated. Her face shifted from sorrow to anger, and back to sadness, yet she was unable to make a sound other than a grunt, which seemed to get stuck in her throat occasionally. Strangely, the old woman was thankful that the body had not been secretly discarded just as the remains of many Negroes and slaves had been that were discovered in other states by contracting companies during new building developments. For as she knew too well, some Negro or slave cemeteries in their path were deemed inconvenient, blocking progress, and setting back deadlines. But the body that sat before the woman was still a spectacle—another undignified display, even more personal than the swinging bodies in trees that she had seen after the picnics and lynching parties had dispersed.

As a photographer's Kodak flash lit up the room, newspaper images of Blacks beaten and sometimes burned at the stake invaded her memory. The sight of adult mobs in black and white pointing at the bodies of the accused with boys and girls grinning at the camera like the grown-ups had done, remained printed in the woman's soul. The smiles at the perceived animal that was killed in sport let her know what her life and those of many others who shared her color were worth to some. The woman looked down at the hardwood floor. "She had a name," she said softly.

"Pardon?" Nelson said as the others also glared at the woman.

Her glazed eyes produced slow, tiny tears. "She had a name," she repeated louder, looking each man in the eyes.

"Grandma Lettie?" Charles whispered. "Would you like to sit down?" The woman said nothing. "Grandmommy, are you okay?"

She finally looked away and nodded insecurely. She spoke somberly, "I survived the effects of the Civil War. I survived the Yellow Fever epidemic. I remained strong when my mother passed on." She placed one hand over her mouth and clenched her eyes shut. "But I don't know how to handle this," she continued. "After all these years."

"How well did you know this woman?" a journalist asked aloofly.

"Sir, please. Don't bother her with questions at this moment," Charles begged, holding his hand up to the reporters.

"Oh," whispered the reporter to another. "One of those uppity Negroes."

The lady sniffled and placed her hand on top of her grandson's. "Baby, remember where we are," she lightly hummed to Charles. She walked several feet away from the corpse and stopped. "I think I would like to sit after all," she said aloud. An officer quickly grabbed a chair and helped the lady into it. The thunder rolled madly, while tree branches slapped against the windows. A reporter sat near her as others stood and began to interview her after writing her name on a notepad—Mrs. Alette P. Dubois. One even made note of the long scar down her cheek.

Mrs. Dubois turned her head toward the body just enough, as if to obtain final confirmation of the woman's identity, but was too afraid to hold her gaze. She looked away and down, more tears falling onto her coarse, wrinkled hands that mapped a lifetime's journey of all that stung, yet all that was darling. She whispered through the breaking of her voice, "Cover her, please," she said. "Please?" she begged one of the guards, who did not move right away but could see the prayer behind the old woman's eyes. He carefully covered the body with the white sheet that lay at the feet of the corpse.

One journalist observed, "You seem to have been very fond of the woman."

"Yes," the old lady said with a brief smile that exposed a tiny dimple in the corner of her mouth. "I admired her greatly."

"What did she look like?" Another reporter asked, hoping for a description strong enough to produce a drawing.

"Like an angel," Mrs. Dubois said, remembering the woman. "I had a daguerreotype of her once, but it was destroyed."

"Do you know who might have done this to her?" a journalist asked.

Mrs. Dubois did not verbalize her thoughts at that moment, although the pain on her face spoke for her. The thunder rolled even greater than it had before, alarming each person in the room who tried to regain their composure.

"Mrs. Dubois," another journalist said, "It appears that you know more than you're letting on. What could she have done to deserve this kind of punishment?" another asked.

Conditioned by her past and the idea that her words are always on trial, the old woman could not trust that her truth would be accepted by the room of white men. She certainly did not want to expose everything to strangers who, with a stroke of a pen, could conform her story to their own perception. She looked at her grandson, who waited to hear her response, realizing how little she had shared with him about the occurrences on the Soileau Plantation and her life with the woman whose body she traveled so far to identify. Mrs. Dubois sighed deeply and shot out an answer before she could stop herself from speaking. "I'm afraid that is something that haunts me to this day," Mrs. Dubois whispered, blankly staring over at the bound woman in the chair. The rain created heavy pats on the first and second-floor verandahs like fistfuls of marbles dropping to the surface. The line of spectators began to yell over the turbulent weather as they dispersed. The gust picked up, winding and weeping severely, causing a blackout of the construction light strings and leaving the elderly lady and the men to sit near the dead woman's body in complete darkness.

Lafayette Parish, Louisiana
Summer 1859

Danielle swiftly struck a match alongside the poorly crafted dressing table her father had made for her before being carted away to a man in Missouri. For a moment, the orange glow seemed to immerse the small cabin and later dimmed, but not without keeping what little glow it had on the looking glass and the soft features of the young woman who stood before it. She lit several of the dipped candles that sat on the table, then stared angrily at the reflection of the girl in front of her. Long loose curls framed the beautiful face that Mademoiselle Simone often said could be mistaken for the face of a French duchess, "If only it weren't the light brown colour it is," she'd add.

She straightened the diamond-shaped piece of tin that she wore upon a strap of leather like a necklace. The only piece of jewelry she owned and treasured was a small, invaluable cracked cameo, secretly given to her as a gift from Monsieur Demetre after several nights of lovemaking.

The young woman inhaled deeply as she peered once more at her full image in the looking glass. She only hoped that her hazel eyes were deceiving her as she noticed that her hair draped past her shoulders and down to her swollen belly. For nearly six months, she never cared to look at such a tender part of her anatomy, although she could hardly ignore it. To Danielle, it seemed to grow with each breath she took. Her stomach sat low as if it was eager to push out the child on its own. A plump-lipped frown sculpted onto her face as she felt the infant kick and move onto its side. She turned away from the mirror furiously, not knowing whether to cast slurs at the innocent babe who occupied her body for shelter, the man who helped to conceive it, or herself, the mother who cannot fully reject the love she carries for the unborn child she never wanted.

Danielle suddenly remembered that she was ordered to be at "the big house" promptly at 6 pm. According to the petite pocket watch she always stashed in her apron, she had twenty minutes to dash across 60 acres of land. She took one last look at her bulging figure, tucked a small obsidian stone into her apron pocket, blew out the candles, and rushed out of her cabin.

The 300-acre Soileau Plantation was encircled with an abundance of beautiful trees and mixed rich vegetation from seeds and buds imported from France and Saint-Martin. It made up one-half of the Soileau & Sons empire, a company created by Master Demetre's late father and run by his heirs and board members, producing fine rum, sugar, and molasses. Refined sugar cascaded into the teacups of thousands of Soileau & Sons' consumers from overseas and northern and southern regions of the United States. Occasional letters of protest from abolitionists warning Demetre of the immoral acts of enslaving human beings for the exploitation of their free labor made their way into the hands of the slaveholder and eventually into the garbage, neglecting to be mentioned to the board. While Demetre and his sole remaining brother, Emile, found it best over the years to discuss business in person, when necessary, they mutually stood by their decision to remain brothers at a distance.

The plantation that Mademoiselle Simone affectionately referred to as "Father's pseudo heavenly kingdom" was inhabited by a mixture of more than 150 one-name slaves with broken families or none at all. Some of whom were Black Caribbeans and Americans, mixed Senegalese and Native Americans with lineage reaching from the Greater Antilles, and "Creoles of Color." The faces of a few elders occupied heavy wrinkles and troubles that made way for the tribal markings they acquired in their youth—reminders of who they are and the people with whom they hope to reunite someday.

The language among the fields swayed like the willows, shifting from Creole French to English. However, the slaves who spoke proper French, the dominant language in the big house, were accused of being "chesty." They each had their moments of torturous days and nights that brought about heartaches, but many believed, as they had been told, that this was their destiny. It was understood, to some, that the best way to survive was to find something—anything—to smile or laugh about.

The sugar plantation was full of activity, as it always was on long-awaited Saturday evenings before the Sabbath. Thunderous debates and music drowned out the many "Bonjours" Danielle offered to others in front of their homes who were shelling peas, braiding hair, and crafting furniture. "Bonjour, Chantal," she said, waving at a slender young lady from afar who conversed among a group of women.

Chantal squinted before recognizing the pregnant figure. "Oh, Bonjour!" Chantal shouted with an artificial grin. "You're looking well today! Take care! ... Arrogant whore," she murmured to her giggling friends. Danielle sensed that they were jealously poking fun at her but decided that a response or a mere look in their direction would be a waste of her time.

The sun, disregarding its job to set completely, beat upon Danielle's neck as she raced through the green pastures and woodlands, swatting at gnats and hungry mosquitoes on the way, before finally arriving at the big house, barely making it at 6 p.m. No matter how pressed for time she was, she always admired the white mansion, bordered with pink roses, wrapped with massive Doric columns and double-tiered galleries. As a little girl, she heard stories of kings and queens and Prince Charmings in dynamic castles and always pictured this home in her mind. Throughout her seventeen years of life, Danielle had seen many homes among neighboring plantations, but she held a prejudice.

For no house could compare to the architectural essence and beauty of the Soileau mansion.

She entered the house through the back of the kitchen. "Just in time," said Corrine, a fellow house servant, searching for something within the room. Danielle washed her hands and fell into her duties, helping Corrine assemble a tray of food. Corrine allowed Danielle to catch her breath before asking, "How is your brother? You have not spoken much about him these days."

"He's...Alysaundre—ornery as ever," Danielle shrugged. "He's gotten worse ever since our father was sold, but I love him still. He has been taking good care of our mother as she recovers quite nicely from that dreadful illness. Aly promised our Pápa that he would take care of me, but I won't let him."

"*Somebody* needs to take care of you," Corrine said, finally standing still. "Here, take this bowl of soup and dish it to the guests. Hurry!"

Danielle floated into the dining room, where she was first greeted by a wave of laughter from the Soileau family and twenty of their guests from the Baptiste, New, and Francois plantations throughout the parish and as far as West Baton Rouge. "That was an exceptional story, Ambrose," said Demetre Soileau, dabbing his watering grey eyes with a cloth as he sat at the head of the long Chippendale table. I haven't had a laugh like that in years." All conversations faded to a whisper when guests at the party discovered Danielle's graceful presence despite her enormous belly, which she attempted to hide behind the large pot of soup. She held her head low, desperate to eye the dazzling silk and lace that the women wore on their dresses. She often dreamt about receiving an invitation to such extravagant supper parties as this, where she could wear lovely pearls and pink ribbons upon a dress created especially for her.

As she traipsed around the table serving pea soup, she caught Master Soileau smiling softly at her before taking a sip of savory red wine from his crystal glass. She nodded at him, trying not to return the smile, but thanking him for it in her heart. Danielle had always enjoyed the looks given to her by Demetre, though she often shifted her eyes modestly. His sharp, handsome features haunted her mind frequently throughout the day and night, sometimes leaving her to wonder whom their unborn child would most resemble.

When she finally lifted her head, Danielle was alarmed to see Demetre's stone-faced wife, Etiennette, gazing hatefully at her from across the table. The thin-browed woman waited patiently for the girl to come around to her end of the table. Before the mistress could find something to quietly scold her about, Blanche New of the New Plantation stated lightly, "I don't remember ever seeing her here before. Is she a new purchase?"

"Oh, no my dear," said Madame Francois. "They have had her for years. She is sure to breed well. By the looks of things, she will have a strong boy to help around the field." She leaned in toward Blanche, "But I would never have such an attractive slave girl in my home." Mrs. New agreed while the other guests continued their conversations. Madame Etiennette glanced around the table, realizing that even in conversation, many of the gentlemen seemed to be fixated on Danielle's long curls, which were required to be hidden underneath a tignon at all times.

"I must apologize for the girl's beastly appearance," said Etiennette, red in complexion, "but we are shorthanded, therefore using what servants we could, even those in such...delicate conditions."

"Dear child?" said Madame Francois to Danielle, resting her plump body against the back of her seat.

"Oui, Madame?" the girl answered bashfully.

"Tell everyone your name."

"Je m'appelle Danielle—"

Etiennette interrupted, "En anglais! In English, girl, not everyone at this table speaks French."

"Oh, excusez-moi, Madame. My name is Danielle S—," The girl caught herself, hoping no one heard her almost share her last name. She said it in her head so many times. She wondered how she could be so foolish as to almost spew it aloud and in front of guests and the mistress. "I am Danielle," she tried to recover. Not every guest heard the mishap, but a few noticed Etiennette's seething anger behind her grimace and quickly spoke amongst themselves about unrelated subjects in a poor attempt to soften the awkward moment.

Demetre escorted his wife out of the dining room and through the sliding doors leading into the main sitting room. "Darling," Demetre said in a firm whisper. "We will discuss this at a later time."

"Why is she here? My orders were that she would not be in attendance this evening. Why must you be so calm? That girl needs to learn her place. And did you hear her almost use our family surname as her own, and in front of our guests—"

"As master of this house, I instructed her to arrive for her duties as a treat to our guests after supper. And I gave her our name several months earlier," he boldly confessed. The woman was speechless for a few moments. Master Soileau spoke harshly without a raise in his voice. "This evening will not be ruined. Now, I suggest we join our guests and speak no more of this. Is that understood?" Etiennette leered at him long and hard with glassy green eyes and a rumbling pout, withholding every emotion that wanted to escape from her body. Had she allowed the hatred she felt for him at that moment to conquer her, she would have spat in his face. "I said, is that understood?" It was not long before Etiennette lifted the bottom of her green dress and returned to the dining room table with her husband behind her.

"Mother," whispered Mademoiselle Simone at the seat on her left. "Are you alright?"

The mistress whispered back, "I must step away. Suddenly, I'm not feeling well." As guests continued to converse among themselves, Etiennette quietly stood to her feet. A servant, Rosezelle, offered to bring the woman a glass of water, but she refused, making a quick exit through the sliding doors.

The party continued, ultimately moving into the ballroom where several slaves were called upon to play instruments and entertain the guests in song. Pushing aside the tin of Soileau & Sons sugar, Danielle's indulgence in an unusual supper of apples, mustard, and roasted pork was interrupted by a serving bell. Had she known that she would be called upon shortly after serving herself, Danielle would have taken daintier bites rather than allowing her cheeks to bulge. The bell rang a second time before Demetre entered the kitchen. "Ah, I should've known you would be in here," he said, smiling at her once again.

"I'm sorry, Monsieur," Danielle apologized, still chewing. "I was too hungry to spit it out."

Demetre smiled brightly, rubbing her cheek with the back of his hand. "You covered your hair," he said, desperately wanting to run his fingers through it.

"Yes. Madòm Etiennette appeared plenty angry with me for not doing so earlier."

"Don't bother with her, you know how emotional she is. And she's not allowed to touch you, you know that."

"I must finish my chores before the mistress—"

"Shhh, enough about her." He placed his palm on her stomach. "How's the child?"

Danielle gently slid his hand from her womb and looked away angrily. "It grows."

"That's good news," he exclaimed. He tried to look her in the eyes, "You are bothered by something. What is it? Tell me and I'll fix it."

"Papa?" called Simone from the kitchen doorway.

"...Yes?" he said, taken aback by the sudden intrusion. The man did not turn to look at his sixteen-year-old daughter.

"The—the guests are waiting," she said, almost in a whisper, while peering at Danielle.

"Tell them that Danielle will be arriving soon. Merci."

Before obeying his command, Simone's face turned bitter at the sight of her father standing so close to a lady who was not her mother and looking at the slave as he once looked at his wife. A slave girl to whom she entrusted her fears, desires, and secrets. What shame Simone now carried. She had suspected many things about her father's lifestyle by the way her mother cried at night when he was nowhere to be found, and how she often carried on whenever Danielle was in their presence. But until now, she never wanted to believe that her father could betray her mother with the teenage slave whom she had grown to love as family. She walked away without making a sound.

"I told the guests that you had the voice of an angel," the master continued, "and that you would be gracious enough to bless us in song." He brought her hand up to his lips and kissed it. Danielle agreed to sing, although she was hardly in the mood.

The guests listened carefully as the sweet soprano voice sent several chills rippling through their bodies with a French song of long ago. Monsieur Soileau sat behind her playing the piano while gazing at the girl, and the head rag that slipped down her curls. There could be no precise match than her perfect pitch that echoed throughout the grand ballroom and the augmented notes of the majestic instrument.

Simone tried to shift her attention to several of the paintings of ancestors in periwigs and dignified expressions, but could no longer ignore the loving smile that her father subconsciously gave to the beautiful brown slave who stood under the dynamic crystal chandelier. Acting as defiant children, her tears disobeyed her wishes, squeezing through her eyes anyhow, streaming down her cheeks, and onto the fabrics of her ball gown. She quickly excused herself from the party. Her actions were mistaken for one of the many individuals at the gathering who cried joyfully at hearing the nostalgic melody. "I find it quite a blessing that God gives our Negroes such gifts to entertain us." Mrs. New whispered to Ms. Francois.

"Yes," Mrs. Francois agreed. "Just as He intended."

Toward the end of the evening, Danielle was released from the party to rest in her cabin. She wished the Baptiste, New, and Francois families "Bonne nuit," as they spoke about their dislike for some of the North's political figures. Demetre secretly promised to visit her soon.

Once outside of the mansion, Danielle pressed forward, inhaling the ever-present scent of tobacco, a smell that conjoined with her growth into adolescence. The girl rushed past the tall sugar canes that looked like rows of tall beings under the starry night. She looked up at the dark sky, able to see the full yellow moon as it stood over the row of rickety cabins. Upon approaching her mother's, she smiled lightly when seeing the face of an eight-year-old girl peek through the door and slip back inside the house. "Danielle is here!" The little voice announced.

* * *

The wrinkles around Alette's mouth deepened as she smiled out at the window and the rainfall, which seemed to indecisively switch patterns, the wind taking it to places against its will. She closed her old eyes slowly, "I did not see her as often as I would have liked on account that she worked long hours in the big house and I was often asleep when she visited, but Danielle was a piece of my everything. She was my comfort with her solitary presence. And although she was a girl, I never saw her as such. To me, she was wise, her answers to my questions were so satisfying and stamped as gospel to my childhood mind. She moved with natural elegance as if she always knew where she was going and what she needed to do. And her voice could make the toughest of admirals cry. I loved her, yet envied her, especially after returning from parties where she was ordered to entertain lovely men and women adorned in fine clothing that I would never get to witness, but through her stories. Above everything, to me, she made all things better. But not everyone felt the same way."

* * *

"Maman!" said Danielle, entering the small, stuffy cabin and rushing to her mother's bedside. "How are you feeling today?"

"Blessed," she said to her eldest daughter.

"Did Master Demetre summon a doctor this afternoon?"

"He did. My illness has gone down to a mild irritation in my throat..."

"Hush then. I'll make you some syrup." Danielle studied her mother's face and the new lines that had taken residence upon it. Her mother, in her opinion, was the most beautiful colored woman she had ever seen—free or enslaved. Once a house slave, Genevieve was the envy of every woman who had ever stepped foot upon the plantation of Old Maîtriser Soileau, Demetre's father. But for many of them, their jealousy lessened when they saw how kind she was to everyone. "A fine image of a good Catholic woman," old master would say about her to other slaves and house guests. He once impulsively stated this to his wife with a twinkle in his eye, bright enough to blind her. Mistress Soileau wasted no time demanding that Genevieve's role change from "a favored house wench" to a common field hand. Now with her skin aged by the sun and muscles beaten by daily labor, Danielle stared into what could be her future if Monsieur Demetre were to tire of her or give in to Etiennette's wishes.

"I have sulfur and molasses if you're having headaches," Danielle offered, beginning to chop red onions she found in her mother's vegetable box. "I have more herbs growing in my garden. Perhaps you could tell me which ones you used to get the mysterious colored boy back onto his feet, so many years ago," she smiled cynically, shaking her head.

Maman chortled, "The boy did exist. Of course, I don't expect you to remember or to have even seen him since you were in the big house by then and were only about 6 years old."

"Likely story, Maman," Danielle joked.

Genevieve coughed and continued, "How many times must I tell you? Ms. Paulina and I cared for the child and watched the poor dear through the night." Genevieve retold how the boy was no more than ten when a Soileau servant, Prosper, found him moaning in pain deep in the woods, barely able to keep his eyelids parted. Somehow, the boy and other colored students had escaped an attack, but he was separated from the other classmates. One lost his life. Genevieve said, "Aly remembers him; they were around the same age. Alysaundre, please tell your sister one final time that the boy existed."

"Why are you here?" Alysaundre resentfully asked Danielle.

The volume of her older brother's voice startled Danielle. "Oh, Alysaundre, I didn't see you in the corner over there. It's so dark. Comment vas-tu? How are you?" Danielle wanted to know.

"Why are you here? You should be at home. I can take care of Maman."

"I don't mind. Besides, you've been busy all day. You need rest just as much as I do."

Alysaundre gawked irritably at her before gesturing his head towards their little sister standing beside Danielle with her arms stretched outward, anxiously ready to receive her beloved sister.

"Oh, I'm sorry, Alette," she said sweetly as she proceeded to perform their daily ritual of a tight hug, a tickle to the ribs, and a pinch on the nose. Danielle then boiled water in the fireplace with her curious little sister at her side. Alette watched carefully, imitating her older sister. She grabbed a wooden comb, loosened her long, thick braid, and began combing her hair in the same style as Danielle's. Next, she removed the hair from her comb and dropped it into the fire. "Lettie, what're you doing?" Danielle asked, stirring tablespoons of sugar into the pot of boiled water.

"Burning my hair," she answered nonchalantly.

"Why?"

"Bonne chance. Good luck."

"Oh, glory. There's no such thing as good luck."

"Then what is there?"

"There is such a thing as God's will. It was God's will that you learned to draw and learn your letters and wait on Maman...why are you rubbing your stomach?"

"Because you're rubbing yours." Danielle immediately removed her hand, not realizing that she was subconsciously petting her womb. "May I touch your belly?"

"No!" Danielle snapped as she stood up to chop more onions.

"Is it God's will that you have a baby growing inside of you?" Alette asked bashfully, twirling a lock of hair around her finger and following her sister around the cabin. Danielle continued to chop the onions and toss them into the boiling sugar water.

"Aren't you going to answer her question?" Alysaundre asked. "You cannot get angry every time she mentions the baby."

"I don't want her getting attached to it."

"Why not?" Their mother faintly asked.

"It's nothing, Maman," Danielle answered with a sniffle. "Get some sleep."

"I didn't mean to make you cry, Dani," Alette said apologetically.

Danielle smiled comfortingly at the little girl, "It's not you, precious, it's the onions."

"Danielle Liana, come here," her mother ordered. The girl obeyed and sat close to her. The woman took the girl's hands and placed them on her belly. "Look at me. Don't fight it," she whispered.

"Don't fight *what*, Maman?"

"Your feelings. Love this child."

Tears began to weld in the girl's eyes, "I can't, Maman. If only you knew...I must go." She said, breaking away from her mother's hands. "The syrup should be ready. Give it time to cool. I will see you tomorrow. I love you." Danielle rushed out of the cabin.

"Danielle, don't go yet!" Alette voiced, running out of the house with a jar of fireflies. "I caught these for you. Here, you can do anything you want with them."

"Thank you," said Danielle, kissing her sister on the cheek. "As much as I would treasure them, let's allow them to continue to bring joy to someone else. Besides, beautiful creatures with wings aren't meant to be captured."

"Oh, all right," Alette mumbled disappointingly. Danielle removed the string and fabric lid, and the two girls watched as one firefly followed another, crawling onto the mouth of the jar where they all flew clumsily above the sisters' heads like a staggering group of blinking stars.

"Here," Danielle said, removing a small bundle of sugar cookies from her apron. "I brought you these. There were more a little earlier, but I was hungry."

Alysaundre walked lackadaisically out of the house, smoking a corn pipe with one hand in his pocket, and instructed Alette to go inside. "I'll walk you home," he said to Danielle. Not wanting to cause an argument, Danielle allowed it. "How has Monsieur Demetre been treating you?" Alysaundre asked after exhaling smoke from his lungs.

"The same way he has always treated me."

"Like a princess."

"My home is hardly a palace."

"But you have the best cabin of anyone here, and he made sure of that. He gives you the best of everything, and he takes the best of you in return."

"You seem upset about his generosity toward me, yet you benefit from the gifts I am given and the food I bring home. I'm just trying to survive the best way I know how."

"Survive?" her brother repeated. "Is that what we call it? You act as if you love him...Do you?"

Danielle said nothing.

"Monsieur Demetre sold our father because he tried to protect you from the master's lust and look at you. I am not able to protect you either, or from the words of others who say terrible things about you...Just tell me if you love him."

Danielle lowered her head and bit her bottom lip.

"I can't stop you from loving him, and I can't stop the things that are to come if you continue this path, so I'll simply stop trying." They arrived at her cabin. As Danielle turned to thank her brother for walking her home, he had already headed back, walking into the darkness.

Two

As much as she fought to proceed with life without thinking of her father, Danielle could not help missing him. At times, she could still hear his laughter above the group of lively spectators whom he attracted in front of his cabin when defeating another challenger in an arm-wrestling match. Before every tournament, he required a kiss from his daughter, Danielle, which he depended on to give him good luck. For a while, Danielle never believed that her kisses were valuable, but thought twice when her father remained undefeated and collected food, clothing, and other goods in place of money.

His absence hurt her deeper than she had ever cared to admit. To her knowledge, he had not passed on, but it felt as if he had. She could still remember how his dark eyes seemed to pierce through the depths of her soul whenever his twinkling gaze locked her into complete submission. He always knew her truth, even if she attempted to cover it up with a carefully woven cape of lies. Often, she wondered if her father had the gift of foresight, for he always knew her whereabouts, sometimes her thoughts. With a sly grin, his explanation of an accusation of such a phenomenon was, "Danielle, you are of my blood, and our hearts are almost one and the same."

His voice was forever etched into her mind. Though her mother's voice was as smooth as satin and her French was as lovely to hear as the trickling of water in a spring, to Danielle, her father's voice reflected the sound of bondage. Somehow, his African and Indian ancestry of the Caribbean coiled twice around his vocals, projecting a thick and unyielding coarseness in his voice as damaging to the ears as a prickly needle on a cactus would be to a human's touch.

She clearly remembered how well he worked on the landscape and gardening around the mansion, close enough to keep an eye on his teenage daughter, whom many of the male slaves asked to marry but were turned down by her protector.

Once, Danielle was invited to participate in games of cricket and cards in the garden with Simone and a few of her closest friends. And for a brief moment, she was simply *Danielle*. She was colorless, role-less, neither rich nor poor, nor slave, nor free, but a girl enjoying the day. But when the tough sound of words sung by a deep voice was heard nearby, reminders of who and what she was in comparison to the elegant, creamy-complexioned girls around her, who cringed at the harsh sound, engulfed her mind. Danielle felt as if fire shot through her veins and made its way to her heart.

"What is that *awful* noise?" One of the guests, Bastienne, asked the others. "You there, slave girl! Who is that?" she questioned Danielle.

"Her name is Danielle," whispered Simone.

"Oh, what does it matter what her name—look hon', what is that wretched sound?"

Danielle knew that it was her father, Edmond, singing an old African chant to get him through the day's work. "Do ba-na co-ba, ge-ne me, ge-ne me," he sang. She frowned upon the prohibited "heathen" language that arose from the pit of his stomach, sounding coarse and choppy, like *gibberish from a swaddling infant*, she caught herself thinking. If only he would be quiet, she could be released from such embarrassment, and the girls, in their fancy slippers and gowns, could stop staring at her, covering their laughter with their lace-trimmed fans. But he never stopped. It was only until Simone snapped her fingers and ordered Danielle to bring the girls lemonade that the slave was unbolted from her internal misery and catapulted into another.

When Danielle moved into her family's cabin after Simone's desire to have her own private sleeping quarters, the Soileau family contracted Malaria. An aunt and a cousin of Etiennette, who stayed with the family for a season, did not survive the early stages of the disease. Danielle was called upon to nurse the master back to health while Corrine and Rosezelle cared for the woman of the house. Simone was in preparation to be sent away to relatives in France, only to receive word of unrest within the country. News of assassination attempts against Napoleon III and the lives of Parisians rerouted her to Uncle Emile in New Orleans, where she remained for several months.

With a positive attitude, fresh air, a wealth of slave-crafted medication and herbs from her garden, and sunlight, Danielle tended to Demetre, speaking nothing of death, but of life, and the life he has yet to continue. When he opened his sunken eyes, the angelic vision of Danielle smiling over him with golden sun rays behind her brought a smile to his pasty lips. He brought his trembling hand to the side of her head and said, "You have been good to me. And if I regain my strength and my life, I will be good to you also." He did just as he promised.

Months of Danielle speaking of Monsieur Demetre with blushed cheeks worried her father. Every day, she had a new story to tell about his adventures or a humorous tale that she heard from him. Edmond warned her not to get too close to the man if she could help it, but she disobeyed. He warned her of a lot of things, such as the day when Simone would turn into a miniature version of her mother. Danielle often credited Simone with allowing her to taste the very thing that slaves often died trying to obtain. Freedom. But lately, Edmond noticed that Demetre absorbed this credit, and Edmond began to see that Danielle's access to temporary wings was nothing more than wax imitations of such, which rapidly melted as she flew closer to the sun. It was not long before a fully furnished cabin, much more handsome and roomier than the others, was erected for Danielle, which infuriated her father.

"Oh, TiFiy, ça ina vèk twa?!" Edmond yelled to his daughter within her humid cabin. She hated when he spoke using "Negro Creole," distorting and switching his words back and forth. Considering it a muddied attempt at speaking a tongue as silky to her ears as the root language of French.

"I'm too old to be called 'baby girl,' Pápa, and there is nothing the matter with me!" Danielle yelled back at her father. She had never seen him so angry. He stood tall and strong, looking down on her with his black loose curls drooping over his forehead, and his dark face gleaming from perspiration.

"Pa d'afær! Nonsense! Then why do you choose to disobey me?"

"I don't have much choice! I must do as Monsieur says at all times, or else I will be punished, or you, or Maman—"

"No, TiFiy," he said, lowering his voice. "Never you mind about the master's orders. You want something from him."

"You're wrong, Pápa, I only want to be obedient."

"No. You want more in life. Do you think that he can give you the things you want?"

"What would be wrong with that?"

"Open your eyes, Danielle! He will *never* be able to give you what you need!"

"Why not?!" Danielle yelled in frustration.

"Because of who you *are* TiFiy! You may be an African Creole, but you are still a slave."

"But many of les noirs libres have nothing but African blood in them, but they've earned their freedom. Monsieur can help me earn mine, then I'd work to buy the rest of our family—"

"He doesn't care for you—"

"He *loves* me Pápa!" Danielle cried without thinking, pausing long enough to see that her words locked her father's tongue into temporary paralysis. "I'm a part of the family, and they love me. They always have since I was little."

Edmond spoke bitterly through his teeth, saliva spraying from his frustration, "A master could love his dog and not think twice about the scraps he feeds his bitch from off of his plate, or the cold floor that she must lie on beside his bed, or the discipline she receives when she is disobedient." Danielle turned away from her father, trying not to cry in front of him until she could no longer hold it in. Edmond knew that his words affected her, but he continued, feeling as though she needed to know the truth. "What would he want with you? You're colored, you're a servant. He only wants to take your innocence. He can't love you."

Danielle faced her father with full anguish and hot, salty tears streaming from her eyes, "He's everything that you are *not*, Pápa!" she raged. "From the way that you talk, with your français Negre, to the rags on your body. From your proud songs of Africa, a land of people who couldn't defend themselves and allowed everything to be taken from them, to the man that you are, just another slave who can't protect his family. Am I to be proud of that, Pápa? You've often asked, 'How can you know who you are when your enemy has defined you on your behalf?' Well, they are *your* enemies, Pápa, not mine. And *I* choose to define who I am."

Edmond breathed heavily, staring hard into Danielle's stone eyes. The cabin was quiet until the sudden whisper of his voice filled the room, and his eyes softened sorrowfully, "Your pain runs deep, TiFiy. My hope is that it's not rooted like that of a sycamine tree. Remember that I have loved you and cared for you all of your days. I have prayed for you and comforted you in all of your trials. To reject your ancestors is to reject me. *I am* the person who loves you and will never stop loving you, even if you stand before me and denounce me. I know what is best for you and our family. Mo va pa lashé—I won't give up, baby."

In an awakening of ignorance, Danielle soon learned the root of previous jealousy acquired by the community of Soileau servants toward Danielle, when her family was the last to be broken. Had she known that her father would be removed from the plantation two days after their battle of broken hearts, she would have made amends, even though the wounds caused by his words continued to nest in her mind. People say that he asked to see her before being carted away. Others say that his ankles bled and were nearly broken by the shackles that bound him, which stopped him from running to Alette when she reached out for him, fighting the overseer who held her back. Some say that Genevieve fell to her knees and wept, while others say that Alysaundre stood motionless, watching, with a hardened face and raised quivering chin. Of course, this and other things regarding that day had to be told to Danielle by others. For she was away, trembling in bed as Demetre touched her in places that had never been touched before, while they satisfied their appetite for one another for the first time.

Three

Abrilliant shimmer of white sunlight reflected off the lake and danced across the water as the calm wind tickled Danielle's face before creating tiny ripples upon the fresh water by which she sat. She could hear someone near her speaking low, but she sat on the grass with an empty clothing basket, looking out at the body of water. On numerous occasions, she witnessed many slaves in the same lake wearing all white, practicing a denomination of Christianity to which she was not accustomed, but respected nonetheless. Some were praying and crying, while others were singing and smiling. Then one by one, with the help of Minister Liam, the people gently fell backward into the water and arose again, drenched with blessings that helped to melt sin, guilt, and shame. They arose, ready to begin a new life.

Thoughts of being washed clean of the past flooded Danielle's mind. She felt an overwhelming desire to rinse away the image of the "dirty little whore" who people whispered about as she passed them daily.

The soft voice that was once drowned out by Danielle's thoughts began to surface, rising in volume by the second. It was coming from behind the white sheets on the clothing line that almost glowed as it was captured by the sun's light and drifted with the wind, moving like a ghost bound by unrest. A black shadow appeared behind the sheets, grabbing her attention. "Did you hear a word I said?" asked Corrine, peeking her head around the sheet.

"Ma'am?" Danielle questioned.

"I *said* that when I went into town to pick up the items ordered by Madòm, I saw that there was a festival with music and games, and

"

desserts, and fine quilts. I even saw Madame Santee, one of the noir libres, and a couple of other free blacks there. We couldn't speak for long, but I heard from the hay man that Mrs. Santee's son asked about you, just as he always does. I heard from a cousin of his that Mr. Santee may try and buy your freedom if the master will sell."

"Those are just rumors," she mumbled.

Annoyed by Danielle's disinterest and sullen brooding, Corrine replied, "What's the matter with you?"

"Hmm? Oh, nothing," Danielle answered, watching Corrine pin up a pair of damp undergarments.

"If I heard that a man like Mr. Santee wanted to buy me or my freedom, my teeth would forever see the light. I'd never have to see this house again. I'd work hard to lose all memory of the happenings on this land...If only we could all be as lucky as you." Corrine tilted her head at Danielle's loss for words. "You know, I haven't seen or heard you laugh in quite some time."

"Well, there hasn't been much to laugh about lately," she said, picking a half-dead leaf from her dress.

Corrine rolled her eyes at the girl, shaking a wet robe loose and pinning it on the line. "Count your blessings, child. You have privileges that none of us are lucky enough to have. You are given wonderful gifts from the master without having to ask for them. You work indoors where you are given nice food to eat—even if some *are* scraps, you can turn them into a meal. More importantly, you have your family." Danielle looked far out onto the plantation and spotted her mother and siblings working with the others in the field. Guilt tugged at her core. Corrine pulled her attention once more. "And you are bringing a child into this world who may receive better treatment than you or all of us. Who knows, maybe his skin will be almost as white as snow, and he may be able to pass when he is older."

"There is one thing to smile about, I suppose," said Danielle, grinning at her friend. "You're soon to be married."

"Yeah," Corrine beamed, looking out at Philippe by the stable as he gently cared for an injured horse. "Finally."

"I'll make the prettiest crown of flowers for you—" Danielle's smile soon faded when she heard a commotion in the sugar field. She saw a small group of people gather around a little girl lying unconscious on the soil, and Alysaundre dashing toward her. The crowd obeyed when the overseers ordered them to disperse. But Alysaundre remained, sitting in the dirt holding the child in his lap, and telling his worried mother that he would take care of the girl.

"It's Alette," said Corrine. "It looks like she fainted again. Poor baby." Corrine helped Danielle to her feet, and they both watched her brother hold the child in his lap and fan her with his hat. Soon, there was movement from the little girl, who was able to stand on her own. Alette nodded as her big brother knelt before her and asked her questions to assess her cohesion. One of the overseers approached Alysaundre with words and pointed to the stalks of sugar cane. Kneeling with his back toward the overseer, Alysaundre held his hand up to the man as if to say, "Wait." The overseer stepped closer, shaking his finger swiftly at the slave who continued to talk with his sister. Alysaundre glanced in the corner of his eyes and held his hand up firmly.

Wanting to shield Danielle's eyes and ears from what she feared would happen next, Corrine tried to distract her as best she could. "Danielle," she said, "Mademoiselle Simone is waiting for someone to assist her, but I seem to be backed up with work here. Can you help her dress?"

"Corrine, I know what you're doing, and we will both get into trouble if—"

"Just go," she said, grabbing the girl by the shoulders. "Look, Alette is fine, and your brother will be too. Madòm Etiennette will be upset if Simone is not dressed on schedule for the birthday celebration." Danielle reluctantly picked up the clothing basket and headed for the big house, glancing over her shoulder several times and entering the back door. It was only a matter of seconds before Alysaundre was punched in the face by an overseer in front of his little sister, who was pulled out of the way by fellow slaves. They rushed the girl to her mother and stood aside with others who couldn't bear to watch Alysaundre foolishly lift a fist to fight back.

The tinkering of Mademoiselle Simone's music box filled her pink and white bedroom, where she waited patiently for Corrine to make her over. Simone sat before her dressing bureau in her undergarments, lifting her brown hair upon her head, then letting it fall past her shoulders, wondering if she would appear older or more attractive with it pinned up. She then twisted her body to the side, hoping to see at least one more curve in her figure than she had seen the last time she peeked at her sluggishly developing body. When she saw that there was not a change in appearance, she sighed, resting her elbows on the bureau and her cheeks on her fists. She picked up a small handbook that her mother requested her to read thoroughly. *Etiquette for Cultured Young Ladies*, it read. Simone tossed the book behind her, where it landed on her canopy bed, barely missing a pale, rosy-cheeked porcelain doll that her father purchased for her while visiting France.

Danielle knocked lightly on the bedroom door. Simone quickly straightened up and cleared her throat. "Come in, please," she said, expecting to see Corrine. She swiftly turned her head toward the mirror and let out a heavy scoff at the sight of Danielle. "Where's Corrine?" she asked with a drop in her voice.

"She asked me to come and assist you," Danielle explained, walking behind the girl and looking at her in the mirror. "She's finishing chores."

Simone looked the slave up and down. "I suppose you'll do," she said. "And hurry, you're late as it is."

"I'm sorry, Mademoiselle. May I help you with your corset?"

Simone arose and held onto the mantelshelf, glaring at Danielle as if to warn her of the trouble she would encounter if she laced the corset too tightly. She followed Danielle with her eyes as the servant began to secure the garment. Simone's gaze volleyed to the mirror on the overmantel, where she continued to monitor the girl who kept her head down.

When the tension was less suffocating, Danielle lulled into the melody of the staccato notes of the music box, humming softly as she had always done at bedtime when the two were small. She had fond memories of playing and staying up past midnight, talking with Simone about things that seemed important to little girls at the time. When Simone laughed at her for expressing her desire to learn to read, attend a ballet, and get married in a cathedral, Danielle knew that things between them were changing.

As the girls reached their teen years, almost overnight, Etiennette noticed Danielle's increasing beauty. Upon traveling, Black, white, and Spanish men threw their attention onto the slave, sometimes never paying mind to the daughter who bears the household name of a popular decadent Louisiana product. From then on, Danielle was no longer allowed to wear flattering colors and styles. But Simone, instead, received an increase in packages containing the latest fashion from Paris and London. More attention to her hairstyles, posture, and skin moisturizer was cascaded upon the girl who cared little for such things. No more were the days when Danielle inherited some of Simone's best dresses and undergarments. Instead, she wore the "plain" attire, restricted from dyeing them or dressing them up in ribbons, apart from the blue and white servant uniform she was ordered to wear when assisting or performing at dinners and parties.

To Etiennette's dismay, Danielle still appeared ravishing, even in common clothes, and was soon ordered to stay on the plantation most of the time, unless it was anticipated that her assistance would be needed carrying items to the carriage while the ladies shopped around town.

Simone listened as the music slowed, fixated on the broken frame upon the floor adjacent to her dresser, which entrapped a daguerreotype of Danielle and herself when the two were younger.

"You're going to have a wonderful time at Mademoiselle Camille's birthday ball," Danielle said, breaking the silence.

"No, I won't."

"Why do you say so?"

"Because my dance card will remain empty all night. Not only do I have the grace of an apple, but I dance like an ostrich." Danielle could not help chuckling.

"Well, I suppose that an apple and an ostrich could both be quite entertaining in their own way."

Simone finally cracked a smile, "Oh, stop trying to make me laugh."

Danielle began to softly sing the very song that she performed for guests at the party. Simone looked down at the carpet. "Arèt," she whispered for her to stop. Danielle did not hear the command. "Stop singing that song!" she demanded, swinging around and scowling at the girl, but failing to cloak her dismay. Danielle lowered her head. Simone's eyes could not avoid Danielle's growing bump. "So," said Simone, forcing a weak smile and swallowing the pain in her throat, which preceded the tears that she fought back. "What is it like?"

"I beg your pardon?" Danielle heard her and knew what she meant, but wanted to pivot around the question and details of the incidents that led to her pregnancy.

"What's it like being with child?"

It took a while for the right words to come out of Danielle's mouth. "Begging your pardon, Mademoiselle, a lady shouldn't—can't discuss such things."

Astonished by her candor, Simone answered, "Well, out of the two females in this room, one *is* a real lady, and the other is a sad impostor. Again, what is it like being with child, Danielle?"

"...It is a bit uncomfortable. A little frightening, Mademoiselle," Danielle admitted.

"I imagine. You have always seemed unhappy about it. And I wondered if it's because you're frightened or inconvenienced. After all, this *does* mean that playtime is over."

"Playtime?"

"Of course. We're not children anymore. I'm exploring the thought of finding a suitor, and you...well. And when this slave is born, what will you wish to call it?"

"Whichever name the master gives it, Miss."

Simone turned around without saying a word and allowed the slave to continue fastening her corset. Simone quickly whipped her head around at Danielle, holding a second glare of warning. Danielle lowered her eyes and gently tugged at the laces, careful not to give off false signs of revenge for the words that were spoken to her.

Danielle despised the person Simone was becoming, but she still loved residue of the old mademoiselle and friend who occasionally shone through. She used to feel alive and appreciated around the girl who too was once transparent. Simone confided in her companion often, without being so consumed by the ideas of her parents and the ways of the South, and Danielle loved her for that. Simone fondly looked back on those days, but now, with her newfound reckoning, she considers them "youth's petals of ignorance."

Though she appeared to be paying attention to her shirtless master, who sat before her on a stool sharing a tale, Danielle disguised her lack of focus behind a timorous grin. Her mind temporarily remained on other things as she repaired the master's shirt that had been ripped for reasons that were "none of her concern." She glanced up at him, able to see the lonely dimple on his right cheek that only appeared when he smiled a particular way. There was something about the way his eyes twinkled from the lit candles in the room that made her swoon and create sloppy stitching in the cotton fabric.

"I was hoping," Danielle said, "that you could tell me about France as you remember it. Please?"

"Again? What more is there to tell? It's not as wonderful as you imagine. If it were, I'd still be there. I don't understand why your heart yearns for a place you've never been."

"I *often* yearn for the things I can never have nor keep," she thoughtlessly uttered, slowly pulling her arm back with the needle and thread.

Demetre watched the girl place strands of her curly locks behind her ear. Her cream-colored nightgown slipped off her shoulder, but she did not bother to pull it up. Her expression smeared into that of distress as she cleared her throat lightly. "Monsieur? *Monsieur?*" Danielle said nervously, watching the vacancy in Demetre's eyes disappear. "I am worried about my sister."

"Is she ill?" Demetre wanted to know.

"She continues to faint in the fields. She obeys your overseers and works hard for a girl her age. But I worry that she may fall ill or even die, unless—"

"Unless she works in the house."

"Oui, Monsieur."

"I believe that there are enough servants working in the house, my dear."

Danielle bowed her head and lowered her voice. "Then, I will take her place, and she will take mine."

Demetre did not consider the thought. By no means would he allow Danielle to work in the field and risk losing her child. He could not even fathom the damage that the labor would do to her body, or the sun might bring to her appearance. "You will work under my roof as you have been ordered to do," he said. The girl nodded. "And if Alette is taken out of the field and into the house, what benefits will come of it?"

Danielle knew her master well and knew the exact words that he loved to hear. "Each time she faints, many of the workers stop to look or tend to my sister, putting the field hands behind schedule a bit. If Alette is removed, then time is not lost. Secondly, she is very bright. She learns quickly. And with her by my side, I will show her how to become as loyal to the Soileau family as I have all these years. And she will serve you graciously. She knows how to clean and is learning to sew. When Corrine or Thadieus or Rosezelle, or any of the others are behind in their work, Alette will be there to assist them. Soon there will be tasks that will be difficult for me to complete," she said, glancing at her stomach. "But if Alette is there, I will not have to burden the other servants in the middle of their chores to help me complete mine. She doesn't eat much, and she's not quick-tempered. And after I deliver, if I can't leave my bed, Alette could be there to take my place."

Demetre pondered over Danielle's words. The girl stared at his face, hoping to hear a positive answer. He responded, "I see that you are finished mending my shirt." Danielle nodded. "Help me into it." She did what was requested of her and stared impatiently into his face again. He grinned at her and said, "It seems unusually warm in here—"

"Monsieur?" Danielle playfully groaned.

Demetre chuckled, "She may start tomorrow."

"Thank you!" Danielle cried, throwing her arms around him.

"She must be at the house and ready to work before dawn."

"Yes, Monsieur. She will do well."

Demetre slipped on his jacket and hat and rose from the stool. Danielle begged. "Please don't leave."

"It's getting late, and a lot falls on my shoulders tomorrow. Don't look so sad. I'll visit soon." Demetre kissed her lips.

The girl wrapped her arms around him, and before Danielle could relax within the tranquil movement of his mouth, Demetre released himself from her embrace. He then touched her stomach, able to feel the unborn child turn. A gleam of gratification appeared in his eyes.

"Monsieur," Danielle uttered sharply and then asked apprehensively. "What is to become of me when our child is born?"

"What do you mean?"

"Will you protect us?"

"Protect you from what? From whom?" Demetre's interest caused him to remove his hat and search the girl's face for answers. She opened her mouth to explain, but no words were formed.

"You're hiding something from me."

"...How will our child be treated after it is born?"

"Your baby will be cared for, and that is all you need to know."

Danielle had more to ask, but felt that it would be best to remain quiet. Demetre stared suspiciously at her, waiting to hear more inquiries. When he did not, he promised to visit her quarters soon as he headed for the door with Danielle closely behind him, able to smell an unrecognizable scent from his body. She watched him disappointingly as he mounted his horse and rode off to the mansion where he slept with his wife by his side.

The exterior of Genevieve's cabin was surrounded by a garden of vegetables and herbs, and pockets of happy memories stored inside. Before Danielle turned the knob, she heard her mother singing a bedtime lullaby that Danielle faintly remembered as a little girl. She thought of all the moments she had missed with her mother when she began working as Simone's companion in the Soileau mansion at the age of six. Thinking of the moments that Alette would lose, she hesitated before making her way into the home.

"Bonjour, Maman," she whispered when seeing her mother kiss her youngest daughter on the forehead as she lay sleeping.

"Is everything alright?" her mother asked, looking to see if anyone was behind Danielle. "It's late." The girl could tell that something was troubling her mother, but did not mention it.

"I wanted to tell you the news." She sat beside the fireplace and selected five ash cakes from a rough wooden plate when her mother offered. She spoke about the conversation she shared with Demetre earlier that night. Genevieve was not as happy as Danielle had hoped. "Are you displeased?" she inquired.

Genevieve wrapped a raggedy brown and red knit blanket around her shoulders and glanced at Alette. "It might be the best thing for her, but I worry when she is not in my sight. And the master..."

"What about?"

"It's his eyes I worry about, Danielle."

"His *eyes*? Alette will be with me. I'll watch her carefully. I thought you'd be happy...Maman." Genevieve ambled to the window and stared out.

"This *would* help with her fainting spells," Genevieve answered back somberly. "But I know you have not been honest in telling me how you are treated by the mistress," the mother said. Danielle swallowed. "Dear, you forget I've seen many things during my life. You can't expect me to be so blind as to think the mistress doesn't possess ill favor of you. I'll agonize about how she'll treat my baby."

"I suppose the mistress does not care for me, Maman," said Danielle, as if 'I suppose' lightened that bit of news. "But she wouldn't hurt Lettie, Monsieur won't allow it—"

"You can't be so certain. And when he is away? Stop putting your faith in that man, Danielle. ...No. I don't want this for her."

"But the master already wishes it, and I can't bear Lettie fainting another day this month. She may not awake next time—"

"Why do you say such things?"

"Because it's the truth. I love her as much as you do—"

"Not possible—"

"She deserves good health and a chance at a better life. What other choice do we have?"

Genevieve sighed. And with further pondering and convincing, Genevieve hesitantly accepted that her little daughter would work in the big house. But soon, her face was weighted with anxiety.

"Something else is troubling you," Danielle noticed.

"No one has told you, have they?" Maman asked. Danielle shook her head, afraid of her mother's next words. "Alysaundre was beaten this afternoon," Genevieve said, still gazing at the darkness outside of the window. "He was taken to the whipping shed, but no one has seen him since. Some of the men are searching for him now." She rubbed her hands nervously. "He would not have run away, he's too much like your father. He'll endure more than what's humanly tolerable for his family."

After asking several questions that Genevieve could not answer, Danielle comforted her mother, "He'll be back soon," she predicted, slipping her hand inside of her mother's. Genevieve forced a smile and gripped the girl's hand tighter. Genevieve had always remained strong for her children, but Danielle worried that years of holding it in would result in an eruption of her soul.

"You should be getting home," said Genevieve. And with a sigh too long to be ignored, she added, "And take Alette with you. I want you to dress her properly in the morning and tell her the rules of the house."

"I'll stay with you until Alysaundre returns."

"I will be fine. Just take your sister. She will need to be prepared for what lies tomorrow. And Danielle, please watch my baby."

On the way to Danielle's cabin, Alette held tight to her sister's hand, happily swinging her rag doll, *Little Danielle*, back and forth. As Danielle adjusted a small bundle of Alette's clothes that she carried under her free arm along with a lantern, Alette skipped beside her. "Can Little Danielle come to the big house with us?" Alette asked.

Danielle looked sourly at the cloth "piccaninny" that an elderly slave had sewn for the child. The tough, repurposed black fabric of the doll's skin collected balls of lint all over its face. Its black yarn hair sprouted upward toward the moon with small red bows, matching the hue of its mouth, clinging to the tips of the hair. Her burlap dress had acquired holes the size of coins. "No," Danielle barked, placing the light onto Alette. "Little Dan—that thing stays at home where it belongs."

"Okay...will Alysaundre be alright?"

"He will, Lettie, he always is," Danielle said, looking around for him.

"Did I make him go away? Was it because of me?"

"Why would you think that?" Danielle voiced, placing the light onto her little sister. Alette shrugged. "You didn't make him go away.

He'll return." She saw the small girl wipe a long eyelash off her face, which stuck to her finger. She clenched her eyes shut and lightly blew the lash off. "What are you doing?"

"Making a wish. It's good luck."

Alette continued to chatter while her sister tucked her into bed. Danielle's stomach brushed against Alette's hand. "Guess what?" she asked. "When the baby is born, I'll be an ant."

"Is that so?" Danielle grimaced. "I always thought you'd be an *aunt*. Now be quiet and get some rest, okay?"

"I said my prayers at home. And I said a prayer for our family." Alette nuzzled her head against the pillow and closed her eyes, only seconds later, she had another query. "How come we can talk to God, but He can't talk to us?" she asked, opening her hazel eyes again.

"He *does* talk to us, you just have to *be quiet* long enough to listen," Danielle explained, maneuvering her hair into a long braid before slipping into bed. The two girls faced each other with their heads sinking into the feather-stuffed pillows.

"What does God sound like?" Alette wanted to know.

Danielle thought for a short time. "Have you ever heard a group of people singing a hymnal together?" she asked. Alette nodded. "Well, when a lot of people sing at the same time, it forms one voice. Perhaps *that* is what God sounds like. Now off to sleep. I love you."

"But I love you most."

Four

Alette's screams in the midnight darkness, followed by the wrestling of the sheets, forced Danielle to jump out of bed and hastily light a candle. She found Alette in a cold sweat, violently kicking and reaching for something. "Pápa!" the child bellowed with tears flowing down her cheeks and speaking in Creole. "Pápa! Révyin bæk!' Daddy! Don't leave me, come back! Leave him alone, stop hurting him! Please, Daddy! S'il vous plaît, Daddy!!"

"Lettie!" Danielle blurted, gently shaking the girl. "Wake up!"

The child jolted out of her slumber, trying to place her location. Crying hysterically, she held tight to Danielle, not wanting to let go too soon. Danielle rocked her back and forth, smoothing her long, disheveled hair and wiping her tears. Danielle saw the pain that the absence of their father caused Alette. She shuddered when seeing the effects of the grief for which Demetre was responsible. "Pápa is not here anymore. But *I'm* here, and so are Maman and Aly," Danielle said sweetly, soothing her pain. "And someday, we'll be free. Pápa will come for us, and he'll take you in his arms, and swing you around, and he'll give you all the kisses he has saved up for you. Don't cry. You'll see him again."

Believing that her statement may never prove to be true, Danielle felt an overwhelming current of guilt rush through her body like flood waters. But in keeping a tightened grip on what childhood Alette maintained, Danielle was reluctant to tell her sister that many separated families would fail to reunite.

Danielle's thoughts of her father kept her awake most of the night after Alette finally calmed and slept. She saw that the wash basin was nearly empty and slipped out of the house with a pail to retrieve water from a nearby stream. Huddled under a cypress tree with bloody whip marks covering his back, Danielle gasped loudly when recognizing Alysaundre, decorated with insect bites. The torn skin hanging from his back had begun to harden, the meat, exposed and glossy.

"Aly!" Danielle murmured. There was no movement. "Aly!" Danielle called, rushing to him. She slipped and fell onto her side, landing next to her brother. Before she could cradle her belly, Alysaundre jumped suddenly, pinning her to the ground, raising his hand back swiftly, and pointing a long stick at her throat that had been sharpened at the tip. His eyes were cold; his face smudged with mud and Spanish moss. "It's me," Danielle said, strangled by her fear while trying not to entice her brother, who appeared to be possessed. His eyes detected familiarity, for his hard expression dissolved into a feeble gaze, which shifted from various places on the moist earth. He removed himself from his sister and returned to the tree under which he slept.

Danielle scurried away from him, catching her back against a tree. She took in small wisps of breath, too afraid to take her eyes off Alysaundre. The girl wrapped one arm around her stomach, able to feel the child moving, and waited for Alysaundre to do the same. "Leave me," the young man said blandly, holding his face towards the dirt, his knees close to his chest, his back stinging and throbbing with the slightest movement. Danielle stared at his hunched profile, scavenging for something recognizable about him, but only finding a broken human being whose body seemed uninhabited by a soul.

"Alysaundre," Danielle breathed, trying to hold her fear long enough to reason with her brother. "Please go home and let Maman care for your back. She worries."

"I won't."

"Then let *me*," the girl said, crawling towards him.

"Stay away."

"Please, Aly—"

"Why do you spend your days trying to fix everything? I'm a man. Let me be one."

Danielle suppressed her rebuttal. Able to see through him, she said with soft poignancy, "You didn't want us to see you this way," she presumed.

Alysaundre's shoulders lowered, and he was once again identifiable. "Father said that the leather slicing his back was not the worst pain he'd ever felt in life," he recalled. "He told me it was the look that Maman and I gave him when laying on his belly." Even in despair, Alysaundre's voice was heavy and stalwart, with a rugged deepness as rough as sandpaper. The smallest movement of his lips projected a large wave of his warm articulation as it did on this night. All of the words and memories that had been cemented came pouring out like rancid water, and Danielle was there to catch it.

"I was too young to know the power behind my stare, but that was the moment I knew that fathers are *not* one step lower than a god, and that sons *would not* always be protected if they remain within the shadows of their fathers.

Afraid that he was going mad, Danielle started to interrupt him but backed down, figuring that his unusual length in oral expression could serve as a remedy for the healing he desperately needed. Alysaundre continued, "Have you seen Maman cry, Danielle?" Surprised, she could not recall. "I have," said the young man. He slowly turned his head to look at the pregnant girl, who also nearly cried. The moonlight peeked through the trees and was magnetized onto Alysaundre's hardened eyes.

Although he refused to verbalize the experience of seeing his mother fight against the emotion, Alysaundre briefly remembered when Genevieve greased Edmond's back with animal fat and later oak of Jerusalem while he swallowed a bottle of rum to numb the pain. She talked to him about the first day they kissed, and about the night they married against Demetre's father's wishes, for he thought that such fine slaves could better "breed" with others that he selected. Edmond took over the conversation, slurring his words as secretion dripped out of his nose and past his mouth, while Genevieve tightened her face and swallowed hard, replying with a sweet, "Uh-huh...Yes, dear heart...I remember." Before a tear could hit her dress, she left the house, hiding her face from her son.

Danielle watched her brother pant heavily, wondering what images soared through his mind, but hearing no more than a hard swallow instead. Finally, Aly revealed his thoughts. "I bandaged Father's back, and he told me that if the day came when I would have to choose whether to protect my family or risk bleeding to death from multiple lashes to the back, to choose family because that's all we have. He tried to ease my mind of the grueling sight in front of me by repeating the stories of the Bible; of Joseph the slave, and of Moses, the man born a slave and welcomed into the arms of the Pharaoh. I believed in those stories...once. I fear no more for men who can cowardly stretch my arms wide and punish me while my back is turned. 'Risk death or fight for your family,' Father said. Oh, Father. He was a hurricane. A warrior," he whispered.

Danielle had never heard or seen Aly grieve for their father in this manner—until now. The man let out a weighted grunt that sounded as if he had taken a forceful blow to the stomach. "But even warriors make mistakes. He loved too much. Do you know what it's like being afraid to love too much?" Danielle *did* know. She knew all too well.

He continued, "And then there's Lettie whom Father loved to no end—"

"What *about* Lettie? What are you saying, Aly?" Alysaundre ignored his sister's yearning to learn more.

"Our father lived for this family, and if I have to, I'll die for it."

Danielle shook her head lightly, "No, don't talk like that."

"But if something happens to me—"

"Stop—"

"Danielle, listen! If something should happen, protect Maman and Alette. They're all you have."

Refusing the help of his sister, Alysaundre washed his face in the stream and stood tall despite the enormous throbbing in his open back. He finally agreed to return home just before the dark sky touched light.

Alysaundre and Danielle discovered their mother sleeping in a chair adjacent to the front door, where she waited for her son to arrive. She awoke at the sight of a battered young man with a black eye and gashes on his face. He was missing a shoe, and his pants were beyond repair.

Genevieve inhaled deeply and stood. "Well, come closer," she said to Alysaundre. She examined his face with her eyes. "Turn around," she breathed. Alysaundre's feet remained planted, and he stared into his mother's eyes. With one raised eyebrow and without having to repeat herself, Alysaundre turned slowly as humiliation ballooned in his stomach. He waited to hear a series of sighs or a gasp. Instead, Genevieve said, "Indeed, you bear a piece of your father's soul."

Five

New Orleans, Louisiana
Autumn 1858

During one of many visits to the vivacious city of New Orleans, the Soileau family was invited to stay with Demetre's nephew, Jeffrey Soileau, a wifeless young man who fell short of his responsibilities working at his father's law firm. When his father, Pierre Soileau II died, Jeffrey suddenly found himself released from the firm by the partners. In a state of relief, he spends most of his days living off his father's assets and collecting proceeds from the small portion of Soileau & Sons in which he takes ownership. He even inherited a few slaves, which many people noticed were very jumpy and nervous around him, watching his every move angrily.

When visiting cousin Jeffrey, Danielle was invited to come along but was made to share a slave cabin with a woman and her three adolescent girls. Jeffrey knew Danielle but did not trust servants in his home overnight. At times, he was impartial to Franklin, his slave companion of five years who was known to attempt suicide at least twice within that time frame.

On the final evening of their stay, Demetre finally agreed to allow Simone and Danielle to attend a French ballet in the heart of New Orleans, "Only if Jeffrey escorts the both of you," Demetre bargained. Jeffrey accepted, and before Danielle knew it, she was riding through the streets of the city with little supervision and a written pass from her master in her possession. The sights, smells, and activity instantly riddled her with exhilaration, for her whole world had been Lafayette Parish. She marveled at the diversity in race and class surrounding her, wondering about the things she might do if she could venture through the city. She could feel the pit of her flat stomach turn as she reflected on the liberty she thought she had, even as a slave, realizing she had none at all. For the first time, she got a true taste of freedom's foreplay.

As Jeffrey escorted his cousin from off the glass coach, Danielle nearly missed a step while staring up at the majestic façade of the theatre, feeling as though she was not fit to enter such an arena. Never in all her life had she seen such a dynamic building that gathered and welcomed as great a mixture of the classes. The girl studied the faces of other attendees and immediately tried to hide her enthusiasm in order to blend in, as much as a servant could. She was relieved that Simone disobeyed Etiennette's rule of style for Danielle and loaned the girl a beautiful gown and accessories to wear for the evening. If this meant that punishment for the slave would follow, Danielle was willing to accept it and absorb every moment at the theatre.

Jeffrey offered Simone his arm and started for the opened ushered doors. "Well," giggled Simone to her best friend, "don't just stand there, silly. Come on!" Simone was excited for Danielle and could not wait to talk to her after the ballet to hear her thoughts on a thrilling evening. Danielle trailed behind the cousins, biting her lip and squealing internally.

As Simone and Jeffrey crossed the threshold, a tall, uniformed usher stood in Danielle's way. "Do you have a ticket, gal?" he snapped.

"Absolutely, she does, sir," Simone defended. "It is a seat ticket."

The usher ignored Simone and looked to Jeffrey, waiting to hear his response. "Certainly, she does, sir," Jeffrey repeated.

"Danielle," said Simone, "give him your ticket."

Danielle removed her pass and ticket from her beaded purse given to her by Simone and handed it to the usher with the pointiest nose Danielle had ever seen. "Niggras must use the side entrance," he briefed. "Take the ticket and go 'round...well, go on." A short breath of wind shifted his hat.

"Danielle," called Simone, "we'll meet back here in front du théâtre after the performance. Will you be alright?" Jeffrey hissed something in Simone's ear. She looked at him sarcastically, "Oh, cousin, please. Just because yours like to run away occasionally doesn't mean mine will. She's not *that* type of Negra."

"I'll be fine, Mademoiselle. Enjoy! Jouir!" Danielle called back. The girl looked around for the correct door but dared not ask the usher who was now assisting white patrons with a smile. As she looked for others entering a side door, her pass slipped from her gloved fingers and onto the ground. She bent to pick it up, but wisps of playful wind returned, carrying her pass several steps forward. "No-no-no-no!" she whispered frantically chasing her lifeline.

"I've got it, Mamzèl," said a voice with dark shoes, a suit, and a handsome face to match. The man bent down and handed the folded paper to the young woman who seemed to hold his speech captive. The two stared at each other for what seemed like an eternity. They couldn't decide which was more overwhelming, the feeling of familiarity or staggering human attraction. The man was the color of coffee swirled with French vanilla cream. And his almond eyes, deep honey brown. His brown hair coiled in light coarseness, almost spiraling like out-of-control ringlets. A small indentation spooned his wide smile and brilliantly white teeth. "Ma'am," he tipped his hat as he turned toward the building, reaching for the arm of the older woman with whom he arrived.

Danielle graciously smiled and hurried the paper into her purse. The man took a few steps but could not help turning around for another glance at the young lady who stood alone. The older woman nudged the handsome man, who smiled embarrassingly, shaking his head. She nudged again. When a coy smile and a drop of the head told the woman that he was not going to speak, the woman whispered in annoyance, "For goodness' sake. I see we've become a 12-year-old boy again...Miss!" she called to Danielle on the young man's behalf.

The man hissed, "Mother, don't start this again. You know I have my reasons—"

"Just because you say you don't have time for women and you don't wish to marry, your reasons should never prevent you from doing what's right...My apologies, dear," the woman later called out to Danielle. "My son has forgotten his manners. We see that you need an escort since your, uh, companions have already entered."

"Yes, Ma'am," Danielle nodded. "Merci, mademoiselle." The man offered each lady an arm as they followed other black patrons toward the side doors. Once inside, Danielle quickly looked up, browsing wildly, taking in every detail of the red, cream, and gold-colored décor. The mother and son glanced at one another, able to tell that the escorted was a virgin of the theatre.

Amongst the chatter of the other guests, Danielle could hear questions being asked of her from the mother and son, but the urge to touch the shiny railings as they climbed the fourth gallery stairs clouded her hearing. Upon reaching the top of the tier, she maneuvered past the well-dressed colored crowd of standing spectators and stepped forward to see the full theatre of four galleries adorned in gilt bronze and zinc ornaments. The man escorted Danielle and his mother to a seat as their tickets permitted.

Once seated, and her heart rate stabilized, the low buzzing of the theater opened a gateway of questions that were previously and unintentionally ignored by Danielle. "I am Mrs. Julia Santee, and this is my son, Mr. Alphonse Santee," asked the kind-faced woman who could have been mistaken for Alphonse's spouse or sister. "What is *your* name?"

"I am Danielle Liana," the young lady answered, suddenly finding interest in the closed velvet curtain on stage. Although she was given a middle name by her father in place of a last name, she hoped that there would be no inquiries regarding a surname.

Alphonse gently lifted her lacy-gloved hand and brought it to his lips. "Pleased to make your acquaintance, Miss...Miss...what is your family name?"

"Soileau," Danielle mumbled, breaking eye contact to view the gas chandeliers. She hoped Simone nor Jeffrey could hear, see, or read her lips. Even among the sea of whites in the dress circles and stall seating, she thought she identified Simone's lavender gown in the second tier near the fireplace and marble mantel, and Jeffrey in the parlor of that same box.

"I beg your pardon?" Alphonse wanted to clarify.

"Soileau," Danielle repeated with a measure of confidence. "My name is Danielle Liana Soileau."

"I'm honored to make your acquaintance, Miss Soileau," Alphonse nodded once, almost bowing. Danielle loved the sound of that. Never before had she thought that having a full name would make her feel beautiful, special, and accepted.

Alphonse struggled to remain reserved, looking straight ahead at the velvet curtain, but catching himself glancing at Danielle in the corner of his eyes as she studied the crowd. Convincing himself that it would be rude to completely ignore the lady, he asked her questions, smiling lightly with indulgence when she elaborated. He staggered in his words when she inquired about him, as women did not pose many questions regarding his experiences. And the two spoke on as if time had carried them together years previously.

Danielle always thought she would be nervous when speaking to a gentleman on whom her feelings would be as sweet as the cane produced on her master's land. But she was amazed by her level of contentment with him. She was not enamored with any of the young men on the plantation, but Alphonse was now her attraction.

The beauty of the stained-glass domed ceiling, with its royal blue and red patterns, almost made Danielle cry, as she was grateful to have seen something that so many of the theatergoers seemed to ignore. Mrs. Santee, who often mentally auditioned young ladies for the role of daughter-in-law, wanted to learn more about this seemingly soft-spoken girl who was not yet a woman, in her eyes, but remarkably poised. Julia Santee particularly wanted to know about Danielle's upbringing; and based on her fashionable style of dress, her family's assets. "Soileau, is it?" she asked Danielle. The name was very familiar to her, but she could not place any Soileau families of color. "Is New Orleans your home, cheri?"

Danielle's stomach dropped as she figured it was best to tell the truth, or part of it anyway. Assuming that the Santees were from the city, her distance would probably serve as an advantage, she thought, and they would never know her secret. "I am from Lafayette—"

"We are as well—" Alphonse jolted, startling the girl. "I have never met you before," he recovered coolly. "While there is a striking familiarity to someone I might have seen before, my memory must be mistaken—I would have remembered you."

"So, you are of the *Lafayette Soileaus*?" Mrs. Santee questioned, almost as if someone had played a distasteful trick on her. Before Danielle could speak, an abrupt applause arose as the orchestra began to play an overture. If this was the same Soileau family of Lafayette known to Mrs. Santee, *could this be one of their slaves?* She wondered. As far as she knew, the Soileaus, a prominent clan in the area for decades, had not freed any of their servants. What on earth could Danielle be doing in New Orleans and unattended for a considerable amount of time? And at a ballet, of all places?

Julia observed her son lean closer to the girl. She finally looked down at the pasture of whites below her in black top hats and glittering jewels, and onto the velvet curtain that had finally lifted, revealing the French dancers.

As Danielle watched the women on stage balance on pointe shoes, Alphonse watched Danielle, internally thanking his mother for dragging him hundreds of miles to witness balls of pastel fluff scurry across a stage. He wanted to know more about the beautiful soul beside him. Alphonse knew that he had seen her before, more than once, but where? He thought for a while. The memory nearly slapped him. *Church!* He remembered to himself. A few times a year, and on the days he was not away for work on the Mississippi, he remembered seeing her in mass when she was a small girl, and when blacks and Creoles of color were allowed through the doors of the sanctuary to sit in the balcony as they were now. Alphonse stared at her features in the dim theater and nodded, confirming that she was the tiny well-dressed girl, who, even then, was unaccompanied and on the balcony.

To him, on this night, she was no longer the small girl with whom he prayed to the same God and worshiped on the cathedral balcony on the Sabbath, but a young woman who evolved gracefully with the passing of time. The moon, which shone through the glass dome, glazed over her, melting across her body like a silver shroud of perfection. If the moon could conceive a daughter born onto the earth sweetly blended with the blackness of the night and the golden sun rays of dusk, and all its mystery and enchantment, and non-masqueraded secrets that nightfall brings, Danielle Liana would be the closest form of its beauty, the man determined. Unable to take his eyes off her, he saw her look from the dancers, onto him and back onto the dancers, smiling bright enough to shame the stars.

At that moment, he thought of all the questions he had yet to ask but would not dare do so. *Is she coupled? Can she cook? How is she with children?* He had heard her French accent earlier and wondered if she could read and write in English as well as French. Without knowing the answers to any of his questions, he already knew that his brothers would be jealous with her at his side.

He smiled lightly at her crown of curls. *How could someone I just formally met make me want to protect and do for her?* Alphonse asked himself, attempting to push away from the feeling that seemed to swallow every bit of power he thought he had, particularly for a man who verbally denounced marriage.

Danielle heard the symphonic notes of a song she had not heard in years. As she hummed the French tune, she removed her gloves and balled her hands to her heart as nostalgia welded within it. She swayed and smiled at the dancers whose choreography gave the song its due justice. She gave a closed-mouth smile towards Alphonse and exhaled slowly through her lips as if returning from a thrilling ride. Alphonse was entertained watching her engulfed in excitement, placing his index knuckle to his lips, wishing that those same lips could touch her bare hand.

Her hazel eyes shifted onto the lower tier from his as her smile melted. Alphonse turned and looked down, investigating Danielle's change in mood. Audience members began walking out in pairs, then small groups, grumbling and turning back to look at the stage. Most stayed and leaned in closer towards the soloist, squinting and whispering peculiarly, and some, almost ferociously the whole while. And there, as if it were an eidolon straight from Danielle's dreams, was a petite black ballerina. Danielle also leaned in, staring at the woman's features. She could tell that the dancer was of color, but with skin painted a little darker than her own. "If this is meant to be minstrelsy," muttered Mrs. Santee, "then I am glad they are going about it all wrong. She's wonderful! And she is certainly a Negro."

Danielle smiled in agreement and allowed herself to be enraptured by the graceful wonder-worker in the green and gold tignon and matching pointe shoes as she seemed to defy gravity, even in her role of a servant. The dancer, with her long neck and limbs, had fooled some of the audience into thinking that she was white, in the role of a colored ballerina, and Danielle could not be any prouder...and jealous. She wanted to hate the French dancer for being born in a country that she had dreamt of all her life. She so desperately wanted to hate the woman for receiving the opportunity to learn an unprecedented art that few could superbly perform, and that even fewer of color were allowed to do. Who did this brown dancer think she was, captivating a paying audience, and not once making them laugh? How dare this pink-lipped phenomenon chase' from continent to continent, etching herself in the memory of so many human beings who may now say that they witnessed such a rarity as a colored ballet dancer and that she was *terrific*, whether or not they chose to admit it. She was not the only performer on stage during that number, but to Danielle and the other people of color in the theater, she was the only one who mattered.

After the show, Mrs. Santee said her goodbyes to the young lady who borrowed her son's arm and heart for the evening, before being helped into the carriage by Alphonse. The young man walked Danielle towards the entrance to meet her privileged party. Alphonse could not believe what he was about to ask: "May I call on you sometime?"

"I don't think that would be possible," Danielle said dimly as if she were a child on punishment.

"I knew it. You're engaged to be married," said Alphonse, exposing his newest fear.

And then it hit Danielle, almost stopping the breath that she took. No matter how violently she fought against the reality that she had little to no power over her fate, the revelation remained that her life was not her own. "That is not it," Danielle stammered, "I'm...I...you and I, we can never...I—can never." Danielle couldn't bring herself to confess. Her lips and her mind refused to believe that she could never choose *her* happiness, whether it was with an educated free man like Alphonse or not. She could either choose to settle with the limited options she was handed or pass them by, while others could create their own destiny.

"Oh, there you are, Danielle," rattled a familiar female voice almost louder than she wanted to hear it.

"I have to go," breathed Danielle running towards Simone and Jeffrey. *Please don't say anything else aloud*, the slave thought to herself of the cousins.

"Who is that nigger man you were with?" scolded Jeffrey. "Wait 'til I tell your master!" Danielle clenched her eyes, unable to turn to see if

Alphonse had heard. But either way, she needed to have one final look at him. She reluctantly turned to see him standing there with vacant eyes, and his mouth partially opened, and the young woman immediately knew that he had heard. Tears pushed through each eye, racing to her chin. And Alphonse, with one hasty blink, changed his demeanor, offering her a nonjudgmental expression and a partnered faint smile. He removed his hat and bowed to the young lady. Alphonse, holding Danielle in his sight as long as possible, pointed to her and lifted his chin and head with his index finger as she climbed in the carriage, still staring at him, and rode away with the fire of the coach lanterns shrinking in the distance.

Danielle said nothing for the rest of the night, feeling robbed of the opportunity to choose her fortuity. At that moment, she knew that a pistol would always remain at her heart accompanied by the order to select life or survival.

Six

Lafayette Parish, Louisiana
Spring 1859

Danielle's heart raced as the two-horse wagon tilted from left to right—its wheels rolling and jerking over rocks on the road to an event she and twelve other rented slaves were ordered to fulfill. Because the job was arranged by the Soileaus' slave leasing agent, the laborers knew little about the person or people who needed their services, but based on their location, it was clear that they were to serve and perform at a party hosted by one or some of the town's noirs libres for a rate of $15 per slave. Normally, Danielle embraced the sound of horse hooves digging into the gravel, or the smell and sight of passing oak trees by nearby marshes and bayous, particularly hours before sunset, her favorite time of the day. However, the girl nervously picked lint from her baby blue serving dress and white apron with lace frills. She tugged at her tignon, assuring that her hair was securely wrapped underneath without so much as a coiled strand exposed. Danielle had never been rented to people who looked like her and wondered if they, too, would have an issue with her hair if it were uncovered.

The group of slaves spoke but only a few times amongst one another for fear that nearby troublesome whites would hear them and stop them, questioning their actions and destination, and occasionally ridiculing them—a constant concern for slaves, even if they all had slave badges and letters of permission from their master.

The wagon soon made a shifty right where it approached a barricade of trees with an equally rocky trail. Birds calling to one another and the quiet running water of a nearby spring joined the chorus of the wagon's squeaks and the clacking of rolling rocks. At last, purposely settled deep into the woods was a white picket fence enveloping a circular clay brick walkway with perfectly round hedges on the inside and another with a sundial in the center of the walkway. Danielle's eyes followed the steps to the six-columned white house with ivy crawling around each towards the dormer windows. They followed a path around the perimeter to the far-right wing of the home. The slaves filed out of the wagon, looking up at the two-story home. "A colored person own *dis*?" One of the men, Bobo, asked. Danielle rang the servant's bell, and a thin, dark woman answered, wearing an apron and her hair slicked tightly back into a bun. She looked around at the lot sternly before her face melted into a soft smile.

"Why, y'all must be from the help sent by Mr. Baxter," she said.

"Yes, mam," said, Bobo. "We're from the Soileau plantation. Our master hired Mr. Baxter's agency to send us out as needed. We all here t'help wit da party t'night."

"But I don't understand," the woman said, turning a little irritable. "The Missus was stiff-footed about only wanting free colored folks working for her this evening. She don't take too kindly to slavery or putting money in slave-owners' pockets. And Mr. Soileau ain't known to rent to no colored folks." The baby-faced woman scanned over the bunch who looked to her for answers. "Well," she sighed. "The misses ain't gonna like this one bit. But since y'all are here, and we don't have time to gather up no one else, I suppose y'all will do just fine. I'm Celeste. The Missus gave me instructions on what she'll have you to do this evening. Come on in."

The group filed into the servant's entrance as the driver was instructed to take the animals to the carriage house. Danielle could hardly pay attention to Celeste's orders as she gave a brief tour of the home. Faint rainbows from the various crystal pieces danced upon the walls in every common room. From the dining room, Celeste swung open the French doors to present an immaculate white ballroom with a baby blue ceiling and white, detailed crown molding all around.

The leased servants mumbled amongst one another, some smiling, others rolling their eyes jealously, particularly at the painting above the mantel of the young colored couple. Danielle was fixated on the young woman who appeared a few years older than herself. Never had she seen a painted portrait of colored people who were not servants in some fashion. The lady, in her light pink gown, had familiar eyes. Danielle followed the waterfalls of lace on the woman's dress and stopped at the swaddled sleeping baby in her arms. She looked again at the woman, not knowing who she was or her circumstances, but knowing for certain that she lived the life Danielle wanted. In the still immortal locket of time, the brown people in the painting were perfect and happy. *What did she have to do to get it?* Danielle wondered. *Was she born into a well-to-do family, or did she marry into one? Did the couple create their riches?* And finally, did the man in the painting love her the way she wanted Master Soileau to love her? Her body rotated as she studied the room, each item, bringing about new curiosities and revealing an ache in her heart, especially the books proudly displayed in a glass cabinet in a corner of the room. Danielle circled back to the portrait.

The sound of shuffling feet did not interrupt Danielle's inquisition of the family in the painting. When Celeste heedfully cleared her throat, Danielle turned around to see Celeste bowing her head as her eyes motioned toward a tall, colored woman and the others, who performed a quick genuflect before the woman. "Miss Soileau," said a surprised voice as smooth as spring water. "So nice to see you again," said Mrs. Santee. Danielle was careful not to allow her mouth to drop as low as her stomach did at that moment. She glanced around at the other slaves and curtsied, a movement she was only required to do in mass, before the guests of the Soileau family, and clients who rented her. She had never done so toward a woman of color. "No, please. All of you," Mrs. Santee smiled sweetly but was uncomfortable with the formality of their actions. "In this house, we respect and acknowledge one another, but you are to bow to no one unless Christ comes through those doors. Is that understood?"

"Yes, ma'am," they all said in unison.

"Celeste has informed me that the agency did not honor my request. And instead, sent you from the Soileau Plantation." Mrs. Santee did not mention her frustration with the monopoly that some booking agencies formed with slave owners, or that they knew that as a black woman, she could not and should not complain against the white man she hired to find help. She was fuming inside, but kept her composure when speaking to the group. "Well," she continued. "Just know that I welcome you, yet I expect hard work. What goes on in my home is not to be discussed outside of it. Not even to your mas—to Mr. Soileau. Is *that* understood?"

"Yes, ma'am," they promised.

"Now, I trust that Celeste has instructed you well?"

"Yes, Madame," replied Celeste.

"Please take your places," Mrs. Santee ordered. "An hour and a half may seem like plenty of time, but it will fly by before you realize." The servants began to disperse. "Danielle, stay behind, please."

Danielle swallowed hard as she watched the others scurry into their ordered positions as they wondered what Mrs. Santee wanted with Danielle or how she knew her by name. Mrs. Santee tilted her head down to get Danielle's eye contact. She smiled warmly at the girl. "Why do you look so terrified?" Danielle replayed their last encounter in her head.

"Because I..." Danielle could not bring herself to say that she was ashamed. Besides, she felt as though she had not verbally lied to the woman. "I've just never seen such a beautiful ballroom," Danielle recovered.

"I'm sure you have. There must be one in that beautiful home you see every day." Mrs. Santee stepped closer to the girl and began straightening the rounded white lace collar on her dress.

"Yes, Mademoiselle, but yours is so, so—"

"Say, no more," Mrs. Santee said, examining the shiny gold painted buttons on her uniform that none of the other slaves possessed. "Well, I do hope that you relax around my guests. After all, I am expecting several prominent people in my home today. But I'm sure you won't disappoint."

"Oui, Mademoiselle."

"And Danielle, if anyone asks your name, I advise that you refrain from using your Master's surname, it implies a number of things that can prompt gossip."

"Yes, Madame," Danielle said, lowering her eyes.

"If you'll excuse me, I have to begin preparations. If you have any questions, you may ask Celeste or any of the other help." Mrs. Santee compassionately inspected the young woman and the sadness in her eyes, embarrassed by the role she is forced to play, but doubtful of the woman she believes herself to be. The one who wants more but doesn't know how to obtain it. Danielle reminded Julia of herself as a youth. "It really is nice to see you again, dear. Take care of yourself." And the woman walked off to her bedroom to prepare for her party.

As time evolved, the Santee home was filled with lively music, and about fifteen dinner guests wearing big French-style dresses lined with silk, supported by caged crinoline. And the men, dark tuxedos and brim-marked foreheads. This number did not include the three Santee brothers, Thierry Jr., Elias, and Nicholas, as well as Thierry and Elias' wives, Flore and Astrid. Nicholas, who was born partially deaf and later completely, could be seen signing and speaking to a guest off in the back garden while the rest of the group gathered on the back Greek revival-style gallery. Bobo and another male slave served hors d'oeuvres as Mrs. Santee twisted her face in frustration. "Where *is* he?"

she hissed to her eldest son and daughter-in-law. "I told him to be here at 4 pm today, not 4 pm the following evening."

"Mama, Alphonse will be here," Thierry assured. "You know he's spent more time getting ready than any of the ladies at this party."

"Stop that," said Thierry's wife, Flore, thumping him on the arm with her folded fan. "But it's so true," she laughed.

"Well, speak of the devil!" exclaimed Thierry. "My little brother has found his way home."

"Heeeey!" The boys yelled in unison and rushed over the do their version of a greeting, which even at their age ranges of 25–35, involved shoving the second-to-youngest and ruffling the hair that took him ample time to shape perfectly. Flore and Astrid giggled towards each other and later shook their heads and rolled their eyes at the occurrence of grown brothers reverting to childhood. In Flore's mind, moments like this allowed her to catch a glimpse into her husband's past. All that was missing was a bag of marbles and a rowdy wrestling match.

"I thought you clowns would have grown out of that by now," said Alphonse, patting his hair to its former style. His sisters-in-law joined the family, giggling. "Flore, Astrid, nice to see you as always." The young man bowed and kissed each of their dainty, gloved hands. He turned to his youngest brother, gripping him in a bear hug. "Nick!" He began to sign. "I'm so glad you made it back from Illinois safely." Believing that they had little to contribute to the conversation, despite Alphonse's ability to sign and translate, the family began to disperse. "How are things with the school?"

"Things are exceptional," Nicholas responded. "We now have twenty colored students who are deaf, but no longer dumb, and have learned to sign and are learning to read and write—I tell you, they're on their way. They *are on* their way."

"Amazing."

"With the funding we have received, the instructors and I are developing a program to teach their families next so that, well, you know—they can have a connection with them."

Alphonse shook his head. "Father would be more than proud of you, but no prouder than I am. Come here!" The brothers hugged again roughly, slapping each other on the back.

"Child of mine!" said Mrs. Santee, embracing her son and leaning into his ear to whisper. "You're late, and someone is here to see you. She has been waiting patiently."

"No. Tell me you did not."

"You will thank me; I'm sure of it. It is Miss Toutaunt. You made her mother and I so happy that you finally agreed to correspond with her after years of her wanting to be courted by you. But her mother told me that her daughter has not received anything from you in a long time."

"Yes, well, perhaps there's good reason. I'm not going to fall madly for every lady you suggest I speak to. It was foolish of me to entertain the idea. And you know I'm not looking to marry anytime soon."

"Did I say anything about marriage?"

"Only on days that I see you."

"Oh, never mind that. I think still, you're only in love with the idea of wanting someone you can't have—"

"That's not it at all—and will you please let me loose? I'd hate for her or anyone else to get the wrong idea about us—"

"Oh, there she is," the mother finally let him go. "Perhaps after you've had an extended conversation with Miss Toutaunt in the flesh, you'll change your mind. And maybe there is more to her that you should get to know. I'll announce you. Come."

Alphonse reluctantly obeyed and escorted his mother, or rather she escorted him, in the direction of a gentle-faced young woman wearing a pink silk taffeta gown with a bertha collar and a strand of freshwater pearls. Her skin was the color of maple-glazed porridge with the texture of hydrangea petals. Her wide eyes were as dark as her wavy black hair, which was pulled into a neat bun. Thierry and Elias nudged each other and watched in amusement.

"Alphonse," beamed Mrs. Santee, "Noelle Medjine Toutaunt. Miss Toutaunt—"

"Mr. Alphonse Santee," Noelle said slowly as the moment she had been anticipating had finally arrived. "Thank you so much for your many letters. I like to imagine the activity revolving around you as you write them to me during your travels." The high pitch of Noelle's voice sent Alphonse on a journey of recollection as one of the many reasons he had avoided her advances in the past. Despite the sound that escaped her throat, Alphonse proceeded to greet her with a gentle kiss on her gloved hand.

"Please excuse me," said Mrs. Santee. "I should really tend to some of the other guests."

Alphonse smirked and stared at his rascally mother, who seemed to glide away.

As Mrs. Santee interacted with her guests, she made sure to keep a close eye on Alphonse and Noelle. She noticed a small amount of flirtation from the young lady but frowned when she saw it was not reciprocated. Occasionally, Noelle would speak or laugh, all the while touching Alphonse's arm as if it were an invitation to safely let down any walls that may have been erected.

The ringing of the dinner chimes ushered all guests as their laughter and conversations continued into the house. Voices of people happy to see one another spilled into the high-ceiling dining room where they all took their seats as light violin and cello music played from a nearby room so as to not drown the conversations of partygoers. Mrs. Santee sat at the head of the massive table, her burgundy satin gown flowing over her chair. Nicholas and Alphonse sat next to one another, now snickering and signing without a spoken word.

Astrid leaned over to observe her brothers-in-law. She said to Mrs. Santee, "I think it's so adorable that your youngest boys have always been so close. What on earth could they be talking about over there?"

"Oh, who knows," says Mrs. Santee, "From the grin on Nicholas' face, something devilish, I'm sure." A couple of the Soileau slaves entered the room, placing various plates of rolls onto the table.

Mrs. Santee looked at Noelle, who spoke quietly to Miss Ivy Santiago. They each took turns glancing at Alphonse, who was now in a friendly, yet heated debate with his younger brother. He rolled his eyes as he signed, "Oh, come on now! Ò, min, ga! Do you truly believe that will pass legislation?"

Mrs. Santee waved her hand at Nicholas. "Nicholas, would you mind trading places with Miss Toutaunt?"

Able to read lips, Nicholas pretended not to see his mother and continued debating. Mrs. Santee scowled. "Alphonse," she whispered loudly. Alphonse made the mistake of glancing at her, and it was now too late to play along with Nicholas. "Since your brother wants to ignore me, be a dear and trade places with Miss Santiago."

Nicholas signed an expletive at Alphonse as Alphonse smiled to hide any expressions that it was an insult. Alphonse signed to his brother, "Forgive me for what I am about to say, Nick, but I have never been more envious of your handicap than I am at this moment." He then took his place across the table next to Noelle. Mrs. Santee beamed with satisfaction.

As more slaves served the first course of seafood, the sun offered a soft orange light behind the long sheer white curtained windows in the dining room. The glow of the crystal chandelier dazzling over the table made Noelle smile tenderly. "Admiring the chandelier, I see," said Alphonse, leaning into her, shifting his eyes from the chandelier to her.

"My grandfather had one similar to it," said Noelle. "Only his was larger." Alphonse smiled politely.

Mrs. Santee asked, "Your grandfather was the French Colonel Toutant, is that right?"

"That's correct," said Noelle. "He went by Saint-Toutant long ago, but once he and my Haitian grandmother bore a son, he dropped the 'Saint.' I'm not entirely sure why. But my mother says that he was anything but, and that he wasn't worthy of carrying such a word in his surname."

"Alphonse? She, too, has Haitian heritage. Isn't that something?" When Noelle was not looking, Alphonse raised his eyebrows, nodding and smiling sarcastically with hard-pressed lips.

"Well, your family has done very well for themselves," Alphonse chimed. "I've been meaning to ask you why there is an extra *U* in your surname," Alphonse asked, knowing the answer but testing her acceptance of her heritage.

At first, Miss Toutaunt looked slightly bothered by such a question in front of the other guests, but quickly adjusted her emotions. "Oh," she casually waved her hand. "That's just my mother's way of wanting to be different while ensuring its proper pronunciation," Noelle explained.

Had Alphonse been ignorant of the real reason, Noelle's flushed cheeks would have given away the fact that she lied. For he knew that the Toutants of color in that family who were fortunate enough to be given a last name were distinguished by an extra *U* in their names. Alphonse was immediately turned off as he had been during their written correspondence, but did not want to embarrass the woman any further by appearing so.

"And how was your childhood?" Alphonse asked.

"I had a very happy Creole childhood. I was sent to a French boarding school as a little girl. Despite what others may believe about boarding school, it was a fun time for me. The nuns and the other children were an extension of my family, well, aside from the slaves who worked there." A slave proceeded to serve Noelle a bowl of soup. "Oh, none for me, thank you." The slave continued, serving each guest carefully.

"Mr. Santee," said Noelle. All the brothers, except Nicholas, popped their heads up in response.

Alphonse smiled, "If you don't want a quartet of brothers in your—*our* conversation," he said with added volume towards his brothers, "you can just call me Alphonse."

Noelle grinned. "Very well then. Mr. Alphonse, do you dance?"

"When the occasion arises."

"So, if music *happens* to be playing later this evening, and we *happen* to be in the ballroom..." Noelle paused, allowing Alphonse an opportunity.

"Then I will ask you for a dance, Miss Toutaunt."

"Splendid. No need to complete my dance card. As far as I'm concerned, you're the only one with whom I want to romp."

Mrs. Santee looked pleased.

As the second course was being served, Mrs. Santee didn't feel the need to chaperone the conversation any further and held lively discussions with other guests. Noelle and Alphonse continued to speak. "Miss Toutaunt," said Alphonse. "I know about your family and upbringing, but you have not mentioned what it is that you want."

The woman looked surprised as she drank a sip of wine. "Well, that is a very general question."

"And it could be a general answer," Alphonse smiled. "What is the first thing that comes to mind?"

"I want to live well, as any woman would. I want to live a life of dinner parties and socials and fine gowns, much like the life I'm accustomed to, only with a husband. And a few children along the way, however many he wants, as long as my figure isn't ruined for good." She took another sip from her glass of wine and continued.

"Children are rewarding," Alphonse started. "But I have often seen many men desire them to ensure that the world has a miniature reflection of themselves."

"Well, isn't that what you would want, Mr. Santee?"

"Yes and no. I feel that children are the purest form of humanity, and at most, demonstrate all that is good when left untaught the negative ways of our society. But if my teachings, morals, and all of the lessons I've learned help make for a better generation, why wouldn't I want to offer my contribution to the world by creating children with the same standards? A problem that I have with many people is that they want children for their own selfish needs, and they do not believe that they owe anything to their offspring. Some want children to make them proud. But do parents have a responsibility to honor their children in the way that they live and treat others? I would say that they do. Furthermore, a mother and father should certainly pass along the knowledge of their ancestors and the land from whence they came. Indeed, parents have a responsibility, just as children do, to continue the legacy of their parents. Therefore, I would ask some of those parents, why willingly bring a child into this world if it is not to help them grow to be sensational?"

"Hmm, that is an interesting male perspective on parenthood. And quite an eloquent way of expressing it. Although, Mr. Santee, it sounds as if you are challenging scripture, as it says that *children* should 'honor thy mother and father'. But perhaps my view is a bit less multifarious. I simply want a family, if that would please my husband. But I would want to give him my undivided attention, so I would want at least five slaves. One to bring up the children and the others to help with the house and cooking."

Alphonse excused her reaction of dismissing his earnest words. Instead, he glanced at his mother, who was engrossed in her own discussion. Had the former slave heard this, she would have taken greater offense than he. The man hid his feelings and asked with a low voice, "So, as a woman of color (and a beautiful one at that) you don't mind the institution of slavery?"

"As a proud *Creole* woman, Mr. Santee, and thank you for the compliment, I do not mind the institution of slavery because it helps our great country to thrive and our economy to flourish. I believe that everything happens in its own time and for the greater good, and slavery is for the greater good." Alphonse was silent. "Are you an abolitionist, Mr. Santee?"

"I am empathetic to those wedged in the system, for various reasons," he said, glancing at his mother and back at Noelle. "But it's easy for any of us to be in their position, regardless of our heritage."

"Well, we had slaves to take care of my home and myself when I was a child. Their situation had very little to do with me. Some people were meant to have wealth, others poor, some business owners, and some laborers. Not all can be privileged and on the same level; otherwise, who else will do the difficult work? I was taught to never be ashamed of my status. I was never shamed then, nor am I now."

"Anyone in your position has the right to be proud if they worked for it. What matters is how a person or their family treats others on their way to obtaining the status from which they now benefit. To gain privilege is to be applauded, but if lives were ruined, then I wouldn't and couldn't be one to participate in the celebration." Too polite to share his entire opinion on slavery and his political views at his mother's party and before her guests, Alphonse, fuming inside, reached for his glass and said, "But one thing is for certain, you are *quite* a woman." He turned his head in the opposite direction as the glass approached his lips, "Quite a woman, indeed."

By the time the third and final course was due to arrive, Alphonse had heard enough from Noelle about her favorite silk and the latest gossip regarding people in the neighboring community. Had he fallen for her, he would have taken offense that she did not ask more about himself or elaborate on some of the mentionings in his letters. Some of his close male friends had always told him that one does not select a wife for her conversation but for her looks, family lineage, cooking skills, and ability to bear children. Alphonse often argued, "If I were expected to live the rest of my life with a woman, *she* is what is left when her looks fade, and her family transitions, and the children have left the home. So, I had better enjoy her companionship."

Noelle rambled on, and Alphonse nodded and repeated the last word of her statement to appear as though he had been listening, but almost despised the shrill of her voice. As he reached for another glass of wine, Elias, shaking his head profusely and with his scrunched face, was enough to advise Alphonse to set the drink down. Alphonse, looking defeated, sighed deeply and obeyed. The young man peered into the round gold-painted mirror that sat above the mantel. He felt his stomach shiver with delight when he saw a familiar face walk into the dining room behind him with a grand display of beef dressed with roasted potatoes and carrots. He stared at Danielle as she made her way around the table, smiling at each guest as she served them. Other slaves followed, serving generous portions of sides, but Alphonse only noticed one. A tender, closed-mouth smile spread across his face as she served the guest adjacent to him. Danielle looked up, finally noticing the man she tried to forget. The bright smile she once had melted into one as warm as his. Alphonse gave a single nod, and Danielle did the same before lowering her eyes. Mrs. Santee watched the two in disappointment.

"A friend of yours?" asked Noelle, bothered by the look she had not received from Alphonse.

He watched Nicholas sign and say "thank you" as she served him last at the table. She placed the tray down in the center and signed, "You're welcome."

The guests who noticed looked surprisingly at each other. "Yes, she is," Alphonse finally replied to Noelle.

Later, as guests enjoyed the courses of their meal, Danielle slipped through the doors to replenish any desired food items, but paused and stood in a corner as Mrs. Santee proposed a toast to the legacy of her late husband, with whom she raised four boys. "And to good friends, family, and lives lost...and the lives that were spared," she said, now turning toward Alphonse.

As the night advanced, the celebration in the Santee home proved to be as vivacious as they were always rumored to be. Several rooms of the house, the back gallery, and the gardens were filled with influential free Blacks, Creoles, quadroons, and octoroons who passed for white at first glance, with no visible signs that there was ever an African engraved in their family trees. Also present were a few trusted abolitionist Frenchmen whose spirits were as high and merry as the wine they toasted. There seemed to be laughter in every nook of the atmosphere, particularly in the overpopulated ballroom, where women stopped caring about who saw them tripping over each other's ball gowns and continued to dance and gleam joyfully.

The piano, drum, and guitar were the first to invite guests into the ballroom, where they took full notice of a soloist who had previously moved throughout the party almost invisibly. Those who had not been dancing suddenly found themselves on the ballroom floor, and those who delighted in movement had an extra bounce in their steps. Noelle broke through a circle of smiling women who claimed the men they deemed desirable to approach the unsuspecting Alphonse, who had been standing on the sideline observing Danielle in song and occasionally clapping and laughing with guests. Unable to wait any longer for him to pursue, Noelle tapped him on the shoulder.

"Why, Mr. Santee," said Noelle as sensuously as one could over loud music. "It seems as though the occasion calls for dancing, wouldn't you say?"

"I am a man of my word," said Alphonse. He gently took her by the hand and led her to an open area of the floor. They danced smoothly to the music, occasionally bumping into other dancers who were smiling and enjoying their partners.

"You're quite the dancer, Mr. Santee," yelled Noelle, smiling up at him. Alphonse responded by smiling back at the woman. When she wasn't looking, he went back to staring at Danielle, who passionately sang, closing her eyes and swaying her head. He watched her intensely when, finally, as if time had not passed at all, "Mr. Santee?" said Noelle. "Mr. Santee," she repeated. "Alphonse." Alphonse looked at her as if released from a dream, with roaring sounds of applause around him. They had stopped dancing, but he continued to cling to her. "The song is over," Noelle informed, appearing beclouded.

At that moment, a slower song began. Alphonse glanced up from Noelle, surprised to see Danielle also watching him. "Shall we?" Noelle asked.

"Of course," said Alphonse, carefully withholding his sigh of disappointment and his desire for Danielle.

The mollifying courting song required dancers to be closer than they were previously. Supported only by the piano and violin, Danielle sang, and Alphonse pulled Noelle nearer. Mrs. Santee stood in their vicinity, briefly turning from her group of guests to see her son holding his potential mate. An endowment of gratification leaped upon her face as she stuck out her chest at her match-making ability and turned back to speak with her friends.

With Alphonse's arm gripping around her waist, Noelle blushed and allowed herself to feel his warm breath slide down her neck. She slowly closed her eyes as he led them around the floor. Alphonse danced, becoming one with the soloist, from whom he never took his eyes. With every turn, he spotted the young lady who too stared back longer than she had intended, so as not to bring too much attention to herself. For she knew that she never excelled at hiding her expressions. She glanced away, watching some of the ladies fan themselves and playfully flirt back at the men who locked them in the proposal of courtship. She scanned the room for Mrs. Santee. Once unable to see her, Danielle peeped out of the corner of her eyes to notice Alphonse still gazing at her while Noelle appeared to be in complete ecstasy. Not knowing what to make of the perceived couple, Danielle looked away and closed her eyes as she ended the French melody.

The girl humbly bowed her head to the applauding crowd before attempting to make her exit towards the kitchen to help the other servants. She had completed the number of songs she was required to perform. The band began to play lightly, allowing the dancers to regain their composure.

Just then, Nicholas walked into Danielle's vision and politely bowed, offering her his hand. Danielle smiled brightly and looked around uncertainly before she mouthed and signed the words, "I can't. I am so sorry."

The band then increased the tempo of the music, and more dancers spilled onto the floor, excited by the banjo, harmonica, and fiddle. Nicholas looked around as well and motioned his head toward the dance floor. He did not allow her to respond before he took her by the hand and waist and twirled her around. The two weaved in and around other dancers, and once by Elias and Astrid who laughed. Nicholas could feel the vibration of the music streaming with the brass instruments, drums, and thumping of the guests' feet. Although they were off-beat at times during the song, later catching up in rhythm and dance, Danielle did not care, for she laughed uncontrollably as Nicholas twirled her faster. While she was having a wonderful moment, Danielle became fearful that Mrs. Santee would see them and could tell her master, if angry enough. Furthermore, she was beginning to feel nauseous and would never live down the embarrassment or punishment of regurgitating in the free woman's home. Still laughing, Danielle tapped Nicholas on his right shoulder, mouthing the words, "Please, sir. Enough." Nicholas twirled her away from him and bowed, allowing her to finish her duties.

Danielle staggered into the kitchen with the six other slave women who watched her cover her laugh and wipe her teary eyes. When inquired about her amusement, she explained the incident to three of the smiling women whom she considered friends, carefully hushing her voice so the other three could not hear.

The friends walked out one by one, still smiling at the story and Danielle's reaction, and continued their chores. Soon, one of the women retreated, leaving Danielle alone in the kitchen with Liza and Jen. Jen was 20 years her senior and often rolled her eyes at the girl; Liza validated Jen's sentiments of pessimism and its coordinated expressions. "As I said earlier, Liza," said Jen, cleaning a countertop, "it just ain't natural for a colored woman to own all of this. And did you see how she turned her brown nose up at us?" She gazed at Danielle, "Reminds me of someone else I know."

Knowing that "Jen could take the glow out of sunshine," Corrine once joked, Danielle chose not to respond. When Jen saw that Danielle would not dance to her tune, she continued to waltz with the only one in the room who would. "And did you see all of those people fanning over her as if she were a saint? Poor thing, she's trying so hard to forget who she used to be—laughing an' carryin' on with those other people who'd be quick to deny they mammy and they pappy if it only meant that they could be amongst white folks and these yella gals, who so light they almost see-through." Jen and Liza snickered, unable to hear the light footsteps approaching the kitchen doors that suddenly stopped when Jen continued, "The Misses seem to already know you, Danielle. Uh, huh. I saw the both of you talkin' earlier. Look like real friends. What can you tell us about her? Can you tell me how a Negra gets a home like this with servants and gowns and still think she above us? Only other Negras I know with fine things like this were selling they bodies back in New Orleans."

"Jen," said Danielle calmly, feeling as though she had had enough. "If given the chance, you would bathe in gloom and drink the bathwater afterward." Not expecting such a response, Liza laughed in amusement as Jen's face distorted in anger at Liza for encouraging Danielle. Liza shrugged and covered her smile. Danielle continued, turning from her chore, "What concern is it of yours how she received her luxuries? Instead of talking about her, learn from her. Rather than wondering about her blessings, if you know how to, be happy for her, that there is one less colored woman in our situation; and maybe one day, you'll stand in her shoes and get your blessing. And as for her turning her nose down to us, that is only what you expect to happen because you're ashamed. There's nothing wrong with accepting that you're embarrassed by your circumstance because most of us know that feeling." The room grew quiet while the muffled blaring of music bounced off the walls in the distance. "But," continued Danielle, "how you're feeling about yourself and the terrible words that you say against people won't change the fact that you're ashamed, it will only make you appear to be a bulging ass."

Liza grit her teeth and drew her bottom lip to one side as she ticklishly looked at Jen in the corner of her eyes. Jen swung herself around and roughly wiped the counters in a circular motion. Given the awkward silence, Liza slid through the kitchen with a tray of small desserts with her head down and lips within her mouth. She was careful not to bump into Alphonse, who stood behind the door listening with one arm across his body and the back of his other hand against his mouth. He motioned to Liza to stay quiet, and with a look of surprise, she dropped her head, curtsied, and continued on her way.

"Watch yourself," Jen blurted without taking her eyes off the bottle of Soileau rum she now wiped down. There was speculation between many of the slaves that Danielle's likeness could be found on the label's picture, standing in the sugar plantation of Saint-Martin with her hair blowing in the wind. Danielle glanced at her and continued to clean the kitchen. "I mean it. Watch yourself. You're here to work, not prance about with these people."

"And I *am* working. 'Prancing about' was not my intent," explained Danielle. "But it *was* fun."

Jen nearly slammed the bottle onto the countertop. "Never mind that. We got eyes and ears on us at all times, and here you are 'bout to get us all in a heap of trouble if word gets out to Master. We ain't all lucky enough to be his favorite."

Danielle wanted to deny it, but she would be fooling no one. It was no secret that Master Soileau treated Danielle better than any other slave on the plantation. "Jen," she said finally. "I told the gentleman that I didn't want to dance, but he—"

"I don't want to hear it." Jen prowled ferociously towards the girl, "Do the job you were told to do. Don't talk to anyone. Don't look at anyone—"

"And by all means," interrupted Alphonse, "don't breathe in anyone's direction." Jen and Danielle whipped their heads around to see Alphonse standing in the kitchen. Jen bowed her head, looking at Alphonse in the corner of her eyes. "She was doing as she was asked. And I'm sure Mother would not appreciate all the implications about her that have been flying out of your mouth. Just know that she is fully aware of her past and present. As for this Songbird's time here with us today, I understand your concern, but from one set of eyes *and ears* to another, please concentrate on *your* tasks while you excuse her; she is needed on the gallery."

"Yes, sir," said Jen, and Danielle followed the man.

The band continued to play energetically as Danielle and Alphonse slipped through the crowd of unsuspecting people. Alphonse felt a heavy hand come down on his shoulder and whirled around. "I'll return shortly," he signed to Nicholas. "Mother knows that I'm stepping out, and Celeste knows that Danielle is needed." Nicholas signed, looking at his brother suspiciously. "No," said Alphonse, "I didn't misspeak." And with a smile melting across his face, making its way to his heart, he turned to look at the young girl who stood slightly behind him, "Danielle *is needed.*" Nicholas patted him on the back as if giving him permission.

As the couple slipped out of the side of the house, Alphonse picked up an unlit lantern near the bottom of the stairs. Danielle stopped following the man. "Monsieur Santee," she whispered. "You told Jen I was needed on the gallery."

"I had to tell her *something*. I couldn't just say how much I've thought about you since our last encounter and how severely I yearned to talk to you at least one more time." Alphonse glared tenderly. He whispered, "What root have you put on me, Songbird?" Danielle cracked a tiny smile. Alphonse reassured, "You won't get into trouble. Celeste knows that you are with me and is giving me time before I have to bring you back."

"Bring me back? Where are we going?" Danielle asked, looking for several routes of escape, and even something with which to defend herself.

"You'll see. Come. I am not trying to trick you if that's what you're thinking. I mean you no harm," said the young man, reading the hesitation on her face. Alphonse offered her his arm just as he did the first night they met. Danielle turned to look at the house behind her and looped her arm through Alphonse's.

The two walked further away, listening as the party sounds, with all of its music, laughter, and conversation, began to fade. Danielle's steps, no longer as confident and definite as they were months prior, immolated her feelings, of slow strides then sudden fast movements. Alphonse looked down at the girl and smiled lightly at her, noticing that something had changed in her, but unsure as to what. He removed a match from his pocket and struck it against a magnolia trunk before lighting the lantern. The dim orange color reflecting off of Alphonse's face warmed Danielle's heart and put her at ease.

"Monsieur," said Danielle. "I want to thank you for that night at the ballet."

"Thank me? For what?" Alphonse asked.

"For your kindness. I always dreamed of attending a theatre and ballet, but didn't realize how greatly I would marvel at it all. But, if I may express myself, monsieur, sharing that moment with you brought me enough joy to last 100 years."

"The pleasure of accompanying you was completely mine, Mademoiselle," smiled Alphonse, beginning to lead their steps.

"Oh, but it wasn't just that." Alphonse stopped and listened to her closely. "I deceived you by not telling you I was a...who...what, I really am. And for that, I am sorry. And rather than condemn me, you encouraged me. And I said that if I were ever lucky enough to see you again, I would grant you my sincerest expression of gratitude. Thank you, Monsieur Santee."

The young man swept the long ringlet of hair that fell from Danielle's tignon away from her face and lightly brushed her cheek with the back of his index and middle fingers. He felt himself lean in towards her, but stopped himself from nearing her plump lips, recalling that she was a slave who had probably had many tangible and emotional possessions stolen from her. Even if Danielle was unaware that she could grant a free man permission to touch her, the last thing Alphonse wanted to do was steal a piece of her or her dignity, even if it was as small but as precious as a kiss. Alphonse leaned back and offered her his arm instead. "Avec plaisir, Mademoiselle Danielle. You are ever so welcome."

They walked on, passing mossy grounds near a rivulet and braiding through magnolia trunks as Alphonse delighted in asking all the questions he wanted to know that evening at the theatre, and Danielle happily answering. He embraced the opportunity to see life as she experienced it, offering a curtained perspective that he had never thought to pull back. This not only allowed him to appreciate his circumstances even more than he already did but also to feel closer to her world and her heart. Listening closely to her speech and conversation, and observing her poised nature, he found the young woman to be more cultured than he had originally perceived.

As the two continued into the night, they approached the stairs of a moon bridge over a bayou. They climbed the steps, and the two stood in stillness with the sound of birds and insects surrounding them. Only liquor and nightfall had the power to make one succumb to truth and vulnerability, unveiling one's naked emotions, or so Alphonse thought. Perhaps the young lady beside him also bestowed this power, one in which he sanctioned. "My father built this for my mother," Alphonse shared. "But I seem to be the only one who uses it."

"Was bridge-building his trade?" asked Danielle.

"No. He was a boat craftsman and later a businessman. But he began as a slave. He belonged to a man named Alain Fontaine." Danielle stood straighter.

"Was he set free?"

"He bought his freedom. He was often rented as a deckhand or under-steward, and later carried people over rivers and to their destinations as a raftsman before getting his master to agree to allow him to buy his freedom."

Danielle leaned in closer. "And how did he accomplish this?"

"Well, my father used to always say, 'It's not enough to say you are a man of a particular craft and have people believe it. You have to dress the part.' So, he bought nicer, sturdier clothing and rented himself to people needing immediate help on the river, giving half of his earnings to Monsieur Fontaine, all the while hiding his gift of crafting boats and the tools he purchased to make them. After he saved enough money to buy his freedom, he rented and hired a crew of free and enslaved Negroes as deckhands, creating his own business. It was not long before he was able to purchase Mother, who was expecting my oldest brother, Thierry Jr., and changed the family surname to Santee. But out of all my brothers, I was the one to take up his craft and take over the business."

"He has given you an amazing gift of freedom and a trade. What a special father you have."

"Had."

"Oh. I'm so sorry. We don't have to continue talking about him if you wish to stop."

"No, it's...it's good to speak aloud about great people every now and again." It was clear to Danielle that he still struggled with the death of his father, but she could not immediately decipher if it was because of how he died or how he lived. The need to demonstrate benevolence weighed heavily on her. But she paused from giving the man the embrace or touch on the arm or back she felt he deserved. Alphonse was not finished speaking as Danielle had thought, "He was killed by a drunken white man who accused him of short-changing him after Father and his crew completed a task for him. Called Father every name he could conjure. Father was stabbed and later died in his sleep due to the injury. If I know anything, it's that Father was an honorable man...but that was a long time ago." Danielle thought about her own father, whose whereabouts were unknown. Alphonse had inspired her to want to talk about him at that moment, but thought the pain would be too deep, and the guilt of treating him as she did, even deeper. Alphonse reminisced, wondering why he was so open with her than anyone he had ever known, aside from Nicholas. "The business hasn't done as well as it had since my father was alive, but that is my own doing."

"And why is that?"

With Danielle being partially sheltered from the rest of society and working beyond the plantation, he wondered if she would understand his reasoning. He decided to share anyway, "Because I—I don't want my family to be a target. It happens every day to successful colored men. Once a Negro does extremely well for himself, things are taken from him. In my father's case, it was his life."

Danielle thought of Alysaundre and their father, who both spoke of this and understood Alphonse's sentiments, but could not agree with how he chose to handle it. "Monsieur, will you allow me to be candid for a moment? And if I've said too much, please express it." Alphonse nodded. "Your father did not go through such trials for you to live of semi-grandeur or have partial success. He taught you something that no one can take away. I know that when you see a bird walking and not flying, it's often because that bird has been wounded. But you. You have opportunities to soar, but yet you choose to stay grounded. Because of the man you call father, you are now a part of a legacy—one in which he has left for you and your lovely family. And to think, out of all your brothers, *you* are the one who took the time to learn a trade that was so dear to him. But to say that you are not thriving purposely, after everything he has given, well, begging your pardon monsieur, but that is undoubtedly tragic."

The echoes of nightly creatures too afraid to have a voice during the day covered the dead air and the seemingly motionless body of water affectionately named *Toujours Bayou*. Alphonse remained quiet for some time as he processed Danielle's words. He wanted to disagree with her and offer further explanation, but knew that it would have only been an excuse to cover his defensiveness. He wanted to be upset with her. After all, who did she think she was, talking about his father and legacy, without ever knowing the man and the things he wanted for his family? Alphonse swallowed hard and, without looking at Danielle, admitted, "You are right. As much as I want to grit my teeth about it, I can't deny that you are correct. My father and family deserve more than what I have given."

Being a noir libre, Alphonse could not count the number of times he witnessed people starting over. Men and women, enslaved and free. He watched people work their entire lives to establish something, only for it to be stolen, burned, or destroyed by those who were often angry at their success or wanted to keep them in their place. To Alphonse, they proved to be more destructive than the storms that frequented Louisiana. He witnessed Negroes start over with the creation of a new or blended family after their own had been sold into different parts of the country. He has seen colored men falsely accused of things and were suddenly denied work locally and starting over in a new town where employment was prevalent.

At that moment, Alphonse decided to live the life his father intended without allowing the struggles of his family's past to be in vain.

He made a decision to accomplish what he needed to do to keep his family safe. Perhaps starting over would serve as a delayed rite of passage for him. Performing the sign of the cross, he accepted the journey and agreed to let his earthly and heavenly Father be his guides.

"So, tell me," Alphonse said, needing to change the subject, especially after seeing Danielle's sad eyes. "Where did you learn to sign? I saw you doing so with my brother Nicholas."

"Oh," Danielle said. "Monsieur Soileau had a deaf aunt whom I waited on when she and her daughter would stay with the family for months at a time. I learned quite a few words in English and French. But have forgotten many since then. It can sometimes be very lonely for someone who can't hear the world around them. So, finding that one person out of many whom they can finally talk to is almost like being noticed for the first time in a long time."

"Well, though it may seem small, the gesture was mighty in our eyes." Alphonse stood smiling adoringly at her.

"Monsieur?" she asked, beginning to giggle, "Are you alright?"

"I am. I just never thought I would see you again...Come with me." Alphonse led her down the opposite side of the bridge and onto a small rowboat along the bayou. He rowed them a short distance before bringing the oars into the boat. Danielle searched around the bayou with her eyes. "I know what you are thinking, but there are no gators in here."

She sighed with relief. "It's so dark," said Danielle.

"I know, but you're safe. Miss Soileau," assured Alphonse. "Tell me, what is it that *you* want? If you could have anything in the world, what would it be?"

Danielle swept her ringlets away from her face and blushingly grinned. "Mr. Santee, I don't discuss such things."

"You don't discuss them, or have you never been asked?"

"I've been taught that desires of the heart were meant to remain there."

"I beg your pardon, but perhaps you were misinformed. Expressing the desires of your heart to those who care could only promote growth and possibly strengthen the desire to bloom into reality. Besides, the best secrets are told in the dark. Please tell me, I'd like to know what is it that you desire?"

Danielle trusted him with her wishes, but did not know where to begin. How could she tell him that she wanted the life that his mother was given, or that she wanted to be the ballerina they applauded that night in New Orleans? With so many untouchable things rushing through her mind, Danielle simply said, "If I could have anything in the world, I would want a changed world. One where we're permitted to care about one another without first having to know the person's lineage." Alphonse nodded, his eyes, with their long, thick, curly lashes, piercing through her and encouraging her to continue. "I want to walk anywhere I please at any time of day wearing whatever I wish, with whomever I desire. I want to live with the idea of knowing that my mistakes or my humanity won't cost me my life. I want a home and safety for my siblings and Maman. I want love, not just to give it, but to receive it. Real love that you can touch and breathe and feel honored that it even came your way. And..." Danielle paused, gathering her strength in her stomach and throat. She slowly pressed her eyes shut. And without tilting her head downward, said, "And I want to know that Pápa is okay. I want to see him again and smell the tobacco in his beard, and tell him all the things I should have told him before he was sold." With her eyes still closed, she allowed a single tear to trickle down her left cheek. "That, Monsieur Santee, is what *this* heart desires most."

The girl suddenly felt Alphonse wipe her tear. Danielle opened her eyes as more tears tumbled down her cheeks. As if awakening from hypnosis, and embarrassed, Danielle shook her head and wiped her eyes with both of her hands. "Please forgive me, Monsieur," she sniffled. "I'm sorry."

"Sorry for what?" he asked. "For crying?" Danielle nodded. "Don't you know tears are cleansing to the soul? To be shameful of your tears is to deny your feelings. They are worth something, but *you* are invaluable. Never be ashamed of *this*." Alphonse pointed to her heart.

Danielle smiled, making Alphonse do the same. He wanted to know more about her mother, and Danielle gladly shared, expressing her deepest respect for the woman whom she felt deserved everything grand. As she neared the end of her mother's description, she added, "I learned about herbs and remedies from her. When the others on the plantation have an ailment, they come to her for recommendations. She has been able to help so many people recover, even a boy who was found in the woods barely alive, or so my family says. I had never actually seen him. I am told there was an attack on colored school children on the—"

"Edge of town," Alphonse completed. Danielle halted her words. "It couldn't be," Alphonse whispered aloud. "Danielle," he said, "I was that boy. Some schoolmates and I were dragged into the woods and beaten as we walked home." Danielle gasped. "The white boys were not much older than us. Our school was burned, and two friends were able to flee. Another died from his injuries. I slipped in and out of consciousness, but I remember waking up and being cared for by two women. It sounds like one of them was your mother! Once my father learned of my whereabouts, he retrieved me. I don't know much about their encounter, but our parents and your master have met. Your mother helped save my life. Please, please thank her on my behalf. Please."

"I will," said Danielle. They stared at one another in disbelief. "I now know that there *was* a boy and what became of him."

Alphonse gained his composure and continued to row for a short while, sharing more conversation and laughs before heading back to the party on foot.

Once at the manner, with the music still blaring and the laughter, claps, and chatter heard sprinkled within, Celeste almost forcefully smuggled Danielle through the side door and accepted the folded cash handed to her by Alphonse. Nicholas, who had remained posted at the servant's entrance, walked with Alphonse around the side of the house and into the back garden and courtyard, signing and speaking as if they had been in deep conversation, making sure to greet tipsy and sober partygoers as insured witnesses. As they made their way up the gallery stairs, Mrs. Santee emerged with Noelle not far behind. "Why, we thought you two disappeared," said Mrs. Santee. "I should have known you would be off somewhere arguing." She wrapped her arms around her boys.

Nicholas signed as Alphonse interpreted, "Not arguing, mother, merely discussing different opinions."

"Oh, excuse me," laughed their mother. "Well, Alphonse, while you were 'discussing different opinions,' Miss Toutaunt here was requesting time alone with you. Come, Nicholas. Let's leave these two to talk. Maybe we'll find someone for *you* tonight if she has not left for home yet." Mrs. Santee swung the heavy French doors wide open before a doorman could do so, and quickly gathered her youngest son inside the house as Noelle stood only two feet in front of the man she was determined to have. As the doors were slowly closing in unison, Noelle opened her mouth to speak but held back after seeing the look on Alphonse's face as he stared into the house. She turned to see what made him awestruck, only to witness the slave from the dining room, now serving guests mini tarts on a platter. Danielle must have felt Alphonse's eyes on her because she, too, looked up and out at him. Their stares were held in suspension until Danielle noticed Noelle perplexedly staring back at her before the French doors clicked shut.

As if the deep inhale and soft sigh did not insult Noelle enough, Alphonse blinked and slowly peered down at the doorknobs. His head, still in the direction of the girl who had just touched him in more ways than she realized. Noelle thought she heard a pant exit from his mouth as if he had been holding his breath while watching her. He appeared to be contemplating something before a suspicion of irritation cascaded across his face. She studied how he struggled with something internally, knowing that it involved the slave who had made him forget that Noelle even stood before him. To Noelle, it appeared as if he had lost something special. Not something that was misplaced, but something that could never be seen or touched again. As if to read Noelle's last thought, Alphonse flashed his eyes down at her with a serious expression. "You wanted to speak to me, Miss Toutaunt?"

Noelle stumbled over her words before inhaling and gathering her composure. "I did." She cleared her throat.

"Right this way, please." Alphonse led the woman further into the garden, where it was quieter. He offered her a seat on a cemented bench surrounded by freshly bloomed ginger lilies and rice paper plants. He watched her as she began to speak.

"I had a lovely time with you this evening and wanted to give you something." She slipped off her glove and reached to hand it to him. "Just something to hold on to until the next time we meet, which I pray, will be soon."

Alphonse did not extend his hand to receive it. "Mademoiselle Toutaunt. I appreciate your letters and the moments that you and I spent here together, and it was a pleasure to see you after all this time. However, I feel that there is a gentleman better suited for you. I'm very sorry."

"Oh," Noelle said softly before looking down and drawing back the glove. "But I thought we were getting along very well. When did you come to this conclusion?"

"That does not matter."

"For me, it does. And you have never told me why, after two years of me wanting you and expressing my interest, why did you suddenly decide to pursue me after a trip from New Orleans with your mother—oh heavens, please don't tell me it was a favor for your mother."

"I wanted to see if you and I could...if I'm being honest, you were a perfect distraction that I thought I needed in life at that time. And I beg for the opportunity to be forgiven."

" 'A perfect distraction?' I have been swooned with words in the past, but distraction was never at the end of a 'perfect' description of me. From what did you need a distraction? Or better yet, from whom?"

"Noelle, you're a beautiful woman, but we are not right for each other. And rather than engage any more of your time—"

"Save your words," interrupted Noelle acrimoniously without raising her voice, the agony of rejection boiling within her. "Your confirmation of my beauty is not needed. I am not a woman to ask what *I* did wrong or what is wrong with *me* on the rare occasion that a man doesn't warm up to me, but rather what is wrong with *him*?"

"Mademoiselle, it would be best if we part ways at this time."

"'Set your sights on someone of higher status and with a stronger lineage,' my family said. But I called myself following my heart, and—"

"Miss Toutaunt, I realize we have exchanged letters for many months now, but do I owe you something of which I am unaware—?"

"You don't even look like anyone who would be acceptable to my family. And to think, I was going to look past your profession—"

"And rivet your eyes on my money instead?"

"I don't need your money, Mr. Santee."

"You don't need my money any more than you need approval, self-worth, acceptance, a husband with the 'perfect' disposition for wiping your feet upon, and the desire to drain the color from your skin. And another thing, Madòm Toutaunt, since we live in a 'great country' that allows freedom of speech, to *certain* people, you are entitled to your own opinions about slavery. But to say in the home of a woman who was once in chains and whipped for picking up a book and now has a passion for business, that slavery has nothing to do with you, that slavery is for the greater good, is as rotten as your foul attitude."

"Well, your family is better for it then, wouldn't you agree?" Noelle responded callously.

With his face flushed with redness and palms accumulating moisture, Alphonse rose and stepped several feet away from the woman, turning his back so as not to react in anger. "Miss Toutaunt," he said, nearly gritting his teeth, "you can stay out here and quarrel with yourself, I want no participation. Have a good evening." Alphonse took long strides away from the woman towards the veranda steps and in the direction of the French doors. Knowing who was on the other side cooled his nerves, if only he could just touch the knob and walk through.

Noelle, amused by his piqued nature, did not allow much time for him to recover from his emotion of the statement before continuing, delivering her words as coolly as before. "Someone else occupies your heart, and I know who it is," she said, making him stop at once at the top step. "I noticed a change in your face from the moment she walked in with her serving tray. And here I thought you wanted *me*."

"Noelle," Alphonse said without turning to look at her, for the temptation of charging her and grabbing her by the shoulders would be too great. "Why don't you demonstrate an ounce of dignity and leave this home? You're no longer welcome."

"Very well then," Noelle said, gathering her large, ruffled dress before standing. She stood waiting for Alphonse to turn around and face her. He turned slowly, waiting for her to move.

"If you're expecting me to see you to the door and your carriage, you are grossly mistaken. I'm a gentleman, but only towards women who conduct themselves as ladies and not spoiled infants throwing tantrums and speaking rudely about my family. Escorting you would mean that I exude a level of respect for you, and I'm proud to say, Noelle, that I have none. I feel for the man who takes you as his bride. But hopefully, you will have grown up by then. Leave."

"I'll leave. But if there's one thing I've learned from you tonight, is that never again will I lower my standards; instead, I'll allow men to rise to mine." The woman gathered the ruffles once more, treading lightly up the stairs. "The good news for *you*," she smirked inches from his face, "is that you've set your standards as low as they could possibly go, so you can only go but up. Good luck with your niggra. Hope her master will let her come out and play." Still staring him in the eyes icily, she floated past him and into the house.

Careful not to appear as a couple and to allow his frustration to simmer, Alphonse waited a few minutes on the veranda as Noelle commanded assistance from a *particular* slave.

"I appreciate you helping me fetch my shawl," said Noelle in the powder room amongst the other guests' apparel. "Please tell me your name."

"My name is Danielle, Mademoiselle. Danielle Soileau," said Danielle with more confidence than she had the night at the theatre.

"Oh, so you have a last name. Well, isn't that nice?"

"You know, I'm soon to have a new last name," Noelle said, turning to the vanity and smoothing the sides of her hair. "Mrs. Noelle Santee. Doesn't that just feel like silk in your mouth?" She smiled to herself in the mirror, then at Danielle, waiting to watch devastation smear across her face.

"Are you to wed Monsieur Nicholas Santee?" Danielle asked with a failed attempt at hiding hope.

"*Alphonse*, my dear. And it'll be so divine. Perhaps we can rent you to sing at our nuptials."

Danielle's face melted briefly as she began to look down, and quickly caught herself and lifted her head. She smiled artificially, which she hoped the stranger had not grasped. Noelle nearly burst with satisfaction, feeling fortunate to have watched Danielle's heartbreak. "I'm sure you'll make a lovely bride, Madòm," it pained Danielle to say. She turned around blankly and removed a shawl from the chestnut wardrobe. The girl stood with her back turned, holding the rose-embroidered item close to her heart as she listened.

Noelle smiled even brighter at the compliment. "Perhaps now, he'll only have eyes for me," she said nonchalantly. "It's all in a man's nature, you know—to crave many women but select one for life. But I'm sure men and women aren't as different as we believe them to be. In *our* case..." Noelle looked Danielle up and down, "In *some* of our cases, there are some men you marry, and some you love...Oh, you found it. Thank you ever so much. Be a dear and put it on me?"

"Certainly, Mamzèl." Danielle securely wrapped the shawl around the woman's shoulders before the two exited the room and into the blazing noise of laughter and song. Danielle quickly retreated to the dining room with her head down, missing Alphonse by a split moment as he turned the knob.

Alphonse charged inside, searching the ballroom with his eyes. The young man felt a rush of sound as he squeezed past guests, distorting his body to get through the many people as he searched for Danielle. "Whoa, slow down there, brother," said Elias, surrounded by a small chuckling audience. "Are you alright?"

Alphonse searched around as he spoke, "I'm fine. I'm just looking for someone."

"Oh, if you're looking for your lovely lady, she is over there, with Mama." He pointed with his drink in his hand.

Alphonse swung around quickly, and in enough time to see the disturbed look on his mother's face as Noelle spoke to her at the front door with an innocent and almost tearful look. Alphonse and Elias watched Noelle continue as Mrs. Santee listened and slowly raised her head to look for her son. Even in a crowded room, she spotted her Alphonse almost immediately. A scowl melted across her face when gazing at the one thing standing between her hopes of marriage for *him* and grandchildren for *her*. Elias sarcastically tilted into Alphonse, "Dare I ask what you have done to make our dear mother so bitter?" They then watched Mrs. Santee look back at Noelle with a look of disappointment. "Whatever it was, you may borrow my horse to escape now."

Not willing to waste additional time wondering what was said, Alphonse continued his quest for Danielle in hopes that he could later clear up any lies or misunderstandings that Noelle potentially caused. Mrs. Santee bid Noelle farewell and dispersed in the opposite direction from where she last saw Alphonse.

Mrs. Santee searched every room until she found Danielle and Elsa, another Soileau slave, in the parlor retrieving used glasses and ashtrays filled with Spanish cigar butts. The woman figured that wherever Danielle was, Alphonse was sure to be nearby. The two slaves stopped and bowed their heads in acknowledgment of the lady of the house. Before a word could be spoken, Alphonse entered the room, appearing flustered, but was taken aback at the sight of his mother occupying the space with the young lady for whom he searched. He looked at the girl who hung her head in habit, and then to Elsa, who seemed confused by the strange silence and stares amongst the other three people in the room. "Carry on, demoiselles," Mrs. Santee finally ordered as she turned around and started for the door. "Alphonse, come with me." He stood motionless, wanting to talk to Danielle. "Alphonse, please. Come with me." The man heard almost a hint of sorrow in her voice and motioned "one moment" to Danielle as Elsa looked even more puzzled at the girl. Alphonse followed his mother onto the back gallery of the home and into the garden, yards away from the now condensed party noise. Seconds later, Nicholas entered the gallery, bringing with him the blaring vibrations of the music.

"Not now, Nicholas. Let me speak with your brother alone," said Julia Santee.

"No," said Alphonse while signing. "He can stay and be a part of anything we have to say. No more pushing him out of rooms and conversations."

The doors shut, and Nicolas stepped aside, staring intensely into the faces of his family members.

"Very well then," Julia sighed, not bothering to do the little signing that she knew. "Miss Toutaunt tells me that you have eyes for another and that you're not interested in her in the least. Is this true?"

"I'm afraid Miss Toutaunt is merely wrapped with a pretty bow, but she is no gift," Alphonse said, loosening his necktie. Nicholas snickered.

"So," said Mrs. Santee, rolling her eyes at Nicholas, "the exchange of letters with her for months meant nothing?"

"I wish she had not reeled you into our affairs—but no, it did not. I suppose I was forcing it, hoping that I would feel something. Or maybe, trying to forget someone. It meant nothing, and after this evening, I wish I had not wasted ink on her. And may I ask why you're so concerned?"

"Because her mother and I had plans for the pair of you. And it's outright embarrassing that you aren't the man I painted you to be."

"Simply because I no longer have an interest in her? I will not discuss the content of our conversations, although something tells me she already has. But I'm grateful that everything occurred the way that it did. She is an example of what we are doing wrong, and I am upset that it has taken all of this to figure it out." The perplexed look on Nicholas's and his mother's faces drove him to further ask. "What are we doing, mother?" He gestured at the house and garden. "We have all of this, yet we have done nothing to help anyone but ourselves."

"What do you mean? Nicholas has the school for colored children, and Thierry and Elias, and I employ a multitude of les noirs libres, not to mention the young women to whom I teach etiquette. And let me correct you; *I* have all of this, and your father and I have earned every bit of it. But I would give it all back if he came walking through those doors one more time. Do you truly know what I went through to establish what I have today?"

"That's well and good, but what have we done to help those who are in the situation that we—you, were once in, Mother?"

"Because I was blessed to be free and earn money, I owe it to strangers to help them? No, no. My responsibility was to help you boys remain prideful of our family name—that you are unapologetically successful, and that you have a happy life, and I've done that."

"And what kind of man would I be if I didn't thank you for everything that you have done and acknowledge the pain you endured to get where you are? Every parent wants the next generation to be a little wiser, a little wealthier, and more gracious, right? While I will always love and be indebted to you and Father, and while you created a path for me and my brothers, without saying the words, someone reminded me of all the things we—I—am not doing."

"And you feel as though you are not helping others?"

"I feel I could do more." Mrs. Santee said nothing. For some time, the clanking of glass goblets in synchrony with the music and laughter during the party filled the silence of two people contemplating, before Alphonse drove to his point. "I'm sure of what I want now... and *who* I want."

Mrs. Santee compassionately looked into her son's eyes for a long time, able to understand her boy's heart but knowing the trouble in which he was headed. She nodded slowly, "Son, I know you think you're enchanted by Danielle, but I don't want you to hurt. And I do not want your livelihood to be affected. That is what will come of this if you pursue her."

"Mother, it is beyond pursuing. I want to free her."

"...A long time ago, I accepted that you never take the easier path to your desires. But I cannot allow you to—"

"I think I want to marry Danielle, mother." Alphonse could not believe the thought formed into words. Nicholas's mouth dropped. "Perhaps someday."

"But you've been fighting marriage for so long. Just hours ago, you told me that you weren't interested in getting married."

"I wasn't interested in marriage to *Noelle*. Everything has become clear to me this evening. I look at Danielle, and I know that I want to be the man who provides for her." Mrs. Santee's disappointment grew, but Alphonse continued, "Do you think I woke up wanting to feel this? I tried to forget her, Mother, but I knew, even that night at the theatre, that I wanted her. There is no other way to say it, but I am sick over all of this, and I am angry. This girl has completely ruined me in the best possible way. She has thrashed all of my plans, and here she is, walking out of *my* thoughts and into *your* dining room." Alphonse paused, turning his back, exhaling deeply. "I can manage an entire crew, run a business, find ways around obstacles, but I have no control over my own heart." Alphonse snickered, "So this is Love...Damn-it." The young man faced his mother. His eyes, almost begging for help, "I can't run any further, Mother. You know me, I don't surrender easily, but something unseen draws me to her; and to her, I yield, and I bow."

"You have spent time alone with her this evening, haven't you?"

Alphonse smiled, "We only talked, Mother, about the things you don't discuss in the day but may keep you up at night. Do you know that it was *her* family who took care of me when I was left for dead? All those years ago on the plantation. What are the chances?" Astonished, Mrs. Santee and Nicholas looked at one another and into the open window, where they caught a peek at Danielle serving food to the guests. "What are the chances that two people who knew nothing of each other's existence were to meet and bond over a life that was saved? Mine." Alphonse slowly approached his mother. "Tonight, Danielle and I spoke about you and of Father. And how he loved you and was able to buy and provide for you. He stood firm when it came to being the man he knew he could be for you and for us."

Tears welled in Mrs. Santee's eyes. "But we were different. Your father went through so much to get me, despite the blood that our master and your father shared. I don't want that same pain and struggle for you. You have made a lot of money taking over your father's business. You are one of the most successful Negro men in Louisiana. You have sailed to places of which most people have never heard. You have so many opportunities to make a life for yourself elsewhere, up north perhaps, and to find a free colored girl to marry. Why not do that and be happy?"

"You and I have discussed this. Now that Father is gone, I stay in the South to look after *you*. And so does Thierry. And we will continue to do so until you choose otherwise. And I have met noirs libres in the South and North, but Danielle, in all of her beauty and tenderness and wit, has been the only one to touch my heart. You've allowed me to pave my own way in life. Now I ask that you allow me to pave my own way in love."

Mrs. Santee exhaled heavily. "Being so much like your father is both a blessing and a curse for you. Danielle is lovely and intelligent, and I see why you would want to make her yours. But I know what lies ahead, Alphonse. Masters don't let slaves like Danielle go. Don't fight this battle." Mrs. Santee looked down and hugged her arms while Alphonse tilted his head downwards at her, hoping to regain eye contact. The mother finally looked up at him painfully and touched his right cheek. "What have I always told you? 'As long as the rain touches the clay and the sea touches the sand, little boy, I will always love you.' Please understand that I want nothing more than happiness for you and a good life. But I cannot give you my blessing. Not this time, son." Mrs. Santee then drifted into the house, leaving her son to contemplate all that was said.

"Well," signed Nicolas as he walked toward his brother, "Sometimes it takes a disruption to take us on our next journey in this world. You were always one to make quick decisions; sometimes I envy that. When you speak of Danielle, brother, I can't ignore the life I see in your eyes. If it means anything, you will always have *my* blessing."

Danielle succeeded in avoiding Alphonse for the rest of the evening. She diverted in different directions upon seeing him, remained close to the other slaves, and did not respond when he requested her. For she knew that he would not discuss anything before the others. As the guests left and the slaves helped to clean the party's aftermath, they all climbed into the wagon to set off for the Soileau plantation. As she turned back to look at the Santee residence, Danielle saw Alphonse step onto the gallery, resting his hands on the railing and peering out at the young woman he knew he must have.

Passing through the pitch blackness of the fields, each slave made their way into their cabins, dreading the 5 am sunrise and the dinging of the cowbell that was only hours away. Danielle climbed up the steps of her planked-floored cabin, still thinking of Alphonse and how deceived she felt by him. She questioned if news of his engagement was true. Was the party at the Santee home in celebration of it? She questioned Noelle and her honesty, but in all, did not know what to believe. She wondered if her time talking in the woods with Alphonse meant anything to him. But she thought of all of the white men she knew who were engaged or married but continued to love or enjoy evenings with other women in the parish, including their slaves. But surely Alphonse was different, wasn't he? After all, he listened to her and even said he needed her. He made her feel as no one had ever done before.

And then there was Demetre, with whom she surrendered herself soon after the trip from New Orleans. His constant advances toward her, even before the trip, were a bit uncomfortable at first. But as his assertion grew, followed by promises and small gifts, so did her heart. As a girl, she had always found him to be handsome and felt a small twinge of pride, with a combination of butterflies, in her spirit when he spoke to her or complimented her on something she did well. And as she grew older, she found it difficult to hide her flushed cheeks when he came near her, although Etiennette had silently observed this for weeks.

Since returning from New Orleans and the months that followed, Danielle unveiled the benefits of putting aside any newly discovered feelings for the young colored man she met at the ballet or the idea of marriage, and of all things, her childish idea of being in love in the way a fair maiden was in the stories she and Simone had heard. She had now been cocooned into a brand-new understanding of the word when it came to Demetre. What began as immense loyalty turned into adoration, and finally sculpted into her definition of love. Surely, if there could be distinct types of love for a friend, a sibling, a parent, or a lover who shares the same race, there could be a love of a slave for her generous master. Love, to Danielle, had turned into an arrangement of favors—a nonverbal understanding between her master, her body, and her heart. A sacrifice for her family and their well-being, as well as her own.

But what was this emotion she felt for Alphonse? Was she allowed to feel this way, and was she allowed to feel it for another man? Even Master Soileau made her feel special, but not treasured as Alphonse did. At that moment, she thought of Master Soileau and all that he could continue to offer her. But could he offer her happiness and the life she wanted? Could Alphonse? In all of her questioning and toyed emotions, Danielle began to feel queasy. Her mouth began to water as she clutched her stomach and ran down the stairs. She sped towards the side of the cabin where she regurgitated in the darkness.

Seven

Lafayette Parish, Louisiana
Summer 1859

Alette had not yet awakened by the time Danielle returned from discovering Alysaundre in the woods and assisting him at their mother's home. The sisters quickly dressed and made their way to the big house while Alette's attention dipped in and out of Danielle's spoken rules. Her listening was preoccupied with the voices of the field slaves singing songs of the next life; some mournful, some gleeful, but both cooperating with the slaves' anticipation to leave a troubled life on earth. The field hands shoveled the soil in synchronization with the songs they sang as toddlers weaved in and out of the line of workers. Old men and women, too weak to work and too old to be of any value to slaveholders, sat outside of their cabins singing what little words and verses they remembered while snapping peas or weaving baskets. Many of them offered wisdom to the young, while others proved to be a nuisance, gossiping and criticizing the ways of their neighbors. Some shared stories of how they were almost free. The elders, aged by servitude and regret, spent their days waiting, with nothing to look forward to but the end.

Before entering the back door, Danielle gasped, thinking only of Etiennette's jealousy and heartlessness. The thought of Etiennette's possible anger towards Alette had numerously crossed her mind, but for the first time, the speculation of Danielle *not* being able to defend her little sister because of her pregnancy fell heavily upon her shoulders. She could only hope the master would protect Alette from Etiennette if anything were to happen. Besides, Demetre was expecting Alette for work today; she could not turn back now, nor could Danielle send her baby sister to work in the fields again under the grueling heat that may further weaken her health. "Did something scare you?" Alette asked as they stood before the door.

"No," Danielle answered. She took her sister's hands. "Be on your best behavior, okay? Do as you're told and stay by my side at all times—*at all times*." Alette agreed.

Soon after sunrise, the Soileau family trickled into the dining room one by one, taking their seats at the grand Chippendale table where they were surrounded by buttered biscuits and honey. They spoke about their well-being and the social events that were worth mentioning. Etiennette saw that her daughter had been noticeably quiet and reserved as of late. "You must get into the habit of smiling, young lady, or else a gentleman won't find you as nearly attractive," Etiennette forewarned, placing a napkin on her lap.

"Is there a young man interested in you already?" Demetre asked, before taking a bite of his biscuit.

"No," Simone answered, dismayed. "There's no one."

"And why not?" Demetre questioned.

"They say I'm too opinionated for a woman."

"*Opinionated*?" said Etiennette.

"*A woman*?" said Demetre with his mouth full.

"Daddy, I'm not a little girl," Simone informed, rolling her eyes onto her father.

"Well, I think you have plenty of time for young men, and I beg you to take it," he said.

"Don't tell her *that*," Etiennette scolded. "Time is a woman's mortal enemy. And you'd better get used to the idea of our daughter growing into her own, her coming-out party is quickly approaching, you know.

Oh, good Lord, Simone, whatever were you opinionated about this time?"

"The rights and education of women,"

"That again?" said Demetre.

Etiennette, who had always thought herself a great teacher when it came to snagging a husband, said, "What did I tell you about sharing your ideas on the subject? You keep this up and you're going to be stamped as unmarriable."

"But, Mother, I'm sure you will agree that if women represent men, and women are the backbones of men, what is the point of having an intellectually weak representative? It only makes men look stupid and standard-free. Should we as women just stay silent about things that matter in this country—*our country*, while speaking our minds behind closed doors and remaining quiet porcelain dolls in public?"

"I'm not certain you should be speaking your minds behind closed doors *or in* public," Demetre said. "You'll get too many ideas rushing through your brains, and we all know how indecisive you are. What business would you have sharing all of your ideas if you're just going to change your minds seconds later?"

"Let this be the end of this conversation," said an agitated Etiennette.

Simone shook her head, "No, mère, if anything, we haven't had enough conversations like this. What else do you believe, Father?"

"Watch it, Simone," said Demetre.

"Stop pouting and sit up straight," Etiennette ordered. "How are your violin lessons coming along?"

"They're fine, mother, but—"

"That's good. I expect to hear you play for me later this afternoon."

Simone dropped the subject as requested. She took a deep breath, "Father, I would love it if you and I could go riding sometime today, just the two of us."

"I have important things to do today. Besides, I must meet with the board and your uncle Emile at Father's home, Evergreen Manor, to further discuss Soileau & Sons' distribution. I'm afraid that horseback riding does not fit my schedule."

"When will it?" Simone snipped.

"What do you mean?" Demetre asked.

"Between discussing molasses and sugar and fighting with your brother about the business and your possessions, when will you find time for me, pére?"

Etiennette interjected, "Simone! Apologize to your father. You know he works hard for this family. And for us to lead the life that he has provided for us, he has to make a few sacrifices. Selfishness is not a good quality, child."

Simone thought that of all people, her mother would understand. She took one glance at Etiennette's face, which had softened from the passing seconds and liquefied into a gaze of understanding.

Simone's loneliness left her craving for any type of attention. Just as she opened her mouth to appease her mother and apologize to her father, Danielle slid through the gliding doors carrying slices of meat with Alette trailing behind her, hugging a small basket of fruit and looking down at her feet. The child had always seen her mother's eyes drop whenever anyone with white skin was around, never questioning that behavior as she got older, only accepting the way things were.

Etiennette glared in rage at the little girl before looking to her husband for answers. Demetre smiled warmly at the child, gesturing for her to come near him. Alette stood frozen for a short time. "Go on," Danielle whispered in her ear. Alette stepped closer to the man, glancing down at her feet and up at him continually. Demetre lifted her chin with his forefinger and smiled once he made eye contact.

"Do you know who I am?" Demetre asked. Alette tilted her head and, in the corner of her eyes, looked at the fancy tablecloth upon which sat real metal utensils and crystal. "What's the matter? Can't you speak?"

"Oui Monsieur," Alette mumbled, "I can speak. I know very well who you are."

"Are you afraid of me?" Alette did not answer. Simone pretended not to be bothered by her father's affection for the little girl. He took a small bundle of grapes from the basket of fruit that Alette handled and put it on his plate. Next, he retrieved an apple from the basket and offered it to her. Alette looked at her sister for approval and was permitted by a nod of the head.

"Merci, Monsieur," Alette said, finally smiling back shyly.

Etiennette poured a thin layer of honey onto a biscuit. "I suppose we're going to have the entire family working here eventually? Why is this girl here? There are no small children she can be a companion to, why do we need this little n—"

"I don't wish to discuss it at the moment," Demetre sternly answered.

"Is she in training to be your next—"

"For God's sake, Etiennette!" Demetre shouted, banging his fist on the table of clanking dishes.

"When I say that we will not discuss it, I expect for you to hold your tongue!"

Danielle tip-toed around the table serving the food. She recognized the look of hatred that Etiennette threw at Alette. From that moment on, Danielle reemphasized to Alette the imperativeness of staying by her side at all times.

"What's the matter, Lettie?" Danielle asked as she retrieved water from the well in the back garden. "You've hardly said a word all morning."

"Why did the mistress look at me that way?" the child asked, selecting purple flowers to place as decoration within the mansion.

"What way?"

"Mean. Did I do something wrong?"

Danielle selected her words carefully before speaking. "No, she's a very unhappy woman. It does not have much to do with you. Just stay out of her way, and everything will be fine. Aside from the mistress, do you like working in the big house?"

Alette smiled brightly, thinking of all the beautiful figurines and other items in the house, and the ones she had yet to discover. "When can I go up the stairs and look in the other rooms?" She asked with a slight perk in her voice.

"There will be plenty of time for that."

Alette scurried towards Danielle when she heard rustling in the nearby bushes and shoes crushing the fallen leaves on the paved walkway. Soon, a man dressed in a brown suit stepped into plain view, swatting and dodging a moth that had just learned to fly, or so it seemed. Alette giggled at the man's funny expressions before the insect sputtered away. "Stop that," Danielle whispered.

"Ahh, there's no sound more precious than a child's laugh, wouldn't you agree?" The man said, brushing off the particles on his suit and removing his hat. "Hello," said the man, smiling nervously. "I didn't expect to see you today, although it is quite a pleasure." Danielle's heart flipped, peering at the handsome man while subtly attempting to hide her stomach with the tin pail. "Well, it's been a while," he said, smiling on the side of his mouth, trying not to look at her belly behind the pail.

"It *has*, Mr. Santee," Danielle admitted, studying his nearly smooth-shaven facial features.

"Has it been *that* long? You're looking at me as if you've forgotten who I am," Alphonse said, still smiling. She tried to forget him and everything that he represented since she knew that she could not have either.

Danielle motioned for them to move further away from the house, which had been known to grow functioning, and often incriminating, eyes and ears. They spilled into the garden within the trees and vegetation. "How did you sneak onto the land without being seen? What business do you have here, Monsieur Santee?" Danielle wanted to know.

Alphonse raised his eyebrow at Danielle's cross tone. "I did not have to sneak, but if I did, I would have entered near the brook west of here. Or near the well several kilometers southeast. Plenty of unsupervised wooded areas there." Danielle looked at him sternly. "Yes, well. I'm here to speak with the man of the house."

"My apologies, but I'm afraid that since you've come unannounced, Monsieur has already left for the day."

"That can't be. We have been corresponding. I had an appointment with him today. Maybe he has forgotten." Alphonse guessed with furrowed brows.

"He will be away until evening," said Danielle. "He did seem a bit anxious when leaving. May I ask what it is about?"

Alphonse grinned at her curiosity. "Business. But I suppose once that subject is taken care of, we can talk about *you.*"

"*Me?*"

Alphonse grinned before his attention was drawn onto Alette, who had unintentionally collected an enormous bundle of flowers while curiously glancing at the two of them and eavesdropping on their conversation.

"Hello," he said, falling to one knee. Alette smiled timidly. "Do you like candy?" Alette threw aside the armful of flowers and would have nearly jumped on him if Danielle had not caught her by the back of her dress and pulled the girl closer to her.

"She hates it," Danielle answered. Alette frowned at her sister for voicing such a lie.

"Well, that's a shame," Alphonse playfully responded. He pulled out a chilled tin containing pieces of candy wrapped in waxed paper. "I wish someone would eat this before it melts."

"Can I have it!?" Alette begged, breaking away from her guardian to approach the man.

"I'm sorry," Danielle apologized. "She doesn't eat sweets, and she's only had candy once in her life and that was last year at Christmas."

"You work on a sugar plantation and she doesn't eat anything sweet?"

"Mr. Santee, I have more of a right to question you or *anyone* who carries chocolates in their pockets during the summer season in Louisiana. Besides, we're not in the habit of receiving or making our own candy or tasting the sugar we grow. But no, she has never had chocolate."

"Well, one piece of chocolate is enough to get anyone addicted, so please accept my humblest apology in advance." Alphonse handed it to a cheerful Alette, who took no time tearing away the paper and stuffing the chocolate into her mouth. "Of course, I couldn't forget *you*, Danielle." He unwrapped another piece of dark chocolate and held it up to the girls' lips. Danielle stared stonily into his eyes, his gentle smile never wavering. After a brief hesitation, her eyes softened and she parted her lips, allowing him to feed her the sweet, rich candy. He slowly wiped some of the melted chocolate off the side of her mouth with his thumb. Alette covered her giggles with her hand, glancing back and forth at the two of them.

"Alette," said Danielle, "do you know your way back to the house?" Alette nodded. "Take this pail and those flowers into the kitchen and give it to Corrine. She will give you your orders at that time. Tout de suite." Alette waddled into the house with the pail.

Danielle inhaled deeply and closed her eyes, "Mr. Santee," she blurted. "Perhaps you should arrange another time to meet with Monsieur Soileau."

Alphonse smiled and paused long enough for Danielle to realize that she was blushing. "Perhaps I should. Or perhaps you should tell me why you were avoiding me that evening, especially after we had previously enjoyed our time together, or so I thought."

"I was not an invited guest of the party and did not have the luxury of enjoying the festivities, Mr. Santee. I was there to work, and that is what I did."

"And somewhere in your orders, you were instructed to open your heart to me while talking near the bayou?"

"I did what you requested of me."

"And sharing your desires, and reminding me of my responsibility to protect my father's legacy was all in a day's work?"

"Oui, Monsieur Santee. I did what you asked." She began to digest his words, thinking that perhaps that night *did* mean something to him. Alphonse took time to study her face. The sides of her mouth bent up slightly as if forcing an obliging look. However, in her eyes, he saw something much different than the annoyance she displayed earlier. He saw a sadness behind them, but the root of her feelings, he could not determine just yet. She swallowed hard. Alphonse nodded slowly. Danielle knew what he was doing. Her father studied her often and was always correct, which frustrated her immensely.

"Please stop looking at me that way," she turned her head. "Just stop it."

"Your lips say one thing, but your soul says another," said Alphonse. Danielle was silent. Alphonse was partially amused by his accuracy. "Since I requested something of you *then*, let me ask something of you *now*, if I may. The truth. Did you dream of someone drinking castor oil?"

"Nooo," she tried not to smile.

"Did something happen that night to make you change the way you did?"

"Yes. I realized that I should have never accompanied you into the woods."

"Why not?"

"You will not tell Monsieur Soileau?"

"Never."

She released her feelings from incarceration. "...Because I did not want to feel the things that I felt for you. I belonged to someone else...as did you."

"Danielle, I don't follow."

The girl became antsy, suddenly deciding that her feelings had no place in the outside world. "Mr. Santee, you should really schedule another appointment with Monsieur Soileau. I must continue with my chores—"

"Danielle." He said sternly. "What did you feel? And exactly to whom did *I* belong?

"You know your way off of the plantation, I'm sure—"

"Danielle, talk to me—"

"And please pardon my late wishes, but congratulations on your engagement."

"Danielle, stop." He whispered fervently, grabbing her shoulders. "I don't have a fiancé, nor a wife...is...is that what you were told?"

"I learned that night that you and Mademoiselle Toutant—"

"We are *not* coupled, nor have we ever been. I despise the woman." Alphonse informed before running his hand down his face. "Who fed you those lies?"

Danielle said nothing to avoid a boomerang of trouble that may come back her way.

"Listen. I don't know what all occurred that night, but I know that I began to love in a way I never have before." He took her hand and led her towards a cast iron bench huddled by bushes that he saw in the distance, and offered her a seat before sitting close to her. Danielle looked worryingly back at the house, hoping the two were unseen and that Alette was following Corrine's orders. The two sat and Alphonse took Danielle's other hand.

"Since we last met, I've taken these past months to better myself for you," said Alphonse. Danielle looked confused. "I almost worked myself to the grave and improved my business tremendously. And I am grateful to you." He smiled and bowed his head. He looked back up at her, getting lost in her beauty and so distracted by her smooth brown skin that he almost lost his words.

Danielle grew uncomfortable by Alphonse's gaze. Although he looked even more softly at her as her master does, she was almost angry at him for continuing to show interest in her, still, even in her current condition.

"Monsieur Santee, I'm happy that your business is thriving, but it was all *your* doing."

"But you awoke something within me," he said. "I have to know. What is it that you felt for me that night?"

"...I felt myself loving you." Unable to believe what she had just confessed, Danielle brought her hands to her lips.

"Well, then our feelings were kindred," Alphonse said, almost exhaling. "But you say it as if it hurts. Do you still love me, Danielle?"

The young woman bit the corner of her bottom lip, then shook her head and smiled a closed-mouth grimace to keep from crying. "Don't you understand? It does not matter that my heart drums harder simply by the thought of you or that every beat pounds your name. Everything that you are fascinates me. You carry yourself the way I would imagine a royal would, and your kindness, laced with the strength of your character, allows me to see the king in you. That evening was the best night of my years because I saw *you*. The window to your soul was open, and there was beauty on the other side. And I fought it, but I desperately wanted to become a part of anything that helps to put a smile on your face.

"I never imagined that the boy, whom I considered a fabrication, would grow to be the man of genuine existence, and ultimately, a conqueror of my heart...but it matters not that our meetings are not accidental. And it doesn't matter that I love you, Alphonse. What matters is that I can't have you. I can't have you."

Ignoring the doubt that she expressed, he held dearly to the words that were in his favor. His feelings burst into several directions as he smiled lightly at his first name being enwrapped in her breath. He wanted to kiss her for affirming her love for him, but his heart ached at the sound of defeat that followed it. He said, "I told you then that I needed you. But I didn't tell you that I needed you by my side. When

I told you that I worked harder than ever, it was with every intention to earn enough wages to buy your freedom in the end."

Danielle gasped. The rumors weren't rumors at all. "You want to buy me?" she asked. "*Me*?"

"No. That would make me no better than the man whose eye you're under. I don't want to be your master; I want to be your husband. Forgive me for not asking your kin first. Please, will you be my wife?"

Danielle could barely breathe. "A proposal?" she questioned in disbelief. Danielle shook her head sadly, "...But I'm with child."

"I've got eyes," he smiled, looking down at her belly. Danielle went to cover her stomach with her arms in embarrassment, but Alphonse stopped her, lightly holding her wrists. He nodded down at her womb and glanced up permissively at Danielle. She nodded in consent and looked away. Alphonse gently rubbed her belly, feeling the baby suddenly move about in response. Alphonse's smile grew, and possibly his heart. He then held Danielle's hands, "You didn't think that I would want to purchase your freedom without the babe, did you?"

The girl whipped her head around at Alphonse. Afraid to ask, she said slowly as if approaching something dangerous with caution, "But, do you know who the father is?"

Alphonse swallowed and shifted his eyes to a nearby bush and back to her. "Danielle, as I understand, the father is your master, am I correct?" Almost completely ashamed, Danielle nodded. Alphonse asked, "What is your concern?" Danielle had plenty but could not voice them, especially Etiennette's promise. "We've all got a past," said Alphonse. "I don't want you to think that you can't marry me because you have one as well. I would not be an honest man if I said that I did not struggle with the idea that the blood of another man ties a bond in your womb. But my family were slaves once too, remember? I know what happens when the master takes what he wants or wants to create more property." Danielle had always thought of her child as being treated differently before and after arrival. But hearing it verbalized that the possibility of her baby—she and the master's child—becoming just another piece of inventory struck Danielle in an unsettling way. Alphonse continued, "But unless you are in love with Monsieur Soileau, and you won't have me, then I'd have no choice but to be on my way. Or does your heart reside in two places at once? If so, choose me to keep shelter of it."

"But there are plenty of other women who will suit you—free women. What would you want with me? I'm no good for you."

"If that were true of the free women in Louisiana or all the other places I've traveled, then I would be married. I can't help wanting *you*. When I conceded to my feelings, I knew that loving you meant loving *all* of you. Not just the *You* who sang in the ballroom, but the *You* who undergoes difficulty, and the *You* who stands before me carrying a life and two heartbeats. I can't choose to love you only during desired seasons... Let me love you, Danielle. Say you'll marry me."

Alette had forgotten her way to the kitchen. Somewhere in between a left turn into the hallway and a right turn past the grand staircase, she found herself in the dim ballroom. She placed the pail by the door and walked further into the room as the eyes of men, women, and children locked in past decades followed her. She looked upon the orchestra loft, mistaking the shadows of the chairs and music stands for a small audience of people. For a moment, she was fearful until a ray of light shone partially through a set of heavy drapes that were halfway drawn to one side. She slid the drapes of all seven windows open, inviting the sunlight to spill into the dance floor and to the ceiling where the crystal chandelier projected a gorgeous sphere of rainbows. She quietly ran her fingers along the ivory keys of Demetre's piano before leaping into the center of the red, purple, and green lights, dancing and twirling in a circle.

Alette peeked out of the ballroom doors to see if anyone was approaching. She then sprinted up the grand staircase in search of an adventure.

The little girl moved about the hall, learning each squeak in the floor as she took swift, careful steps to Mademoiselle Simone's unoccupied bedroom where she quietly turned the knob and entered. The pink curtains danced among the wind of the open window and appeared inviting to the eight-year-old girl. She was awed by the number of dolls on the bed, to whom she rushed and immediately played. Never before had she seen pink-cheeked dolls so white and elegantly dressed. Amazed by their likeness to actual people, she traced her small fingers over their sharp facial features, feeling the grooves of the eyes and red mouth. She tightly hugged a baby doll dressed in a Christening gown and gently laid her back on the bed. Alette explored the room, finding perfume, a blank dance card, a curling stick, and a book of short poems on top of the bureau. She picked up the sticks and tapped them together before one flew out of her hand and landed next to a daguerreotype of her sister and Simone. She was amazed by the never-before-seen invention. The girls looked small, and their eyes smiled. To her, Danielle looked just as pretty as she always did. Alette quickly stuffed the picture in her dress pocket seconds before Simone walked into the room after spending the day with her tutor.

"What are you doing in my quarters?" Simone demanded to know as she stacked her books on the mantel.

Alette's voice disappeared along with a reason behind her curious actions, "Cleaning!" She finally blurted.

"Cleaning what? My room hasn't a speck of dust in it. And with what are you cleaning? I don't see a rag." Alette twiddled her fingers, hoping that Simone wouldn't discover the missing picture. "Go into the bathing room down the hall and empty the pots outside...well, go on."

In the bathing room, Alette saw a porcelain bowl with two handles on the sides and a painted picture of a flower and vines all around it. Inside, it contained urine with several flower petals floating in it.

Alette walked softly down the hallway on the balls of her feet to avoid spilling the yellow substance onto the floor and herself. She was certain that her heart skipped a beat when she saw Etiennette coming in her direction, walking hard on her heels. "Why aren't you using the servant's stairway?"

Alette gazed up at the woman, who had a sinister yet attractive appearance to her face. "I beg your pardon, Madame," she said, "but I lost my way."

"Well, this should help you remember." Etiennette hit the bottom of the pot, causing the urine to splash onto the child's face and into her mouth. The girl gasped loudly, dropping the pot and watching it shatter into tiny pieces, and her headscarf hitting the floor after it. The mistress calmly said to her, "Clean up this mess. And the next time you walk around here, move out of my way. And put that tignon back on your pathetic little head. I don't care if it *is* soaked in piss."

She retrieved a rag from a pocket of her dress and sopped the bodily fluids and chipped porcelain, wringing it into a pail, creating small knicks on her fingers. When all was cleaned, she headed downstairs and into the back garden where Danielle remained talking to Alphonse. She wandered around the trees and bushes before they saw the child, who was now searching frantically. They walked briskly towards her and stood in shock at the sight and smell of the girl. "Lettie," Danielle said, hurrying to her and kneeling, "What happened?" Upon seeing their faces, the child felt safe enough to surrender to her tears and cry silently.

In the moments that passed, Danielle explained to Alphonse that she needed to quickly take Alette to her cabin to change into fresh garments and return to the mansion to resume their chores. The man hated to depart in such a manner, feeling angry about his helplessness and the cruelty that the young child endured. He promised to return after completing a big job at sea.

* * *

"I could still taste it," Alette said, clenching her fists and shuddering. "I continued my silence for the remainder of the day and into the night at home with Maman. For the first time, I was angry at Danielle for letting me leave her side. It was then, and every day after, when the abuse in the house progressed. Prior to working in the house, I was not completely shielded from witnessing some of the cruelty that occurred on the Soileau Plantation. But after becoming a domestic servant, I finally saw all of the suffering through a lens that was polished and buffered by the dying souls it captured. But I did not expect to encounter it within the house.

"When blowing dandelions and wishing for a better life did not work, and wearing a grigri did not grant me the luck I needed, I finally believed Danielle when she said that there was no such thing as good luck. I became numb, which was my best remedy for survival. There was no time or sympathy for feelings or words of comfort when in the presence of my owners or overseers.

"Children often went unembraced and uncradled on the plantation when there was work to be done. And adult bodies would be brutalized if it was not completed." She looked at Charles, who stared at her with hard eyes, angry at the overseers who made loved ones choose work over their hurting little ones. Alette continued, "I never thought about how painful it must have been for the adults until I became one. And after a while, the children learned—we learned—that there was no use of a public display of tears... Hugs, Charles—that is one thing your mother and her brothers can never say they were denied."

***

After preparing for a night's rest, Danielle knelt beside her bed and performed the sign of the cross when her cabin door creaked open. No one visited her late at night except for one person. "Oh, Monsieur, I was about to begin prayer—"

"Well, stop and listen to what I have to say," said a female voice. Danielle whipped around, struggling to stand to her feet. The silhouette of a woman stood motionless in the doorway.

"Prayer, for you, is about as useless as a one-legged horse." She took two steps inside the cabin and shut the door. Danielle began to shake as she offered Etiennette a seat, but the mistress refused, claiming that their business "will not absorb much time."

"A lot has changed since I last paid you a visit," Etiennette calmly stated with half of her face covered in shadow. "And yet, a lot has remained stagnant." As she spoke, she wandered around Danielle's cabin, peering at her belongings and occasionally picking them up for inspection. "Why do you choose to anger me, Danielle? I don't know how you convinced your master to allow your sister to work in my home, or if it took any convincing at all, but you're a poor example to your apprentice, my dear. Alette was poking around in places she had no business. I think she now understands not to make a habit of it. She is very similar to you—gallivanting around a home that is not yours, doing as you please. Like you, Demetre insists that Alette works within our home. However, I would hate to have to teach her another lesson.

"And just what are you attempting to accomplish, girl? What do you want from my family? What do you want from my *husband*? Do you think you can get all that you desire from him? Well, I assure you that nothing he gives to you has not already been in my hands first," she said, picking up the broken cameo and tossing it back onto the dressing table.

"I see how he looks at you, and I noticed it that evening at the dinner party. But don't fool yourself into thinking that salt is really sugar. I've seen how flushed your cheeks become when you are near him. He *is* handsome and seems to have that effect on a lot of women. But don't think that my Demetre loves you," Etiennette added with a shaky voice. "I have seen whores like you, putting your tails out there, just waiting for an opportunity at a better life for yourselves and the worthless little animals you breed.

"But you don't seem to understand that there are severe consequences for doing what you please. I have said it previously, and I meant every word of it—if that slave you are carrying enters this world with white skin or resembles my husband in any way, I will not hesitate to kill you, that child, and anyone in your family of my choosing. You may bed whomever you want on this plantation—if you have not run through them all. But there is a cost for touching my husband and crossing my family." With that said, Etiennette left just as quietly as she had arrived.

Eight

❦

Soileau Plantation
Fall 1859

The sweet smell of almond verbenas and other flowers and their nectar engulfed the Soileau mansion on the first day of autumn. Fast-paced footsteps and rustled clothing of the help and the linens they carried became the home's heartbeat during the preparation of one of the grandest occasions to occur within its walls. Over one hundred guests were expected to arrive, including family members who traveled great distances in support of their dear Simone. But some were motivated by materialistic curiosity. The neighing of decorated horses and the clipping of hedges were as soothing as a lullaby outside of Simone's bedroom windows where she was accompanied by cousins, Gloria and Bella Soileau, and two childhood friends, Leala and Bastienne. Corrine, silent and forcing herself to be expressionless, succeeded in blending in the floral wallpaper, serving as her backdrop as she waited to style Simone. She could not help but be amused by the naivety revealed in the girls' conversations and almost laughed at the gossip she had heard about some of the other young women in the parish.

Unfathomed by the dislike that their fathers have for one another, Simone and her two curly-haired blonde cousins did as relatives often do when they have been kissed by passing time; they interacted as if none had escaped. Both sisters, now in society and wanting to be pegged snuggly with the ways of other American girls their age, rarely spoke French, and as Simone noticed, barely retained their accents.

Too much was changing in Simone's world that she could barely keep up. The only thing that didn't seem to be immutable was the figure that she sulked at in the mirror at least twice a week. Even the curve of her 17-year-old cousin Gloria's hips made her popular with several men of class and wealth, to one she favored and carefully wrote letters while sprawled across Simone's bed. And even cousin Bella, who was only months younger than Simone, was sure to take after their round great-aunt Estelle. But her body revolted, deciding it would develop a delicate feminine shape, and her face would clear, making a number of young men in various counties finally notice her sparkling blue eyes and call upon her. The teenagers, lounging in their white undergarments and rag curls and updos, ate delicate snacks strategically selected to avoid any bloating or bad breath.

"But you're *supposed* to open your mouth a little when you kiss," Bastienne explained to Simone. "Don't you know anything?" Simone and the other girls looked upon her as an expert. After all, she *was* newly engaged. But little did the girls know that Bastienne had only recently learned this well-known fact herself.

"But what do you do with your hands while he's kissing you?" Leala asked, arising from *The Scarlet Letter*. "Should you keep them folded in your lap?"

"Well, that depends," said Gloria, halting in her letter to Francis D. Edwards III who was finishing his studies in Europe. "If he's a good enough kisser, enough to make you melt, you'll suddenly find yourself with your arms around his neck." She smiled devilishly, "And if *you're* a good enough kisser, it just may make him *rise*."

Bastienne and Gloria giggled as the other girls gasped, turning red. Wide-eyed, Bella drew out her words disappointingly, "Why, Gloria Vignette Soileau." Corrine wondered if she should indirectly intervene by dropping an item loudly or asking an unrelated question before the discussion turned to filth. However, she kept quiet, untangling Simone's brown hair from the loose rag curls. Besides, what would stop them from discussing sex at a later time anyway? She thought.

"Well, she's right." Bastienne still giggled. "But it doesn't take much for a man to rise."

Leala placed her hand on her chest. "Don't tell me you two no longer have your pearls," she said almost in a whisper as if parents might be listening nearby.

"I still have mine," said Bastienne.

Everyone whipped their heads around to Gloria who remained quietly smirking, lying on her stomach with her heels kicked up and blowing on the wet ink of the rag paper. Their eyes widened as Gloria took her time to respond. "Oh, collect yourselves. I still have mine as well," she said without looking up. "But I know that on my wedding night, it'll be divine, and sweet and slow." Corrine withheld a snicker and the knowledge that "the first time" would be nothing short of the opposite of what Gloria imagined.

"When it comes to kissing," said Bastienne, smoothing the edges of her auburn hair, "before Harrison and I were engaged, I watched enough of our servants sneaking about and kissing to see how they did it. And when they weren't kissing, they were always off somewhere getting each other pregnant, like bunnies. But it's not their fault. The females are disgracefully taught to always keep their legs open."

Simone could feel Corrine's hands slow down when Bastienne said this. *Getting each other pregnant?* Simone thought. Out of the girls in the room, she wondered who else's Papa was suspected of fathering slave children. Did their fathers also look at their slave women the same way they used to look at their mothers? She wondered. Bastienne continued, "They start having babies when they're merely children themselves. It's as if something suddenly comes over them and they forget that we ever taught them the gospel. Sometimes I feel like they're better off not knowing it at all, like on my aunt's plantation. And from then on, most of the girls are always looking evil for no reason. Barely smiling, even when one attempts to be nice to them. Hmm, so sad."

Leala slunk back into her book as the room remained quiet. Simone could feel the speed in Corrine's hands pick back up again.

"Here you are, my dear cousin," said Bella, presenting Simone with a pink velvet box tied with a light blue silk ribbon. "It's from Daddy. He bought it specially for your big evening."

Simone had forgotten for a moment that Corrine had a hold of a lock of her hair that was seconds away from being yanked as she uncoiled the hair from the rag. "This is from Uncle Emile...for me?" Simone asked unassured.

"Of course," said Bella, pulling up a chair in front of Simone. "Our fathers may not get along, and possibly never will, but that doesn't mean that Daddy doesn't have the deepest affection for his lovely niece."

Simone's heart fluttered with joy at the sound of that. She slowly untied the ribbon and opened the box. She gasped lightly as the other girls drew near to look at the golden dangling earrings and hair combs encrusted with pink diamonds. "Do you love them?" Bella asked, delighting in Simone's happiness.

"Oh, I do. Very much. Oh, I don't know what to say....Oh, Corrine, look! Be sure to put the hair combs in when you're finishing up."

Bella clasped her hands together and drew them to her mouth, smiling greatly. "I knew you would. Here, let me put the earrings on for you." Simone quickly removed the old cameo earrings that her father had given her and allowed her cousin to insert the sparkling new ones. Bella inserted the shepherd's hooks before kissing Simone on the cheek. Simone didn't know which was greater, the excitement of being in possession of the most beautiful earrings and hair combs she had ever seen, or the idea of her uncle thinking enough of her to purchase such a presumably pricey gift.

"Be sure to thank him for me. Or rather, I will write him a letter of gratitude."

"You can thank him yourself," said Gloria. "He'll be here this evening for your party. And the urgent business meeting."

Simone smiled at the news, for she had not seen her uncle in almost a year. "I'll be sure to thank him to his face then," she said. "And there will be an urgent meeting?" A hint of concern showed on Simone's face. "Oh? Is everything alright?"

Bella and Gloria glanced at one another, silently deciding who should share the news. Bella spoke, "Uncle Demetre did not mention anything of it?"

Feeling anxious, Simone said, "No, he rarely makes mention of any of his affairs."

"Well..." said Bella before turning to the two friends sitting on the chase, "please excuse us."

Leala and Bastienne protested, mentioning that they were insulted by the lack of trust, promising not to tell a soul. "And we're not dressed properly," said Bastienne. "What if someone sees us?" Gloria threw sheets at them and wrestled them out of the bedroom door.

Bella began to explain, "As you know, we used to have the sugar plantation and mill in Saint-Martin as well as Louisiana. But since the abolition on the island long ago, and the demolition of our hard work there, each year, it has been harder to compete with other sugar companies in the states. Therefore, our fathers have lost a lot of money, Simone—"

"Oh goodness," Gloria interrupted, leaning back onto her elbows. "Bella talks as if we're destitute. Our family has plenty of money. Besides, they are resolving the issue as we speak."

"What if it's worse than they're making it appear?" asked Bella.

"It's not," said Gloria. "You're just doing what you're best at—worrying. Father and uncle have everything straightened out. Now stop it, you're taking away from our sweet cousin's day. Look at her, the poor girl can barely sit still now." The girls watched Simone nervously bounce her leg. "Now let's put an end to this conversation once and for all, and let the men handle it. Agreed?" Simone and Bella nodded as Gloria opened the door to let in the others who fell onto the floor of the bedroom after eavesdropping.

The girls spoke on, eating snacks and reading as Simone sat quietly, auditioning different seating positions and wondering about the evening's outcome and if she would get any attention from desirable men.

"My goodness, Simone," said Bastienne, "will you hold still while your Negra does your hair?"

"It's humanly impossible for anyone to sit at such lengths," Simone complained. "And is it absolutely necessary that one head should have so many curls, Corrine?"

"I'm sorry, Miss," said Corrine, untying the thin white rags. "Your mother made certain that you should have lots of lovely ringlets so that you look your very best tonight."

"Uh!" Simone grunted. "Mother has taken part in my sheer embarrassment again. Two ringlets and I can get away with being sophisticated. A head full, and I may as well have some milk and take a nap."

Simone's maidens chortled. "The embarrassment has yet to begin, dear cousin," said Gloria, making her way to the mirrored bureau, fluffing her blonde updo before prancing back to the bed and rippling upon it.

"Really?" Simone moaned.

"Yes," the girls mumbled and nodded in agreement.

Simone cringed at the mass verdict.

Bella asked, "What is it, really, sweet cousin?"

Simone's truth deflated, "I just don't understand why I can't consider marriage on my own terms. Should I not be allowed to fall in love naturally and marry *when* I want? And once married, I can never sleep diagonally or in the shape of an X ever again until death parts us." The girls looked around at one another and smirked. "Isn't anyone bothered that our lives are not our own? We are in a prison of our own existence. Why, our clothing alone keeps us from being as free as we wish—tight corsets, long huge dresses allowing us limited movement, preventing us from running as we wish, leaping if we wanted—"

"Climbing trees and hanging upside down from the branches if we desired," Gloria over-exaggerated in her dramatics before melting out of character. "Hmm," she said, "that's adorable. It's time to grow up and accept what is." The young woman propped herself up onto her elbows.

"Tell me if I'm correct," said Bastienne. "You want a man to court you, but you're not yet ready for marriage. You have dreams of traveling and learning vast subjects, even goals of being an expert in them one day."

"Yes," Simone said sharply as if someone finally understood her.

"You want your mate, but yet you want to stand alongside him and claim your independence."

"Yes, yes!"

"You know that your life is worth far more than running a household, supporting your husband's career and his public opinions, all while being expected to look radiant and please him as many times as he wants."

"That's exactly it, Bastienne!"

"You don't want a lifetime of constantly elevating your man while the world forgets about you and the good that you have to offer."

"Absolutely!"

"And what about the sacrifices that you'll be expected to make? It'll be hard enough to say goodbye to your family name, let alone saying goodbye to your family and destroying your figure while you push out his future."

"Yes, that's it. Yes!"

"Well, too bad, Simone. You have two choices. Either sabotage your *own* future and security by becoming an old maid, or learn to love your role as a woman of prestige and rich heritage and do it with grace." Simone frowned at these options.

"I see things quite differently," said Leala, setting down the book. "There's nothing wrong with allowing a man to be a man while stepping back as he creates a certain lifestyle for me. As long as he is just and good."

"There is nothing wrong with that unless your happiness ceases to exist because of it," said Simone. "Why *must* we sacrifice almost everything about ourselves, even our ambitions, because of the gender God has selected for us? Do I forget who I am because of whose arm I cling? My fear is that the moment I walk out of those doors in curls and pastels, I'm in jeopardy of losing Simone Soileau, only to adopt my new name— 'The wife of...' And it will be then that I gradually become someone's possession. Will my knowledge of culture, music, languages, and mathematics hold value and merit after I'm set upon the block and taken into matrimony? So, forgive me if I take little joy in being primped and paraded about for my beauty and intellect like a show pony or a prize slave."

Corrine pursed her lips harder than she intended while her hands continued to work.

"Hush now," said Bella, in the calming nature that only she could provide to her favorite cousin. "Don't you think you should be a bit more optimistic? What if, amongst all the pageantry and people, you find a man who doesn't want you to change? What *if*, to him, your spark and independence and grand ideas are the very best part of you?" Simone said nothing, only thinking of the possibility of meeting someone like that in just a couple of hours. Bella continued, scooting her chair closer to Simone and touching her hand. "You can't go into this thinking the worst. You have been privileged to be a daughter of fortune. Take this opportunity to enjoy it. Take pride in the idea of men coming here to see *you* and to get to know the beautiful, intelligent you that *I* know."

Flattered and embarrassed, Simone's light pink thin lips smiled a little over Bella's new perspective. "Well, perhaps I *have been* a little apprehensive. But partially because my meeting with gentlemen thus far has not been a happy experience. Mother has ensured that I received the proper training in etiquette, but it has not done a bit of good when it comes to capturing the eye and heart of a good man."

Gloria moved to the edge of the bed with Bastienne now joining her. The two closed in on Simone. "Poor lamb," said Gloria. "I wish we had gotten to you much earlier. Etiquette lessons can only show you how a lady should conduct herself while in public. But it cannot teach you how to charm a man, nor the art of flirtation."

Bastienne added, "Some of it will come naturally if you are encountered by the right gentleman, and by 'right' I mean one who makes over $37,000 a year."

"Don't tell her that," hissed Bella. "We don't want her to focus solely on money or dismiss a good man if he makes short of that amount."

"Well, if he were a 'good man' to begin with, he would make well over $37,000. And what's stopping him from thinking about the money and assets he would receive after taking Simone as his bride?" Bastienne responded. "They all think it, even though they don't verbalize it. Now, Simone, tonight, we will be your court of ladies and will guide you throughout the evening. But you should at least know the basics in how to capture a man's interest and eventually his heart."

From how to bat her eyelashes in a lady-like, "less whorish" fashion, to techniques on how to walk, draw out her speech and even laugh sensually yet fetchingly, the girls took pride in sharing their wisdom with their newest pupil. With her head up and shoulders back, Simone exuded a confidence that sat dormant until now. She felt a new spark of life and optimism race through her veins, making her excited about the gifts that the night could bring. After all, it was her evening, and she made the decision to enjoy every moment of it. Her newfound courage sparked a rebirth of energy in the rounded room.

Danielle entered the room with a platter of light hors d'oeuvres before distributing them. The girls delighted in the fruit and stuffed cucumbers for a short time until their smiles thawed when observing the servant's condition. Simone scowled, gazing away into the looking glass and allowing Corrine to continue pinning her waist-long brown curls in an updo. Danielle could feel the girls' curious eyes on her and her stomach, but the room remained quiet for several moments. With breasts larger than anyone had ever seen on her and wide, curvy hips, the girls instinctively swept curls to one side or smoothed down parts of their hair. Some blushed as their bodies looked like those of small children in comparison to Danielle's mature frame.

Danielle looked at their faces without holding eye contact. Not one smiled at her as they used to when she arrived; however, she had long since accepted that things were different between her and all the girls with whom she had grown up. She no longer dwelled on the days when they laughed until they cried or performed in original Soileau presentations of plays where Danielle was often cast as a servant, villain, or talking animal rather than a damsel, fairy, or princess of a neighboring country, as she used to when the girls were smaller. "Bonjour Danielle," said Bella, breaking the silence.

"Mademoiselle," Danielle nodded. "It is lovely to have you as a guest again," Bella replied with a smile that faded as the intrigue of Danielle's new fragile condition grew.

Gloria glanced at Bastienne, who must have shared the same thoughts and questions as she by the heavily concentrated look on her face. Her eyes wandered over to Simone, who, only seconds ago, was happy and relaxed. But now, her cousin was visibly embarrassed, with cheeks nearly a deep maroon. Not sure what to make of it, Gloria asked what the other girls surely wanted to know. "Danielle?" said Gloria. "How long have you been with child?" Leala slowly slid her book down below her nose, listening and watching.

"Well, Miss," said Danielle. "It has been about seven months now."

"And the father—is he a slave here or on a neighboring plantation?"

Simone interjected, glaring angrily at her through the mirror. "Gloria, if you don't mind, I would rather you not ask our slaves about the sins they commit when the sun sets."

"Oh Simone," Gloria waved, "stop being so huffy and just worry about getting beautiful for the evening. Danielle, is the father here on the plantation?"

"Miss Gloria," Danielle replied, "perhaps I should follow Mademoiselle Simone's wishes and not speak on such things."

Displeased by the secrecy, Gloria, who had always thought the scandalous and unorthodox lives of slaves were juicier than any of the gossip about her white counterparts, felt as if she would burst if she did not know the details of what she asked. "What is it with you two?" Gloria wondered. "I simply asked about the boy's whereabouts, and you're both turning this into a mystery. Now I demand to have my question answered."

Danielle detected the suspicion that crawled upon the girls' faces. Her eyes flickered upon Simone, whose anxiety almost brought her to tears. "The father," Danielle answered, "Is on a neighboring plantation but may have received his freedom papers, I think."

Wide-eyed and without blinking, Corrine looked up at Danielle and back down onto her task. Simone exhaled slowly. Gloria said, "My father allows our slaves to marry, especially the ones who are with child. Says he doesn't want to be responsible for morally leading flock astray. He says he wants to set a good example. Does Uncle Demetre permit you all to marry?"

"No ma'am. To my knowledge, there has been no mention of us having that privilege under his permission."

"Would you want to marry if given the opportunity?"

"I suppose if Maîtriser Demetre insisted upon it."

Bastienne asked, "And the father of your unborn child has not attempted to claim you as his own but rather left you as he made his way into society?"

Danielle remained quiet, feeling guilty for having lied in the first place. The girls accepted her silence as a solid answer to Bastienne's question. "Do you see?" Bastienne asked the girls, "Negro men are like dogs, happily planting children in Negras and walking away to join their next female. Disgraceful."

Corrine grit her teeth at Bastienne's lack of knowledge regarding the sexual exploitation that really occurred on most plantations, including her own. Gloria moved towards the wardrobe where her blue and pink dress hung. She opened it, unpinning a silk rosary from an inside layer of her dress. Walking over to Danielle, she took her tray of snacks and set it aside. "Because I care about your salvation, I want you to have this and use it to repent when you pray at night," Gloria said sorrowfully as if helping a wounded deer. "And when you pray, ask for forgiveness for the beast who did this to you, forcing your child to be a bastard. I think it's so wrong that so many of you people are without fathers. Just so sad."

Danielle settled on the words, thinking of all the fathers she knew on the plantation who wanted to be with their women and children. Some traveled miles on Saturday night and Sunday to visit their families on other properties. Some were purposed as bucks, while other fathers she knew were sold away from their families or killed if caught fleeing. She thought of Demetre, who had in fact made her child a bastard. Giving a pseudo smile of gratitude and one of pity for Gloria's belief, Danielle accepted the rosary. "Merci Mademoiselle. You are so kind to care about my soul and salvation."

"You're welcome," Gloria said, curling the rosary into Danielle's hand. "Now be a dear and help us get ready. The hour draws near."

Corrine worked meticulously on Simone's hair and wardrobe before she and Danielle assisted the others into their corsets and dresses. The excitement swelled as they began to hear music and the arrival of carriages. They listened intently as each guest was announced and escorted into the ballroom. "Mr. William Duponte, Mr. Bouchard Duponte, and Mr. Jean-Paul Duponte," the French marshal resounded.

"I did not know that three of the Duponte brothers were coming," said Leala. "Oh, Simone, you're so lucky to have your pick of them.

They're some of the finest men in the state of Louisiana." As the girls raved over the family of five sons whose father's military involvement added to the old money and status acquired in their lineage, Corrine and Danielle glanced at one another. They had overheard from the men speaking in the cigar room, that one of the brothers, and many of his acquaintances, had gotten some of the slave women "in trouble" at the University but that no charge would be brought against them for "damaging" another man's property since there were no white witnesses who would profess to the incidents. After all, "Boys will be boys," they heard Demetre say. "They have to get practice somehow."

When every hairpin was neatly in place and every ribbon securely tied, the ladies heard a hurried knock on the door. "Mademoiselle Simone," Liza said softly from the other side of the door. "Il est temps. It is time."

Danielle and Corrine lined up near the door side-by-side, as the sisters, Leala and Bastienne, aligned in a row with Danielle at the end. "We are ready. You may open the door now," said Simone. Liza gently opened it only to reveal two rows of well-dressed slaves standing at attention, including Alette, who watched in awe at the most beautiful gowns she had ever seen float past. The slaves smiled and bowed their heads as the ladies began to pass them. Simone looked over at Danielle and held her gaze, one of fear and joy, yet conveying a look that things were going to change for her from that moment on. Danielle once again saw the old Simone—her friend and sister, her keeper of secrets—and gave Simone the warmest smile, as if to say both, "good luck and farewell." Simone returned the smile as Danielle bowed and allowed the girl to follow her court through the hall and down the stairs, where a crowded ballroom of guests awaited her arrival.

Nine

Laughter and the hoofing of shoes could still be heard over quick-tempo music, and later, the symphonies of Chopin drifted into the sky like feathers. Alette dragged her feet, resisting as she looked back at the house. Wishing that she could be a witness to Simone's coming-out party, Danielle held tight to her hand as they made their way into the darkness that swallowed them whole.

Alette had only spoken a few sentences per day in the previous weeks, but even her desire to stay and watch a party involving whites for the first time could not strengthen her tongue enough to move. She tugged at her sister's hand. "I'm sorry Alette, but we're not—I'm not allowed to stay. Maîtresse Etiennette and Mamzèl Simone insisted upon it. I'd like to poke my nose into the party as much as you, but these are the rules." Alette frowned, frequently glancing over her shoulder at the brightness of the seemingly thousands of flickering candles and lanterns that provided light for the sisters as they entered the slave grounds.

This Saturday night was not much different than the usual with visiting slaves who were allowed to travel miles to see what few loved ones they could still locate. The smell of hominy grits and fish traveled through the air just as quickly as the steam from iron pots or smoke from chimneys.

"Perhaps once we get to Maman's house," said Danielle, "you can tell her about the things you saw while preparing for the party." Alette shrugged. "I wish you would speak more." But Alette had lost her desire to say many words. She figured that spoken words, for a slave, served no purpose. They were either used to incriminate or confirm a command of obedience. If words were meant to express oneself, and an enslaved girl, such as herself, was not allowed to express her emotions the way she wanted without being punished, then her words too, were captives. Throughout her eight years on the plantation, she witnessed several acts of brutality by the French and American slave drivers, predominately due to the replies of the slaves. And numerous incidents and run-ins with the mistress of the house throughout the weeks were enough to make the child create her own rules: *Say nothing. Do what you're told. Remain hidden.*

The sight of Genevieve's brightly lit cabin warmed Alette's spirit. She detached herself from her sister and ran into the small house where she saw her mother and brother dishing four meals onto thin metal pans. "Hi babies," Genevieve greeted. She handed Danielle a tin cup of hot water and crushed chamomile with a small sliver of sugar cane inside. "Alysaundre traded for fish today."

"Thank you, Aly," sighed Danielle, sitting upon her mother's lumpy bed and removing her tight satin shoes. She sipped her tea, wincing with each swallow. While Genevieve noticed her daughter's red swollen feet and ankles, Alysaundre watched Alette give him an airy hug and mopishly grab a plate. Throughout the weeks, he saw that she was losing color in her face, and she clung to Genevieve each morning, yet she never verbally expressed her troubles.

"Alette," Alysaundre called. "I no longer see you and Missy together. Are you not friends?" He asked about her favorite rag doll, who at one time, was only separated by the day's work.

"She doesn't like Missy anymore," said Genevieve, sitting on a stool, rubbing Danielle's bare feet. "Says she didn't know how beautiful 'real dolls' were until she began working in the house."

Alysaundre scowled. The child sat on the floor in a corner with her back against the cabin walls and her plate at her crossed legs. She performed the sign of the cross over her food, prayed, and quietly began to eat as her brother watched. Without taking his black shiny eyes off the child, "What else has been happening in the big house, Danielle?" he asked fearing the answer.

"Well, we're preparing to have members of the Soileau family as guests for a number of days—"

"Which ones?"

Danielle recited a list of cousins, "...and Mr. Jeffrey—"

"Mr. Jeffrey?" Alysaundre shook his head and blinked excessively before looking up. "If he attempts to handle me in the same manner as his own slaves...well, I've been told of the inconceivable things he has done to them."

"I can attest to him being obnoxious and sometimes harsh with his words, but what inconceivable things has he done?"

Aly addressed his mother before revealing the source of his ire for Jeffrey, "I'm sorry for speaking about this in the company of you and Alette, but he uses to his advantage the dominion he has over his male slaves, forcing himself upon them, even those with wives and a family." Everyone remained quiet. Aly shifted, "And Alette, how is she being treated?"

"She won't say much to me or Corrine," Danielle said with a low voice towards her cup. "She just does her work as she's told and usually in half the time it takes to complete. I've tried to get her to speak—to answer me, but her response is limited."

"Lettie?" said Alysaundre, softening his voice and face as he always did with his little sister. "Come here." Alette looked at her brother and paused before placing her plate on the floor and walking to him. He lifted her up and placed her on his knee. He stroked her curls. "I know you haven't been saying much, but it's important that you talk to your brother, okay?" Alette said nothing. "Has Monsieur been hurting you?" Alette shook her head.

"Aly," Danielle interjected, "Monsieur would never—"

"Don't defend him. If you don't know what he's capable of by now, you're more of a fool than I thought." He turned back to Alette. "Has anyone in the big house been hurting you?" She looked around the room at her family, lowered her head, and shook it no. "You're not being truthful, Lettie."

"I am," she said.

"Then what is the matter, baby?" asked Genevieve.

Alette wished that she could tell her family how much she hated being a servant, after seeing the lifestyle in which the Soileau family lived. She wanted desperately to tell that someone, Etiennette, had been hurting her every day, for sport, and how much the mistress enjoyed it. She prayed that she could explain the threats that she had received if she told. And she wondered if she had been told the truth by Etiennette about the man whom she called her father. Was he really her stepfather as she had been told, and was he truly dead, as she was informed? The child looked at all of the faces of her family members. She had always thought she looked like them, and a little like her father, but now, she wasn't sure. With the current issues brewing inside, she did not want to be the one to cause them any pain, while an intricate part of her being knew that as slaves, they would not and could not resolve any of these issues. She saw the trouble that resulted with Alysaundre in the field when she fainted and could not bear to imagine the punishment he would endure if she exposed her secrets.

"Dani needs water for her feet," said Alette, sliding out of her brother's lap. "I'll get some from the well."

"Alette," said a frustrated Alysaundre, "I'm not finished talking to you!" But Alette had swiftly taken a pale and left the cabin. "How could you allow this to happen, Danielle!" he yelled.

"Allow *what* to happen?" Danielle replied.

"That's *not* the same child! That's *not* our sister! And if you hadn't insisted upon her working in the house, perhaps we would have our sweet girl for a little longer."

"Not that much longer, Aly, she would have died had she been in the fields a second more. And we still don't know what's wrong with her—"

Genevieve calmly interrupted, "It seems there's very little spirit left in her. I watched it happen to the both of you." The mother sighed and shook her head helplessly.

Alysaundre calmed himself. "I still say I'd rather her work with the children her age in the fields, fetching water or cane bundles, where we know that the only eyes upon her aren't undressing her." He paused and looked at Danielle.

Hurt and furious, Danielle straightened her posture, "Please go on. What else do you think, brother?"

"I just don't want her to end up like—"

"Like me? And how is that?"

"Stop it, you two," Genevieve intervened.

"Tell me!" Danielle demanded.

"Get some air, Alysaundre," said his mother before he could put salt in Danielle's wounds.

"Yes, like you, Danielle," said Alysaundre.

"And how am I, Aly? Really?"

"Alysaundre, please," begged Genevieve.

"You know, Maman," said Danielle angrily, rising and slipping on her shoes, "he doesn't have to leave, I will. I have an idea of all the things he thinks about me. I just thought that the brother I love so much would one day stop killing me inside for what I've done and for who he thinks I've become." Danielle stormed out of the cabin as Alysaundre rushed after her and away from the cabins.

Alysaundre presented his truth: "You're a girl who would rather be anyone else but Danielle." Danielle stopped without turning around. "At times, I question if you really want to be seen with us, or if it's just guilt, so you're trying to fix everything. You've tried to create the person you wanted to be most. Poised, worldly, speaker of multiple languages, established, white—"

"Spending years as Simone's companion has made me those things Aly, and I won't apologize for who I am."

"No, but you're wrong for *what* you've become. It's a dangerous thing when white men love the sugar on their land, priding themselves on turning it from brown to white. And I see in Alette that she now hates who she is." Danielle started to lower her head, but would rather stand tall than give Alysaundre the satisfaction of knowing that he was right. "Things don't always turn out the way we want them to. People don't always become who we hoped they would be, and now, you're having Monsieur's child, and you're stuck. You now have ties to his bloodline, and still, you can't be that free girl that you dreamt of becoming. You're just another one of his dolls whom he gets to play with because he has you right where he wants you—here with him, on this plantation."

"I'm no doll—"

"No. You are just *one* of his dolls. Oh, you didn't know that he has his way with other women? He has been known to visit them on his brother's plantation, and there's some here who can describe every inch of his body better than you can."

Danielle inhaled deeply, still unable to face her brother, "Why are you so cruel? You try to ruin me every chance you get when all I try to do—all I've *ever* tried to do is help this family and love you. You telling me these things, is this truly about me or something else?"

Genevieve went after them, finding the siblings in an isolated area, "Alysaundre, enough," she ordered.

"No, Maman, she needs to hear this," Alysaundre protested. "While I prefer to teach Alette to be strong, you want to teach her to lie on her back—"

"Enough!" yelled Genevieve.

Danielle began to cry, "You're disgusting."

"This is as much about Alette as it is Father," Alysaundre continued.

"Don't you dare throw that at me again," Danielle said, turning and charging towards her brother.

"Then you'd better duck. He was sold because of you—"

"That's not true," Genevieve said, stepping between the two of them.

"It *is*, Maman!" shouted Alysaundre. "Everyone knows it, including Danielle."

Danielle placed her hands on her teary face. She sobbed. "What do you want me to do, Aly? I live with this pain every day of my life, and I regret it. But I can't do anything about it."

Alysaundre stepped closer. With a lowered stabbing voice, he rattled through his teeth, a confession that he had never shared with the girl. "He and I were planning to free all of us, and you ruined it!"

"What? Maman, did you know?"

"No," said Genevieve. "And thank God nothing came of it. You two could have gotten caught and killed.

Genevieve took her daughter into her arms. "There's nothing you could have done differently, dear heart. You must accept that, just as Alysaundre needs to accept that his father is gone." Genevieve kissed the top of Danielle's head. "Don't let this kill you slowly. You must accept *its* lessons." Danielle hugged her mother tighter as Genevieve stroked her hair. The woman glanced up, doing a double-take when seeing the silhouette of a man with a pail in one hand and the hand of a child in the other. She recognized her baby immediately, but who was the tall man with her? She stared and loosened her grip around Danielle. Alysaundre stepped past his sister and mother to stand in front of them and ultimately towards the man and child.

As the two stepped closer, Alysaundre recognized the bounce in the child's step as Lettie's and aggressively started toward the stranger whose hand she held.

Danielle squinted, "Alphonse?" she said, wondering what brought him to this side of the plantation and how he snuck onto it without notice from anyone but Alette. For a moment, she was embarrassed that he could see her family's living conditions compared to his own. She looked around, ensuring that he had not, in fact, been seen by oth-

ers. He looked solemn when walking toward the women and Alysaundre.

Without removing his intense gaze from Alphonse, Alysaundre reached his hand out for Alette to grab and let loose of Alphonse's. When she did so, he tugged her arm behind him to join his mother and sister. "My sisters know you, but I don't. Who are you and what business do you have here?"

Alphonse removed his hat, staring at Genevieve and almost reaching to hug her. "Pleased to make your acquaintance," he said to Genevieve and Alysaundre, nodding at the two of them. "I am Alphonse Santee, and you saved me when I was a boy." Genevieve pressed her hands over her mouth, her eyes wide. Alphonse continued, "But there's something else." Alphonse lowered his voice and looked around with his eyes. "May we speak privately?" Before Alysaundre, who trusts no one immediately, could question why they needed to speak privately, Alphonse gave eye contact to each family member, sighed, and said, "I have news from your father."

Ten

Genevieve, eager to hear news of her husband, invited the man out of the heavy humidity and into her cabin, away from hidden ears that could potentially travel to undesirable lobes that may not have her family's best interest at heart. As she marveled over the handsome man who was once a frail boy close to death, she offered Alphonse a cup of well water or cooled mint tea. He chose the tea as he sat in a chair Edmond had built with roped carvings along the headrest and claws at the bottom. Alysaundre leered at Alphonse intensely, biting his tongue from saying anything about this man sitting in his father's chair. Leaning against the warm wooden cabin, chewing on a cob pipe that dangled from his teeth, he sized up the free colored man, while almost daring him to say or do anything that would warrant a physical attack. He glanced over at his frizzy-haired sisters, whose bodies sat still upon the bed as if frightened. However, Danielle, wide-eyed and anxious, agonized at the thought of the wrong words or the tiniest incident that could launch at any moment and overpowered her initial, yet fleeting, embarrassment of having Alphonse as a guest in the scanty cabin. Alette's face was no different, except tears were already forming in the child's eyes.

With shaky hands, Genevieve handed the tin cup to Alphonse, who accepted the drink with his right hand and calmly laid his left hand on top of hers for assurance. She purposely took her time in all her movements, fearing that her life could change the moment Alphonse opened his lips to speak, but she yearned to know what had happened to the missing piece of her heart she called Edmond. She joined her daughters on the bed, allowing the small beads of sweat to trickle into her bosom.

Alette, Danielle, and Genevieve held hands while watching Alphonse retract letters from his leather satchel. The man looked at everyone in the room. When no one came forward or reached for the letters, but looked to him beseechingly to read them, he cleared his throat and spoke.

"The nautical world in the States is small. But the maritime world among coloreds is even smaller. I met Mr. Edmond at Martin's Wharf in southern Louisiana. He was one of the boat hands removing cargo from a ship called *La Andanza*." The ladies looked at one another, exhaling briefly before turning back to look at Alphonse to continue. "I was supervising my own workers when I heard a commotion from a white man. He had become belligerent after telling Mr. Edmond that he had loaded too many crates onto one of the wagons. Mr. Edmond looked puzzled but continued loading the items. Assuming that your father and *your* husband was ignoring his command, he yelled louder, and Mr. Edmond responded. Recognizing what Mr. Edmond had said, and realizing that the captain had—um, secured female companionship, and was nowhere to be found, I felt it my duty to intervene and explain that Mr. Edmond's tongue was of Creole. I translated for the pair of them and extinguished any further anger or confusion. I then left to tend to the job I was there to do, still keeping a watchful eye on Mr. Edmond as he had reciprocated.

"While he and other colored boat hands were required to plant themselves on the main deck until the ship sailed the following morning, Mr. Edmond formally introduced himself to me and invited me to watch him in an arm-wrestling match." Danielle scoffed and smiled. "After winning each match, we conversed later that evening, where he questioned something very familiar about me, learning that Lafayette Parish was our common home."

Edmond could barely breathe. His mouth became dry, and his heart palpitated dangerously. Careful not to assume and risk disappointment, he asked, "Lafayette?"

"Yes, sir." The music of a freshly tuned banjo began to play as the volume of the main deck occupants increased.

"I'm sure you've heard of the Soileau Plantation?"

Alphonse sat up in his chair, "Yes! Yes, I have."

"That was my home once. My family is still there, and I would give anything to be back with them." He wanted to say more, but found the pain too much to share with his new associate. Edmond felt small and wounded next to the young man who reminded him so much of his own son. He figured that no noir libre would have access to any of the Soileau slaves, and therefore, Alphonse could not possibly know of his family. Or could he? He wondered. "Do you know anyone from there?" His eyes, begging.

Alphonse spoke with much animation, explaining that he knew a beautiful young woman whom he strongly desired. He mentioned her younger sister and that their mother saved his life once.

"No," Edmond said in disbelief. He stared at the strong young man before him. He then said, "Please tell me you know of my girls Alette and Danielle," Edmond said, his voice shaking, his eyes pleading as moisture surfaced.

Alphonse leaned in. "You are their father. Danielle, she has spoken of you, questioning your whereabouts, suffering so deeply, but how much, I'll never know."

"My TiFiy—she suffers inside because of my absence?"

Alphonse nodded and carried on in discussion. He hadn't the heart to tell him the magnitude in which Danielle struggled or that his daughter was with child and due to deliver soon, but shared what he knew about the family.

Edmond could not speak. He listened to every word about his loved ones, soaking in each golden syllable and turning them into smells and images that he hoped would never fade. Without realizing it, Edmond had his hand tightly over his mouth with tears swiftly rippling over each knuckle. He shut his eyes tightly and wept silently, not caring about the loud, rugged whiskey-drinking men upon the smoke-filled deck. Alphonse allowed him to weep for some time before he heard a sound escape—a sorrowful raspy moan which he figured Edmond needed to release, for perhaps it had been bottled so tightly for his own protection since being carted away. Alphonse looked down at his lap and swallowed hard, carefully trying not to cry himself. When the tightness of Edmond's throat lessened, and his tears phantomed away, he wiped his eyes with his shirt and spoke softly. "Tell me what it is that I have to do to return to Lafayette Parish with you, and I will do it!"

Alphonse watched the family as they waited for more details. "We attempted to strategize in code, but our options looked bleak. And he could not run on a whim and in plain view at this port. I told him that I would do all that I could to maintain the shipping schedules to keep sight of him. But then I asked if there was anything he wished to share with you. And these letters are what he wished to discuss, exactly as he spoke them." Alphonse held up the parchment and began to read Edmond's statement aloud:

***

"Family...family. I've never put into words what I have felt and have stormed through. I'm afraid that what I am about to share will reveal all of me. And since this is no time to allow pride to limit my words for you, I ask that in listening to them, that you hear me, but know that I will never sink so deep as to give up finding my way back to you.

"The day that I lost my world, my soul screamed with anguish. When God gave us dominion over the animals and the beasts of the fields, he gave man power to remove a calf from its mother or the eggs from a hen's nest. But never did He intend for man to remove fathers from sons, sisters from brothers...husbands from wives. At the time, had I known that I would experience such great pain, I would have chosen death if it were offered to me. But my anger would never allow me to die. Whatever had to be done to kiss my wife's sweet lips again, or tussle my son's head of curls, or throw my Lettie into the air, or...or sing to my TiFiy again, I would do it.

"I was driven to two other plantations in Louisiana where we picked up two Negro men, whose only tongue was Spanish, and a mulatto boy, dressed in grand clothing, about 8, who couldn't stop crying. Said his Papa was his master. His face told us all that he didn't know why he was being sold. My wish to be left alone with my sorrow would not be granted. I hoped that it would drive in me a plan on how I could return to my family. The men said nothing during the ride, only looking at their surroundings, heads turning at the crackle of a branch.

"No sooner than I would start to think of my son's face, I would hear the clanking of the mulatto child's chains. As I thought of my darling TiFiy's stare, I would hear those links. I tried everything to not look too hard at the child. But when I did, I saw in the boy a great likeness in all my young ones, especially of my little daughter, Alette, whom I wished to be with at that moment. What tiny shackles were around his wrists and ankles. Not caring about the ones around mine, or even realizing the depth of the wounds on my ankles, I cursed the blacksmith and welder who could create these demonic instruments, especially for children who are birds of the human race. My heart, still sore for my own babies, overpowered my ferocious agony until the one thing left to add to the symphony of chains were his sobs. To hear a child tortured with heartache is like listening to purity in human form being wounded. I heard the echoes of my very own Alette in his cries, and with that, I couldn't help but to console the boy who was scared and had no one. In doing so, he became my saving grace from the madness in my head and my strength to continue.

"I tried to memorize every road, every house, every pond—until night fell upon us and I could no longer tell apart my surroundings. The boy, asleep in my arms, jolted awake when we were told to get out of the wagon and onto a large boat at a pier on the Mississippi. We were then loaded onto the boat where we sailed for about two weeks, cleaning and serving, barely eating or sleeping. Once we docked, we were back in our chains and roughly pushed into a wagon where we rode for a day or so, passing towns and plenty of flat land.

"The boy had since become calmer than in previous days, occasionally weeping and talking about his Mama and brothers. His eyes thanked God that I was there to help him with his grief, and his desire to never leave my side within those past weeks made me value our friendship. I thought back to when you were a boy, Alysaundre, and the things I taught you at his age. If we were to live on the same plantation, someone would need to help look after him, teach him, raise him up like a man. No sooner than deciding that I would be the one to do it, the wagon stopped, and I was pulled out by my arm by two overseers. I looked behind me and reached for the boy, only to be yanked harder and kicked for not moving fast enough onto what was to be my new plantation. The child, wild-eyed and confused, tried to hop off too, but was yanked back by the driver by his chains. The boy yelled for me as the wagon rode on and I struggled to reach him until a blow to the gut crippled my chances to get near the boy. Riding further away, I suddenly heard abrupt silence from the child as if someone had knocked him over the head to hush him.

"And there I was again, wallowing in my anger on a new, much smaller cotton plantation in Missouri, not at all like the Soileau plantation in appearance and in spirit. The slaves have no allegiance to one another and float around like angered ghosts, forever living in the moment where their souls were unwillingly snatched. So that I don't cause any more damage to your hearts I will spare you details of some of the treatment received and witnessed on this land.

"I rarely saw the master, but one day, to my surprise, Master Sterling Delaney visited the field with some of the overseers. The Negroes were told to line up so the master could inspect our hardiness. The blonde-haired man stepped to each of us, without giving you a full description of his face, I can tell you that his noticeable limp looked out of place with his firm, strong stature. Hands, uncut and smooth-looking, accent, with barely a twang, as I had heard from others claiming to be from Missouri. Already puzzled by this man and how he came into the fortune he possessed, I heard him weed us out of the line with a confident 'yes' or 'no' in American English. I was to be a 'Yes.' In three days' time, I and fifteen other men in line that day would be on a boat where we labored and transported traded goods, mainly cotton, on the shores of the Atlantic.

"With the winds gusting and the sounds of splashing waves, the birds flying overhead on the open ocean, the wind across my face is freedom's kiss, and I have been tempted. Understand that my work is hard and days, long, but I am grateful for the chance to look up from it all as we travel throughout the States. My senses come alive when on the water, granting me a little joy that I never knew still existed, but it's nothing if I can't share it with you.

"Once I awoke with a familiar taste in my mouth—a taste of warm sweet grass, sugar, and earth and I jolted from my cot, flying onto the deck. And there they were upon the horizon and blessing my very thoughts about my whereabouts, Spanish moss, and indigo—oak trees, and allamandas. I knew at that moment that I was back in Louisiana. I wanted to leap off of the ship and into the water and swim to you, my love, and my babies. But in which direction, I knew not. How to swim, I knew not but was willing to learn while trying to get to you. Instead, I remained and sought Chance for an opportunity to flee.

"We finally docked in what I later learned was New Orleans. Its busy loudness was just what I needed to somehow make my escape. I was witness to many Negroes at the dock, some with their own boats. Their freedom, I could not confirm, but I would need their help if I were ever to be by your side. While unloading crates of goods from boat to wagon, and boat to boat with my own fellow mates and the blacks at the docks, I spoke heartily in Creole French with a Negro who worked for a fishery in the neighboring town of Lafayette. I learned that he was a noir libre. We seemed to be kindred spirits, both speaking of family, hard work, music, and travel. I hinted that I needed to see my family again and that I would do anything within reason to have you. Being one who was snatched from his family, whose whereabouts are still unknown, and having a rooted hatred for white owners and all whites who turned a blind eye to our condition, he said that he could help me. He told me that he was unable to take me the full distance, but that he knew others who made it their mission to help slaves get to their destinations by land, even if that meant all the way to freedom. We bargained and strategized, and by sundown, the plan was complete. The details of our plan and the people involved cannot be written, but I could almost taste the sugar from our plantation again.

"Before any of my plans could take flight, I had been chained within the belly of the ship for the remainder of the journey. I learned that betrayal came in the form of one of Master Sterling's slaves, who received no gain other than the satisfaction of seeing another Negro denied of the one thing that gave him life again. Perhaps his greatest tragedy is never having befriended Loyalty but wanting to see Misery remain in one another. Or maybe, I was young-minded to think that something of that nature would come so easily to me. It's sad, isn't it? To think that if something that should be rightfully ours approaches us with ease, that something is wrong. Whereas others would not give it a second thought. Without sharing details, that slave met my rage on several accounts once arriving back in Missouri. So much so that his fear for me is greater than that of the overseers. He now understands what he took from me when he parted his lips to the master.

"My tears fall for you. There are some Negro men who don't know where their children's heads lay at night and long to discover that place. There are others who don't care because it's easier not to. I am not that man. My tears fall for you, and I am no less of a man for telling you so. The great I Am entrusted me to be your father, and it's been an honor to carry out His will. I remember hard days in the fields, and gentle nights once at home. I have no riches in the world, but I am a wealthy man. I had always feared that someone would discover what jewels you were and remove you from my arms - that you would belong to someone else, forgetting who I am, the sound of my voice, the look in my eyes. When you were each birthed, I placed your little heads on my chest, hoping that you would know the thumping of this instrument is for you, just as you knew in the womb that your Maman's beating heart told you that you were hers. But I decided then that when Infinity blew her breath on our union that no one else gets to watch you grow.

"Genevieve, my darling. My mind and spirit have not abandoned yours. As you and I are one, your pain has been felt, even at this great distance. Your fears have been silent, and I'm having this kind man write these words so that they are stitched into the fibers of your heartstrings. My devotion is to you and only you. Though we are apart, and unsure as to when we will touch, I am yours. Never will I create a new marriage and family and begin anew. Just know that I reach out to you before closing my eyes at night because one day, I will again lock fingers with yours, feel your hair and face in return. There are some words that I wished not to be written. They will be revealed to you in time. Know that your love and gentleness of your words have brought me through dark days. If I have never told you before, thank you for choosing me to be held captive in your soul. If ever you handed me the keys, permitting me to free myself of our union, I would swim across the rocky shark-filled ocean just to drop them in Mount Liamuiga, wishing never to be released from your love. Thank you for mothering my children. Remain strong for you and for them, and when we meet again, I will pick up in strength if ever you fall weak and carry you as long as I live.

"To my sweet Lettie. My little fuchsia flower. You picking the roses around the big house had nothing to do with my departure. Your screams as I was leaving haunt me, just as I know my being removed still terrifies you. Please, let go of any guilt you may feel."

Alette stood with tears in her eyes and redness in her face. Her spirit rejuvenated. She walked slowly as if meticulously choosing her steps. Tears streamed down her cheeks as her gaze locked upon Alphonse. She stood at his side, looking at him, then down at the perfect script handwriting. Alphonse pulled her close to him, allowing her to rest her head on his shoulder as the tears quietly rolled onto his vest.

"My Flower," Alphonse continued to read, "Some Negroes would say that it is more trouble—that it would hurt you more, in the end, but as much as I want to bottle your innocence, it, along with a strong mind, is something I pray will remain longer in you than any other Negro child. When you have a strong mind, no one can change it, only influence and inspire it. Every inch of you bears greatness. Those who are not for you will tell you lies. They will tell you that you're not smart, beautiful, worthy. Know that you are cherished, and you are a light.

"Son," Aly uncrossed his arms and stood tall as if his father had just entered the room. "By now, you are enraged. You hate white men. You hate being the patriarch of this family while having little power. You may even hate *me*." For the first time in months, the family saw a mudslide of humility on Alysaundre's face. "To that," Alphonse continued to read, "I say, it is okay. Sometimes with anger comes action. But my prayer always for you is that you act in wisdom. Let anger propel you to change your circumstances, but let wisdom guide you. When anger is in action, it silences any messages meant to be received. Anger is wild and wants to be seen, heard, and felt. It becomes an arrowhead gone array. Anger is selfish, not caring who it hurts in its path. Wisdom is steady, precise, keeping sight of the target, consequences, and everyone it affects. Be the good man I know you are. Until my return, protect our family and make wise decisions. Mo linm twa mô gaçon.

I love you, my boy." Alysaundre swallowed hard. His eyes, vulnerable and unable to decide whether to be his father's son in that moment or protector of the women in the room. He looked down at his feet and then strongly into the eyes of each female.

"TiFiy," Danielle sat straighter, eager to hear what her father had to say to her, but unknowing of his temperament towards her. "I won't share the words that were last spoken between us, but I hope that you are well. I am not angry with how you chose to survive. But I do hope that it is also for the benefit of this family and that your allegiance remains with us. There is so much I want to tell you, but Time and I are not comrades.

"I do not wish happiness for you, but instead, share with you my desire for your joy. Happiness relies on circumstances, while joy is a gift that is long-lasting. So, I pray that joy is what you seek. I don't know where your heart roams these days, but I wish it to be in one piece. Now, whether my presence would determine if that always stays true, I do not know, but I do offer my acceptance for whatever the outcome. Alphonse tells me that he loves you, wants to take care of you. Well, my blessing is yours. You know that I've turned away many suitors for you, but there is none more deserving of your love than him. Please let it settle with you that he will make a fine husband and be prayerful that Maître Soileau will allow it."

Danielle looked down at her swollen belly, feeling ashamed. *He doesn't know*, she thought.

"No more seeking, Danielle." Alphonse continued to read, "Love is yours; Love is in your family, it is in Alphonse, and it's in the things that you do daily. You care for others; you mend people and plights. Please, see all that is before you and hold tight to it.

"Family. With all that I've said and all that this good man has written, know that we will see each other soon. I won't give up. My fight is strong, and freedom is near. Keep your eyes open and your feet swift. My love to you all."

* * *

Alphonse folded the papers as everyone stared impatiently at him. "Is there more?" Lettie asked.

"I'm sorry, no," said Alphonse. "By the time we finished, the sun was rising, and your father had to prepare to set sail."

"Did he say where he was going?" asked Alysaundre.

"He didn't know, but I learned that he was going to Maryland. But I promised that I would deliver this message to you."

"And we thank you," Genevieve said, clasping Alphonse's hands. "You've risked so much to do this for us." Danielle could have listened to Alphonse read her father's words all night and, like Lettie, wished there were more. She was quiet as the others rambled around her.

Alysaundre whispered to himself, "Keep your eyes open, and your feet, swift."

Overhearing him, Alphonse said, "That reminds me..." he took the folded letter, walked to the fireplace, and without hesitation, threw the evidence of his and Edmond's exchange into the fire. The women gasped and Alette made a move to retrieve them.

"No Lettie!" yelled Genevieve, grabbing her daughter before she could reach into the flames. "This is the way it has to be. If anyone finds out about what was said or planned, it will be hell for us and Monsieur Santee." Lettie yanked herself from her mother's grasp, angrily watching her father's words and hardship crackle. And just that simply, she had lost him again. Too angry to cry, Alette threw herself onto her bed, not wanting to be bothered.

Alysaundre pulled out his pipe, stuffed tobacco into it, and lit it with straw from the fireplace. He tapped Alphonse with the back of his hand and with his head, motioned the visitor to follow him outside. They moved quickly, looking over their shoulders and traveling through the night and into a secluded wooded area of the land, the moon illuminating brilliantly for the two of them. Alysaundre took a few puffs of his pipe, slowly blowing out the smoke. "I want to thank you for what you've done," he said, turning to look Alphonse in the eyes. "It sounds like my father approves of you, but I can't let you drag yourself deeper into our troubles."

"It's too late, my friend," said Alphonse. "I'm involved and I'm going to continue this struggle with you."

"What are you trying to gain?"

"Nothing."

Alysaundre said sternly, "You want something."

"...So, what if there *is* something I want?" Alysaundre continued to listen, and Alphonse confessed. "I want to help the little girl in mass, now a grown woman, who lifted my soul as she sat unaccompanied in the balcony singing hymnals with an incredibly angelic voice so many years ago. And because you are all a part of her, I want to help. I *need* to help. And I want to try for the woman who healed me, your mother. Without her care, I would not be here."

"How do I know that when things ignite, you could still be found?"

Alphonse paused, then stated, "There's nothing I can say at this moment to convince you of what I will do in the future. I don't know what more I can do to gain your trust. I risk my life every time I sneak onto this plantation, but I do it and will continue to do so because I love your sister. I pray to Saint Raphael and Saint Joseph that she loves me just as much. I want her as my wife, and the babe will be treated as my own. The little one won't have to question who his father is because I'll be right there to do as a père should.

"Now, from one man to another, feel no shame in what I'm trying to provide for your family. You are much more important to them than I could ever be, and you are so much more needed. You're able to help them in many ways that I cannot, and I'm asking that you allow me to help in another. Accept the help I'm offering."

Alysaundre boiled in anger at Alphonse. He said nothing for some time, allowing himself to feel less than an ounce of humility. When

Alphonse saw the shift in Alysaundre's expression, he stuck out his hand. Alysaundre took a long puff of his pipe and squeezed the man's hand. Alphonse said, "I have to go. Please tell Danielle that I will return soon. Tell no one that I was here or about what happened tonight."

Alphonse walked several yards north into the woods toward his horse and unraveled the reins from a tree branch as Alysaundre followed. "Wait," said Alysaundre, "Did you and my father have anything planned?"

Alphonse mounted his horse. "Yes. But there is no time to share details. Just know, I am going to need your help soon. As your father said, 'Keep your eyes open, and your feet swift.'"

Eleven

The passing ghostly images of buggies and chaperoned ladies gliding through town went ignored by Simone, who gaped in amazement at the reflection of the maturing young woman before her in the window of Miss Prideaux's dress shop. Normally, she would never bring attention to herself by wearing such a large, stylish hat. But recent events have allowed her to regain confidence, even if the fashion made too bold of a statement for her. The baby fat in her cheeks was no longer present, and the freshwater pearls framed her slender neck elegantly. Her mother tried to assist in maintaining the girl's figure by constantly reminding her that "not even hoop skirts could hide tree trunks." Simone's body was maturing, and she had to admit that she loved it. Standing on the inside of the fabric-filled shop, which smelled of vanilla and lavender, Simone bit her bottom lip, recalling the changes in her life that brought her to this moment.

In the weeks prior, her cousins, Gloria and Bella, along with their cousin Jeffrey, had remained house guests since the coming-out party. With the three teen girls staying up later than Etiennette's recommended time, according to their charm school instructors, the Soileau mansion engulfed a girlish giddiness not experienced since Simone and Danielle ran the halls as adolescents; for Simone caught the eye of a young man from a "good family." With high status and income, Demetre and Etiennette deemed him worthy enough to court their daughter. Matthieu, the nephew of a wealthy steel tycoon, had just completed college in Virginia and had plans to travel abroad to his various places of business, making a holiday of the visits while monitoring the growing plantations that his family owned. Such places as the Bahamas in the winter with Simone and escorts of her choosing meant sleepless nights of excitement for the young woman. She secretly enjoyed the idea that her cousin, Gloria, might have been a little envious of the upcoming trip, as well as others in the works, which would expose Simone to exotic lands and new languages. With her newfound power, she learned how far her status could carry her, and the weightless journey looked endless.

In town, the girls and Cousin Jeffrey helped Simone shop for garments to be unseen in the same dress or pattern twice by Matthieu or anyone in town watching their courtship from afar. In Miss Prideaux's dress and pattern shop, Simone was overwhelmed by the many selections within the store. This new pressure to select the perfect fabric, patterns, and colors made her glad to be in the trusted company of family who would give honest suggestions. "Hmm," pondered Gloria as Simone turned from the window and held up two unflattering patterns to her chest. "The prostitutes on 4th Street would welcome you in as their sister if you were to wear that in public."

"Oh, Gloria," said Bella, removing the patterns from Simone's hands and holding a yard of lace below her face. "Saying that you don't like something is never simple enough, is it? Simone, I think this lace would make Matthieu swoon for you ten times over. It gives you an even softer look. Miss Prideaux," she called to the fine-dressed woman folding material behind the counter. "Can this be dyed pink?"

"Absolutely," said Miss Prideaux.

Simone twisted her face and scratched her neck. "But it's so itchy," she said.

"Must be Italian lace," Jeffrey murmured to the girls.

"What kind of lace is this?" Bella asked Miss Prideaux.

"Italian," she answered.

Gloria rubbed the texture of a piece of plaid material between her fingers. "Everyone knows that French lace is best. Couple that with a beautiful hat with a pink satin bow, and you will be engaged in no time. We shouldn't be wasting our time *here*; we need to visit the high-fashion dress shops in New Orleans." Miss Prideaux overheard her comment and rolled her eyes.

"I'm afraid she's right," Jeffrey agreed. "I'm sure the man is surrounded by beautiful women who want nothing more than the son of a steel tycoon on their arm. You, sweet cousin, are not only dressing to win his engagement, but to show other women why he selected *you*."

Simone looked to Bella, who sheepishly nodded in agreement. Gloria instructed, "You simply must ask Uncle Demetre for more money or insist that he purchase items from Paris or New York."

Simone turned a little red as she thought about her family's finances and started to whisper to the girls when she saw Miss Prideaux who was doing a terrible job pretending not to eavesdrop. Without wanting to discuss the details of her father's money in public, Simone suggested that they all leave at once in order to plan the trip to New Orleans.

Once outside, Bella offered to purchase pralines for everyone five stores down. With the sisters and Jeffrey in the candy shop, Simone slowed her stride to admire a display of beautiful bonnets in a store window. She then overheard two Negro Creole women behind her whispering. "Isn't that one of the Soileaus?" Simone heard a woman say. "You should tell her."

"Yes, but I can't approach her with this news," Noelle said. "Not here anyway."

"And why not?" Noelle's lanky friend pressured. "Do you realize how much you have lost in Alphonse? His money would have granted you security. You should tell Mademoiselle; she has a right to know the type of slave that is among her."

Simone turned around, "What exactly do I have a right to know?" she asked sternly.

Noelle jolted at Simone's directness and cleared her throat, "Good day, Mademoiselle," she said. She introduced herself and inquired about Simone's association with the pregnant servant of whom she was about to speak.

"Yes, Danielle belongs to me," Simone confirmed. "Go on."

"Last spring," Noelle explained, "Your Danielle sang at a ball where a free gentleman was supposed to propose to me. And instead, he disappeared with Danielle. He followed her all night. News is that she may be carrying his child," said Noelle who became dangerously comfortable in her speech and smug expression.

Simone felt a glimmer of happiness to learn that Danielle may not be carrying her father's child. "Continue," Simone ordered.

Noelle gladly obliged, "As I mentioned, he is a free man; however, he has chosen to concern himself with a slave, and I understand that his mother does not approve."

"And who is this free Negro of whom you speak?"

"Alphonse Santee," Noelle blurted. She proceeded to discuss his bloodline and rising success in business, omitting any mention of feelings of betrayal.

"What does he look like?" Simone asked.

Noelle began to describe him, almost falling in love all over again. She blinked rapidly, returning to the marketplace. "He comes and goes," said Noelle. "In Lafayette for a short while before returning to sea. As for Danielle, she completely changed the heart of the man who courted me."

"Oh, come now," smiled Simone. "Danielle and I aren't necessarily on the best terms, but no one can change the heart of a man in one evening." Noelle frowned as Simone continued, "Either he was never truly yours at the start, or Danielle and this Alphonse have met before…" Simone listened to her own words.

"Well, Mademoiselle Soileau, it sounds like there are a few things that need to be uncovered about Danielle and what she has been up to when your back has been turned."

Simone said, "Noelle, you have given me good information. I do hope your heart mends. Good luck and good day." Simone walked away to join her cousins as they filed out of the candy store seeing the two Negro Creoles and the arrogance they projected, Gloria vaingloriously scanned Noelle up and down.

Constant laughter and chattering encircled Simone during the carriage ride home. She stared out the window, thinking of all the new information she carried.

"You're not being sensible," argued Emile, too discombobulated with Demetre's stubbornness that he could no longer puff his Hernsheim Brothers cigar. "There is no pride lost in letting go of the distribution of one of our products."

Demetre calmly puffed away at his Turkish cigar.

"And once again," said Emile, "you are not concerned. Listen, if we focus on our sugar and molasses and do away with the rum, we can cut the cost of bottles and repurpose the labor towards the other products and double our volume and remain afloat."

"I don't want to 'stay afloat,'" Demetre said, finally standing to cross the smoking-room floor. He looked out of the window to his lavish courtyard. "We didn't put in so much work to scrape by—that's not the type of family or business we are. We take risks and we win. We stumble, but we never fall."

"Brother," urged Emile, rising to face Demetre. "Have you even looked at our books? We are declining as other companies are offering the same amount of product for half of the cost."

"Sure," said Demetre. "How many companies prostitute themselves, selling for less than they're worth?"

"Well, as mentioned in the last two meetings that you did not attend, something different needs to occur. You and I aren't going to settle this today, but understand that there are changes coming; and whether you're present or not, the board and I want to meet and make decisions next week."

"You can't make major decisions without me," Demetre disallowed sharply, stepping towards Emile.

"We need to agree on a solution, and you need to be there. However the board decides will be the direction of this company, you know that. We also discussed meeting with our artists for new packaging."

"New art is unnecessary and is not a priority."

"I'm not debating with you on this. A slave in the middle of the nostalgic Saint-Martin plantation that no longer exists needs change. Customers in the north like sugar, but they don't want to be reminded of how and by whom it's made. And as more abolitionists are breeding up north, they're certainly not going to support our product with this type of image thrown in their faces. We were thinking, a finely dressed French woman pouring our sugar into her tea."

"As if there aren't enough of those types of images. Artwork of a slave on our plantation reminds customers that it comes straight from the source."

Emile smirked, knowing full well of his brothers' intentions. "Very well then. Let's propose to the board an image of a different slave on Father's old plantation. And we'll use one of my house Negroes serving a guest."

Demetre's lip curled in disagreement. "I've seen *your* slaves, and none of them are worthy enough to be rendered on our advertisement. It should still be Danielle, but in a different setting."

"If by 'worthy enough' you mean good enough to take to bed, then is that why you're insisting on Danielle?" Demetre took a couple of puffs of his cigar and sat on the edge of his desk. "You know, most men occasionally have their pleasures with their wenches without involving them in their businesses, let alone plastering their images on brands of sugar and molasses." Demetre stood to straighten his smoking jacket and sat back down on the desk's corner. "I hear she is with child. Congratulations? Not only is she the face of Soileau & Sons, but you have boldly given her our name, and now she is going to have a little Negro...with our name. Do you have any idea what that will do to us and our business if people learn about your affection towards your slave? It could ruin us. All because your loins pulsate for your daughter's playmate."

Demetre grew angry over Emile's choice of words but could not externally confess his emotions. He took another puff, blowing the smoke in the direction of his brother. "What I do with my 'loins' is none of your concern. I can count at least 30 of your slaves who can sniff yours out of a line of cocks while blindfolded. I just happen to purpose the ones I choose to bed."

Red with anger, Emile responded, "Well, when purpose and your loins collide, it, unfortunately, becomes *my* concern and affects everyone on the board. Do not let this or any other obsession get in the way of everything we've built."

"It is not an obsession. I'm merely doing what I want with my possession. You're growing my personal business into a larger situation."

Emile stared at Demetre for a long while before finally scoffing and sitting on the couch. He smashed the tip of his cigar into the glass ashtray, crossing his legs. "Do you know what makes sugar so dangerous? It's addictive. It's like opium—the first taste is innocent. The second is more enjoyable. And the third is familiar and pleasurable. Before long, it becomes a part of you, believing that you need it to function. The things and the people around you don't seem to matter as much. And while you're getting taste after sticky taste, things are crumbling around you due to your foolish decisions. Do not let Danielle's sweetness cause you to lose sight of our company, or I will have the board vote you out. I'll send for Bella and Gloria tomorrow." Emile snatched up his writing pad and swiftly left his brother's home.

Twelve

By midday the following week, Corrine helped Danielle and Alette remove the clean linens from the clothing line and bring them inside the house. They walked along the path to the back of the mansion and garden when they saw Alphonse amid the vegetation wearing his finest navy-blue suit and hat, holding two flowers, waiting for someone to arrive. Alette dropped the clothing basket and ran to him. "There's the chocolate princess," he said, removing a piece of chocolate and holding it out for her to grab. Gently pushing his hand out of the way, she hugged him tightly, and he returned the gesture. He looked up at Danielle's concerned face and Corrine's bashful grin. He smiled lightly in acknowledgment but appeared more serious today.

Danielle desperately wanted to straighten her uniform and tignon without Alphonse seeing her do it, but his eyes panted for her and appeared worried. Corrine glanced back and forth at the two. Their love was evident. Corrine said, "Come, Alette. Let's give them some time. Y'all don't be too long, you know this garden can suddenly attract mockingbirds in human form." Corrine gently tugged Alette away and into the house, but not before Alphonse could gift each of them with a flower. Alette moved hesitantly but was reassured by her sister that Corrine would remain by her side.

"Is all well, Monsieur?" Danielle asked quietly.

"Yes," Alphonse cleared his throat. "I sent Monsieur Soileau a letter prior to my visit today. He knows that I am here to discuss a matter of business. He agreed to meet with me in person. I have not mentioned you or your family to him, but you and I know what is needed out of this encounter, and I will do my very best. I am praying that favor leans on my side today. Monsieur Edmond gave me his blessing. But I need to hear your words. I need to know that I have your love and that you grant me permission to keep your heart. Let me make you my bride. Will you have me, Danielle?" Danielle was silent for far too long. "Did you give your heart away?" he worried.

Danielle swallowed hard, thinking of Etiennette and her threats, as well as her treatment of Alette. The conflict shook her to tears. Danielle wondered if she were to be sold without the mistress ever knowing for sure who fathered the child, she wondered, would her family be free to live?

"Is that a tear?" Alphonse asked, falling deeper into her hazel eyes.

Danielle spoke, "I love you. My heart is yours, Alphonse. But if Monsieur Demetre agrees to sell me," she looked around and lowered her voice, "I can't leave my family. I must stay and see that they are treated well."

"Will you have power over their treatment if you remain? If your master is willing to sell, I will see that you are not away from your family for long. All I asked is for your trust." Danielle stood in silence. "Your past decisions can no longer define you or hold you prisoner. You deserve love, just as that child you are sheltering deserves a chance to be cherished, no matter who the father is. I'm not a pleading man, but you've made me a willing beggar if only it means you'll be my always. Before I stand face-to-face with your master, I need to know, will you be my wife?"

Danielle, with tears rolling down her face, nodded. She nodded again more assuredly, this time smiling and later covering her giggle with her hands.

Alphonse smiled greatly, doing everything possible not to leap and yelp, but laughing quietly instead. He then gently held the face of his love and slowly kissed her full lips. Danielle had longed to be kissed that way. She felt true love behind the curl of his lips as they caressed between hers. Not wanting to ever stop, Alphonse forced himself to do so and wiped the tears from Danielle's eyes with his thumbs. Kissing the fingers of both of his hands, Alphonse pressed them to his new fiancée's belly.

"I'm ready," he said. "Take me to him."

The girl led Alphonse down limestone stairs leading through a tranquil courtyard, passing a well and a small gated garden of blossomed flowers surrounded by a statue of St. Catherine of Sweden along the way. They arrived in an open grassy garden where Demetre was spotted wearing a full fencing outfit, practicing on a long white strip against a masked wooden fencing dummy holding a Spanish foil in its right hand in an upright position. A young male slave stood by, holding a tray of pineapple juice. Demetre traveled back on the strip before striking the dummy in what would be its heart. The slave traded Demetre a cool beverage for his foil mask.

"Hmph!" Demetre said, swallowing his drink while noticing Danielle and the guest. Alphonse removed his hat in Demetre's presence.

"Excellent form, Monsieur," said Alphonse. "Parfait. Perfect. It's no secret that the French are masters at the sport."

The head of the estate motioned for them to come closer. "I figured it was such a nice day, I'd bring my practice out here. Are you Monsieur Alphonse Santee's boy? Has he sent you to give me a message?"

Alphonse smiled lightly, careful not to seem amused. "Monsieur, *I* am Alphonse Santee. Pleased to make your acquaintance," he said, his head nodded into a bow.

Demetre stood expressionless. "I'm in no mood to jest. Where is your master?"

"Sir, I am not here to waste your time with jokes. I am the owner of Santee Sails and the one with whom you've been corresponding. Here are my identification and freedom papers."

Demetre reached for them while staring into the face of the only known colored businessman to encounter him. Alphonse's gaze remained on the papers as he felt a slight flash of anger from Demetre.

He yanked the papers, almost eager to find any sign of fraudulence in the seemingly legal documents. His eyes volleyed from the papers to Alphonse, who was still careful not to change his expression to avoid accusations of being uppity, as Demetre couldn't help but feel as if he had been tricked. Without moving his head, he focused on Danielle, searching for any familiarity between her and the handsome free Negro who owned his livelihood. Feeling a twinge of jealousy seeing them near one another, Demetre quickly hid any mien of concern and shoved the papers back to Alphonse with a sneer.

"So," Demetre said, "Alphonse, is it? Your letter mentioned that you wanted to discuss a business matter." He brushed Danielle away with a single motion, and she quietly disappeared behind trees within earshot of the men as Demetre was given another glass of the juice.

"Monsieur," said Alphonse. "Thank you for agreeing to meet with me today." Demetre's unblinking eyes urged him to get to the point. "Yes, well, I wanted to offer you an opportunity to make a considerable amount of money without lifting a finger." Demetre continued to stare at Alphonse and drink his pineapple juice. He heard a twig snap behind the trees, noticing Danielle was still close by, and he motioned for her to leave the garden. She did as she was told.

"Any business that requires me to earn money without lifting a finger, I want no part of," said the slave owner. "No one can thrive without putting in the effort. But I'm willing to hear you. What are you asking of me?"

"Well, sir, I assure you that—"

"Do you play?" Demetre interrupted.

"Pardon?" Alphonse asked, taken aback by the abrupt question.

"Fence. Do you fence? Or perhaps Canne de combat is your sport?"

"I'm more familiar with fencing, but only a little," Alphonse modestly responded, although he was awarded champion at several Creole fencing competitions.

Still holding his glass of pineapple juice in one hand, Demetre snatched an extra sabre mask from his butler with the other hand and tossed it to Alphonse. "Tomas can get you suited."

Tomas, a tall, gangly, and bearded slave of a peanut complexion, helped Alphonse out of his suit jacket and vest and into his white padded canvas fencing jacket. As he fastened the bone buttons down the side, he locked eyes with Alphonse, as a warning to play wisely and not at the expense of the slaves who may potentially be punished in frustration. He gently placed the sabre mask onto Alphonse's head, although his glare was fierce. He then turned and nodded to Demetre with a smile to show the opponent's readiness. With one arm akimbo, Demetre quickly steadied himself.

Tomas, who acted as president of the jury, called out, "Messieurs, we'll have a clean game." Alphonse and Demetre took their positions. When he saw that they were prepared, Tomas yelled, "En garde!" The men took their positions and began their match. The opponents dashed and darted until each one gradually gained a stronger force behind each blow. Demetre became desperate in his movement when seeing that Alphonse was getting close to defeating him. Upon noticing a subtle shake of the head from Tomas, Alphonse weakened his game, remembering all that was at stake. Finally, putting aside his skill and ego, Alphonse clenched his teeth, allowing Demetre to win the match.

Demetre basked in his glory, sticking his chest out a bit more than he had prior to the match. He wished he had not sent Danielle away so soon, for it was always beneficial to have a female around to share in his victories. Tomas handed him a glass of water as Demetre took his seat, still smiling. "Thank you, Alphonse, for that wonderful match," he said with a tone of "nice try."

Before Tomas could help him out of his gear, Alphonse began removing it himself, yanking away at his anger of always having to diminish himself, his abilities, and God-given talents to appease whites. Usually, a master at masking his anger, Alphonse had a particularly tough attempt at doing so. Alphonse breathed deeply, drawing back his emotions and focusing on the reason for his visit. He painfully smeared on a smile, "Splendid footwork, Monsieur. Wonderful match indeed."

"Tomas," ordered Demetre. "Gather a scoop of water for Alphonse."

Alphonse did not wait for Tomas to return with an iron ladle from the field hands' water trough before he started in on his requests. "As you know, Monsieur, several of your slaves were rented for an event hosted by my mother. She found their work to be impeccable, and I wanted to make you an offer on her behalf and partially my own."

"Go on," said Demetre looking up at the free Negro. "But step back a little."

Without question, Alphonse stepped back to where Demetre did not have to raise his head or eyes to look at the colored man and continued. "She was interested in purchasing some of your inventory."

"Surely you mean a horse, some pigs, barrel of sugar, perhaps?"

"Your slaves, sir. But only a few."

Demetre never sold his slaves unless he saw it financially necessary, or if they were a physical threat to him or his family. He thought about the money he'd lost but questioned whether this was a perfect opportunity to reclaim a small quantity of funds. Demetre said nothing, only listening further to the proposal.

"She has a list," Alphonse removed parchment from his inside jacket pocket. "But if you don't mind, I'll begin with mine. You might find my request strange, but I'm seeking an ornery slave to be another hand on my boats to haul lumber or goods. I've found that the more troublesome the slave, the more aggression they let out in their work." Alphonse leaned in, "Especially if you step on their necks long enough."

Demetre smirked. "An ornery slave?" he repeated, slightly entertained by the idea. No one had ever asked for a troublesome Negro, though a few of *his* came to mind. He nodded without naming the slaves. "And what do you have on the list?" Demetre questioned.

"Ah, yes," Alphonse jolted, holding up the list. "Let's see here." His eyes scanned the paper. "Mother mentioned she'll be needing a small child to be a fan girl—one she can groom to be a good house servant—perhaps 7 to 8 years of age and well-behaved. Her current one is growing far too fast and is particularly lippy and forgetful. It's time for a replacement."

Demetre did not recommend a child, only nodded. "What else?" he questioned.

Alphonse quickly held up the paper again. Wrinkling his brow, he said, "I'm sorry, I'm reading my mother's poor attempt at trying to recall a slave's name. She thinks her name is Danielle."

Demetre's eyes quickly widened and returned. "Are you sure it's Danielle she's requesting and not Devereaux or another with a 'D' in her name?"

"I asked Mother the same, and she said there was only one slave whose name began with a D." He read off the features of the girl as she appeared months prior at the Santee party. Based on that description, Demetre was definite that it was Danielle who was being requested. He noticeably clenched his teeth. Alphonse continued, only offering limited praises before reaching the bottom line, "She was impressed by the diligence of this slave girl and wanted to apply her services to her household. Therefore, Monsieur Soileau, I am willing to pay your asking price for what I've described."

Demetre was silent for what seemed like minutes. "I will not honor your request to purchase." Alphonse's heart sank, but his face was unmoved. "I will, however, grant permission to rent, not for your mother's household, but for your company."

Expecting his plea to sell or rent to be turned down completely, Alphonse was eager to launch his second proposal, but only after approval of the merchandise. "Oh, thank you, Monsieur. I am pleased to know that your willingness to rent will benefit both you and me." A sweating and fully clothed Tomas had finally returned with the dripping ladle and offered it to Alphonse, who held up his hand and shook his head. Tomas cut his eyes at him before turning and taking a sip for himself. Alphonse continued, "I will have to find the words to tell Mother that her wish cannot be granted at this time."

Demetre explained, "There are plenty of slaves to pick from, but I do not dispose of my finest, with the exception of the ones I'm willing to send your way."

"Ah, yes." Might I take a look at them before we negotiate?"

"Tomas!" Demetre called to the slave, who turned to wipe his mouth. "Fetch me Rubar, Seven, and Alysaundre." Danielle gasped then smiled, recalling the good that could come of this offer if all goes well.

"Oui, Monsieur," said Tomas once again, heading into the fields.

"Monsieur Soileau," Alphonse requested, "I know that you will not sell, but I wanted to have a look at the prospects my mother listed, if I might, particularly since she spoke so highly of the help she received and the cleanliness of the workers. You understand my curiosity, don't you?"

Demetre did not see the harm in that. Actually, it was a way of boasting and dangling desired goods before another's face, which he enjoyed. He rang a bell as house slaves filed out to greet him one by one. The first to emerge was Danielle from her hiding place, nervously holding her fingers before subconsciously rubbing her stomach.

Alphonse said, "She escorted me to you. Which one is this?"

"That is Danielle," said Demetre, waiting for a reaction.

"*That's* Danielle?" he scoffed. Danielle couldn't help but be engulfed by insecurity.

"You are alarmed?" Demetre asked. Alphonse did not comment. "You can share your criticism without consequence."

Alphonse looked Danielle up and down smugly. "It's just that she is quite different from what mother described. I question how much work could get done with a woman who is on the verge of explosion, despite how well she performs. Pardon my candor, but what should occur after she has the child? A working slave with a baby latched to her teat is not ideal, in my opinion, but it may not be bothersome to others. Perhaps choosing not to sell was its own blessing. I don't expect my mother to watch the child, but I would hate for you to free up one of your slaves to watch the babe and pick up her lacking chores."

"You seem agitated by her pregnancy."

"No, only by inconvenience. A female who is with child can be good, but not when there is work to be done and money to be made." Although slightly offended by the welcomed series of statements, Demetre was beginning to like the Negro who stood before him and shared similar thoughts. Alphonse took another glance at Danielle's stomach and back at Demetre, who smiled slyly. Alphonse mustered a smile in return. Feeling as if each man were stripping away layers of her clothing, Danielle felt disgusting and hurt by the role Alphonse played. But she knew it was necessary.

The two men and Danielle were soon joined by Rosezelle, Corrine, Alette, and two other slaves. Bewildered by their summoning, Demetre pointed to the appropriate slave, calling their names out to Alphonse. Alette tried desperately to read Danielle's face, which teetered from confusion to offensiveness. The women and Alette were soon asked to depart.

Demetre slowly paced, "My boy," he said. "You've given me something to think about. Although I'm not going to sell to your mother, I have changed my mind about renting to her. However, she may not have Danielle. I want her here," he said, gently looking to Danielle. "With me." Alphonse fumed internally while Danielle, looking down at her belly, couldn't help feeling flattered, believing that she was still wanted and that Demetre still took interest in her child. "I will share with you the dates and seasons that I can spare any of the house slaves you saw. But you will need to make arrangements through my rental agent. Is that understood?"

"Yes," said Alphonse, "That is a very generous offer that I will accept. However, I would like to put my mother's requests to the side and discuss those whom I can use on my boats."

Just then, behind wrestling vegetation and crackling dead leaves came Tomas, followed by two overseers, two field hands, and Alysaundre, whose eyes shifted wildly to his sister, Alphonse, and Demetre. Ready to defend the girl, he stood with his knees bent as he always had whenever the overseer or Demetre was in proximity. Alphonse strolled musically to the tallest darkest Negro who was at eye level with Alphonse. He stared him in the eyes for seconds. The slave, unwavering in his glare, did not give off any indication of danger to Alphonse, only the need to survive with dignity. The only thing stamping him as ornery to his master, besides his glare, was his darkness. "This one," Alphonse said to Demetre, who found the interaction between a free colored man and slaves fascinating, almost entertaining. "What is this one called?"

"Rubar," replied Demetre.

"Aggressive, is he?"

"Very. I've never seen anyone that big and black who isn't. But Peter's got good control over him and the other scoundrels," Demetre complimented the young overseer who was only months into learning his trade.

Alphonse circled around the slave, looking him up and down, opening and closing his brown vest, lifting his pant leg to reveal strong muscles. He went to the next slave. "And this one?" he asked.

"That one is Seven. I changed his name from something gibberish to Seven after learning that he ran away from previous owners seven times. But he has been broken and has stayed here for over 5 years. But still manages to give the overseers grief sometimes, due to his mouth."

Alphonse stood inches away from Seven's freckled tan profile. The red-headed slave stared out into the courtyard for only moments until the agitation got the better of him and slowly turned his head to challenge Alphonse by looking him square in the eyes. Neither man blinked. "Seven times, eh?" asked Alphonse.

"Yes," replied Demetre.

"Where to?"

"He's trying to get to his wife and child. By now, I believe they have been separated and sold to different masters." Seven blinked numerous times and looked down. "And see, for that reason, I don't allow my Negroes to marry. It's pointless, not recognized by God, and only becomes a problem for me."

"Sir," said Seven to Demetre, still looking at the soil. "My wife and my boy separated?"

"At last I heard," said Demetre.

"Who they masters?"

"That's none of your concern. One good thing about the state you are in is that you can always start anew—have other children with some of the females on this plantation. In fact, I encourage you to have your way with them, and perhaps it will help to ease your anger." Demetre and the overseer laughed. Seven's lips quivered, and his eyes welled with tears. His nose, red. He bit his bottom lip and managed not to let a single tear drop in front of his master. Demetre turned to walk away.

"Who they master?" Seven asked again.

Demetre whipped around. "Didn't I tell you that you don't need to know? You will move on to another girl." He turned to walk again.

"I don't want another, sir. I only want my Lorraine and my Azacca Jr.—"

"If you don't want lashes, I suggest you hush, now."

Seven opened his mouth to speak again, but Alphonse purposely interjected. "—And who's this Monsieur?" heading for Alysaundre. Strange sounds emerged from Seven's mouth. Sounds of mourning trying to pound their way out, breath by breath. Alphonse halted but did not turn around. He did not want to see another man break down, although he knew Seven had ample reason to.

"This is Alysaundre," Demetre said. Seven yelped. Alphonse examined him with his eyes, then squeezed his cheeks together with his hand, exposing Alysaundre's teeth. Looking into his mouth, Alphonse angled his head to see further. Alysaundre balled his fists, losing trust in the man whom he had met only weeks ago. He loosened them when Alphonse gave his future brother-in-law eye contact and a quick nod. He then circled Alysaundre, slapping him several times on the back to feel the sturdiness of his muscles.

"What kind of trouble has he been in in the past?" Alphonse asked, inspecting Alysaundre's loose sandy hair for lice or other bugs.

"He defiantly lifted his finger to Peter and was punished severely for it. But he's learned his lesson, haven't you, Alysaundre?" Alysaundre remained silent, glancing in the corner of his eyes at his master. "And *that* is typically the cause of his troubles—his unwarranted anger. The sneers he gives to his superiors."

"Any fights or deaths at the hands of this ma—boy?"

"Fights, plenty, murders, none."

"I choose this one," Alphonse decided.

"Well then, it's settled," Demetre confirmed.

"My boy," Alphonse said to Aly, "you're going to be working for me on my boats. The labor is hard, and I expect nothing but your best work. My overseers and I have little patience and won't tolerate a defiant Negro. You want to be angry? Be angry at the waves as we're rowing against the tides. You want to attack something? Attack those trees that are blocking your boat's path through the river. The test you give me or your overseer could be your last."

Alysaundre looked straight ahead, giving a quick nod. "Monsieur Soileau," Alysaundre said finally. "And Monsieur..."

"Santee," said Alphonse.

"And Monsieur Santee. Send another in my place...please."

Demetre looked to Alphonse. "No," said Alphonse. "I've made my decision. You will work for me."

Alysaundre shifted his glance from the direction of the free Negro's fine dusty leather shoes to Demetre's glossy fencing boots. "Monsieur Soileau, I need to stay here... please."

"You know, Alphonse," said Demetre. "I believe I am better off without Alysaundre on my land. What would you say about *purchasing* him today? $700?" Although Alysaundre's price was listed at $600 in the slave schedule.

Alphonse pretended to be affected by the steep asking price. He tried bargaining the price down, but Demetre did not budge. After a brief deliberation, Alphonse held out his hand, and the men shook.

Demetre said, "Wait here. I will draw up the papers." He took a few strides toward the house.

"Monsieur!" Alysaundre looked up and called out. He lowered his head as Demetre pivoted sharply. "If I am to be sold to another man, I ask, if it's all the same to you, that you please sell my mother and sisters to this man as well."

"No," Demetre said coldly. "It's *you* I want to rid of."

"Please, will I be allowed to return to the plantation for visits to see my mother and sisters?"

Alphonse looked at Demetre. "Danielle," Demetre explained, "is one of his sisters. Alette, whom you saw earlier, is the other." Demetre looked at the sadness covering Danielle while Alphonse watched Demetre's face nearly succumb to a softness for the girl, which he had not seen previously. Alphonse didn't know whether to be concerned about the unspoken communication between slave and master or to be grateful because of its potential to benefit Alysaundre.

"His sister is Danielle, huh?" asked Alphonse. "I should have seen the resemblance. Although after a while, most slaves start to look alike to me anyway."

Demetre smiled lightly, "I'll get the papers," he said as he headed toward the mansion. "And I will add a pair of shackles."

"Thank you, but I won't be needing them," said Alphonse.

"Trust me, you will," Demetre insisted without turning around.

The overseers wrestled Seven and Rubar back to the field by their torn shirts. Seven snatched away, running to Alphonse. "Take me," he pleaded. "Alysaundre doesn't want to go. Take me, please!"

"Get back over here!" screamed Jeremiah the overseer, grabbing Seven by the back of his neck.

Alphonse wished that he could buy the freedom of another man for the purpose of allowing him to locate his family. But knew that he would destroy the plan.

Danielle hiked up the hem of her dress and quickly walked to Alysaundre, pausing at the sight of Peter beside him. He simply looked at her, granting permission to approach her brother. Trying to hide tears, she gave him a tight, lunging embrace. With all of their disagreements, Alysaundre could not remember the last time he hugged Danielle. He slowly began to feel his arms rise and wrap around her shoulders. He squeezed harder, bringing her tignon-wrapped head closer to his chest. The weight of Danielle's curls caused the dark green headpiece to wither onto the orange fallen leaves. Not knowing what the future held, Alysaundre stroked her hair, taking in the smell of berries and light honey. Remembering all that he could of his sister.

Demetre reached the top of the stairs. "Danielle!" He called out without turning his back. "I'm certain there's a lot to be done before sunset."

"Oui, Monsieur!" Danielle responded as she reluctantly pulled away from Alysaundre.

He stared widely into her eyes as if he wanted to tell her something. But all she could gather was, "I'll be back," he murmured.

"Good luck, Aly," Danielle whispered. She waited until Demetre had taken a couple more steps toward the mansion, until Tomas or Peter were not looking, to walk closely past Alphonse. Danielle extended her pinky in an effort to glide it along Alphonse's hand, hoping to feel his skin for as long as possible within the brief moment allowed. When he could not feel her, without letting anyone, aside from Aly, witness, Alphonse stepped a little closer in an attempt to reach out for her with his middle finger. They reached desperately, missing each other's touch by a fraction of a centimeter. Alysaundre distracted Peter by making a sudden movement in the opposite direction. It was then that Danielle was able to glide her fingertips along her lover's hand as if to say, "Thank you, and I love you."

After signatures inked the drawn contract and authorized passes, and the currency was exchanged, Aly boarded the back of Alphonse's empty wagon in the provided shackles securely on him for show. Alysaundre looked out toward his Maman in the fields, as she extended her kissed hand in his direction. She whispered, "Keep your eyes open, and your feet swift," as the men journeyed off the Soileau Plantation.

Thirteen

Alysaundre sat quietly at the edge of the raft as his new coworkers joked and smoked tobacco after a 3-day job of clearing cypress trees and debris to create a path through bayous and rivers. Weeks after being purchased by Alphonse had scrimmaged by as Alysaundre tried to learn the rules of his new world. He and the other watermen frequently presented documents to white men who stopped them en route to their job sites, although half of the workers could read the contents of the papers Alysaundre was told to hold onto so dearly. "This one," Alphonse told him in his home only a few days after the purchase, "grants you permission to work on water," he said as he dipped his fountain pen into the ink and signed his name next to his embossed company seal at the bottom of the document. He blew onto the ink and handed it to Alysaundre, who accepted the parchment with both hands, careful not to smudge Alphonse's signature, gliding over the cursive words with his eyes. Uncomfortable in his vulnerability towards a more established young black man, Alysaundre said, "It doesn't feel right to hold a paper so close and I don't know what it says. Read it to me?" Alphonse began to feed the contents of the permit to Alysaundre as he digested each sentence.

"And *this*," Alphonse said warmly, handing over another document, "will be registered and filed at the Recorder of Deeds." Alysaundre held the heavily printed paper. He looked at Alphonse, waiting to hear more. "It reads:

'I, Alphonse Renaud Santee, of the town of Vermilionville, in Lafayette Parish, Louisiana, do hereby certify that I manumit and set free a male slave named Alysaundre Soileau, of about 21, fair-skinned and 5 feet, 10 inches, medium build, sandy brown hair. I relinquish all claims to the said Alysaundre Soileau, his person, and services from this time forth and forever, given under my hand on this thirtieth day of September, eighteen hundred and fifty-nine.'"

Alysaundre swallowed hard. He never imagined this day. He always believed that he would gain his freedom by running away or by death. With a balled hand and eyes to the ceiling, he listened to Alphonse's words. "You take this and put it in bonded leather. Only reveal this when you must. Do not let anyone borrow, hold, or rent it. Life out here for a free man is hard, too. People will try to fool you, charge you more, pay you less. White men will be jealous of you or cast anger upon you for the way you look.

"Do you know how to fight?" Alysaundre nodded, finally looking at Alphonse. "Good," Alphonse continued. "Hold your temper until it is necessary to unleash in order to protect yourself. You want to fight a white man just enough to get him off of you and long enough for you to disperse.

"I am not asking you to stay away from spirits, I am demanding it. No alcohol. And let's not pretend that liquor is delicious because it is not. It doesn't erase your worries but enhances them. Very few people like to drink alone and will offer one to you. Let *them* get drunk, but you—you keep your mind clear.

"Beware of kidnappers who are always looking to fool and capture us, especially near the docks.

"I won't have time to teach you how to read, but I will show you a few words here and again. It's up to you to learn; learn it well and continue at it. Not knowing how to read will leave you in the dark.

"Have you got a woman?" Alysaundre shook his head. "Good. Keep it that way until you are ready to have a family or care for someone other than yourself. And just like on the plantation, stay away from white women, especially those who may tempt you intentionally.

There are several well-dressed ladies at every port waiting to bait you in many ways. Some want you to take them to their beds, others want to have you beaten and your money stolen. They may take your papers for profit too. One may say that she is different, but the moment white men learn of any comradery between you and a white woman, you will be killed.

"I don't tell you all of this to grab away at your happiness at this moment, I tell you this because freedom for us is not complete, nor is it just. But there are ways around obstacles. Promise me that for your family's sake, you will remain focused until your exit out of the south for good."

Alysaundre held out his hand. Alphonse grasped it, tugging Alysaundre closer and hugging him ruggedly, followed by a hard slap to the back. Handing over the piece of paper, Alphonse stated, "Here you are, my brother," and slapped Alysaundre on the back once more, leaving him to stand alone in the living room staring at the paper. Alysaundre could not believe that the eight-by-ten-inch piece of parchment which he held determined his freedom. That something so fragile had so much power over his life, which in turn, could affect the lives of his family. He carefully looked over the words again and once more, wishing that he could read them rather than memorize sounds and syllables that flowed out of another person's parted lips like the Red Sea. His mind teetered between pure joy and fear. Triumph and loneliness. Gratitude and vulnerability.

He thought about his father, then Lettie, and all that it would take to free them. He thought about Maman, and tears welled up in his eyes. The beautiful woman who raised him and cared for him with such grace did not deserve to belong to any man except Edmond. And then there was Danielle, for whom he secretly confessed his indebtedness. He walked outside onto Alphonse's porch quickly, exhaling deeply. Clutching his new freedom papers, he looked into the blue Louisiana sky and closed his eyes. He knew all that he had to do.

The rocking sensation of the boat and the scent of alluvial in a still clouded aroma of earth and humidity was pleasing to Alysaundre, who opened his light brown eyes towards the sky as the men approached the banks. They filed out of the boat, some making their way to a freedman boarding home just outside of Vermilionville, where they were less likely to be harassed by Irish watermen on strike. Sounds of heavy boots against the planked wooden porch alerted the cook of the men's arrival as she prepared two-cent bowls of crawfish soup and bread in the back of the house. They all lined up before the open fire and cast-iron pot, talking and joking loudly.

Alysaundre listened to each dialect, recognizing most he had heard on the plantation. "We just missed 'em," Alysaundre overheard a lodger say. "They came sweeping through here, telling them to show their papers. They didn't snatch up nobody, but I sure as hell wanted to stomp the sons-of-bitches," the man said, sitting on a table at which his friends ate supper. He removed his tattered-brimmed hat and began to light a corn cob pipe. "Don't think they just want us as bounty. They also looking to see what we got and how they can take what they want."

With bowl in hand, Alysaundre took an empty seat at the table where the man with the brimmed hat sat with friends. He listened as their conversations hopscotched from women to hobbies, to whites, to women, to future plans of moving to the North, to music, and back to women. "Shiiiiiiit," said the man with the brimmed hat, "I'd lick her toes if she asked me to." The men rumbled with laughter, and Alysaundre chuckled and glanced over occasionally, trying not to involve himself in the conversation. "I won't be getting anywhere near those toes without first getting my money right." He pulled out a folded newspaper from his back pocket and leaned into the men. With a lowered voice, he read, "You see what they're offering Negroes up north? *Room and board, wages, and 3 hot meals a day.*" Alysaundre had not heard much after. He simply stared at the paper with bold letters and heavy columns of text. The image at the forefront of the publication name bearing a star with an empowered Negro woman holding up a ball of light in the palm of her hand. Drawings of men's suits, ladies' hats, and jarred products fell between the content. "I said, here you go, Beige," the man said, shoving the paper in Alysaundre's face. The others had left the table a short while ago, leaving Alysaundre and the man alone. "You've been looking at this paper, so I figure something in there must have caught your eye."

"Oh," Alysaundre said, glancing around, not expecting to converse.

The man slid a little closer to Alysaundre, examining him with his eyes. "Fascinating," he said. "You actually *are* Beige...well, here you go. The paper is last month's edition, but we lucky to get any information from up north, right?" Alysaundre did not lift his hand to accept the publication. "Oh, I'm sorry. You can't read. Well, I ain't reading the whole paper to you, but I can read a section if you like."

"Can you teach me to read it instead?" asked Alysaundre, who did not seem as timid as the man perceived. "I'm willing to pay you a penny for every two lessons. And, you teach me to write my name and the names of my family. I'll pay you at the end of each class."

The man rubbed at his small beard, pouting his bottom lip while nodding slowly. "You want *me* to teach you?"

"Yes."

"In English or Français?" asked the man.

"Tu parles Français?!" Aly asked excitedly.

"What?"

"I asked if you speak French?"

"Just joking. Yes, I speak French. It will be double if you want me to teach you in two languages."

"English for now. I need to see how good of an instructor you are." Alysaundre said, cracking a smile.

"Yeah, well, you just do as I tell you, Beige, and there won't be a problem." He rolled up the newspaper as if he were about to hit his new pupil.

"Alysaundre, Lafayette Parish," he stuck out his hand.

"Chatlie Rivers, Kentucky by way of New Orleans. But you can call me Chat." The two shook hands. "Alright, Beige, we start tomorrow."

"I just told you my name."

"I know, but I do as Americans do. We learn the true name of something and decide to call it what's most convenient for us instead. Just ask them Indians."

Chat lived up to his promise of teaching Aly to read, first by recognizing the letters in his name, and later spelling it. "Ain't no sense in you learning how to spell other things before you know how to spell your own name," said Chat in the cloudy smoking room of the boarding house as Alysaundre stood before a chalkboard, carefully crafting each loop in the letters. Of course, he had always heard his name in various ways and projections, but had never been introduced to it in this way. He felt as if he were finally gaining a little more sense of control over his very being.

Over the weeks, Alysaundre removed folded pieces of newspapers from his pockets to practice reading during his lunchtime. "Keep working at it!" his mates yelled from the other side of the encampment on any given break. "Shit," said one worker, with a cigarette dangling from the side of his bottom lip as he sharpened a stick with a pocketknife. "Watching you, I might need to take up reading."

"Make the time, my friend," Alysaundre encouraged.

"Ah, I don't know," the man waved. The desire to want to read was frequently thrown at Aly by others, but he never witnessed anyone taking action to accomplish such a task. For many chose to push learning to the side to survive and find additional income.

When traveling, up and down the Mississippi, Aly accompanied his coworkers into any general store that would have them. With stares from white shop owners and customers, Aly learned that his money was wanted when it came to less intimidating items such as jams and marmalades. But upon asking to purchase a pen, paper, and ink, anger ensued from clerks who often called him a nigger and kicked him out before reactionary customers could gather and later ruin the reputation of the shopkeeper. Others would deny his request but allow him to purchase anything else in the store.

"Man," said Chat while tying lumber to the cypress boat near a dam. "You got to go to a store owned by one of us to get that stuff."

"I didn't know there was such a thing."

"Yeah! Ain't got no other choice sometimes. They hard to find, though."

Chat was right. While in the hills of Virginia, Aly and his mates entered a town of free Blacks and entered Graham's General Store. "Afternoon, Miss Sally. How ya doin', Miss Sally?" they said to the young woman at the counter as they entered and removed their hats. Some of the men wandered off in search of jerky and preserves, their boots rhythmically beating the hardwood floor with every step. Others stood in line to purchase items behind the counter, while some pretended to be interested in the items for a chance at Sally's attention. However, conversations were kept to a minimum as Sally's father stocked the nearby glass cases and items behind the counter, occasionally sliding looks of displeasure or outright intimidation. Alysaundre was next to approach Miss Sally. For a moment, he struggled to recall his reason as he stared at the rich, deep beauty of the young woman who looked to be his age. Her eyelashes were the longest he had ever seen; her dark coffee complexion had neither bump nor blemish. Her thick black hair was in a loose bun upon her head. A look of pleasant unfamiliarity came across the woman's face. She liked the way he stood, straight-backed and confident, although his expression said otherwise. She nodded, "Hello, sir," she said to Alysaundre.

"Good day, ma'am," Alysaundre said, with as much gentility as he could muster. At that moment, he realized that this was his first time interacting with a woman who was not a slave or resided on the Soileau Plantation. Careful to avoid sounding foolish or uneducated in front of the pretty woman, he continued with a delicate tone. "I am looking for writing supplies. Would you happen to have any that you could sell to me?" His heart anxiously awaited a reply.

"Well," she said with a slight smile, "we seem to have sold out of pens, but I do have paper and ink that I can sell you if you'd like."

Alysaundre was enamored by her voice, which sounded similar to a *trickling brook. How does one's speaking voice sound so soothing? He asked himself.*

The woman raised an eyebrow with a questioning smile.

"Oh," chuckled Alysaundre, embarrassingly, "I will have the paper and ink. Please."

The woman turned to collect the sealed bottle of ink and the paper. "You planning on doing a lot of writing?" Her father shot her an irritated gaze as he continued to stock the next shelf without looking at what he was doing. His eyes shifted to Alysaundre.

Alysaundre dared not let his eyes fall upon the woman's body, although he desperately wanted to look. "Uh, yes mam, I am."

"In French? Your accent tells me that you mostly speak French."

"You're correct, but I plan on doing my writing in English."

"Well, I hope she will enjoy getting your letters." The woman turned around with the items, locking her eyes on him.

Alysaundre broke eye contact, noticing her beautiful, blush lips. He looked back at the woman. "She?" He asked. "Oh, I'm not—there is no 'she,' presently."

The father cleared his throat.

"Oh," she said, almost dancing to the register at the corner of the counter closer to her father. She smiled even bigger as she wrote the contents into the sales book and the store's address onto a piece of paper. Alysaundre smiled out of the side of his mouth at the wonderland of the woman's face, which revealed its latest feature, dimples. *How could one face be so blessed?* He thought. "I'm very sorry that I didn't have a pen to sell you."

"That is alright," Alysaundre said. The numbers on the register rang up $0.40. "I am grateful to be able to purchase this today. Thank you." The father cleared his throat more obnoxiously.

Alysaundre handed the woman the money.

"You're welcome." She handed him the ink and the papers tied with string. "Here," said the woman, "this is the address to the store. "If there is anything that you need when you return, just drop it in a letter and I'll be sure to have it waiting for you." She handed him the address. He did not want to let on that he could not yet read it.

"Trust!" The woman's father barked at her.

"Daddy!" The woman barked back, revealing those dimples that Alysaundre was careful not to fall into. Her wide eyes told her father that he was embarrassing her, while his crossed arms stated that he did not care.

"I don't mean to get you into trouble with your father," Alysaundre said, unintimidated.

"Oh, not to worry. Daddy does this to every man who walks in here and assumes I might fall in love with just anything in trousers," she whispered. "I have better sense than that. Mama says, 'Not every man deserves your smile.' So, I don't throw my smile at just anyone."

"Wise ladies, you and your mother," said Alysaundre.

"And Daddy, well, he's just protecting his girl, that's all. And he's got a cute way of going about it. Just look at that face," she pouted. They both looked at the bearded man, who was now fuming. Alysaundre turned his head so as not to laugh or smile in the man's direction.

"Now, I heard the others call you Miss Sally, but your father called you by another name."

"Trust," she said. "My first name is Trust; my middle name is Sally. I tell people I'm not fully acquainted with to call me Miss Sally. There's something about being called Miss Trust that I find unsettling."

"And what shall I call you?" he asked, placing his purchases in his satchel.

"Trust. Just Trust," she responded sweetly.

"Well, I thank you for all your help, Mademoiselle. I hope we see each other again."

"As do I. Don't forget to write—if you need to order anything."

Alysaundre felt something upon his face that he rarely experienced, a full-toothed smile. "Yes, ma'am. Goodbye," he said to Trust. His smile vanished. "Goodbye, sir, and thank you," he said to her father, still staring angrily.

As he walked out of the general store, gleaming with his chest poked out, several rolling eyes and teeth-sucking met his glance as he and his comrades headed out of the town and back to the boat. "Don't pay them no mind," said one of the mates. "Miss Sally don't hold conversations with many men. She certainly don't smile at everyone. Somethin' about you she like. She's a good one right there. If you smart, you would go after her before another man do."

Alysaundre's insecurities began to settle in. How was he going to write to her when he just learned to write his own name? What kind of life could he give to a woman when he was just learning his limitations as a noir libre? And then there was his family, on whom he needed to focus. He looked at the address, thinking about the prettiest face that had ever made him smile. He tucked away the slip of paper thinking that if he never pursued Trust, it would be all the better for both of them.

Several days at sea gave Alysaundre cravings of owning a pen and learning to write to someone, anyone who could read and write back. Plantation life led him to prefer being alone, except for Maman and Lettie. But out on the water, his transformation was unsubtle. He thought he held his head high as a slave, often getting kicked by overseers passing by, but now, freedom allowed his head to be elevated to a height he thought unimaginable. He shared stories with friends and gained trust in some, but held tightly to his gift of discernment, for his survival depended on it.

When their schedules allowed them to meet, or if they were working on the same project, Chat and Alysaundre resumed their lesson wherever they could, "Sh-sh-i-i-i-t-t-t. Sh-it. Shit," Alysaundre read the word written in the dirt beside the bridge under which they and other crew members worked. The men nearby laughed. "Chat!" Alysaundre snapped, "Why are you teaching me bad language?"

Chat took a drag from his cigarette, "You need to know how to *read and write* the everyday words you hear, right? And you also need to learn words that begin with sh, ch, th. One of the easiest to learn and for me to explain, is this here word," Chat underlined the word with a stick, "shit!" Alysaundre shook his head. "Alright," laughed Chat, "Let's try something else. Something you should know how to write above anything—your name."

Confidently snatching the stick from Chat, Aly began to write his name in the dirt, carefully crafting the most important group of letters yet. Upon finishing, he tossed the stick to Chat who stylishly caught it with one hand while holding his cigarette with the other. He examined each letter, took a drag, and nodded with approval. "Not bad," he said with a smile. "Not bad at all. Say, you ever thought about changing your name?"

"I didn't know I could," Aly said.

"Of course you can. You free, ain't you? Who named you?"

"My father. He named all of us. Said that if a white man ever decided to change it later, by then it wouldn't mean anything, our rightful names were already embedded into our souls, and that would be the name by which God calls us."

For a moment, Chat was speechless. "Damn, Beige," he finally said. "Was yo Pap a preacher?"

"In his own way, I suppose."

"Well, my name used to be Jordan, like the river. So, I changed it to Chatlie Rivers no sooner than I got my papers."

"Why?"

"Why what?"

"Why did you change your name?"

"I ain't really free if I carry the name that some white man gave me. I'm forever bonded to him. And what if I took a wife? I can't let her take the name of that white man. And you can forget about any of my children bearing his name either." Chat looked hard at Alysaundre and was probably the most serious that Aly had ever seen him. Chat took a drag and broke his glare. "You should think about changing your last name if you got one, or making up a whole new one," he said finally.

Aly looked out at the earthy water as some of the men knelt beside it, washing their hands, smoothing their beards, or preparing for the continuation of the job aboard the boat. While he wanted to rid of any connection to the Soileaus and their plantation, he could not change his name until he was reunited with his family. "Yeah," he nodded simply.

With the cigarette now dangling from the corner of his mouth, Chat wrote another word in the dirt. "Well, c'mon. Now how would you read this word?"

Aly studied the one-syllable word for a moment, "F-f-f. U-u-u. F-f-u-u-u..."

Thirty miles outside of Lafayette Parish, Alysaundre walked into a general store with a reputation for serving Negroes, but only selling the products in the small colored section toward the back of the store. He saw bottles, jars, and packages with bold words, others with images of men or children; however, any products featuring white women were reserved for patrons of a snowier hue. His eyes glanced over the items within his area, where he spotted a familiar name. He focused on the poster pasted on the hogshead of sugar and bottles of molasses, recognizing the image of his sister on the Soileau & Sons products. He had seen the finished result of the hard work that he and other slaves had accomplished. The plowing and harvesting, the hot distillery, the tears, the long hours laboring in the suffocating humidity, the whippings—they all came flooding back into the compartments of his mind which he had intentionally blocked for his sanity, or so he thought. And to see his sister on the packages, not with her hair covered in a tignon as required or molested into a style similar to that of white ladies he had seen. He had never visited this tropical plantation on which Danielle stood in the picture. Had Master Demetre taken her there before? What were his ties to this place, he wondered? For how much did the sugar and molasses sell? What was the cost of products responsible for splitting up families, bondage, and so many other monstrosities—products with his sister's likeness—what was the cost? Did *she* know she was on these packages? Did any of his family know?

Reluctantly, Alysaundre picked up a bottle of molasses and examined the label, softly rubbing his thumb over Danielle's face. Despite his bitterness toward his sister's exploitation and likeness on items so sweet and often addictive, he took the bottle along with a small can of coffee to the counter, where a 12-year-old boy stood alone waiting to make a sale while his father visited the outhouse. Alysaundre acknowledged the boy with a head nod. Receiving one in return, Alysaundre then saw writing utensils behind the counter, in neither white nor colored section. "I'll have a pen and pencil, please," he said, hoping his request would not be rejected. The boy hesitated, for he could not recall if he was permitted to sell those items to Negroes.

Wanting to make a sale for his father and believing that items used for writing were not detrimental to anyone, the boy brought them before Alysaundre and rang them up, along with the coffee and molasses. After the exchange for money, Alysaundre nodded again, "Merci beaucoup Monsieur," he said before scooping up his purchase and whisking out of the store with the boy offering a slight smile.

With the sun setting, equipped with a pen, paper, and ink in his possession, Alysaundre felt freer than he had in weeks and was ready to learn or work towards whatever came his way.

Fourteen

Lafayette Parish, Louisiana

Etiennette and Simone waited in the foyer, getting one last look at each other before Simone's departure. The mother could not help but notice the raised head and broadened chest of her daughter—her glow, almost blinding. Was it her new love, her upcoming freedom, or both? Etiennette questioned. She took offense to the inkling that Simone's anticipation of freedom was the drive behind the minute-by-minute smiles and nimbleness to pack upon receiving her father's consent to leave for months. "You don't have to go all the way to New Orleans for an education, Simone," Etiennette said, cradling a care basket of fresh fruits and Corrine's biscuits wrapped in a white cloth. With a small case in hand and a satisfying gleam, Simone patiently listened to all of her mother's reasons to remain in Lafayette Parish. The entrance began to clutter with additional carpetbags and trunks belonging to her cousins, Gloria, Bella, and Jeffrey, who, one by one, entered, accompanied by a slave assigned to help with the luggage. Each of the slaves bustled through the foyer and out of the porte-cochere to store the belongings in the carriages.

"Mother," sighed Simone, "we've talked about this. There is nothing here for me anymore. Even Father agreed—right Father?" she asked as Demetre entered from the library.

Demetre placed his hand on his wife's back, "What are we going to do, dear, keep her here and stunt her knowledge of the world? Besides, she'll be with Emile and her cousins, and *will be on her best behavior, because there is no other option, correct?*" he said, directing his question to the teens who now stood behind Simone.

"Oui, oui, bien sur oncle Demetre," assured Gloria.

Not accepting of any such response from Gloria, Demetre turned to Bella. "You'll look after one another? And see that she does the right thing?"

"Yes, of course, Uncle," Bella said, moving towards Simone and hugging her. "She is like a sister to me more than a cousin, so I will always care for her well-being."

"See?" said Demetre to his frowning wife, "There is nothing to worry about. And we have raised a good girl. I trust her decisions."

Etiennette mumbled, "You shouldn't; she is still a young girl in need of guidance."

Demetre turned from his daughter to mumble in return, "There was no mention of her youth when you were seeking a suitor for her."

"Father is right, you know," said Simone. "Listen, we must be off now. I'll be sure to write."

"We will be in New Orleans to visit soon," said Demetre.

Emile motioned for his daughters to head toward the door before taking his top hat from the hat rack. "Well," he said. "We will meet soon with the rest of the board to speak about what's ahead for Soileau & Sons."

"What *is* ahead?" Etiennette asked.

"Nothing to concern yourself about, really," said Demetre, also shifting toward the door.

"Perhaps limited production," Emile interjected. "Possibly new advertising—"

"Oh, thank Heavens," said Etiennette. "I never understood why a pretty French woman could not be on the packages. Simone would be a fine young lady to print in the advertising."

Jeffrey said, "Yes, because a white-skinned girl epitomizes the dark sugary sweetness of molasses." Gloria nudged him and laughed under her breath.

"Emile," said Demetre, leaning into his brother, "This is why business should be left between us." Demetre snapped his fingers at the slaves to open the main doors.

Simone hugged her parents and received her mother's basket, warmed with her body heat. As the heavy doors slowly swung open, Simone saw two parallel rows of seven house slaves and the carriages waiting to whisk her off to her new future.

While she wanted to leave, she wasn't so sure now. The sight of all of the people in her daily life made her a bit hesitant. The reality of her leaving tugged at her heart, causing her to cry silently. She took a deep breath and ventured forward to bid farewell to each of the men and women with whom she grew up. The second-to-last face peeked past the tall columns of people and at Simone as she made her way to her. Simone smiled at once upon approaching the child who had grown on her. "Alette," Simone said sweetly. At that moment, she began to see Danielle when she was of the same age. Memories of the games they played and the secrets she shared flooded Simone's mind. She thought about how they held hands everywhere when they were little and helped decorate the house every Christmas. Before Simone realized it, she began to cry. "Soyez sur votre meilleur comportement. You be good now, okay? Listen to Danielle and your Aunt Corrine."

"Yes, ma'am," Alette said, almost in a whisper.

Simone smiled at the sound of the precious little voice she rarely had the opportunity to hear. She bent down next to the child. "I'll tell you what. You may select one doll from my bed."

Alette lit up, "To keep?!"

"Yes. To keep."

"And you won't want it back when you come to visit?"

"No, it will be yours to have."

Alette balled her fists and squealed, but not nearly as loudly as she wished. "Thank you!"

Simone stood to meet Danielle, who offered a pleasant smile in appreciation of the gift given to Alette. "Mademoiselle Simone," said Danielle. "Thank you. That is very kind."

"Well," sighed Simone. "Perhaps this is where our journey ends?"

"I hope not."

"I will be home occasionally."

"And I'll be waiting."

And with that, the girls smiled cordially at one another as Simone lifted the bottom of her blue hoop skirt. She looked down at Danielle's belly and up at her again before boarding the carriage. As the others climbed aboard, Simone waved to her parents and at the slaves, but only thinking of Danielle and the discussion they exchanged days before.

Hoping to find Corrine in the kitchen, Simone encountered Danielle canning preserves. "Oh," Simone said. "Where is Corrine?"

"She went to collect some spices in the garden," said Danielle. "I can get her if you like, or is there anything I can do for you?"

Simone looked behind her, hoping to see Corrine, but settled for Danielle. "Well, I'll take some of those cookies on the counter over there."

Recognizing that those were the very cookies that Simone vocally banished from her life prior to her coming out party and thereafter while in front of her family, Danielle smiled and said, "Oui, Mademoiselle." She prepared a plate of pecan lace cookies for Simone and started back to her chores. Surprised to see Simone still standing on the threshold with her plate, Danielle inquired, "Would you like more? Some tea perhaps?"

"Join me, Danielle," Simone insisted. Before Danielle could rightfully use her chores as an excuse to avoid further discussion, Simone raised an eyebrow. Danielle set aside her broom. "Don't let me be the only one eating pastries," said Simone. Danielle made a plate with a modest amount of the dessert and followed Simone into the parlor.

With the shades opened, the girls internally marveled at the multicolored sky and vapes of clouds amid the sunset. Danielle waited for Simone to take a bite before partaking and ate accordingly. Finally, a sound emerged from Simone, "Mmmm! Delight baked into a single cookie. Why did I ever deny you?" she asked the half-eaten dessert.

Danielle chuckled lightly, "I'm happy that *you're* happy." Simone took another bite, closed her eyes, and swayed in ecstasy. "I wish Corrine could see the joy that her cookies have provided." The girls chuckled once more. Danielle could see that the girl was forming her words before speaking. Simone finally said, "You know, I will be leaving soon to expand my education."

"Yes, Miss," said Danielle, lightly pricked with envy. "You have a life of excitement waiting for you. Congratulations."

Simone offered a nod of appreciation and a swivel in conversation. "I often think about *us*. I mean you and I." Danielle put her plate of cookies onto the small round tea table between them. "We were the best of friends...family really. And at times, like sisters." Simone thought about the misery of going places without Danielle and the events and milestones that happened without her. "This is the most we have spoken to one another in nearly a year, and to think, we won't see much of each other for a long time."

"Yes, Mademoiselle," Danielle agreed. "I do miss our talks."

Simone could not believe what she was about to admit next: "It took some time for me to come to this, but I want you to know that I am trying to accept what has happened." Danielle could barely breathe. Feeling shame, she quickly looked at her belly and shifted her sights to other items around the parlor. Simone continued, "I am still angry that it was you whom my father chose, but I know I cannot do anything about the circumstances." Danielle finally looked at Simone, who, in her eyes, suddenly carried the grace of a woman far beyond her years. "But, if I am to fully accept...this, I *do* need further understanding about something." Afraid of the questions that may arise, Danielle nervously waited. Simone whispered, "Are the words of others true about you and Alphonse?" Danielle felt a chill roll down her back. *Has Jen told in retaliation? Thought Danielle. And what else did Simone know?*

"Mademoiselle?"

"I know about him. I know that you two have the deepest affection for one another. But is it true? Does the babe you carry in your womb belong to Alphonse?"

Danielle simply looked down, unable to speak. She certainly did not want to expose any information, truth or otherwise, in the house. She began to tremble. Although stating untruth about Alphonse being the father would make Simone and Etiennette happy, and could possibly save the life of the baby and Danielle. But if the news spread to Demetre, what would become of her or her family? What revenge would he plot? "Danielle?" said Simone, leaning in with genuine concern. "Are you okay?" Unable to find words regarding this, even if she wanted to, Danielle shook her head. Simone suggested, "Let's go into the garden."

Under the gazebo amid the violas and forget-me-nots, Danielle wrapped herself within the warm fabric of Simone's borrowed pink shawl that carried the scent of her childhood best friend. The girls sat side-by-side, but only one of them was unable to look at the other. "Are you ready to talk now?" Simone asked. "You know how well I keep secrets." Danielle *used to know* how well Simone kept secrets. But so much had changed within the lives of each of them that Danielle no longer trusted Simone or her words. She knew the magnitude of pain that Demetre's appetite for Danielle had caused Simone, but she wanted to avoid worsening the matter. Unaware of the transaction between Mr. Santee and Demetre, Simone tried again to get answers. "Danielle. Does the child belong to Alphonse?"

"Mademoiselle," the slave began. "While you are asking me the father of my offspring, you are also questioning who has bedded me. I understand that we shared everything as young girls, including every thought and dream. I am sorry for everything that has happened, particularly those that I had control over. And while I want nothing more than to be your confidant once more, and your friend, I simply can't share aloud the tapestry of such intimate moments." Simone no longer leaned in but sat up, rather disappointed and a bit offended by Danielle's response. She took a deep breath and set aside her offense to listen once more. "I don't know what you have heard about Alphonse, but he is a gentleman, and he respects the law...and me. He is a good man." And for the first time, she turned to look Simone in the eyes, revealing both love and fear. "Yes," she reiterated, "he is a *good* man."

Simone's gaze softened as she began to recognize the girl who sat before her and learned that she must be satisfied with the given answer. "Well, I don't know if you were instructed not to tell something, but even in my asking, a part of me feels as though I *should* know, while the other doesn't *want* to know." Danielle, looking desperate in her need for Simone to forgive her, never veered her eyes away. She hoped that with every word that came from Simone's mouth, there was acceptance in Danielle's answer.

Simone continued, "If I may share my full heart, I wanted to hate you for all eternity. In fact, I wished that I could. But I realized that I only hated the way I felt when all of this transpired, and I blamed you. Truthfully, every thought circled back to us and where my life would have been without you. But until recently, I never thought about what life is like *for you* and the decisions you must make. Everything in me told me to hate you. But instead, Danielle, I see you. I may not know the depths of it, but I see that you are frightened, but you're trying your best to carry forth because that is all you *can* do." Simone paused, noticing that her words exposed Danielle by the strength with which she swallowed. Simone tried to regain the girl's eye contact.

"You have my word that I will not speak of this moment or conversation to anyone." Simone could see Danielle's shoulders relax as she tried to hide her deep exhale. "I don't know this Alphonse, but I can see in your eyes that he is very special to you. But what I know for sure is that we have grown up. And we're both in love at the same time." Simone placed her hand on top of Danielle's and squeezed gently. The girls laughed, and without realizing it, they were crying.

As the sun completed its job for the day in the Louisiana sky, the girls talked and walked arm-in-arm, bringing their conversation, and ultimately, laughter, into the house, hidden in the wings of the mansion away from everyone.

Simone heard the door of the carriage shut. She stared out of the window at her parents and back at Danielle, and was thankful for the encounter they had had days prior. She felt a gloved hand on top of hers and turned to see Bella's warm smile over her left shoulder. "I'm okay," whispered Simone, as she put her hand up to the glass, offering Danielle a farewell for now, as the horse and carriage rolled away.

Fifteen

Hours before the passenger steamship, Le Voyaguer de l'eau, was to set sail from St. James Parish to Missouri, Aly, Chat, and other free sailors of color loaded equipment, vessel supplies, and the furniture of passengers sent by their butlers and slaves before the arrival of the ship's guests. Men could be heard on the decks above shouting instructions to one another as they secured ropes and knots, polished windows, and poured dirty mop buckets of water over the side of the ship and into the river. Alphonse had arrived hours earlier to deliver his men and sign documents. When speaking to the captain about the shipment schedule and the crew on the steamer, he waited until the captain had gone, before throwing a peculiar look at Aly. Alphonse then checked the time on his watch before setting off to complete the day's work. At last, when all of the items were on board and bolted for the long journey, Alysaundre started to retreat from the decks of the ship, leaving Chat to continue smoking and joking loudly with many of the workers on the dock. A twinge of excitement and nervousness tossed about within him while looking around a vessel that he would be riding for the first time.

Just above him, he saw the sun beating off of the shiny wood railings and brass portholes and wanted desperately to explore that privileged level of the ship. He could hear the stomping of boots and conversations in English and Cajun above him from the men going about their routines. He could hear a cluster of them further along the deck, with one voice carrying over the others.

As he neared the back end of the ship, to look out upon the river, he listened to the seagulls call to one another as the cluster of men dispersed and the sound of something scraping against sandpaper intervened. The scraping was then intertwined with song. "Do ba-na co-ba, ge-ne me, ge-ne me," the voice sang out boldly. While standing at the rail, Alysaundre lifted his head slowly wondering why his imagination would play such a trick on him. "Do ba-na co-ba, ge-ne me, ge-ne me," the voice rang out again.

Aly gripped the banister. His eyes widened. Feeling as though someone knocked the wind out of him, Aly called back toward the deck above, "Ben d'nu-li. Do ba-na co-ba, ge-ne me, ge-ne me!" Aly heard a metal object fall to the floor followed by the shuffling of feet.

"Do..." the voice hesitantly sang. "Do ba-na co-ba, ge-ne me, ge-ne me."

"Ben d'nu-li," Aly sang quietly.

"Stay where you are!" The raspy voice shouted. "Don't move!" The man's boots seemed to shuffle about before running down the deck and a flight of stairs. "Ge-ne me!" he called in desperation as he walked from under the threshold and turned to his left. And there, at the end of the deck stood a form, and no mirage or hallucination could receive the credit. With the Mississippi River and squawking seagulls behind him, Edmond saw his firstborn, Alysaundre staring back at him.

Aly was the first to move as he panted and started toward his father. Edmond joined but walked slowly from the shock as Aly gained momentum on the deck which seemed like miles. Finally, the two had met and connected in a hardy embrace. Edmond spoke, but his words were muffled in Aly's arm. The young man would not let his father loose, sobbing as if releasing the woes of all the moments he had sealed. Edmond held the back of his son's head, "Thank you God. Mèsi Bondje," he whispered in Creole. He repeated it, each time shakier than the previous until he too was crying.

A couple of chambermaids had witnessed the reunion outside of the cabins they cleaned. One of them approached the men, "Edmond," she whispered. "It's best if y'all come inside. This ship is huge, but it's got a mouth to tell on you." The men followed. "I'll give y'all some time," she said with a smile and glassy eyes. "I'll knock before I come in," and she closed the door behind her.

They studied each other for any new bodily imperfections but found none that were visible. Both blurted, "How are you?" and smiled.

"You look well, son. You're wearing sturdy clothes. And where's your beard?"

Aly ran his hand down his neck, showcasing his new shaved look. "Oh, Alphonse requires all workers uniformed and clean-shaven. You're a barber now, I see."

"I am. I worked in the boughs of ships for months and cut hair and shaved men on and off of the ship before my talent was realized by others. This is my new job aboard ships now...You look better than I've ever seen you."

"I'm much better, Father." He whispered loudly, wrestling to loosen the buttons of his inside jacket pockets for his papers. "And I'm a free man! I'm free!" He handed it to Edmond, who handled it delicately. His father's mouth dropped open. "And I can read it, Father. I can read now!"

"My God," Edmond said in a light voice. "Alphonse stuck to his word. He freed you, did he not?"

"He did."

Edmond looked around. "And your mother? And the girls? Are they free too?" Edmond hoped that they would emerge through the door.

"No." He was only able to free me."

Edmond nodded disappointingly. He leaned into Aly and whispered. "We will continue with our plan, but we will not discuss it here." Speaking quickly, he asked about the family and learned of Genevieve's sadness due to his absence, but was pleased to hear of her strength, and that she too had not moved on to another man.

Aly added, "Lettie is growing. As is Danielle. They are surviving, but they both need you. And that is all I will say until there is more time to talk."

Edmond studied the strife in his son's eyes as only he could. "You have more news hidden. Whatever it is," Edmond sighed, "I am ready to listen."

Aly sensitively divulged information about Danielle's pregnancy with Demetre's child, unpeeling additional details as Edmond's face smeared with disappointment. Edmond slowly sat on the bed, staring at the floor as if frozen with defeat. "Alright," he finally said, accepting the pain and calculating a pivot in plans. "And Master Demetre," Edmond began to ask, "does he know about Alphonse and TiFiy?"

"I don't believe he does. And Father, you do not have to continue to call him Master anymore. He doesn't own you."

"Oh, but he does. He never sold me. Only leased me. He is losing money and finding ways to bring in more of it. I heard Master Sterling talk about it while drunk and shooting cans one evening. Be sure to inform Alphonse, as this is now a part of our plan."

He paused, noticing Aly's stare of disbelief that his father was before him. Edmond stood, placing his hand on his son's shoulder. "I know I have been speaking a lot of Alphonse, but I am proud of you. You've been the head of our family when I could not be. You've protected your family the only way you knew how. You could have gone north after gaining your freedom. But you remained here in the depths of earthly hell for a black man. And you did it for your family. And I am thankful. Here you are, standing tall. My beautiful boy."

There was a light knock on the door followed by a soft voice, "You best be heading out now," the chambermaid said.

Giving his son a hug, Edmond whispered, "I'll come find you during our journey when I have the chance. And remember, keep your eyes open and your feet swift."

The two exited the chambers, heading in opposite directions, both looking back at one another.

The ship sailed for two weeks, temporarily docking at two regions of the south in order to pick up supplies or food. Many of the slaves and freemen were thankful that they did not have to be jailed until the ship set sail like on previous trips.

During the journey, Edmond and Aly received the opportunity to discuss happenings on the plantation and family matters. The end of the trip proved to be a success, returning to Louisiana hours earlier than scheduled.

* * *

As the sun melted into the balding east Louisiana oaks, Alphonse led a horse and wagon down familiar roads leading to the Soileau Plantation. Alysaundre remained quiet within the cart, looking around at the area that had been his residence for years. He wished the captain of the Le Voyaguer de l'eau dead when he refused Alphonse's request to rent Edmond for several hours, bolting the invisible chains that kept a man 20 miles from the family he yearned to see and breathe. Unfortunately, Aly began to remember that torture as anger bubbled within him as it had when he lived on the plantation. It didn't help that they were stopped twice by local patrollers demanding to see their papers or having guns drawn on them before laughing and permitting them to carry on. "Those sons of bitches," Aly said after several moments of being silent. "Anfand-chyen! Wish I could slit their necks, every one of them."

"You think that would solve our problems, huh?" asked Alphonse.

"They enjoy being evil," Aly said through his teeth. "I wish I knew why. That way, at least, I could follow through with life knowing that there is a reason."

"You have a lot of wishes today. Good thing I'm not a Genie." Aly looked perplexed. "Never mind," said Alphonse. "Power."

"Huh?"

"Power is why they are cruel. Even poor whites can obtain it if they are cruel to Negroes. They can go so far as to terrorize their own who are guilty of treating us with dignity; the kind ones— those are the ones you have yet to meet, but you will. When grouped together, that power gives the evil ones a togetherness, a brotherhood that they crave or never had from the start, and they take it out on our skin. You take away that feeling of belonging and what do they have left? They have their own problems to deal with. It is frightening to think that they believe they are doing the right thing. Many of them have the nerve to pray to the same God as us and ask for favorable treatment."

"Yeah," chimed Alysaundre. "Either they're praying right or we're praying wrong. Or perhaps we're cursed."

"I never want to hear those words ever again," Alphonse said, nearly stopping the wagon. "Our blackness is not a curse, although we're made to feel as if it is. Things that are cursed wither and bear no fruit. Things that are cursed don't continue to step upon the evil that is thrown down to us, helping us to rise." Alysaundre said nothing. "In all," Alphonse concluded, "we don't have time to get them to love us, something that might never happen. And as for me, if I am not dead, I keep moving forward. But again, I warn you. Hold your temper when you're around them. Nothing gets accomplished once they see your infuriation."

Perhaps it was Alphonse's response that allowed Aly to tuck away his animosity piece by piece, or the thought of seeing his mother and sisters again. The pair were each deep in thought as the horse occasionally blew through its nostrils or shook its mane, rattling the metal on the harness. Remembering the occasion for their travel, Aly looked over at Alphonse and patted him hard on the back, awaiting a response. Alphonse smiled nervously before drifting back into deep concentration.

Smoothly entering a discrete path onto the plantation, the men parked the horse and wagon in the nearby woods and walked to Danielle's cabin, as hers was the furthest away from the others.

Luckily, she had not yet arrived, and Alysaundre offered to retrieve Genevieve and Alette from their cabin while Alphonse awaited Danielle's arrival.

Aly knew that Monsieur Demetre and Etiennette were visiting her aunt Olivia several parishes away, as they had done every year at around this time. Without being noticed by the slaves or overseers, Aly managed to enter his mother's cabin. He memorized everything as it was—weaved baskets, pottery, crushed spices, and mint leaves in a cement bowl by the wooden table Edmond had built and carved so long ago. He rushed to Alette's bed where he saw an ivory-skinned doll wearing frills and feathers. He whipped around to find something of Alette's childhood that brought him fond memories of her. Delighting in the sight of her rag dolls in the nearby rocker, Aly picked one up, caressing it gently and later squeezing it in anxiety. A broom leaning against the newly whitewashed walls stood next to one of Edmond's old straw hats as it hung on a hook. Aly smiled and tried it on. He then gathered wood from near the fireplace and proceeded to lay the logs in preparation to light a fire. A pot of beans with hog fat had slow-cooked over the now charred wood below. Careful not to alert others or the overseers, with smoke floating from the chimney, Aly lit candles instead. Muffled voices were heard in the distance. As one drew nearer, Aly took an anxious breath, straightening his clothing. "Alright, then!" Genevieve called out to her walking mate before parting ways. Her shuffle up the cabin stairs was a bit slower than Aly had remembered, or perhaps, it was simply his excitement causing things to seem slower than they were.

Genevieve walked into her home with a pail of well water and saw before her her son, Alysaundre, standing by the fireplace. He removed his hat, "Hello Maman," he said with tranquility. Genevieve dropped her pail and screamed into her hands.

"It's okay," Aly smiled as he sped to her.

"Is this a dream?" Genevieve asked in shock, studying every feature of his face and body intensely.

"It is not," Aly said, locking her into his arms. "I can't stay long, but I needed to be here with you today." Genevieve cried uncontrollably. "It's alright Maman."

Genevieve grasped the side of his head, "Oh, look at you! You look wonderful. You've thickened. And your clothing. My, is that leather? I can't believe you're here—are you okay?"

Alysaundre gleamed, "I'm better than I've ever been." Alysaundre shared most of what had occurred in his life since leaving the plantation—his freedom, literacy, his job, and Edmond.

"You were *together*? You *saw* him? You *touched* him? How is my love? Is he well?"

Not knowing whether Genevieve was relieved, happy, or jealous, Aly confirmed, "Yes." Aly detailed every moment he could remember with his father. "And before you ask, he has kept to his word as he stated in the letter. He is still in love with you, Maman." Genevieve hugged Aly and sighed. For the first time, Aly thought about what life would be like if he chose to find a love as strong as his parents.

Before stretching deeper into conversation, Alysaundre said, "Maman, you have to get Corrine and Minister Liam and meet me at Danielle's cabin. Tell Minister Liam to bring his Bible along. And you, bring flowers. Go in secret. You will learn everything soon enough."

With Danielle leading the way to the cabins, Alette practiced her new talent of doing a one-handed cartwheel without dropping the cornbread tied in a handkerchief. "Lettie, that's not ladylike."

"Well, once I'm a lady, I'll stop," replied the girl.

Expecting Genevieve to be at home with wooden bowls of beans already prepared for the sisters, the two waited for some time before venturing over to Danielle's cabin. Under the door slit, Danielle saw waves of light motioning. She looked at the windows and saw the movement of a person, which she figured could only be Maman since the Soileaus were away.

"Maman," said Danielle, creaking open the door, with Alette trailing her. "We waited for you so we could have supper together, but—" Danielle's mouth dropped at the sight of her cabin, fully lit and with all who were present. Danielle and Alette both yelped Alysaundre's name before rushing to hug him. "How?" Alysaundre motioned toward Alphonse as if to present him. Danielle lightly touched her mouth when seeing Alphonse take a deep breath and smile while standing alongside Minister Liam. Turning to Corrine, Danielle asked, "Did you know?"

Teary-eyed, Corrine shook her head and laughed, "No," she whispered. "I would not have been able to keep this from you."

"But I'm not presentable," Danielle whispered back, looking at her soap-covered dress and bulging belly.

"He thinks you are, that's all that matters," Corrine quivered with excitement as Alphonse swallowed nervously, his smile never wavering.

Corrine began to unwrap Danielle's tignon and watch her curls tumble down near her waist. She smoothed and fluffed before placing a single purple flower in her hair. "It is no crown of flowers, but you look very pretty. One more thing," she then pinched Danielle's cheeks for additional color before nudging her friend to turn to her mother.

"Maman!" Danielle laughed, accepting a bouquet of flowers.

"Your Pápa has given his blessing," Genevieve whispered, "and you have mine. I've seen you when he's near you and when you speak of him. Now go."

Alysaundre offered his arm, "We know he is a good man," he said. "But is this what you want? Do you want to marry?"

Danielle squeezed her brother's arm and nodded. She nearly giggled like an adolescent. "Yes. I'm ready."

"Okay," Aly smiled back and walked her to Alphonse.

Neither Danielle nor Alphonse could take their eyes off one another. Once directly in front of Alphonse, Aly looked at the two of them, who seemed to ignore Aly altogether, and finally offered Alphonse the hand of Danielle. "Thank you," Alphonse said, staring Aly in the eyes with the utmost humility. Aly nodded and stood aside.

"Monsieur," Alphonse said to the minister. "Before starting, may I speak?"

"Yes. Please," Minister Liam allowed.

"Danielle," Alphonse started. "I'm sure this is not the wedding that you envisioned. But if you give me a chance, I promise to give you a life you can't imagine. If we had to, I would marry you anywhere so long as there was enough room to stand beside you, and enough space in your heart to allow me to become your husband. If Christ enables me to be with you for all eternity, I will catch every tear that has fallen in anguish and wash away your worries. Your glow makes me the warmest I've been, Danielle. You have opened my eyes to things I once chose to be blind to. Every day, since that evening at the theatre, I needed to see you, to touch you, to breathe you...to love you. To love you in a way that only you, me, and God can understand. To care for you and the babe, to ensure that you want for nothing. And although not of my blood, that child will no longer just be your baby, but mine as well to love, protect, comfort, and teach until God removes me from this earth. Excitement runs through me when I think of the world you and I will build for this child.

"It would be a terrible mistake if I stood before this man of God and said that I am not afraid, not of man, nor circumstances, or even of the future's outlook. But I'm afraid because you have all of me, Danielle. Except for the Lord above, I have never offered myself to any being; but I am privileged to share my soul, my tears, and my laughter with you. And so, that is why, on this day, I knew that I could not continue life without knowing that we were bonded by marriage. Without anyone's permission but that of your parents, and sanctioned by the Father, the Son, and the Holy Ghost, I stand here, ready to make you my wife. And I am ready to love you, even after my final breath." Alphonse allowed his tears to fall, as Danielle wiped them away. Bringing her hand around to meet his lips, Alphonse softly kissed Danielle's palm and inhaled deeply before nodding to Minister Liam.

The minister opened in prayer, blessing the union of the man and woman who stood in his presence and acknowledging those who were witnesses to God's ordinance. Reading Ephesians 5:25 from the tattered bible that he kept hidden underneath the floor of his cabin, the minister recited several passages, holding rosaries made of coiled string and later anointing their heads with his hand.
He asked each of them if allowed control over their circumstances, would they uphold the sanctity of marriage.

"Alphonse?" Minister Liam asked, "Will you, before me and witnesses, take Danielle as your wife, solemnly pledging yourself to discharge towards her the affection and all of the duties of a faithful husband?"

"I will," Alphonse promised, staring at his bride.

"Danielle?" Minister Liam asked, "As you stand before myself and witnesses, do you take Alphonse as your husband, solemnly pledging yourself to discharge towards him all the duties of an affectionate and faithful wife until distance do you part?" "I do," Danielle promised.

"In the book of James, we are told that all things good and perfect come from the Lord. In His eyes, the union I see before me in Holy matrimony is good and it is perfect. You walked through these doors as two solos meant for the same symphony. And it is so that I am honored as God's humble servant to bless you in the name of the Father, and of the Son, and of the Holy Spirit," the Minister concluded performing the sign of the cross. And without instruction, Danielle and Alphonse kissed with all of the bottled love and anguish they had experienced while they were apart.

Their evening together was treated as such, as their longing to explore every peak, ripple, and curve of their bodies became sweet reality. Alphonse slowly peeled away Danielle's hands and sheets, which she used to hide her insecurities. The woman stared into his face for approval, receiving a smile and a kiss upon her lips. In addition to soothing fingertips flowing across her body, Danielle encountered a gentility that she never knew was associated with lovemaking. Alphonse continued to smile at her often, whispering tender words as he mapped every place on her body that pleased him. He, in turn, allowed her to participate in their experience equally, and however she wished, as she had never done before. That moment defied her previous definition of sexual intimacy, causing her heart to swell with even more love for her man. Alphonse secured her in his tight arms and pressed. Her eyes widened at the initial contact, later softening and closing, lulling her to complete ecstasy, thankful that no one was near to hear her moans. She allowed herself to be present, fully immersing herself in every moment she had with him, allowing her body, especially her belly, to be loved and accepted, and loving his in return. While showing absolutely no signs of inexperience, Alphonse was careful with his bride, his full lips, addicted to her skin as he caressed her neck, breasts, and back with them. He handled her well, testing her limited flexibility— asking her several times about her well-being. A gentle pant or light laughter permitted him to continue his rhythmic waves. And that they did, multiple times throughout that beautiful night, where the stars seemed to gravitate closer to the unworthy earth.

Later that morning, Danielle awoke to the dark sky as she normally did. Fearing that her marriage to Alphonse and the evening with him was all a delicious dream, she smiled and sighed when seeing him lying beside her, sleeping peacefully. Rolling out of bed, Danielle grabbed peppermint leaves from a jar and chewed on them. She added more wood to the fireplace, watching the flames grow. Although it was Sunday, a day of rest for the other slaves, she began to groom, preparing herself for the day's work in the mansion. Her eyes wandered on the beautiful man still lying quietly in bed. She bit her bottom lip and grinned as she slipped back beneath the blanket with him. The young woman stared at every feature of his face and the curls in his hair. She thanked God for every scar, birthmark, and imperfection on his body, as they all now belonged to her and were perfect in her sight. She lifted the sheet, needing another peek at every bulge, every muscle.

Silently, she prayed that they would never be parted by distance and that she would be a good wife while allowed. Her words to the Lord expanded as she prayed for Alphonse's leadership in the marriage and his strength and patience to be married to a slave. She concerned herself with his safety, praying that he would be kept whole when returning for her; that no harm should come to him, especially because of whom he loved. And lastly, for herself and her family, she prayed for freedom from the Soileau Plantation. Not just to loosen ties with Demetre, but to rid herself of Etiennette's threat of murder. Danielle found herself having so much more to live for than ever before, to take up and make a life, a genuine life, with the man who lay beside her. She cradled her belly and rubbed gently, feeling the child roll in comfort.

At the conclusion of her prayer, she tried to put her troubles to the side, focusing on her husband. As badly as she wanted to please him again, she settled on awakening him with light kisses on the chest, her hair tickling him as he stirred and smiled at his new wife. Alphonse said, "Seeing a sunrise over the ocean is beautiful, but it doesn't compare to what I see before me."

Danielle smiled lightly. "Well, good morning to you too, my love." The newlyweds were playful in their kissing, knowing that it would lead to a continuation of lovemaking. Danielle laughed as she threatened to rip away the sheet that covered Alphonse's naked body should he take another step toward her. Alphonse smiled wickedly and ripped off the sheet himself. Danielle concealed her laughter as Alphonse grabbed her from behind in only a couple of steps, finally kissing her neck and shoulders. "Vrémen, shou-shou. Really, Honey. I must go, and so should you."

"I don't want to," Alphonse said.
Danielle turned and kissed him passionately. Alphonse caressed her hair, and he began to rise. Danielle laughed, "We mustn't do this again."

"You are right," Alphonse agreed, scooting away from his wife and locating his underwear. He quickly grabbed his clothing, giving her instructions as he slid them on. "Do you remember what we talked about?"

"Yes," she said, wrapping her hair in a tignon. Alphonse grimaced.

"Is something the matter?"

"It matters not, but it has always agitated me that the full beauty of Negro women cannot be exposed simply because it makes some people uncomfortable. But perhaps it works in my favor; I obtain the benefit of consuming all of your beauty."

"We're forced to do a great many things, and this is the least of them; therefore, I have no choice but to be content with doing so," Danielle responded, completing the head wrap. "You were saying?"

"Until I can secure your freedom, no one on this plantation must know about our union. Only your family, Minister Liam and Corrine. In the interim, I'll continue with the arrangements. I'll try to return in a couple of days at nightfall. If by chance I arrived early, or we miss one another, you'll know I was here if you see this gemstone." He showed her the aquamarine and tucked it in his shirt pocket, buttoning it securely. "It's always brought me good luck. More news and instructions will come—"

"Alphonse, it's time for us to go," Alysaundre whispered as he knocked lightly on the other side of the door.

"I'm on my way," Alphonse whispered back. He continued speaking with Danielle, "Your brother and I will be staying away from New

Orleans, as I've turned down jobs for my men and me there. It will be safer around some of the other docks in Louisiana—"

Corrine's voice could be heard almost singing behind the door next, "Daaann-iee-elle?"

"I'm coming," Danielle called.

Alphonse continued, putting on his last boot, "So if you hear about trouble in New Orleans, rest assured, it won't involve us, ma che're. Corrine knows how to get a message to me or your brother for any reason." Alphonse cracked open the door to see Corrine and Alette holding lanterns. He opened it fully and saw a peeved Alysaundre almost staring a hole through him. Alphonse cleared his throat. "Good morning."

"I'll be in the wagon," Alysaundre sneered. Corrine laughed under her breath.

Alphonse turned to Danielle once more, making a point to kiss her stomach. He later said, "I wish I could take you away from here now. You do understand that it is not yet time?" Danielle nodded. "Uh, it pains me that I can't leave you with a gift, at least, my shirt, my watch—"

"You've given me plenty...thank you." Before forgetting, she pushed cloth-wrapped bread into his hands and kissed him.

"I love you, okay?" The seriousness in his tone made Danielle pause. She nodded, and Alphonse continued. "Things will be difficult for us but I don't give up. No matter what happens, I'm still yours, and you're mine. As you know, I don't believe in the word 'impossible,' and I don't want you to either. I may not be in your presence, but you're never alone. I don't regret what we've done. You're my world now, and I thank you for allowing me to be a part of yours. I won't judge you, and I'll continue to pray for you as I did when you were sleeping. I love you, Mrs. Danielle Liana Santee." And with that, Alphonse kissed his wife one last time, stepping backward and Danielle forward, down the cabin steps, and finally in different directions as their lips parted. Alphonse hurried into the woods and

Danielle arm-in-arm with Corrine. The newly married couple looked back at each other until hidden by the vegetation.

The silence was deafening, and the tension thick during the wagon ride to drop Alysaundre off at the boarding house for colored mariners. However, Alphonse had not noticed or cared. All he could think about was Danielle. While already motivated to do right by her, he mentally double-checked his strategies for her freedom and his husbandry.

"Something wrong?" Alysaundre asked. "You're legs, they're restless."

"All is well," lied Alphonse, "Only thinking."

"Well, congratulations again...brother." Aly extended his hand and received a tight grip from Alphonse. "I can't remember seeing my sister so happy..."

"Since we are brothers now," said Alphonse, "we should be able to speak plainly. I understand that you worry for us, particularly Danielle, and if she hurts, you all feel the pain. It is my solemn promise that I will do everything in my power to make sure she remains happy. I love her too much to see her any other way. You may think that I'm taking a chance on her because she is in bondage. But she's taking a chance on me, in all my offerings and even in my flaws, and I owe her my best. It is not a burden for me to show it or to say it a million times a day if I have to, but without any agenda, I love the girl."

Satisfied with Alphonse's words, the men grew silent, later finding other things to speak about until they arrived at the boarding house. After Aly refused Alphonse's invitation to attend mass that morning, the men tipped their hats to say goodbye.

* * *

In fresh clothing and driving his finest carriage, Alphonse arrived at Mrs. Santee's home, smelling the sweet flowers several yards before approaching. Alphonse retrieved his mother and escorted her to the carriage. She did most of the talking, sharing ideas to improve the boarding houses, happenings in Lafayette, and a little gossip to top it off. "You'll see once we get to church," she said. "A giant knot right on his forehead. I guess that will teach him to stop gawking at other women." Alphonse scoffed with a smile which quickly faded as he drifted back into thought. Julia stared at her son. "Are you alright? I'm used to you returning withered from long trips, but you look exhausted and so serious."

"I'm fine, Mother," Alphonse insisted, keeping his eyes on the road as Julia continued to inspect him.

"Mmhm," she said. "You can barely look at me." Agitated at her prodding, Alphonse briefly looked at her for her gratification and back to the road. She looked at his neck, discovering a blemish. She pursed her lips and joined Alphonse in looking at the road. They saw the white peak of the church approaching, towering over the trees until the full building was in sight, framed with pristine landscape artistry. Les noirs libres in Lafayette and neighboring parishes took great pride in their church, as they were forced to combine their money to purchase the land and build the cathedral themselves. For the archdiocese refused to fund a Catholic church for Negroes. Years of tampering with the colored church ensued, as some of the local whites disapproved of the ownership of the church being fully operated by free colored men.

Outside, the church bustled with les noirs libres in big hats and sharp suits, some of whom wished to hear a word from the Lord, others desperate to socialize or arrange meetings and tea later in the week. A lake of pastel dresses rolled among the crowd with the occasional bobs of all-black hoop skirts with lace.

Hellos and handshakes gravitated toward Alphonse and Julia, who barely stepped yards from the parked wagon. A hive of women quickly whisked Julia away. With his hands in his pockets, Alphonse people-watched among familiar faces. Mr. Abrams strolled past arm-in-arm with his wife and tipped his hat at Alphonse. Alphonse returned the gesture. Several of the young men greeted Alphonse, catching up in jovial conversation after Alphonse's typical monthly work-based absence before returning to their families and mates. A tall, thin gentleman approached him with much delight and shook hands heartily. Julia saw as Alphonse leaned into him as if speaking in secret. Their faces, masked in complete stolidness as they intensely discussed and planned something. Soon, Mr. Wilks and Alphonse shook hands and sauntered away in opposite directions. Julia returned to the conversation but still questioned the interaction.

As Alphonse headed into the church, he suddenly felt burning eyes on him. Already knowing the source of the flames, he turned to see a group of three women gazing at him about 10 yards away while speaking under their breaths. In the middle was Noelle. "Ladies," he said to them. "Hello, Noelle." She simply stared. Unbothered, Alphonse opened the heavy oak doors of the church and walked inside.

Drifting whispers seeped through the walls of the parish as Alphonse took a moment to perform the sign of the cross and genuflect towards the larger statue of the white Jesus dying on the cross in the pulpit. Prayers of health, family, and finances from the few early worshipers bounced off the stained-glass windows of saints bearing the French versions of their names. On one side of the altar, a statue of a pale Virgin Mary looked down adoringly at those kneeling below, while her son extended his arms, welcoming all who prayed at his feet at the other end of the altar. Finding a seat towards the back, Alphonse sat and silently prayed for discernment, success, and direction in leading his new family and guiding them to freedom. He prayed for a covering over them, himself and his immediate relatives, that they would not be subjected to suspicion, violence, or death.

The sound of shoes shuffling into the church intensified. Alphonse cleared his throat and straightened up. He watched in the corners of his eyes as members filed in to take a seat in the pews. Alphonse stood, nodding towards some as they passed by. Summoning her son with a look, Alphonse retreated from the back to join Mrs. Santee in the second row. Her eyes still fixed on him in suspicion, Julia and the rest of the congregation remained standing as the priest led the procession of the deacon and servers to the altar to begin mass.

The church bells rang simultaneously with the bells of the colored church and white cathedral across Lafayette Parish. Though apart, the people of both sanctuaries knelt and sang, praying to one God synchronically. While one priest preached about power and promise, the other preached about pleasing God in word and deed.

Throughout the service, Alphonse was barely present, occasionally bouncing into the service, and participating in the acclamations and responses in habit. However, he was pulled in when hearing the priest mention continuing to pray for the strength of slaves and the hearts of their masters. Alphonse never thought, nor did he have the desire, to pray for Demetre. He inhaled in preparation to do so and began. He got as far as praying for Demetre's heart to be merciful when his mind wandered, thinking of all that he had put Danielle and her family through. He began to question how he could pray for this man who had tortured them, not with whips and chains, but with threats and heartache. Alphonse figured that the prayers would not stop there. How could he pray for Demetre's heart and not the heart of the entire Soileau family, the overseers, the pattyrollers, those who watched, pointed fingers, or lied? And finally, the entire system of bondage that enabled the idea of humans being treated like animals, or even worse, people whose children were not their own. A system that stood strong in the belief that certain humans were not worthy of love, marriage, family, education, and wealth. "No," Alphonse unknowingly said aloud during the sermon. Mrs. Santee and a few others in neighboring pews leered at him. Oblivious to Alphonse's outburst, the priest continued.

Mrs. Santee kept her head down and whispered through her teeth, "What *is it* with you this morning?"

Alphonse said nothing, only thinking of his beautiful new wife and wanting to rid her of enslavement.

On the way to Mrs. Santee's home, the sun seemed to follow the woman and her agitated son as it bristled through the trees above them. "My God, Alphonse," said Julia. "If there is something I should know, you had better talk now." Alphonse was silent. "And you didn't have to walk out in the middle of Father Saint-fleur's sermon."

"I just needed some air."

"You couldn't wait until a man of the cloth was finished delivering a message from God?"

"Because Heaven forbid God should strike me down for choosing oxygen over Father Saint-fleur's sermon."

Julia paused. "Does it have anything to do with that blemish on your neck?"

"You're examining me now, Mother?"

"Whether you like it or not, I know your body from top to bottom—"

"No, Mother, you *used to* know it from top to bottom, and quite frankly, at my age, I'm disturbed by the idea of you knowing anything about my body."

"Well? You might as well say it."

"'It' *what* Mother?"

"Whatever it is you've done."

The coach approached the port at the Santee home. "Who all is here?" Alphonse asked in a way that jolted Julia's nerves.

"I gave them the morning off to attend mass or visit relatives. Why?"

"So, no one is here?"

"No, not yet. You're scaring me, is it serious?"

Alphonse helped Mrs. Santee out of the carriage and onto the landing. "I'll meet you in the parlor," he said before steering the horse to the carriage house.

Mrs. Santee nervously stood by the window, grasping her hands, bracing her heart for the impact that was about to occur. Once inside, Alphonse got to the point as his mother whipped around to hear the news. "I will have to leave, Mother. And I don't mean on an extended trip for work."

"Why? Are you in any trouble? Did you offend a white man?"

"No. I'm in no trouble."

Julia sighed in relief, but quickly rebounded, "Did you get someone in trouble?"

"No. I just need to leave Louisiana and the south altogether, and the time is approaching."

"Why? What do you mean you 'need to'?"

"You and I know that the South is no place for a colored man. It's certainly unkind to Negro mariners. Work here is not settled, and every day it seems as though more laws are created against seamen. It's only a matter of time before one of my men or I drift toward the wrong imaginary lines within the waters, with legislation allowing white people to sell us into slavery. I understand that the sea isn't paved with gold for a schooner full of colored mariners in the North, but it's easier to maintain a decent living without being subjected to jail for almost every assignment, passport or not. I have had a lot of time to consider this. My mark has been made here, but now it's time for the grids of my life to succumb to a new path."

"With the exception of Thierry, your brothers have all moved north, and I figured you would follow."

"I want you to come too, Mother. I saw a house off of Lake Erie that I want you to have."

"You expect me to just leave everything I've worked so hard for and move? And why Lake Erie?"

"Give it some thought at most," he suggested. Alphonse did not tell his mother that in the last few months, he had worked to establish a business of the same nature in the north called J.T. Brothers & Co., giving homage to his mother Julia, his father Thierry Sr., and his brothers. His days absent from Louisiana were spent recruiting residents of boarding houses for colored sailors. He purposely omitted any information regarding the counsel he received from antislavery societies that extended assistance and resources. Instead, he shared, "And to add, your concern for wanting me to give promise to the idea of matrimony was considered. Which is also why a colored man with a wife and family has fewer opportunities for peace in the South."

Julia slowly sat in the walnut parlor chair and listened.

"And," Alphonse continued, "if I am going to have to protect and provide for the family I wish to have as a man, I can't continue to live someplace where I am not seen as such."

Julia looked hurt, looking up from the rug and into her son's eyes. She spoke quietly, "I don't know how you did it, but you married her, didn't you?"

Alphonse nodded. And with a slight smile, he admitted, "I did. I did. Danielle is my wife now." He began to describe the wedding.

"Well," Julia deprecated, "good thing it's not recognized legally. But unfortunately for you, you'll have a lot of confessing to do."

"I can't confess if there was no wrongdoing, guilt, or regret. And I certainly will not be doing so to a priest. Besides, if you intend for me to confess to God, then I'm certain His reaction to marrying my heartbeat personified and allowing her to bless me with a 'blemish' on my neck would dissatisfy you."

"Alphonse, I'm simply saying that your marriage to her is void to the world as if it never happened. You didn't marry in a church, or before your own family, or...me. It's not recorded in the bible—it's not lawful—"

"This should not be a debate, but we have the law of the Father and the law of white men, and somewhere along the line, people have adopted the two as one and the same. Our marriage, Mother, is legal in the only eyes that matter, the Lord's. Your marriage to Father was never considered legal simply because you received permission from your owner, nor was it after you became free. If I'm not considered a whole man, according to the law, what makes you think that the same people who created the law care about or respect who we love and who we marry? A legal marriage, to them, makes us more human than they intended. So, I would rather look to the sanctification of the Lord, because at least He can see me in return." Mrs. Santee remained silent in her anger. Alphonse continued. "I'm not telling you this news to hurt you or to receive your blessing. And I don't expect you to be happy for me. But I feel that you should know. And all I ask is that you don't tell anyone until the time is right."

"And when will that be?"

"You will be the first to know."

Mrs. Santee stood to look out at the fading green of the banana leaves in her garden. "This isn't what I wanted for you, my dear."

"You have told me what you wanted. Right before you walked away from me—"

"To consume from the same plate of another man, to love in secret, to duck and hide from the man who tells your wife when to eat, sleep and shit and in which order—"

"Ahh! Damn-it, Mother! I knew it was a mistake to tell you!"

"And it sure as hell is a mistake for you to be yelling at me in my own home," Julia seethed, stomping towards her son.

Alphonse took a breath and lowered his voice, "I'll see you in a few weeks when I come to say goodbye." Alphonse grabbed his hat and jacket off the coat rack by the door and touched the knob.

Mrs. Santee called out from the parlor, "Are you happy?"

"I beg your pardon?" He asked, thinking he had heard her incorrectly.

"Besides being tormented, are you happy?"

"I'd be tormented if I didn't take a chance and marry her. I am incredibly happy to call her my wife. But I won't stay and listen to you stab me with your words about her."

"My lips will not disclose anything you've shared with me; not about your marriage or your...wife—sounds so strange to say," Mrs. Santee smiled lightly. "But, if you plan to move North, which I'm not ready for you to do, I doubt if you would be content with the distance."

"I'll see you soon, Mother," Alphonse said, refraining from sharing further details.

"Alphonse, whatever you're planning, it affects this family, remember that. Please don't do what I think you're going to do."

Alphonse quickly kissed his mother on the cheek. "I'll see you soon," and he sped out the door, almost bumping into Miranda as she approached the door.

"Alphonse!!" Julia cried out after her son as the church bells rang in the distance.

Sixteen

White smoke transcended into the sky from the stove, nearly touching the birds frightened away by the chimes of the Cathedral bells. The smell, almost boasting to those on the field that Sunday dinner would soon be ready for the newly arrived occupants in the mansion. The near silence in the house frustrated Etiennette, whose meanness had heightened lately, especially when Danielle was near. Her devious antics of mentioning false stories to Demetre about Danielle ranged from theft to entertaining slave men, and escalated to pokes with knitting needles or attempting to trip her onto her stomach. Danielle had learned to be intentional in avoiding Etiennette and even taught Lettie to do the same.

Today, however, no threatening looks or nasty words could dampen Danielle's spirits. She was noticeably glowing, nearly prancing when setting the dining room table meant for 16, which she thought was silly since only two would be dining. Etiennette floated past the double doors, catching a smile on Danielle's face.

After notifying the other servants of her next move, Danielle walked through the sitting room, humming a beautiful melody, unaware of Demetre sitting in one of the tall velvet chairs with his back to her. As she hummed her way onto the garden terrace, he sat up slowly, smiling as he listened to the song that he had not heard her sing in over a year. Inspired by the soprano voice and melodic intervals, he wondered if he remembered how to harmonize the chords on the piano. Danielle made her way into the garden to pick flowers for the dining room table. Far enough away from the house, she released the lyrics from her lips, carefully monitoring her volume.

As she detached each angel's trumpet from its stem, she felt the passion arise in her voice, and the baby nestle within her womb. She cradled her belly, and sang downward to the child, supporting the flowers underneath. The baby moved once more as if responding to its mother's touch. Her voice faded to a whisper. And not knowing why, Danielle cried a single tear. Soon another joined, followed by another. She soon learned that surrendering to her baby meant a sudden and ill-prepared combination of joy and fear, responsibility and determination, angst and love.

Piano keys softly played in the parlor, picking up volume within certain areas of the song. Danielle knew that Demetre had heard her attempt to sing in secret, and she blushed in embarrassment. Quickly wiping her eyes, she continued picking flowers until she heard an abrupt stop. Demetre soon joined her in the garden, but Danielle pretended not to notice. "I wish you wouldn't stop," Demetre said, appearing behind her faster than she expected.

"I'm sorry, I didn't mean for anyone to hear me," she simpered. "I thought you and Madame might want fresh flowers while you're enjoying supper."

Demetre moved closer, as the girl disguised her discomfort with a pleasant smile. He looked her over, surveying her tignon, figure, and clothing. "I remember that song," he finally said. "You sang it as you nursed me when I was ailing."

"I didn't realize you were awake most of the time," she said, inching back.

Demetre nodded once. "I've never spoken of the times I was on death's door and the songs that strengthened my soul."

"Thank you, Monsieur. It is quite a blessing that Madame Etiennette regained her strength." Demetre halted in speech. Danielle added, "I thank God that your life was spared."

Demetre nodded again in an unusually quiet manner. He smiled and turned to walk away, and without thinking it through, Danielle blurted, "Monsieur?" she could not back out of her question now, as he was now looking her in the face. "It is an honor to have served you and the Soileau family throughout the years. My closeness to Mademoiselle Simone is a bond that I cherish. My intended purpose, since I was small, was to be her playmate. However, she has left the plantation, establishing a life for herself in New Orleans, leaving her childhood behind. And I am left, clearly not a child, but still a faithful servant who is grateful to have learned so much from all of you. You mentioned the time when you were ailing and close to death, truly giving us all a fright. I have always felt it a blessing to be an instrument of your recovery. And it is with that that I humbly stand before you and ask for my freedom."

Demetre was taken aback. Little did he know that his conversation of music and life-changing memories would lead to Danielle's request for freedom. "Has someone been putting these ideas into your ears?" He asked her.

"No Monsieur," Danielle said. "Just you." Demetre raised an eyebrow. She continued, "Just now. I would not be far from you at all, for I don't know that I could bear it."

"Then why leave?" He asked. "Have you not been given the finest of any one of the servants here?"

"Oui Monsieur."

"Have I not given you my name?"

His comment unraveled another seam of his feelings toward her. As always, Danielle masked her aggravation—that he would believe that her happiness would only be fulfilled by material items and a last name. "Oui, Monsieur," she said, "and I thank you. I was hoping the baby would be born free, and I could raise the child as a noir libre while you visited whenever you wished." She knew that the plan to run away was set, but naively thought that doing things "the right way" and asking permission might somehow protect Alphonse if Demetre were to ever find out about them. Also, she had known of other slaves who ran away unsuccessfully. She was terrified by the idea of being pregnant and possibly chased by barking dogs conditioned to smell fear and hate anyone who looked like her and with an eagerness for sovereignty. She did not want to envision the punishment that she or her family could receive. If she were emancipated, she had no intentions of continuing anything with Demetre but vocalized her false devotion to him to display her veneration toward her master. She almost shared concerns for her mother and sister remaining slaves on the plantation but feared that it would possibly entice him to hold their fate over her, locking her or them, into a sinister bind or elevating surveillance.

"Your proposal to me," Demetre summarized, "is that I free you on the basis that your role of Simone's companion has expired, because you saved me from death, and lastly because you want the child to be born into freedom." Danielle nodded, her heart nearly leaping out of its cavity. Demetre thought about Danielle's reasons for wanting to be free, as well as his personal benefits or financial gains of freeing her from bondage or keeping her enslaved. There were current murmurs from others about Demetre and his slave girl which he had always ignored. However, he considered whether setting her free would make his feelings for her apparent. It would certainly ease the tension between him and Etiennette.

Setting aside reasons, he caressed her cheek with the back of his fingers, and down to her neck, "Do you know what fascinates me about melodies and songs? Once they're heard and others adore it, they want it also. But the composer knows that he is the only one who will take exceptional care of each note, as it was intended. His pride allows him to share his creative brilliance with others, but the music is not theirs to keep. It's his." Demetre captivated Danielle into an unsettling sweat, unknowing the direction her master wavered. "Give me time to think," he responded before walking away. Surprised to hear those words, Danielle swallowed hard and wrung her hands before looking up and seeing Etiennette watching from the second-story window.

There was great disquiet during dinner, as two pairs of eyes took turns flashing upon Danielle in between silver forks clanking upon the floral plates and the sipping of wine from crystal goblets. Even Corrine looked around, wondering the origins of the discomfort in the room.

By nightfall, Danielle was happy to be in her home, preparing seasonings for the week's meals. She hummed, thinking of her Alphonse as beatific emotion rushed over her. Her smile broadened when she heard a footstep at her bottom stairs. The second and third were with certitude, and Danielle's heart dropped once the door opened. "Monsieur Demetre," she said, forcing a smile, hoping it passed as genuine. "How are you?"

Demetre only smirked as he removed his jacket and handed it to her to hang on a nearby nail on the wall. "Since we last spoke," he finally said, still smirking, "I have been thinking about you, Danielle." He stepped deeper into the cabin; the young woman slid out of his path. He continued, "You questioned your purpose here since your days of being a companion have set. And indeed, you did save my life, helping me to envision the days ahead when I thought I would never do so." He stepped closer to her, and she continued to step back. Demetre withheld that local law allowed slaveholders to set free a slave before age 30 if the life of a master was saved by the slave. "You're too young for me to set loose into the world."

"Monsieur, the date of my birth passed five days ago; however, you have the power to release me whenever you see fit. And I am knowledgeable enough to survive the world on my own," pleaded Danielle.

Demetre said, "And it is because *I* say who goes and who remains that I have made the decision that you will stay."

Danielle opened her mouth to speak, to breathe, anything that would allow air to enter her lungs. "But Monsieur, could I buy my freedom? If I were to be rented or saved any small wages given to me by the renter, could I buy my freedom?"

"My dear, you're forgetting that you would be purchasing the freedom of two."

"How much are we worth?"

"$1,000 for you, $200 for the child, and $100 more each year the baby grows older."

Danielle swallowed hard, despising the demon she never knew lived within him. Never mind that the child was his own. Never mind that there was a price on the babe. "What if the babe were free?" she asked, hanging her head, afraid of his words exposing a truth about him that she had ignored. The girl did not look up to see Demetre ponder the idea as if amused by what had become a game for him.

"That," he said, "might be a consideration." Danielle was surprised by his words once again, but quickly blew out the light that lit within her. "But," he said. Danielle looked up in curiosity. "Suppose I free your mother or Alette, only *you* choose who stays and who goes."

"But Monsieur," Danielle panicked, "They need each other. Couldn't they both be free?"

"Dear," he began, smiling and nearing the girl whose back was now pressed against the cabin wall, "Just as I'm not usually in the habit of discussing legislation with my slaves or women, it is also not customary for me to negotiate with anyone whose name is in my book of assets. While I was only jesting with you, I am quite serious about you remaining here with me. I am disappointed that we are having this discussion, but it's time that you realize where my boundaries lie. Anything I do for you is out of my very goodness, and not because you are owed something of me. Is that understood?"

An abundance of saliva formed in Danielle's mouth. Never before had she felt the urge to spit in Demetre's face until that moment. But instead, she simply nodded. "As for your purpose," Demetre added, "We both know what that is, don't we, Danielle?" Demetre leaned into her, tugging one side of her neck and pressing his lips onto it.

"No, Monsieur. We cannot."

"Now you're refusing me? You are acting strangely, and I don't like it."

"I mean no disrespect, but my body changes weekly, and I'm sure at this stage, it might cause you great discomfort." She tried to free herself of his intentions and his grasp.

"We've been together many times since learning of your pregnancy."

"Begging your pardon, Monsieur, I've never been *this* pregnant before, and—and you will receive no pleasure from our actions," Danielle lied.

"What is with you?" Demetre raised his voice in frustration. "I have never questioned your devotion, and I've been confident in your love for me and your life on this plantation until today."

"No, Monsieur, there is no need to question my loyalty. I was just wondering if we could wait. Please."

"Until after the birth? No, I need to have you before you spoil." He grabbed her by the wrist, swinging her toward the bed. He yanked at her undergarments as she pleaded. Neither her tears nor her sobs could stop him from penetrating her forcefully.

"Please, Monsieur. No... Please."

In the day following, Demetre did not speak to Danielle but extended leftover scraps to eat and extra linen. Danielle displayed gratitude but screamed internally over the joy that was stolen from her, and the violation of her body, which made her replay every grunt, spread, rip, and eventually, every drop of tears. Danielle did her work around the big house and obeyed orders as normal, but it was evident that she was a shell of a woman, walking around in a fog, noticeable to Alette, who asked Corrine to come outside and "help us pick vegetables?"

"I don't understand it, girl," Corrine whispered after sending Alette off to do another chore. "One moment, no one can reel you down from the clouds, and the next, you're in a well of gloom. What has happened in between?"

"Oh, Corrine," the girl confided. "He's not the man I thought he was."

"What has Alphonse done?"

"No. I mean Monsieur Demetre." Danielle proceeded to tell him about how he mocked her for asking for her freedom and that of her family, then forced himself upon her.

"He did that to you? *You*?"

"Why do you ask that way?"

"Well," Corrine configured a falsity. "Because you're—you're with child and with *his* baby. And I've always seen him delicate towards you." Danielle knew when Corrine was lying to protect her, and this was one of those times. "Is that why he hasn't said a word to you today?" Corrine saw the tears welling in Danielle's eyes. She pulled her friend close, allowing her to weep in her arms. The rushing wind swept through the trees shhhing and partnering with Corrine, who nurtured the young woman and was sensitive to the ordeal and battered idea of her self-worth. "You're going to get past this," Corrine said. "And you'll heal each day. Mr. Demetre is no different than these other masters around here, and there's nothing we can do about that. Be upset if you need to, but never let *them* see it," she said, pointing to the house. "The heart of a servant woman holds so many secrets, as you already know. Let this be one of them, especially when you're speaking to the Negro men who love you."

"But Alphonse will know," Danielle worried.

"Not unless you tell him or you stop allowing him to touch you. You didn't deserve what happened, but you deserve luck and all the wonderful things that come your way. Look towards your new husband. You have something beautiful that many would spend three lifetimes trying to grab hold of, and I'm glad I'm a witness to it. With so many ugly things in this world, it's nice to see something as pure as the love between a man and his woman. Now, you still have to work in this here house and around that man. Try your best to put on a different face. I'm here if you ever start feeling bad again." Corrine gave the young woman a squeeze and waited for her to loosen her grasp and dry her eyes.

Accepting Corrine's advice, Danielle proceeded with her work, hiding her emotions when replenishing Demetre's plate of cheese and glass of wine, "Is there anything else I can do for you, Monsieur?" she asked.

"No," Demetre said, slowly sitting up straight. "You've done enough." With pleasantry on her face, Danielle nodded and turned to walk away. Demetre inspected his glass with his eyes before dismissing her for the evening. Urged by Corrine to go home and rest, Danielle made Alette promise to stick close to Corrine and obey her.

The rhythms of cane knives severing the sugar stalks were off-beat as Danielle walked through the plantation on her way home. Now and again, the tempo would sync with the addition of the sound of the shears swiping away at the flags in between each blow. She watched as men and women worked as a trio, all knowing their parts within the orchestrated system of cane cutting in preparation for the sugar mill. Little children, as young as three, played a role in assisting each hand. Tiny bare feet ran in syncopation to gather and remove excess debris, careful to stay out of reach of swinging blades and older children who helped lay the stalks neatly in the carts. On days when no one was looking, at least for a little while, these same children would play and hide from each other within the forbidden grounds of the cane fields. For if any stalks were destroyed without permission, trouble from their parents, guardians, on-looking slave, or overseer would ensue.

East of the row, an overseer on horseback cracked his whip when a slave cut too far past the ripened shoot, causing the juice to potentially sour. The others flinched at the sound but continued to work without so much as lifting their heads in curiosity.

There were fewer slaves in the field than Danielle remembered. Groups of teenage boys, who gained pounds of muscle prematurely from the everyday fieldwork, were tasked with carting away the chopped cane to the sugar house and mill for grinding. A couple of them noticed Danielle, whom they admired but did not see regularly. Their instantaneous looks of disappointment were fleeting as a head nod or wink caused Danielle to acknowledge them in return with a humble wave.

She saw her Maman out there tending to the bleeding and callused hands of others. It was not long ago that Aly and Alette were in the very field with her. Every time Danielle got the nerve to ask Genevieve about her feelings of being without her family in clear view, Danielle paused, not wanting to contribute to sad thoughts and memories. However, Maman had a way of presenting a surprising response to difficult questions.

The cry of an infant interjected Danielle's thoughts. A high-cheeked slave woman, the color of Alphonse's favorite chocolate candy, addressed an overseer. She was a tall woman, but appeared small when looking up at the man on horseback carrying a whip in one hand and a pistol at his hip. She pointed in the direction of an older woman sitting on the porch of a cabin holding a hungry pink baby with dark wavy hair. The overseer made a motion for her to "git," giving the mother permission to sit on the porch alongside the older woman, lift her blouse, expose a breast, and offer nourishment to her child. Danielle tried to move along but found herself bound in that spot. Her feet, feeling like lead, were unable to move from the soil. The baby drank heartily as the woman massaged her breast for repetitive milk flow. All that was currently happening or had occurred on the field did not matter to the mother, for she appeared relaxed when bonding, looking down at the baby as his jaws moved up and down.

The mother's eyes wandered before catching Danielle's. The woman stared at the pregnant lady with resentment as if she had taken something from her, of which Danielle was not immediately aware.

Danielle had seen her before, but did not know her or her name. The woman broke first, rolling her eyes away from Danielle and onto her baby. Every intuition that Danielle had had came barreling through her mind. She began to despise Demetre even more, not only for assaulting her but for every dismissed question Danielle had previously asked. She now knew for certain that other women on the plantation were involved, but the amount left her unsure. She questioned the number of seeds he had planted and why her unborn child was chosen to be acknowledged. She surveyed the fields, narrowing in on the lighter-skinned children who toggled in sight between Creole, mulatto, and white. With the many mixtures of enslaved people among the plantation, it was difficult for her to truly tell which ones belonged to Demetre, but she had her suspicions. Were the others acknowledged without her knowing? What was his plan for his offspring? And did Etiennette know?

Danielle's feet became lighter as she could feel herself move away faster from the fields and into her cabin. She had no appetite for the vegetables and beans she had gone home to cook earlier that day. She simply bolted her door, rolled sideways into her bed, and fell asleep, exhausted from the emotions of the day.

The light tapping on the door and a familiar voice awakened Danielle, who was alarmed to learn that she had slept into the night. The tapping recurred. "Songbird? Zozo shantè?" she heard him say. Relieved, Danielle rocked twice out of bed and opened the door, pulling Alphonse inside as quickly as she could. She started to step away when he came near her, but she remembered Corrine's advice. He held her face with both hands and gently kissed her lips.

"I didn't know I could miss someone so much," she said, embracing him tightly. "Are you hungry? Can I warm up a meal for you?"

"And I, you," said Alphonse, reading the quiver in her voice. "Is something wrong? Here," Alphonse lit his lantern, and Danielle lit a fire and candles. "You don't sound like yourself," he said.

"I'm just anxious to leave this place," she said, holding his gaze. "I'm ready for us to go now. You told of potential dangers, and I wasn't sure about the journey, especially in my condition, but I don't care. And Maman is strong, and Lettie is spunky. I'm more confident than I've ever been about the idea—"

"What's happened, Danielle? How did you get these bruises on your arm? Who's done this?"

Danielle wanted to tell him about the rape, *but what if Corrine was right?* She thought. Although bothersome, the idea that Demetre and Danielle had previously slept together was nothing new to Alphonse, but if he knew that Demetre forced himself on her as his *wife* and did so violently and recently, perhaps Alphonse would not stand idly by and allow it to happen again. Just as she was afraid of his actions, she was afraid of the look he would give her, as someone or something broken or tainted. Instead, she decided to tell him another truth. One she had only shared with Corrine, "Etiennette," she started. "Etiennette has been rampageous towards me. Most of it I can handle, but she has threatened murder upon the baby and me if the child is...of Demetre's blood."

Alphonse listened as Danielle revealed every disturbing detail and had to sit for a good bit of it. When Danielle concluded, Alphonse took a moment to process all that he had heard and felt. With prayer hands to his mouth, he uttered, "A week and 3 days, Danielle. That is when we will flee. Just as everything is planned precisely, every detail is counted to the second for this to work. Many trusted individuals will be assisting to bring you and your family to freedom. Do you think you can hold on?"

Overwhelmed by the approaching escape time frame and the thought of several people—strangers—rallying to help free her family and herself, she said, almost in disbelief, "I'll try." Danielle folded into her husband's arms.

Danielle apologized multiple times for not telling him earlier. And just as she began to push him away with her words, stating that she would understand if marriage to her was all too much for him, Alphonse interrupted and assured her that he would stand firmly by her side and that he meant every word that was spoken when they married. "How many times must I prove to you that I love you? You're stuck with me, Songbird," he smiled.

Discussions of logistics and occasional kissing sessions followed by mutual foot rubs, conversations of travel, and verbal acquaintance followed the two well into the early morning. For Alphonse, it was never easy parting with Danielle. He greatly enjoyed her company, and she, his. Retrospections of what-ifs consistently entered his head, which he forced himself to block for his own sanity. However, this time, leaving her, if only for a few days, gave him reason to worry more than ever. "Alphonse," said Danielle, stopping him from touching the door, "I'll never truly know what you feel every day when you face the world, but I know it's not easy, even though you're free. But I look at you in wonderment when thinking about perseverance and the dignity you uphold. When I am free, I promise I will do everything in my power to uplift you so that you will never have to come home doubting yourself, your actions, or your purpose. Thank you for working hard and for being my burst of joy that flutters in my soul. You are the love I didn't know I could have." Before leaving, Alphonse passionately kissed his wife and sweetly kissed her stomach before fleeing into the woods hours before the sun arose.

Seventeen

Danielle managed to get more rest soon after her husband left to supervise a crew set to work off of the river. When she awoke, she felt a small contraction. "No, no, no, no," Danielle whispered. "It's too soon." Cradling her belly, she took a couple of quick breaths to avoid panic. She waited and the contraction ceased. As she washed and dressed, there were no additional pains. Relieved, she grabbed an ash cake and ventured to Genevieve's house to walk with Alette to the Soileau Mansion.

"When is Alphonse returning?" Lettie asked.

"Soon, why?" Danielle wanted to know.

"Because he's your husband now and you two should be together."

"I wish it were that simple."

"I know...When am I allowed to tell others about him?"

"Who are you wanting to tell?"

"No one really, I just don't like keeping my new brother a secret. People aren't meant to be kept a secret. Especially good people like him. Maman said that she prayed for him for you. She said she's been praying now for a husband for me too when I'm older...You're happiest when he's near. I'm glad you chose to be nice to him."

"Me too, Lettie."

"...I don't think I want a husband, not if I'd have to keep him a secret. There is not much sense in Maman praying for a husband for me to fall in love with just so that I cannot walk arm-in-arm with him outside. I'd rather not fall in love to begin with. I wonder if anyone has ever asked God to allow them not to love."

Danielle looked down at her belly for a short while.

"Hmm," Lettie reckoned. "But if God *is* Love, and He has the power to do anything, could He, would He, prevent a person from sharing a piece of Him with someone? Well, if He can, that would be my prayer."

"Don't say things like that. Suppose you'd want to love again."

"Then I'll pray to love again."

"But you would still be facing the very thing that you were trying to avoid—keeping someone a secret."

"I would hope that by the time I pray to love again, things will be different."

"One could only hope. Fortunately, and unfortunately for us, that is not how the heart works."

Using the servant's entrance at the rear of the house, Alette and Danielle hung their shawls and began work with some of the others. Later, Danielle visited the hen house to gather eggs when she felt another contraction about the same strength as the last and held onto the fence. The hens scratched and clucked as Danielle breathed deeply. Careful not to get upset, she continued gathering the warm eggs until the pulling stopped. She thought of the women she knew who had contractions at different stages of pregnancy or a month prior to having a baby, so she went along the day working, keeping hope that she was like the other women. She shared with Corrine the feelings she had had all morning. Alarmed, Corrine quickly changed her facial expression to protect Danielle from anxiety. "I am sure it is nothing to worry about just yet. But I'll stay close by when I can," Corrine whispered, as they sat on the back verandah steps mending socks and other small stacks of clothing. "I will get a message to the hay man to alert the Fortune's the next time Philippe or I go into town. I know they will take good care of the baby."

Corrine had been the only one to know of Etiennette's plan to do harm. In the days after Danielle revealed the secret, Corrine used to her advantage, the monthly access into town to pick up orders of food and supplies for the household. There, she learned of the Fortune's, a childless free couple in the parish who was highly respected by many of les noirs libres within the community. Through the hay man, who arranged the secret communication between Corrine and the couple, the Fortunes agreed to house the baby until it was safe for Danielle to be with her child. But seeing Danielle in her current condition, Corrine worried if their plan would work at all but mentioned nothing of her fears to Danielle.

Danielle looked out into the garden, watching the squirrels chase one another. "I should say it more often, Corrine, but thank you," Danielle said.

"For what?" Corrine asked.

"For being my friend. For telling me when I've done wrong. For holding Alette and me under your wing when you don't have to."

"Girl, you don't have to thank me for doing those things. I've always told you you're like my little Tilly and Elle. Who knows how much closer us sisters would have become had I not been sold?" Corrine grew quiet as she sewed the hole in Demetre's sock. She swallowed hard, breaking her thoughts. "Thank *you*," she said to Danielle, "for letting me be your sister."

Danielle reached for Corrine's hand and squeezed it with a smile.

By mid-morning, Etiennette and friends, Margaret and Lucille, enjoyed the latest gossip over tea and cake, putting aside the book they were supposed to have read and discussed. Danielle had been banned from serving during any of the mistress' functions months before, so as not to become a topic of conversation. Attempting to remain out of sight, Danielle had taken all of the servant entries. But as the ladies continued to speak passionately about the legal troubles of Mr. Gainer, they moved from the study to the garden without notice, causing Danielle to rush to hand parasols to Jen who followed them outside and remained several feet away.

As Danielle retreated to the courtyard stairs to head indoors, she felt another contraction, this time stronger than all the others before. She quickly clutched the banister with one hand as she bent over and cradled her belly with the other, making a faint sound. Etiennette looked over her shoulder and saw Danielle in this position of struggle and pain. When the contraction stopped, she witnessed Danielle stand tall. Etiennette quickly returned her focus to the conversation in progress before Danielle turned to look at Etiennette, never realizing that the mistress was now aware that Danielle was in labor.

On the pregnant woman's behalf, Corrine asked for Danielle's dismissal after complaints of feeling faint and sometimes dizzy from lack of food. "Sir," said Corrine, "all she needs is a little broth and a lot of rest and she should be as good as new," she reassured, minimizing the circumstances.

Demetre showed concern, as she has never fallen ill or had to be released in advance. "Take me to her," he said.

Leading him out of the cigar room and to the second-floor sitting room, Corrine alerted Danielle before their arrival to avoid being caught casting attention toward her belly. "Really, she has not been eating and just needs food and rest. I have broth prepared that I can give her once she is in bed," Demetre and Corrine walked in to find Danielle sitting in a conventional chair with her head in her hand.

Demetre hurried to her. He stood over her and placed his hand on her shoulder, "Are you ill?" he asked.

"I'm a little dizzy at times," she responded without looking at him. "But I have herbs at home that will help, and Corrine has some fine broth that is good for the body."

"Are you certain it's not the baby?"

"I haven't been eating much, Monsieur, and that is what is ailing me."

Demetre's long pauses always worried Danielle, as she always questioned what he was thinking or what he knew but chose not to disclose. Finally, he said, "Very well then. Let Corrine walk you to your cabin and get rest. Corrine, the ladies will also be joining Etiennette and me for dinner. When you return, you will assist with the cooking and serving along with Rosezelle and Jen."

"Yes, sir," said Corrine.

"Thank you, Monsieur," said Danielle.

The women crossed the plantation and into Danielle's home where Corrine ordered her to remain in bed. She returned with broth and without the knowledge of anyone in the neighboring cabins, secretly summoned the plantation midwife who examined her, paying close attention to the timing of the contractions and believed Danielle was in false labor. Corrine promised to retrieve the seasoned midwife if anything were to change. "Would you like me to leave a signal for your Maman?" asked Corrine.

"No," Danielle responded while in bed. "There's no need worrying her just yet. Although, I felt certain that my labor had begun."

"You rest well anyway, and I will see about you once I am dismissed. Alette will be escorted home by myself or Rosezelle if I am held up. Are you certain I cannot alarm Ms. Genevieve?"

"No, she will be awake all evening serving me. She needs her rest as well."

"Very well. I'll return when I'm able. And close your windows tightly. Smells like rain." Despite Danielle's wishes, Corrine, before returning to the Soileau mansion, dropped one fist-sized rock in a pail outside of Genevieve's door. Genevieve knew that one rock meant Danielle was in labor and two rocks meant the baby had been born.

Corrine rushed back to the mansion where the preparation for supper had begun. When no one was in sight, she told Alette of Danielle's dizzy spells and that she was home resting. "Your sister is fine. Rosezelle or I will carry you home this evening," she told Alette.

During supper, Etiennette and her friends spoke with as much energy as they had hours before, only hushing to take a bite, chew, or drink. Demetre flashed open his pocket watch, throughout the meal. As Rosezelle and Corrine served slices of cake, Etiennette ordered Rosezelle to pour her husband a glass of wine from the cellarette.

"I'll have some too," said Margaret, holding her glass.

"Sorry, my dear friend," said Etiennette. "This is Demetre's favorite. Margaret, we can continue to enjoy the bottle on the table here." Rosezelle poured Demetre's glass of sherry and later, Margaret's wine from the crystal wine bottle on the table.

By the third large glass of spirits, Demetre had joined in on the dining room conversation and laughter. Etiennette kept a watchful eye on the kitchen door, never having seen Danielle enter or exit.

Before nightfall, Lucille and Margaret loaded their carriages, thanking Etiennette for a lovely day and making plans to meet and discuss the next book on their reading list. No sooner than the ladies trotted off, Etiennette rushed to Demetre who was stretched on the sitting room sofa. She tried to help him sit up, "Uh," he groaned. "That's not my regular sherry. What was in it?"

"Yes it was, dear," said Etiennette who mentioned nothing of the opiates she slipped into his bottle before dinner. "You just drank yourself into oblivion. Now, up you go." Realizing that she could not lift him alone, Etiennette called Corrine and Thadieus for assistance. They hoisted him up, walking him up the stairs where he was undressed and placed in bed.

"Corrine," said Etiennette, "I need you to finish some of the ironing."

"*Tonight*, Madòm? Begging your pardon, but ironing is reserved for Sundays."

"Who do you think you are? I didn't ask you the day of ironing. I'm ordering you to do as you're told. Have Rosezelle, Jen and Alette help you until it's done."

"Yes, Ma'am," Corrine said. She scurried away, hoping Etiennette had not seen her glance at the grandfather clock in the room on her way out.

While rushing to the laundry room, she found the women and Alette and told them of Etiennette's sudden orders to have the ironing completed that day. "She's wanting us to stay *longer*?" asked Rosezelle. "Why?"

"It has everything to do with her punishing us for Danielle leaving early," Jen said, rolling her eyes.

"She didn't leave early," corrected Corrine, "she was dismissed due to illness."

"And why would that matter to Madòm?" Rosezelle asked, "She doesn't even care for Danielle, and would prefer not to be around her."

"Stop talking bad about my sister," said Alette. "None of this is her fault."

"She's right," said Corrine. "We will finish sooner if we work now and talk later. Besides, the winds are beginning to howl." All agreed and worked well into the night to press the sheets, clothing, curtains, and tablecloths.

Not long after Corrine had left, Danielle wished that she had told her to alert Genevieve and carry back the midwife, for her water broke and she suffered in pain for hours. She tried yelling out for them with no response. She stumbled out of bed and onto the cabin steps, only getting as far as a few yards on her hands and knees. The contractions were excruciating, and she knew she would not make it safely to her mother's cabin for help. Deciding to deliver the baby on her own, she wobbled to her feet and struggled back into her home. To avoid infections, she removed her gown which was covered in clay and bodily fluids, only wrapping herself in a sheet. She made a soft pallet onto the floor beside her bed for her to squat over in preparation for delivery, occasionally yelling out for Maman, Corrine, or the midwife. She soon discovered a rhythm of breathing that helped her manage her muscles and anxiety a little better, giving her the ability to focus on the weight that was now slowly easing towards the birth canal. She could hear the winds blowing in an inconsistent pattern as if it ran out of breath and silenced in a moment of thought, just to begin again in a decoration of leaves and debris while forcing metal pails, such as Genevieve's to tumble multiple times, tree branches to knock into cabins and shutters slamming back and forth.

The time had come for Danielle to take a deep breath and push. On her aching knees, each gradual push was no easier than the last. She twisted the nearby blankets, screaming into her cotton-stuffed pillows that were soaked with her tears. She pushed for what felt like an hour, stopping and starting in exhaustion, giving up briefly and encouraging herself to continue. And so, she did. Feeling the head first, then the weight of the shoulders, followed by the chest and the full body and the gushing of the afterbirth, Danielle had prematurely delivered a baby girl.

Once cleaned and wrapped in warm blankets, Danielle examined her new baby. Ten small fingers and toes, hair—a sandy brown and too early to tell if it would ever curl, eyes—green, skin—white as a dove, with a birthmark on the right side of her torso matching Demetre's.

The child's calm demeanor did not last long, as she cried for food. Danielle gently removed her right breast and nursed the baby. She thanked God that the child took to the nipple quickly and was content. During feeding, Danielle strategized how to get the child into safe hands during the storm that now involved rain. With the baby's premature arrival, the new mother did not know where to find the Fortunes or Corrine. In the meantime, she needed to keep the child safe while locating Maman, a midwife, or any of the elderly female servants who she knew could nurture the newborn.

Under the floor of Danielle's cabin, were two square doors on opposite ends. One was an exit leading to the bottom of the cabin. Built by her father, he was never comfortable with any place that offered one way in and one way out. The other was a compartment to place keepsakes that could be detrimental to her life or well-being if one were to discover something found there, such as a book or money. Enduring the pain that Danielle did not have time to focus on at that moment, she lifted the door and lined the deep wooden casing with blankets, temporarily hiding the sleeping baby inside. She closed the door which blended with the floorboards, allowing air to circulate in and out of it.

When the women and Alette had completed the ironing and any additional chores that they felt Etiennette may require them to do before they could leave, they were finally dismissed into weather conditions that failed to subside as they retreated for home. Corrine escorted Alette home and ordered her to go to bed. "I will see about Danielle," she told her. As she climbed the steps to Danielle's cabin, the door swung open, causing Corrine and Danielle to jump at the sight of each other. Their astonishment turned into relief, and they embraced. She saw that Danielle was dressed in clothing for traveling.

As she walked into the cabin where a warm fire burned, Corrine asked, "Where were you going?"

"To find you or Maman or anyone who could take us for the night," Danielle said.

"*Us?*" It was then that Corrine saw the blood-stained floorboards beside Danielle's bed. Corrine's eyes widened. "Oh, my Lord, wind and stars, you delivered the baby. Alone. I'm so sorry. I signaled Ms. Genevieve, against your suggestion. She must not have seen the pail. And I tried to come back for you. You will stay with me. Where is the child? We must move in haste."

Danielle struggled towards the hiding compartment in the floor. "Do you think Etiennette knows or will try to come tonight?"

"She knows *something*. But I'm not certain if she would come tonight in weather such as this. Monsieur is too ill to even stand on his own. I believe something toxic was slipped into his drink. But we will have to continue hiding the baby until we can get the child to the Fortune's." Danielle lifted the door and reached for the infant bundled in blankets. Corrine came closer, ready to meet the child.

Just then, the door creaked open. "Danielle!" Alette screeched in horror, standing in the doorway, looking at the blood-stained wooden planks.

"Shhh," Corrine said, then whispered sharply. "I told you to go to bed! Lettie, you can't be here. Come on, we have to leave."

"I was so worried about Dani," said Alette. "And why do we have to leave? And what's happened?" She then saw the baby in Danielle's arms. Her jaw dropped.

"Come," said Danielle.

Corrine helped Danielle as she hobbled down two of the five steps when someone on horseback approached. For an instant, Danielle hoped it was Alphonse, ready to take them away. However, it was Etiennette wearing a large dark hat and men's clothing.

"Corrine," said Etiennette. "Be a good girl and go home. Danielle and Alette, inside." Danielle and Alette backed their way inside before closing the door and locking it. Danielle ran and lifted the exit door, motioning for Alette to drop through. Once doing so, she handed the infant to Alette and whispered for her to run to Corrine's cabin without letting Etiennette see or hear her.

"Mam," said Corrine, her voice shaking. "I beg you, please let me stand with them—"

Etiennette pulled out a pistol and aimed it at Corrine, "I recall a girl questioning my authority earlier this evening. Do you remember, Corrine? Now, I said go!"

Corrine began to cry, "Please Mam, don't do this, you're a Christian woman. People respect you—"

Etiennette shot at Corrine, who felt the rush of the bullet whiz past her ear. Corrine screamed. "Please, Mam!" she ran, fearfully screaming for anyone to help.

The angry mistress dismounted the horse and tried to enter the cabin, only to hear the baby whimper close by. She ran towards the sound several yards away where she caught Alette, grabbing her by the hair, and bringing the little girl and baby back to the cabin where she banged on the door for Danielle to let them in. "Open the door, Danielle," she said in a melodious-like manner. "I have Alette and your bastard!"

Danielle was about to drop through the floorboard when she heard this. Devastated, she hoisted herself up and prepared to face Etiennette and protect her newborn. She unlocked the door to find Etiennette holding a knife to Alette's crying face.

Danielle took the crying baby and tried to grab Alette, but Etiennette refused to let her loose. "Please let her go, Madame. She is innocent," Danielle pleaded.

"Show me the child," the mistress demanded.

"I'll do so if you allow Alette to go home...please—"

Etiennette took the knife and made a long incision down Lettie's right cheek. Alette screamed in pain as blood poured down. The baby screamed louder, even after Danielle placed her in a nearby basket behind her for safety while she ran to aid. Etiennette put the knife to Alette's neck and Danielle halted. "Show me the child," Etiennette repeated without raising her voice.

"Okay," Danielle cried. "Okay." She began to hear people approaching, calling her name, and for "Mam" to "calm and come on out." Danielle backed towards the crying baby without taking her eyes off Alette. She scooped up the infant, standing at a distance as she unwrapped the blanket from the child who had yet to receive a name. Etiennette inched closer, still pressing the knife onto Lettie's neck.

She revealed the pink screaming baby. Danielle needed to say something—anything to prevent Etiennette from harming the infant or further injuring or possibly killing Alette. "The babe," said Danielle, "is not his. She belongs to a slave from the Collier Plantation, an octoroon who has since run. The babe—she will grow into her color, Mam. Look—her ears. They—they are darker at the tip. That is her true color. And beneath her nails are brown. Please, Mam, she and Alette hold no fault in this. If it is me you want to dispose of, then have me, but the children are innocent."

"I see nothing of the sort. Disrobe that babe fully," said Etiennette, looking over the child. Danielle complied, conspicuously covering the baby's birthmark with her hand as she held her close. "Hold it up by the pits of its arms so I may see its full body," Etiennette ordered. Danielle looked into Lettie's wide eyes with sorrow. "Hold-it-up!" Etiennette yelled. Danielle obeyed and the baby's birthmark was exposed. "That mark!" she shouted as she accidentally loosened her grip on Alette. "That *is* your master's child!" Danielle clutched the baby and turned, using her own body as a shield as Etiennette lunged at them. The baby continued to scream as Danielle tried to run towards the exit door in the hopes of saving the baby or both of them. She was only able to touch the door before Etiennette grabbed Danielle by the hair and twisted, yanking her toward her and onto the floor. Danielle could only place the baby beside the door before turning around to grab Etiennette's leg, causing her to fall and release the curls she held in her hand. Enraged, she scrambled towards Danielle who slapped her across the face and pinned her down by the neck with her hands.

"Run, Lettie!!" Danielle screamed.

Alette did as she was told while the women tussled. Etiennette scratched at Danielle's neck and face and jerked the post-partum woman off of her and onto her left side. Danielle tried reaching for the pistol on Etiennette's hip but could not get it out of the bolster at her angle. Etiennette stomped Danielle in the chest who only had time to gasp twice before punching Etiennette in the eye when she saw that the mistress was aiming to grab the child.

"Don't you dare touch her!" Danielle screamed, grabbing hold of the crying infant as she tried to race past Etiennette and out of the door. Etiennette wrestled with Danielle over the child whom Lettie heard the loudest as she ran crying approaching a crowd of servants and overseers on horseback brandishing whips to control the matter.

The crowd was in a frenzy when they saw Alette's bloodied face. "My baby!" Genevieve screamed, "Alette!! What's happened!?"

Alette ran into her mother's arms, "The mistress has gone mad!" she hollered. She spoke quickly, "She's trying to kill Danielle and the baby and tried to kill me and Corrine! Please, someone, help!" Genevieve instinctively ran in the direction of Danielle's cabin with Alette closely behind her when an overseer hit Genevieve with the tail of his whip, splitting the back of her dress. Some of the men distracted the overseers with shouts as the others followed Genevieve, for the overseer could not whip them all at once.

The slaves heard the shouts of Danielle and Etiennette as they ran closer. They heard the child and could not seem to run to the cabin fast enough.

"Give her back!" They heard Danielle scream, "I want nothing from you or Monsieur! I only want to care for this child."

"I've always hated you," they heard Etiennette say. "You've inserted yourself into my family—"

"Give her to me!" Danielle pleaded.

"You flaunt our name as if you've earned it."

"I no longer identify by the surname—"

"And I have to see your face on our family products daily. And here, you have my husband's child to wave before him—"

"I will keep my baby away from the both of you, I will—noooooo! Oh, God! Oh, God!!"

***

Alette twisted the handkerchief but preferred to let the tears stream from her old eyes. "To this day," said Alette, "I can still hear the tortured screams of that baby. I can hear my sister's repetitious ululations, 'What have you done?' and later she begged Madame Etiennette to kill her too. She kept saying that she couldn't live like this. But with all of the weapons that Etiennette had on her that evening, she didn't have to use them to kill Danielle. She opened the door before one of us could touch the handle and slowly walked out, battered, crying, and stunned by what she had done. She had brandished so much hatred towards my sister and anyone affiliated with her, that she never imagined that she would feel anything after going through with her plan to commit murder. She never thought of the infant as a precious child or even human until that moment. I don't know if she was ever remorseful. I only know that while she walked from Danielle's cabin to her horse, it took 5 people to hold back Maman from attacking that evil woman for what she had put her children through. My mother was almost beaten for it once the overseers caught the tail-end of it. And even then, Etiennette didn't flinch or look our way." One of them escorted her home, while another rounded up some of the others and forced them back to their cabins. A few of us were allowed to stay.

Alette squeezed her eyes shut and took a deep breath. Charles placed his warm hand on top of hers. The old woman grabbed hold of it using her other hand. After more tears flowed, she continued. "But Maman didn't know *all* that had occurred until she followed the smell to the cabin. She was scared to open the door. But when she did, she saw Danielle kneeling beside the fireplace rocking back and forth. The front of her dress was charred. She had tried to rescue the baby, but the flames were too hot." Alette balled. "Danielle was inconsolable by Maman and Corrine. She wept and moaned into her burnt hands. I don't know if she even noticed we were there. Amid all of Danielle's infinite, 'I'm sorries,' towards the baby, *I* felt as though I swallowed the most guilt."

"But," Mr. Nelson said quietly, "you were just a little girl who did nothing wrong. Why would you feel guilty?"

"When you're *that* young, you question whether everything traumatic that has happened to you or family is somehow your fault, as I did. I felt guilty for disobeying Corrine when she told me to stay home with Maman. I felt guilty for Etiennette catching me and the baby. I felt guilty for running when my sister instructed me to, and not at least trying to bring the baby along...Someone may have said, 'Take Lettie home, somebody,' but I was fighting to stay within that cluster of pain. Perhaps in my eight-year-old mind, I felt I needed to remain there to accept my punishment.

"Then, as she continued to rock and cry staring into the fireplace, Danielle apologized to the infant for being too afraid to love her baby to full capacity in the beginning but said that she was loved, so loved in the end. And that baby *was* cherished, not just by Danielle, but by me and Maman, Corrine, and Alphonse. I don't know how Demetre felt about the unborn child or the idea of Danielle carrying his baby, but I'd catch him touching her belly when they thought they were alone. Maybe Etiennette saw this too and it infuriated her, especially since she could never give Demetre more children. The babies who didn't survive years prior were all buried in a special garden that we were forbidden to enter unless we were watering the flowers planted there."

"Grandmommy," said Charles. "You've never told me the full details. You've always said that Danielle lost the baby or that she didn't make it through the night."

Alette dabbed her eyes, "The idea that something so heinous happened to someone in our family, well, I suppose that at the time, I didn't want you or others to be haunted by the thoughts, images, and emotions that come with knowing the details. And in a way, for me, not speaking about it meant not reliving the pain and the guilt. However, it stayed with me, quietly and mournfully."

Charles answered, "Thank you for wanting to protect my heart. But we're family, Grandma Lettie. If you're in sorrow, let us mourn and heal together." Alette offered him a faint smile before nodding. "What happened thereafter?"

Alette continued, "The following day, Danielle, Maman, and I, along with Corrine and Rosezelle were allowed a burial for the baby. Her remains lie here on these grounds within the slave graveyard, stacked with field stones and dressed with flowers and a white painted rock with a baby drawn on it as her headstone. I had learned my letters a year prior from one of the fieldhands, so I desperately wanted to paint a name onto the white rock but was forbidden to do so for the safety of myself and the other slaves on the plantation.

"We cried with Danielle in the days after. Maman cried to herself in the fields, Corrine and Rosezelle in the house, and I mourned with Danielle in our cabin as I looked after her. She stayed with Maman and me, as she had fallen ill soon after the birth. If a broken heart was an ailment, she contracted that too."

Eighteen

Many women on the plantation had visited Genevieve's cabin to bring meals, extra bedding, and bandages to the young lady who had suffered through great pain and tragic loss. Some offered their condolences and handmade items of practicality. They chose not to step foot inside the home, for their convictions from previously speaking terribly about the girl for years would not allow them to face her.

The elderly women, who could no longer work the fields, assisted in caring for Danielle when Genevieve tended to the sugar. They draped trinkets and burlap satchels of mixed herbs for luck and healing around her neck while medicating her with asafetida and oil, and other remedies within soups and teas that their African parents and grandparents used. They prayed Christian prayers over her in English and chanted heart-mending prayers in Creole tongue. The old women were not alarmed when Danielle awoke screaming and crying and sometimes fighting; they expected it and knew how to calm her. Perhaps they permitted the best medicine, one which Alphonse once told her was cleansing. They allowed her to cry. With wrinkled, rough hands on top of her wounded palms, they offered words of comfort, passing along their secrets for making it through deaths and murders of *their* children or other loved ones.

While she wished many times to awaken in the arms of Alphonse, she took comfort in seeing the stone in her fist and a shirt with his scent draped over her when she opened her eyes.

Demetre did not learn of the birth until three days later. Still recovering from the alcohol laced with small amounts of poison that Etiennette poured into his wine, he noticed that neither Danielle nor Alette was in the house working. He also saw that Etiennette was not herself. She was nonverbal, disheveled, and stared off frequently. Demetre thought he saw bruises on her face and body, but she would not hold still long enough to allow him to confirm it. She would not divulge to him anything that had happened after going to bed that evening.

He asked Corrine of the sisters' whereabouts. "Alette is tending to Danielle, who remains ill," Corrine said.

"She still is not well?" Demetre asked, surprised. "And the baby, how is it?" Corrine could not get her words out. She stammered and looked sorrowfully at the floor. "No," Demetre said.

"I'm sorry to have to tell you, Monsieur—"

"No!" he yelled, grabbing her by the shoulders.

"The—the child is no more. Monsieur. I'm so sorry, sir." Corrine began to cry as Demetre slowly released her.

"You may carry on," he said lightly and dazed. Without giving it much thought, Demetre soon prepared his horse and made his way towards Danielle's cabin.

Outside of her door was a reef of wildflowers picked from the outer fields of the plantation. Expecting to see her resting, Demetre, instead, saw a made bed with a rosary on top. The floorboard beside her bed had been scrubbed, yet Demetre could only stare at the bloodstains and piece together the events that might have happened while he was out of commission. He could not fathom why flowers lay at the fireplace.

Demetre traveled the plantation in search of Danielle, passing familiar slave women along the way. He had shocked plenty of workers with his presence on the field and questions as to where he might locate Danielle. They hesitantly pointed in the direction of Genevieve's cabin, where he went inside and found Danielle curled in bed, asleep, and Lettie brushing her sister's hair. The little girl heard the cowbell from the fields and saw Demetre fixed on Danielle, slowly approaching from over her shoulder. "Monsieur!" Lettie jumped. "What can I do for you?"

Demetre squinted at the bandage covering Alette's wound. "What has happened to your face?" he asked.

Alette stammered, "I-um, when-uh—"

Soon, she heard footsteps sliding up the stairs, followed by, "Lettie, fetch some water from the well while I—" said Genevieve, surprised at her master's presence. "Monsieur," she acknowledged.

"Genevieve," said Demetre. "It's been a long time. I've come to see about Danielle. I heard she was...ill."

"Yes," said Genevieve, staring him in the eyes as she moved and stood between him and her girls. "She caught chills not long after giving birth," she informed him as she discreetly shifted Alette behind her.

"Is she recovering well?"

"She is, sir. Her fever has diminished, and she is doing as she is told and resting."

"I will call on the doctor to have him examine her."

"Very well, Monsieur, thank you for that." Genevieve removed her satchel. "Can I offer you anything to eat? Or tea, perhaps?"

"No," said Demetre, trying to sneak a peek at Danielle. "I don't have much of an appetite." Genevieve smiled politely. "Tell me," said Demetre, with eyes that almost mirrored his desperation for information. "Was the child a boy or a girl?"

"Lettie," said Genevieve. "Take the pail and bring back water so that Danielle will have something cool to drink when she awakens."

"Yes, Maman," said Alette, scurrying out of the cabin with the metal pail.

Genevieve relaxed only a little. "It was a baby girl, sir."

"Oh...and what did she look like?"

"I wouldn't know, Monsieur."

"How do you know that it was a girl, yet you had not laid eyes on her?"

"Because I was only told the child's sex. She had been...carried off to God by the time I was at Danielle's side."

"Was the child born alive?"

Genevieve's voice trembled. "...Yes. Yes, she was, Monsieur. She came into this world early but sounded healthy, strong lungs and all." The first of three cowbells echoed throughout the plantation. Genevieve gathered her dress in preparation to return to the field.

"So, you *heard* the child, but did not see her?"

"Yes, sir."

"Besides Danielle, how many people saw the child?"

Genevieve took in a deep breath and exhaled before answering, "Please, sir, we are all in mourning over that terrible night. I especially, because of the loss of a precious grandchild and the pain that my girls endured." The second cowbell rang. "Please, sir, I don't want to get behind in our planting schedule."

"It can wait, and I will escort you to the fields myself when I am ready." Genevieve dropped the hem of her dress. "So, Alette was there. She saw the infant." Genevieve drifted over slightly, allowing Demetre to see Danielle. "Why are Danielle's hands bandaged? And what happened to Alette's face? Why is everyone swimming in this lake of secrets?"

The mother locked eyes with her master, "My girls were attacked, sir, on the evening of the birth. Alette's cheek—slashed. Danielle—beaten and previously threatened with death. I thank you for taking an interest in the health of my daughter and her babe, and I will welcome the doctor when he arrives. It is recognized that you are wanting to fit the pieces together. While your whereabouts during that evening is no business of mine, I'm afraid you will have to ask others who are closest to you for details, as they could provide more, and they have less to lose than I." As they stared at one another in silence, Demetre and Genevieve heard the ringing of the third cowbell. "I do pray for the heart, mind, and soul that is within you, Monsieur, just as I prayed for your father. If your proposition to lead me back to the field so that I may work is still available, I beg for my release to return to work so that I am not punished, please."

In his frustration and confusion, Demetre nodded once and exited with Genevieve behind him.

After leading her to the field to join the others and ordering one of the overseers not to punish her, he attempted to rush home. "Good day, sir!" an overseer called from several yards away. He began to approach Demetre.

"Not now Jeremiah—"

"Oh, I only wanted to make sure you and the Missus were feeling better." Demetre looked perplexed but allowed Jeremiah to continue. "I wasn't sure whether to call on the doctor, as I had never seen the mistress in that manner. But don't you worry, things have settled down here."

"Settled down? Doctor? And in what manner have you *not* seen Etiennette?"

Jeremiah removed his wide-brimmed hat. "Oh...you don't know what took place."

"Tell me. Please."

"Your wife had it in for your negress. Me and Solomon heard gunshots, got us up in the dead of night. There was a big commotion and that nigger who works in your house, Corrine, came runnin' and screamin' for help. Said *your wife* shot at her. Now, I've never known Mrs. Soileau to be totin' no guns, but you would know better than myself."

Demetre did not reveal that Etiennette enjoyed guns and hunting before she became a wife. He was captivated by her skills as a sharpshooter but made her retire her guns and hobby when they married, as it was not "lady-like." He listened to Jeremiah's encounter as his heart thumped harder and faster.

"Corrine said Danielle had delivered and that the mistress wanted revenge. I didn't think such a kind-souled woman such as the Missus would have it in her. Now Solomon and me, we got the rest of them slaves in line until Alette came runnin' towards us in hysterics, face bloodied and all. The lil' bitch came blamin' Mrs. Soileau for the slashin' on her face, claimin' she was 'mad.' Alette's mammy decides she wants to run past Solomon and me, so my whip caught her in the back. Then, believe me when I tell you all them darkies at once resisted and defied me and Solomon and ran past us. One of them got stomped on by Solomon's horse (but he was all right, just a broken arm, he was out here working the field the very next day). Some of the wenches ran to Danielle's cabin, where there were all kinds of screamin' and hollerin' and by that time, Mrs. Soileau came out real slow, traumatized, it seemed. We asked how she felt, but she didn't answer us. Just as the Mrs. was mounting her horse, your negress' mammy came runnin' towards her. The mammy's friends stopped her from harming your precious wife. Had she touched a single hair on her head, I would have nearly gutted her, sir, I'm sorry. Solomon stayed behind to supervise them coons who went in to see about Danielle and I escorted the Missus back to the main house. Her eye was swollen, face bruised. I tried to ask her questions along the way, but it was as if she couldn't hear me. I asked her to tell me everything that happened and what went on in the cabin, and nothin.' The only words she spoke were 'thank you for escorting me.' (Now if it turns out that your negress knocked your wife around, you just say that word and I'll beat her).

"Anyway, Solomon later tells me that he went into the cabin and that the babe had died. Don't nothin' really affect him usually, but this one had him messed up in the head. Said the babe had...burned to death, sir. He let them have a ceremony for it. They did and got back to work. We didn't lose any time. But I been keepin' watch for any further signs of defiance or an uprising, and there have been none. Now,

I'm sure your wife only came to check on Danielle or talk to her, and at some point, early that night, had to defend herself against her. But in the end, your wife had it in for your Negress."

If there was a way that Demetre could have processed that information without it resulting in rage, he was not aware of it. He instructed Jeremiah to keep his hands off Danielle and any of her family members, and that if there is injury to any more of his property, that he should be notified at once. "And I am sending for a doctor to examine Danielle," he informed. "I will also need him to examine the boy with the broken arm."

"Yes, sir," said Jeremiah. "Good day, sir."

Toggling between angst and disgust over that horrendous evening and Etiennette's apparent involvement in it, Demetre stormed into the house and was first met by Felix, whom he ordered to take Philippe and go into town and request a visit from the doctor. As he wrote down instructions in his letter to the physician, he saw Etiennette enter the room behind Felix with a cup of tea. "Hurry now," he commanded to Felix. Demetre briskly approached Etiennette.

"Your health has returned, I see—" said Etiennette as the back of Demetre's hand came clear across her face and the teacup and saucer crashed to the floor, as did the mistress.

"You vile, wretched woman!" He seethed as she fell to the floor. The servants ran in once they heard the commotion. Jen helped Etiennette to her feet while two of the men tried to calm Demetre. Rosezelle and Corrine, however, retreated to their tasks upon seeing Etiennette wipe the blood from her nose with the back of her hand. "Never," said Demetre, "would I have ever imagined that you were capable of murder." Jen gasped lightly, releasing Etiennette's arm, and stepped back when hearing this. "Everyone, get out," Demetre said to his slaves. They stood grounded. "Get out!" he ordered. They fled but remained within earshot. Etiennette grabbed a sharp piece of porcelain to protect herself. "Oh, you're going to cut *me* as well?"

"Don't dare put your hands on me again!" Etiennette said. "I can't continue to stand in the shadows while you allow your concubine to parade about. Daily, I watched her pregnant belly grow knowing that your bastard was inside. Every day, the sister of your whore walked these halls as your life continued, uninterrupted. I've told you my stance on the matter, yet you continued to ignore my plea—"

"If you're insinuating that I made you do it—"

"You've disregarded me for too long, Demetre—"

"And I'm on the verge of disregarding you altogether."

Etiennette wiped her nose once again. "If, by your definition, you mean to ignore, disrespect, push away, you've done that."

"*You* know what I mean."

"And how would you explain our dissolution of marriage?" Etiennette sneered. "It matters not; the newspaper editors, from Mississippi to Florida, will print that the 'co-owner of Soileau & Sons, has participated in a long-term affair with his slave, for whom he has separated from his wife of 19 years."

"And I will tell them and those who know you, you dastardly bitch, of the sin you committed."

"I doubt that they would believe you."

"The judge would."

"Judge? I committed no crime—"

"I can fix it so that you're out in the streets penniless with only your gossiping friends to take pity on you to your face and whisper about your downfall behind your back."

"Not before they see my bruises and swollen eye and read my public recounts of the night you beat me, followed by the money you would lose and possessions you would need to sell to stay afloat. There is no dragging me down without you coming along for the ride." Demetre lunged at the stranger before him. She neither flinched nor stepped back against the hands that reached for her neck, but never took hold. "And your precious Danielle, well, she admitted that the child may not have even belonged to you."

Demetre balled his fists and grunted before throwing down his hands. His eyes scorching. "Then why would you kill the babe? Enough with your lies, Etiennette."

"You don't have to believe me. The truth will always reveal itself."

The hatred between the once lovers was almost enough to fill the sitting room as neither one wanted to take their eyes off each other, ready to strike with a stab or a blow at any moment. When neither acts of violence were presented, Demetre said, "I suggest we separate immediately. Your actions have gone far beyond that of a demon."

"Perhaps Simone will understand why her parents are no longer under the same roof."

"You will move to Evergreen Manor until I am ready for your return. Jen can help you pack, and Philippe can drive you."

"You will not banish me to your father's house. I am not leaving—"

"Woman, if you do not leave my home, I'll have to bury you in the garden with the rest of our unborn children you couldn't carry."

Etiennette's hardened red face loosened briefly, and her eyes welled with tears. Without contesting, she dropped the sharp ceramic piece and retreated to the bedroom to pack her belongings and a combination of her inheritance and Demetre's money she had been hiding from him for years.

The doctor arrived later that afternoon just as Etiennette's carriage had rolled away. "She's on her way to visit family," Demetre explained.

Dr. Guilford had examined Danielle, who was awake but remained quiet. Feeling as though she were a bother once again, she curled away from Genevieve and the doctor, wanting to hear no more about her condition or any parts of her ordeal, which, other than the explanation of "losing the child during labor," had not been shared with him. "From what I recall you saying, she delivered on her own, is that correct?"

"Yes, doctor," Genevieve nodded.

Dr. Guilford continued. "Her vaginal area is healing well. No tears or infections that I can see. Continue to change the dressing often. Also, that brandy that I gave her oughta help. Other than an occasional cough and dehydration, she is recovering quite nicely. Whatever you've been doing seems to be working a lot better than some of my other patients, and *they're* white. But then again, you people are as strong as oxen. You can withstand things more than anybody I've ever seen. Funny the gifts the good Lord gives to *some* folks."

He wandered to Genevieve's table, which had been scattered with wooden bowls of various crushed and torn plants and herbs used for medicine. "I see you've got your own concoctions over there. If you don't mind, I'll just take a sample."

Genevieve protested with tact, "I understand how you would think that, but if you would like extra seasoning for your wife to *also* sprinkle onto your vegetables or poultry, I welcome you, Dr. Guilford."

The doctor examined the medicine a third time and gave Genevieve a smug reaction. He sifted a large portion of some of the medicinal plants into cloth satchels and stored them in his doctor's bag. He tapped his bag and said, "This will help or even save many people. You're doing your Christian duty, Genevieve."

On his way towards the door, he asked, "You wanna tell me what happened to her hands now?"

"She was boiling water as she was growing ill and didn't realize what she was doing when she picked up the pot with her hands."

The doctor shook his head before placing on his hat. "Yep, I've seen it before. A lot of gals become absent-minded, even insane, after giving birth, sometimes to the point of idiocy. Happens to white women too." He took a couple of steps down the stairs, "And thank you for the ipecacuanha roots. I had to clip some before coming in. That plant is very hard to come by."

Genevieve watched as the doctor headed in the direction of the Soileau mansion to report a summary and diagnosis to Demetre. She heard movement behind her, only to see Danielle walking about the cabin, searching ferociously for clothing to put on. "Get back in bed, Danielle," Genevieve ordered.

"No Maman. I need to move around—where have you placed my clean gown?"

"I agree, you *do*, but you're not well enough to go about the day."

Danielle continued to move briskly, searching through baskets and a wooden chest made by Edmond. "Well," Danielle rebutted, "you heard the doctor, I just need more water and something to rid this cough. You think Alette knows where it is? Where is she, by the way?"

"She's in the main house—"

Danielle paused. "Without me?! Maman, she can't be there, not with that demonic witch, sòrsyèr!"

"Danielle, Etiennette is not on the plantation; she is at their other residence. Demetre insisted that she remove herself from the home."

The young woman stood still for a short while, processing what that meant for her going forward. Suddenly, she continued her search for the gown.

Genevieve stomped to Danielle and grabbed her wrists. The young woman struggled. "Danielle, stop. Stop! What're you doing?"

"I can't be here, Maman. My husband is waiting for us in the upcoming days—Aly and Papa are too, and we have to go. I can't stay here any longer. I'll help you prepare—"

"Go? We are not going anywhere, especially you—"

"Oh Maman, this can't stop me, I need to regain my strength, and I can't be in this place. I don't want to leave you or Alette." Danielle burst into tears, "Don't make me leave you. And Lettie deserves a chance. Her heart is as pure as the day God created it, and she is so smart. She is so much more than this. Even if I don't make it, *she* should."

"Why are you talking like this? And why do you always think you know what's best for Alette?" Genevieve spoke sternly, tugging her daughter towards her.

Danielle angrily snatched her wrists away. "Perhaps I don't always know what's best for her, but I know this is not it. And in the end, I'm going to try. And when I make it, I'll come back for you." The mother and daughter continued to tussle their words. "I have always felt the enormous rush of love that you have for us. But the moment I became a mother, all I could think was, 'Maman loves us *like this*?!' While *I* inherited a mother's love, *you are* not given your daughter's *pain*. I don't expect you to know what *this* feels like."

"'This' what? To lose a child? And I never want to know. I wish I could mend your grief, but know that I'm grieving with you. I lost a grandchild, and I'm afraid of losing you. If we run, we could be killed—you—you could be killed, Fiy."

"Or I could live. Either way, I would be running toward someone I love."

"Stop this talk, Danielle!"

"Even if you are against the idea, I'm still going. I know that Ruby would have wanted that."

"Honey, poupe,' who is Ruby?"

Danielle's face softened. "She at least deserved a name."

Genevieve relaxed her shoulders. She spoke tenderly, "Oh, Danielle. Is that what this is about? Are you wanting to be with her? Are you *trying* to die?"

"On the contrary, I'm trying to live. But the fact remains, I feel I have died once already, I no longer fear the thought of doing it again."

Nineteen

New Orleans, Louisiana

She felt at peace more than she had in weeks of attending the Sacre Coeur School for Girls in New Orleans. Simone was surprised at the number of friends she had made quickly. Like-minded girls, who too came from wealth and lived a sheltered life, were enthusiastic about being on their own. While some wished to receive an education in hopes of contributing to the progression of female accomplishment in art, literature, and mathematics, others saw it only as an opportunity to escape the watchful eyes of their parents and "mammies." However, the steamboat ride to Lafayette Parish gave Simone an opportunity to release herself of the hurt, at least a little, caused by her suitor who explained to her that they were, "just two different to continue courtship." Dreams of wedding bells and rooms filled with gifts and best wishes were washed away.

While Simone was a little homesick, she made no plans to remain in Lafayette Parish but to throw her gathered sorrow and love letters into the Mississippi River and carry forth in her studies and travels. With Bella by her side, she remained encouraged and was able to vent whenever she needed. Uncle Emile chaperoned the trip but did not look forward to conversing, or feuding, with Demetre regarding Soileau & Sons.

Simone, Bella, and Emile arrived on the plantation in a horse and carriage in the evening with supper and everyone in the household awaiting their arrival, including Etiennette who received a note from Demetre telling her the date and time to arrive to welcome their daughter home. "Furthermore," the note read, "any mention regarding our disagreement will result in serious and unfavorable consequences." Demetre greeted his brother and niece as they entered the vestibule. As his daughter approached him, Simone smiled, quickly dropped the expression, and sighed before walking into his embrace. Etiennette quickly entangled her daughter, as if to apologize for her heartbreak. "I'll be alright, Mother," Simone reassured her. "Mmm, the food smells divine! How I've missed the meals here." The new arrivals were exhausted from the trip, but far too hungry to pass up the dinner that was prepared for them. As their luggage was taken to their rooms, the travelers quickly refreshed and sat at the dining room table.

As the servants presented their plates, Etiennette, Bella, and Emile spoke among themselves. Simone looked around for Danielle and little Alette. "Papa," said Simone, "where is Danielle?"

"She was rewarded some time to herself," Demetre answered as Etiennette sipped wine.

"Tomorrow, I will see her."

Demetre warned the mistress with his eyes.

Etiennette noticed, "...You are losing your accent, my dear. Is that intentional?"

"Maybe," said Simone.

"Everyone at school speaks English," defended Bella.

"But," asked Emile. "Does that mean that you have to change who you are?"

"Not changing, simply trying to fit in, uncle," said Simone.

"—Simone, Bella," Etiennette interrupted. "What about the academy do you enjoy the most?"

"I enjoy learning about poetry and literature the most," said Bella.

Eager to say that she thoroughly enjoyed her freedom, Simone instead settled for, "World history and current affairs."

Demetre raised an eyebrow, "Oh? I thought you would say poetry as well. A young lady who knows the greatest works of literature presents a fine exhibit for culture."

"Fine exhibit? Sorry Bella—but Papa, what am I going to do, constantly recite the works of others, haiku my way through life? No, I want to travel the world—and do what? I have not yet figured it out, but I want to see other lands, other people, how they live."

Etiennette shook her head, "I don't see much success in that, particularly as a woman."

"Uh, you sound like Matthieu, telling me what a woman is and isn't good for." Her parents said nothing, only waiting for her to mention more details about the broken courtship. Simone's eyes volleyed at Bella and Emile who also stared at her. She sighed. "He was particularly upset after many balls and dinner parties as we conversed with his friends and his father's acquaintances. He said that I speak too much of my mind and that if I am to be on his arm, I must know my place. He said that he expected a girl of my status to know better. Then he insulted my upbringing."

"Did we not discuss this?" said Etiennette. "I knew your mouth was going to be the demise of your destiny. Good Lord. What all did you say to make him change his mind about you?"

"Does it matter, Mother? He simply wanted me to be his doll when around others and I was not willing to do that."

"Tomorrow, you will send him a letter and apologize for your behavior—"

"I will not. I felt like a prisoner, Mother—" Emile quietly removed himself from the table, taking Bella with him. Demetre soon followed. "If I find a man of quality on the way to my destiny, I'll be sure to not let him distract me. If he wants to come along for the ride, he'd better be prepared to hand me the reins."

"That is not what you should expect out of life, child. Do you know how difficult it is for women without a husband? And here you have one handed to you on a platter, and you find a way to destroy it by opening your mouth."

"Should I have waited until we marry to speak my mind?"

"Yes!"

Simone laughed. "This is ridiculous. So, a man should not know all of me or who he married until standing before God?"

"Listen, you are going to beg his forgiveness and ask him to take you back."

"Did you not hear what I just said, Mother? I don't want to feel imprisoned in my own marriage—"

"So, you'll find another outlet—"

"There are other men who will accept me as I am, Mother. Why is it so important that I marry *this* one?"

"Because your father is losing assets." There was a still hush over the dining room. "He doesn't think I know, but it's been happening for several months. We recently had to sell some of our cattle. Next are the slaves, then the land, unless Soileau & Sons sales increase. But for now, another sugar plantation is dominating in some areas."

"Gloria told me that money was lost, but I didn't know to what extent."

"I just want you to be taken care of. What you are feeling is nothing different than what generations of women before you have experienced. For us, it is not a matter of knowing your place. It is survival. And with this man, you will have the opportunity to see the world. But don't sabotage your future meanwhile."

Simone thought silently about the direction of her family and their livelihood. She offered no verbal promises of sacrificing her happiness, although it was a consideration.

Several marks and blemishes on her mother's face became more apparent as Simone squinted and watched Etiennette shift in her chair. "What happened to your face, mere'?"

"Oh, nothing. Just an accident."

"It doesn't look like it. Your eye, it looks like it was once struck, and your cheek, bruised."

Etiennette looked around and whispered, "Do not repeat this to your father or anyone. Danielle did this to me. She has gone mad over the last few days. If Solomon and Jeremiah had not intervened, who knows what would have happened? I didn't want to mention it in your father's presence, but I don't want you to see her. She might hurt you too."

"Danielle attacked you? That does not sound like something she would do. And why can't I tell Papa? Does he not know anything has happened?"

"No, he does not. And I suppose her jealousy got the best of her. With her being with child, I'm afraid that Demetre might have her hung, and I couldn't live with myself if the blood of a child were on my hands."

Just then, Demetre slid open the dining room doors. "I hope you ladies have had an opportunity to speak on courting and marriage and mending hearts," he said.

"We did," said Etiennette, "And I think our daughter has a better understanding of 'the world.' Don't you, Simone?"

Staring at the dinner glasses, Simone was perplexed but stated, "Um. Yes, Mam."

"Perfect," said Demetre. "We will speak more on this tomorrow if we need to. However, Simone, ma chere fille, you have had a long day of travel and I need you to get sleep."

Simone agreed and excused herself from the table, passing her father on the threshold. Etiennette retreated from the table following Simone. As she passed Demetre, he slithered his hand down her arm until reaching the point of his destination, grabbing tightly onto her wrist and yanking her arm downward. He seethed into her eyes as she pursed her lips to hush herself. Demetre squeezed harder, digging his nails into her skin, causing Etiennette to make a faint shrill. Simone turned around, only to see her parents holding hands, looking intensely at one another.

Later in the evening, Demetre requested a word with Emile in the cigar room. "Really Demetre," Emile said, holding his head in his hands as he slumped on the couch. "We're not as young as we used to be. Men our age need sleep. I don't understand why this can't wait until morning."

"We don't have to discuss everything tonight, but I have to get a few things off of my chest." Emile waved his free hand motioning Demetre to continue. "My marriage to Etiennette may be coming to an end soon."

Emile perked up with concern. "Was the decision made by your head or your loins?"

"This is serious, and this could affect the business," Demetre said pacing and smoking a cigar.

"Does this have anything to do with Danielle?"

"Yes, but not in the way you think."

Emile raised his voice, "I knew your personal affairs would get in the way of the family business—"

"Lower your voice."

"I will not. This could ruin our livelihood. And I don't care what other masters do concerning their slaves, we have more to lose. You don't think of anyone other than yourself—"

"You haven't even heard what's happened—"

"I don't need to. Man strums slave repeatedly. Man falls in love-lust with slave, (which came first, the love or the strumming, I don't know). Man flaunts his young, impregnated slave around his wife. Man is suddenly surprised that the drapes are closing on his marriage. The end—"

"Etiennette has committed murder."

Emile studied his brother's face. His mouth dropped and his eyes widened. His expression then settled into cynicism," No," said Emile shaking his head. "No. I may not know her as you do, but Etiennette wouldn't go as far as to murder Danielle."

"Not Danielle. The infant. Danielle delivered early days ago." Emile sighed slinking into the couch as Demetre recounted the details as they were told to him.

Emile shook his head and exhaled. "And she threatened to go to the papers about the affair?"

The brothers spoke longer than intended into the night regarding family and the distribution. They agreed to redesign the packaging in an attempt to lessen rumors and to appeal to those in midwestern and northern states. Demetre finally agreed with Emile and the others on the board, to reduce cost and discontinue one of their three products. Their decision to end production of the Soileau & Sons rum brand was sealed over two poured glasses of alcohol and a clank of farewell to the additional cost of production.

Traveling into town with a list and a pass secured to her bosom, Corrine rode with Philippe in the wagon and set out to complete a mission of her own that she had accomplished many times before. Through a trusted slave with easy access to Alphonse and other water-men, loading bales of hay onto the bed of the wagon, Corrine, relayed an oral message to Alphonse about Danielle as she had successfully done previously when alerting him of the delivery and the tragedy be-hind it. "Now that her illness is gone," Corrine said with her back to-wards the hay man, "and her strength restored, her hunger to get away is immediate. But she won't be alone." Despite Genevieve's firm stance to remain on the plantation, her feelings towards the attempt at free-dom changed when looking at Alette's scar, triggering reminders of that night and the helplessness tied to the lack of freedom to protect her youngest daughter. She spent a restless night thinking of Danielle's words and determination that struck her soul so deeply, that the pos-sibility of dying while or after attempting freedom was not an option for Genevieve. It was at that moment that she would use the power of manifestation to reach freedom.

Corrine continued. "There will be three of them, they know the plan, they know the timing, and they are ready."

The hay man nodded as he continued to work without providing Corrine with eye contact. "Alphonse will have this message today and everyone will be in place as he promised." Corrine closed her eyes and exhaled as Philippe clicked his teeth, jiggled the reins, and drove off.

Etiennette's temporary return prompted a shift in Alette's duties. Rather than working in the big house, she served by assisting with the livestock, a job that Lettie preferred. Danielle too, was satisfied with her role, as she tended to the laundry. Hidden away from the mistress and Mademoiselle Simone, Danielle—dodged the young Miss who had been seeking her obsessively. Finally, when no one was around to see her do it, Simone opened one of the panels in the wall of the ballroom and followed the narrow servant's stairwell. Images of running up and down the stairs as a child, hiding from Danielle and other children during her birthday party reappeared vividly. The humidity of the enclosed space and the smell of wood remained as she quietly spiraled up the stairs with paths that eventually steered in several directions. Simone continued to the attic, one door leading to Rosezelle's small quarters, and another used for storage. Relying on her memory, she entered the door leading to storage.

Inside, she saw all of the furniture, toys, and oil paintings of French landscapes and disgraced family members, mainly from the maternal side of her genealogy. She noticed that space had been cleared away for the table displaying folded laundry, freshly pressed garments, and woven baskets of clothing to which had not yet been attended. Feeling that this was Danielle's hiding place, Simone decided she would wait until she returned.

She slowly walked around the attic, the soft morning sun peering into the small windows past the sheer white curtains. She felt herself smile after pulling back the sheets that covered her childhood. She ran her fingers across the chiseled details of the rocking horse that she loved so much as a little girl. The sandy mane and tail of the horse were heavy and still intact. The leather pink saddle and reins with silver studs held nicely, given the number of times it had been ridden, flipped, and pulled to various places of the residence.

A large dollhouse with miniatures and a white family with colored servants no longer towered over. She picked up the white family, their painted pink smiles, eternally expressing their exuberance for one another, even if their owner tossed them into situations of turmoil. The slave women, with their cream-colored headscarves and red grinning lips, were always happy to serve all who dwelled in the miniature home, even the Topsy-Turvy doll who used to frequently visit.

Simone brushed her fingers along each old or broken item until she stopped at the empty wooden doll cradle which creaked at the touch. Once the rocking stopped, Simone still heard creaking, followed by light footsteps. As she whipped around Danielle gasped at the sight of Simone in the attic. Simone gasped in response when she saw Danielle with a smaller frame. "Mademoiselle," said Danielle. "Did you lose your way?"

"If I lost mine, you've lost yours in return," said Simone. "And when did you give birth?"

"About a week ago—shouldn't you be preparing to go on a ride with your father?"

"But Mother said you were still with child. She said you attacked her. Did you attack my mother, Danielle?" Simone's voice escalated.

Danielle did not cower at the volume of Simone's voice. "My baby did not survive, Mademoiselle."

"Oh. I'm sorry," Simone did not know what else to say, however, Danielle filled the silence.

"I don't think I'm healed enough to relive it. Not even in memory, Miss. If I may, please allow me to work. I have to keep busy."

"But," Simone said, listening to the pain in Danielle's voice. "I don't understand. No one mentioned the birth, and Mother said you attacked her. I saw the bruises. Did you attack her?"

"I realize that I hardly answer any of your queries when we meet, but I cannot speak on this. I'll accept whichever punishment you have for me, but I beg you to look for answers elsewhere."

"You look pale and not yourself. And why are your hands covered in bandages? Your eyes—it's as if your soul has fled, Danielle. What has happened? —"

"There you are, you two," said Rosezelle hastily grabbing Danielle by the arm. "I beg your pardon Ma'am; your father is looking for you and Danielle's assistance is needed. Please, tell no one of her whereabouts."

"Why?" Simone asked.

"Your father awaits, Mademoiselle," said Rosezelle. Simone sought answers within their faces, but neither revealed their truth.

Finally, Simone retreated, and Danielle worked harder to move within the walls of the mansion, working, storing food for Lettie, Maman, and herself, and resting when she needed, in preparation to escape.

Twenty

Demetre yelled out after his daughter, who raced away from him down the grassy hills on horseback. "Simone!" He yelled, tapping his thoroughbred to gallop after them, but they had reached a distance too far to catch up with no signs of Simone slowing down. As the sun was setting, he only hoped that she would return home before nightfall. But after receiving the answers to her questions about Danielle and Etiennette, and seeing the turmoil of horror and sadness looming upon her face, he was not certain.

Simone slowed her horse, Cinnamon, once she reached Le Etoile Creek, dismounting and allowing the horse to drink from the trickling water that would have been relaxing had she not been distraught. She promised Demetre that she would keep his words a secret from those unaware of the occurrence, even family. She wanted to find Danielle but didn't know how she could face her, to tell her, a slave, that she was sorry for the lifetime of pain she must endure. Even after her father's warnings, Simone wished she had never asked as many questions as she did and never left New Orleans, where at least she would be learning to build strength after ending courtship with her first love. She composed herself as best she could and readied herself to return to the plantation, without the power to stop thinking of Danielle the whole way.

When early evening fell two hours later and Simone had not returned for supper, Emile and Demetre set out to look for her along with Phillipe, who rerouted them by suggesting a different direction away from the plantation and Danielle's cabin where Simone was visiting.

The door of the Soileau mansion slowly opened to reveal an exhausted, red-faced Simone who had no desire to hastily speak to Etiennette or Bella when they asked her whereabouts. "I'm fine, Mother. I'm fine, Bella," is all she said. She refused food and started up the stairs with Bella following behind.

Soon, the men returned, rushing through the door, checking to see if Simone had found her way back. "She's here," Etiennette said faintly. "She is heading to bed. What is the matter with her?"

Demetre falsified, "Lest we forget that she is still nursing a broken heart?"

Bella stared worryingly at Simone, who slipped on her nightgown with the assistance of Corrine. "Thank you," Simone said almost in a whisper as Corrine nodded and left to go home for the evening.

"Sweet cousin," said Bella, rising from the chaise to hold the hands of Simone. "Did something happen today?"

Simone answered, "I have never been unsure as to how I should feel, Bella. But right now, I am straddling every emotion possible, and my heart is not adorned with armor for what I've learned today." Despite her promise to Demetre, she shared all that he told her. However, she kept to herself that she wept in the presence of Danielle as the two hugged in her cabin, Danielle, having no tears left to cry. Simone did not talk about the encouraging words Danielle had given her regarding school, life, and the advice to "humble yourself before your heart." Simone scoffed with a smile, "You sound as if I'm never returning." Danielle remained silent.

For the first time since entering the cabin, Simone looked around, seeing strips of cloth pushed under the bed, onions in the pockets of clothing draped across her chair. While she did not question any of those items or know to do so, she saw that Danielle was peering into her eyes and onto her face, as if she were memorizing every detail of Simone's features. Although difficult to keep to herself, Simone could not tell Bella that Danielle and Simone locked eyes. As a part of their connection since childhood, they had an unsettling understanding that this was likely the last moment they would see one another.

"You know, Bella," said Simone. "I think I want to reside in New Orleans. I may even accept someone's advice of showing my heart a little humility."

* * *

Before the sun could barely peek through the balding trees, the male slaves systematically moved like machines to load the hogsheads and 75-pound burlap sacks of sugar from the boiling house onto the wagon. The sugar transporter squinted at his inventory sheet as his driver held a torch near for light. "Philippe!" yelled the overseer, Thurman. "Your feet bolted to the ground, boy? Get your ass over here and help these niggers with this sugar. Stop starin' and start rollin' a barrel!" The hogsheads, marked *Soileau Plantation, Soileau & Sons*, thundered up the tilted wooden planks as Philippe kept a watchful eye on the speed at which they moved. He found one branded with an S that had not yet boarded and tapped twice on the lid as he paired with an unsuspecting young man who helped with the load. Philippe opted to handle the third barrel among the bunch to have the brand and worked to help load it. "Careful with those sacks!" Jeremiah yelled to the slaves as they stacked them onto the wagon next.

As the loading of the products was complete, he saw Corrine watching and moving in the distance towards the mansion as the sun was beginning to light her path. She had already said her goodbyes earlier in the twilight with Danielle in her cabin, along with Lettie and Genevieve. Phillipe waited for them in the darkness near the boiling house. Hugging each of them, Corrine encouraged Genevieve and Alette with compliments of bravery and assuring them of the short distance needed to travel until they were in the safest hands.

"Be your best," she whispered to Lettie. "And remember the wise words of your Papa; when your enemy tries to define you on your behalf, lift your head and know who you are. I'll hug your doll baby every day. I love you, sweet girl."

Perhaps the hardest to let loose was Danielle. Holding her tightly and crying, Corrine's words would not escape her body. Danielle, through her sorrow, could only whisper her words in song:

> *How do you repay a well that gives, that loves, that flows,*
> *For only God knows,*
> *How one blesses others with a drink, restoring life anew,*
> *An endless chain of blessings, a destiny full of gratitude.*

Danielle squeezed Corrine tighter, "When I reach freedom, I will find you. I love you. Be well, sister."

Once the family arrived behind the boiling house, Philippe helped them crawl through a hole of loose bricks and into three padded hogsheads with breathing holes covered with a dark flap of cloth on the inside to disguise the hole. They were provided with a flask of water, an apple, and hush puppies. With only minutes before the overseers were to arrive, the three scrunched down for Phillipe to place a compartment layered with sugar snugly within the barrels and the lids on top. "Until we meet again," he whispered before exiting the house through the hole and replacing the bricks.

The transporters drove the wagon to the front entrance of the mansion, where they spoke with the Soileau brothers and handed them a copy of the sugar distribution schedule. "I thought I smelled onions back there," one of the transporters told Demetre as they started on the path. "I just hope it ain't the sugar." Corrine watched as the wagon picked up speed. She took several deep breaths as they rode out of the gates and whispered, "May the Almighty protect and grant you your right to freedom."

Alette lifted the flap of material inside the barrel and saw that sunlight sprinkled onto the trees and road behind the wagon as they trotted into town. The men delivered three bags of sugar to the general store and a bag to the drug store. Danielle could tell by the bumpiness in the road and the broadening smell of earth and algae that they were near the bayou. She soon heard the sloshing of water and the voices of men in Creole and English. "Alright, boys," one of the transporters said to the watermen. "Hurry up and get these on the boat. I want this shipment to the levee early, not on time, understand me?"

"Yes, sir," said Chat. With the bed of the wagon facing the flatboat, several rivermen helped to unload the bags and later directed the hogsheads onto the watercraft using the planks. Alysaundre worked swiftly but gently, with his head down, as he recognized the men from his time on the Soileau Plantation, but did not want to take a chance at the possibility of being placed by them.

"Fine day, Mr. Fortier, Mr. Guidry," said a man emerging from the boat, smoking a cigar. His white skin, freckles, and sandy red hair stood out from the group of ebony, brown, and "beige" bustling men he supervised. He approached the men and the wagon.

"Fine day, Mr. Santee!" Mr. Fortier repeated to the freckled man. "I didn't expect to see you for this mission. You usually pop up around the northern bayous." The men shook hands.

"Well, you know," said the freckled Mr. Santee. "All missions are important, but folks have been giving my boys a hard time lately, causing them to get behind in their routes and deliveries. So, I thought I'd come along and see that they get to the levee on time. So, if you'll excuse me, men, we'd better get goin'."

"Well, we won't hold you," said Mr. Fortier. "Alright, Guidry, let's move on out."

The transporters wheeled away, leaving the rivermen to secure the sugar on the boat before drifting away from the land and into the

Bayou Vermilionville. Alysaundre guarded the three hogsheads with the "S" brandings as he looked around for any white faces that might be peering from the distance. The men worked quickly to drive the boat down the Vermilionville Bay, where the crew seemed to exhale in unison when reaching an area of safety. Alysaundre, Chat, and a man wearing a large hat and covering rushed over the barrels, each quickly removing the lids with crowbars. The man in the hat looked inside. He removed his hat, extended his hand, and a smile. "There's my Songbird," said Alphonse.

Genevieve and Lettie soon rose out of the hogshead with hesitation and eyes sensitive to daylight. Danielle followed. Alphonse lifted her out of the barrel, damp with sweat, and held her as their spirits whispered to one another, perhaps more articulately than words of any language ever could. Each of them squeezing tighter, Alphonse's heart pounding in Danielle's ear, his hand caressing her hair and later bunching it in his palm, thinking of all she had been through and the frustration that he could not protect her from it. He then cradled her face in his hands and kissed her, their breaths quivering.

Although they were safe for the moment, floating in the direction of Cote Blauch Bay, Aly was too nervous to speak as he embraced Genevieve and Alette. The little girl looked up at him, "Thank you," she said, "for coming to get us. And I love you so much." Aly inspected her scar with his eyes, catching himself from presenting any expressions of anger and disappointment, but Alette had already noticed and touched her face in response. "Oh. This," she said.

"I already know what happened," Aly said. "We've all got scars. You and me just happen to show ours on the outside. But this, here on your face will never diminish your beauty. Nor is it to be seen as a reminder of hatred, but one of strength and of life. Do you understand?" Lettie answered with a smile.

As a few crew members steered the boat, Alphonse introduced the man known to the transporters as Mr. Santee. However, to Lettie,

Danielle, and Genevieve, he revealed his full identity as his cousin, Udonis Santee, an octoroon within the family's tree, who enjoyed the advantages of passing as a white man. Having some maritime experience, allowed him to be recruited and apprenticed by Alphonse, particularly when Alphonse apprehended a challenge for an all-colored crew to cross borders or complete jobs without harassment or the threat of extra fees and imprisonment.

Alphonse quickly spattered nautical instructions to the men. He also enforced directions regarding keeping their stowaways and any knowledge of them under surveillance, if or when they were to encounter anyone with queries. He informed the women onboard that while they are in a known safe spot within the river now, it will not be as such in various locations during the journey. There should be little movement from them, he explained, as they might stand out to those unseen persons upon the shores. "Whether it is their business or not," said Alphonse, "there are always eyes upon us." Aly struggled with the idea that the women would eventually have to climb back into the hogsheads, particularly his mother, whom he had witnessed being treated like cattle and now, the plantation produce. Genevieve voiced that she did not mind if it meant bringing her family closer to safety and freedom.

By dusk, Alphonse had ordered Chat to take the Creole skiff kept on the craft and a few coins to a nearby maroon community in search of any additional food while they were in the area. They had rationed enough food for the journey but always felt it better to have more than just enough. He found it especially beneficial to have a stash of their own and one for any riverboat Cajuns who surfaced their true need for food with threats and thievery. Chat returned to the boat with an abundance of vegetables, fish, frog legs, oysters, and a smile. "I knew you had a way with words," said Alphonse, helping him onto the boat, "but I didn't expect you to talk your way into their harvest." Throughout the years, Chat had befriended many of those within the community and found that some of the ladies expressed their generosity by keeping his belly full.

By night, they pushed their way through Cote Blauch Bay and exited Morrison's Cut. The crew of 7 were assigned shifts for resting, steering, and keeping watch. But like Alphonse, Alysaundre chose to remain awake with such precious cargo in tow. He placed thick woolen blankets over the women as they slept huddled in a corner of the boat among the bags of sugar. He placed a burlap sack over them as added protection from the elements. He stepped back and stared at them without noticing Chat studying him. "You feel it?" said Chat, sitting on a crate, shaving wood into a sharp stick. Aly looked puzzled. Chat elaborated, "You know, the burden of having a family, but not knowing how you would ever get along without one? Every man with a family has felt that punch to the gut at least once in his life."

"How would you know?" asked Aly. "I thought you didn't have a family."

"Ain't never said that. Had a woman—a good woman, who was carrying my seed and everything. Master said under the eyes of God, he would never separate us. I reckon he thought God wasn't watching 'cause soon as he fell on his financial knife, he sold my girl. Ain't found her since. Don't know if she alive, or how my lil' boy or girl looks. I just know he or she would be around your lil' sister, Lettie's age. I look at you with your family—even as you're helping them to freedom, and all I can say is, 'that's one lucky bastard.'"

Through the night and the light fog, the crew and runaways traveled through the Bayou Lafourche. Genevieve had awoken before dawn with a rush of anxiety, for she knew that she and the other field hands would be on their way to work during this time. She saw Alphonse tying knots with rope, and he motioned for her to come near, so as to not wake Danielle and Alette. "Good morning, Madòm," Alphonse whispered. He pointed to a basket of salted fish, bread, and a cup of water. "You're going to need your strength this morning." He saw that she was cold and found a blanket to wrap around her.

"You're a good man," Genevieve said. "How far do we have until we reach the steamboat?"

"We should reach New Orleans by mid-afternoon." When he saw that Genevieve remained standing, looking around in nervousness, he tried to calm her, "It's perfectly normal to be uneasy right now."

"Uneasy?" said Genevieve. "I'm petrified. By now, they must know we're gone. I don't know if those are horse hooves I feel pounding or my own heart. And I can almost hear those hounds barking on our trails now—oh Jesus, I don't think I can do this. And to bring my girls along—"

"You can," he reassured, gripping both of her hands. "We have a full day ahead of them, and if Mr. Soileau chooses to place an ad in the paper, which he will, it will take until tomorrow for it to be printed and distributed. You must stick with the plan. Don't let fear reroute you. Besides, Monsieur Edmond would be disappointed." The wind of his words was enough to lift her head.

She retrieved the food and began to eat. Alphonse joined her. He soon shifted to look at Danielle and saw that Genevieve was smiling. "It is as if you were meant to be part of our family at the start. You've given her heart a million reasons to beat," she said.

Alphonse looked out onto the lake. The sun barely started to peek onto the water and create a golden path. "I feel the same for your daughter." He said finally. "At my mother's ball, she sang a song that instantly took over my whole being, where its meaning and her presence allowed me to have definition in life, and has since been a part of my journey. She's the melody I didn't know I needed to hear, and the chorus I want to hum for the rest of my life. She is enough."

Genevieve smiled at his confession, satisfied at knowing that freedom and happiness were within reach for her daughter.

Alysaundre arrived and kissed his mother on the cheek. Next, he gently woke his sisters with orders to eat and prepare to climb into the hogsheads until safe to emerge, as the canal was more populated than the previous bodies of water, and risking the possibility of being seen by one person could ruin the mission.

The crew carried on, saying very little among each other, and even less when boats of white men were near to tauntingly ask questions, and steal food or supplies, but were diverted upon the appearance of Udonis, who demanded that they disperse.

By midday, and after occasional exits and re-entry of the barrels, Danielle heard the thunderous population of peddlers, sailors, and passengers along the levee in New Orleans, just as she'd remembered during her last visit. Her heart raced when hearing the hundreds of men yelling various things, but only making out the commands to "lift higher" and "dépêchez-vous!" She then felt the boat bump and cease in a forward motion.

"Songbird. Zozo shantè," Danielle heard Alphonse whisper close to the breathing hole. "This is it. The steam packet is but a few kilometers. Alysaundre will be nearby to get you out. You know what to do from there. I love you, and I'll see you soon."

"I love you, too," she whispered back.

Alysaundre briefly whispered to Alette and Genevieve before they were rocked and rolled off of the boat. Even over the crushing of the gravel, Danielle heard a familiar voice above her talking to Udonis. "Get those sacks of sugar, boys," barked Jeffrey. "Steady, now. Put them in my wagon. Hurry it up. Are your darkies always this slow?" he asked Udonis.

"They're precise," defended Udonis. "If you want your products handled with the greatest care, you best let me handle them and give direction where I see fit. You'll have your sugar stacked and ready for sale shortly." Jeffrey swelled with irritation.

In their large hats and working clothes, Alphonse and Alysaundre, Chat, and others kept their heads down and rolled the barrels past and toward the ship's attendant guarding the main deck. They pointed to Udonis and showed the attendant their freedman papers and an inventory list. The attendant pointed to the sugar, and the rivermen carved open the lids, revealing the sugar compartments. He inspected the sugar, then nodded once and motioned for them to proceed onto the main deck to store the cargo.

Jeffrey lashed at Udonis, "This product is the livelihood of my family and me. And when it is in jeopardy of being outsold by others who will arrive at any moment, I will speak to your niggers any way that I see fit. Don't tell me how to proceed with my business, or I'll see to it that this is your last day of being contracted."

Udonis saw that Chat had emerged, giving him eye contact and a quick nod of the head. Udonis gave Jeffrey a side-mouthed smirk but was careful not to insult Jeffrey any further. "Yes, sir." He said, placing his hat on his head. "Alright, boys!" Udonis said to the crew, "You heard the man. Let's get this sugar-loaded so this fine gentleman can get his orders." Jeffrey's nose lifted a bit higher as he waited for the completion of the transaction.

The steamboat's horn blew as the final warning of its departure, and Udonis watched Alphonse emerge on the deck with his paid ticket and papers in hand. Both Chat and Udonis were discreet, trying not to stare at the family they hoped would meet freedom in Ohio. Chat would especially miss Aly, whom he adopted as his brother, and now witnessed presenting his ticket as a passenger to the agent. Aly tried desperately to hide his anxiety, along with Alette, whose gloved hand he held like that of a father. The dress she wore, of a previous passenger who had long forgotten it on the ship, was almost a perfect fit, much like the coat Alette timidly carried and hugged to the right side of her face to hide her scar. Her forged papers were handed back to Alysaundre as they were granted access to the ship.

The lively music, cheers, and laughter of guests of a nearby showboat blared as Jeffrey carted off with his merchandise in tow, with, unknowingly, Danielle and Genevieve two decks above him dressed as chambermaids. Escorted by the steward, Mr. Wilks, the women were instructed to appear as if they were within their rightful place of employment, but to never offer attention to themselves. "Do not work too closely," the tall Negro Creole man whispered to them as they quickly changed behind crates below deck. "Simply give passengers proper service. You may keep any gratuity offered. Speak when spoken to, but do not say much. Pardon my vulgarity, but your papers must remain close to your bosoms. They are borrowed from free negro women who were paid handsomely for you to use them."

"Yes, sir," said Genevieve. "Thank you."

"You're welcome. And your little daughter will and must remain at Alysaundre's side at all times. He knows what to do."

Police patrolled the docks, giving hard looks to those working, free or enslaved, as the steamboat began to move. A paperboy weaved in and around the crowd of merchants selling eggs and loaves of bread. He eventually stopped to sell one to Chat, who nudged Udonis and pointed at the advertisement and reward for three missing female slaves of the Soileau plantation, particularly one that may be recognized as the girl in the Soileau & Sons sugar ad art.

Twenty One

The Mississippi River

Traveling the high brown waters of the Mississippi brought about great excitement from the boat's local and out-of-state passengers, some of whom were visiting, others looking to make Ohio their new home. For several minutes, guests stood at the banisters gazing out at the river, the artery that connects both north and south in trade and opportunity. To know all that the Mississippi had witnessed and heard, some thought could increase or diminish one's respect for humanity.

As a part of the captain's orders in his need to prevent disease from entering his ship, immigrants were not permitted onto the large steam packet, except for some of the regularly employed crew members. The tight schedule did not allow for time to remove deceased or sickly passengers who could potentially spread illness to his crew.

Danielle worked assiduously with her head down, blending in with the other colored chambermaids, only acknowledging one another in eye contact and gesture. Her productivity slowed when cleaning staterooms with open doors and hearing the music from the saloon band. Her subconscious hums to the lull of the piano and flute soon formed words that unknowingly escaped her lips. Soon, inquiries from passers-by and invisible musical notes floated into the chambers, followed by peeks of curiosity to find out "Who is providing that beautiful singing?" Danielle immediately stopped and finished her work before closing the door to the deck and slipping out through the cabin door, disappointed that she could not escape in song for the rest of the trip.

Following Mr. Wilks' advice, Danielle and Genevieve separated from one another, but just enough that they would know if the other needed assistance in any capacity. Danielle had become skilled in dodging the advances of white men as they reappeared in their rooms, some drunken, most sober. Both women learned ways to avoid the casual groping and hand sweeps of the ship's passengers. However, occasionally, an unsuspecting hand could be felt across their backsides. On the second day of the journey, Danielle polished the banisters in the early morning when a man wandering the decks with his wife and looking at her as she spoke, reached and touched Danielle's behind, never taking his eyes away from his wife nor looking back at Danielle's embarrassment.

Upon completing the cleaning of one of the chambers, Danielle stepped out to breathe in the cool November air. Just as she wished to feel her husband, he appeared on the lower deck, walking and paying close attention to every detail and action on the ship. Feeling her eyes on him, he looked up and found her. Her light smile let him know that she was well, but her eyes told him that she needed him...badly. Alphonse signed to his wife; *Freedom is near.*

"You there, girl," said a female voice behind Danielle, "come and make my bed." Danielle turned to the petite curly blonde. "Well, come on," she said, snapping her fingers. Danielle entered and began making the bed while the woman dressed for the day behind the folding room divider. "Help me into this dress," the woman ordered as she referred to the pastel green morning dress hanging on the divider. Danielle did as she was told. The woman reached for her hat, humming as she placed it upon her curls. Danielle wished she could trade places with the woman at that moment, who was free in every way possible—humming when Danielle could not, wearing beautiful attire, and waiting to be escorted by a gentleman or simply dine in the saloon.

"I know it's not traditional," said the woman, adjusting her hat. "But I do wish women could wear colors other than pastels. I've always enjoyed how I look in black. But I would hate to have to wait until there was a death to do so." The woman picked up her purse and reached into it, handing Danielle a coin. "Here you are. I do hope we meet again."

"Merci, Mademoiselle," said Danielle as she left the room with money in her possession for the first time.

Alphonse knew and accepted that men of color remained on the lower deck. However, being a passenger aboard a steamship as a husband whose wife had experienced so much took an exceptional toll on him. But he was comforted in knowing that she was only one deck above with Genevieve and Mr. Wilks not far away.

Within their first moment on the packet, Alysaundre and Alphonse scrambled to set up sleeping arrangements within the quarters near that of the crew for their group to remain together and privy to any happenings that might involve the ship or other passengers. Lacking bugs and unidentifiable stains, the bunks were nicer than others that Alphonse had seen. Yet, the smells of unbathed fellow travelers and salted pork circulated the deck, often mixing with the aroma of the fish courses and vegetables from the grand saloon. While some of the guests brought onboard their own food to cook or prepare, others like the Soileaus and Santees packed light and purchased food from the rafters and food boats selling to steamers and people aboard other watercrafts making a journey along the river. Aly had underestimated the amount of food that Lettie could devour, but was happy that he had the means to provide for her.

Just as quickly as they learned the culture of the boat on day one, and the ways of their deck mates, Aly and Alphonse gaged the gamblers from the typical passengers. As they did on the ports, docks, and levee, they avoided the many games of chance. Like Alphonse, Alysaundre wore a money belt hidden beneath his long shirt. Alysaundre heavily protected his little sister from potentially dangerous or "handsy" guests. He wanted desperately to sneak to the upper decks; however, the surveillance from guards was unyielding in the need to keep the classes and races separate. During day-to-day activities, the opportunity to check on Danielle and Genevieve's well-being presented itself as they passed by one another. Alette held back her desire to talk, reach for, or exchange a familiar look with them, but Genevieve's heart lightened at each glance that she was able to see her children at least twice daily.

"Ah, shit," muttered a deck passenger as he swatted his rolled-up newspaper at a mouse running out of the men's washroom. The animal did not get far from the paddle wheel before the man bopped the mouse and picked it up by the tail, throwing it overboard, and tossing the paper behind crates. Alysaundre watched as the agitated man adjusted his suspenders and his testicles before heading to the other end of the deck. Surprised to see a newspaper on the lower deck and a person who could read it, Alysaundre quickly retrieved it. He shuffled through the classified section of the *New Orleans Chronicles,* where he found fugitive slave ads. He clenched the paper upon seeing bold letters that seemed to lunge at him from the page:

> *$300 REWARD*
>
> *RAN AWAY, from the subscriber,*
>
> Mr. Demetre Soileau and his lawful wife, were three **NEGRO WENCHES** who escaped from the Soileau plantation, all related. Alette, child wench about 8 years of age, fair complexion, stands at about 4'9 feet, has a long scar down one side of her face. Genevieve, the mother wench, about 40 years, brown complexion, medium build, about 5'8, dark brown eyes, bow-legged, has a crooked pinky finger, a grey streak in her hair as a result of a birthmark. Danielle Soileau, is said to have a likeness on the Soileau & Sons sugar and molasses advertising art. She is of 18 years, light brown to fair complexion, curly brown hair to the waist, petite frame, 5'7 in height, eyes hazel, talented at singing. They may be in search of a sibling to the daughters, Alysaundre, recently sold and may be working as a riverman. All mentioned speak French and English. Reward and expenses will be paid upon the safe return of all three. Offer will be abolished if property is returned damaged and the law will be called upon. $50 will be given for any information as to who aided the runaways.
>
> D. Soileau

Aly showed the publication and ad to Alphonse, who removed the entire section of the paper and ripped it in secret, tossing it into the river. Alphonse then recruited the assistance of Mr. Wilks to discard the classified page of the newspapers that contained the advertisement, or any abandoned paper that was located on the ship's upper decks.

Opportunity struck when the horn of a rival steamer with trophied antlers displayed on the boiler deck sounded its horn, challenging the

SS River Runner to a race. Passengers on the main and boiler deck cheered on the captain, and most crowded to one side of the ship, bantering with the passengers of the rival steamer. Working on opposite ends of the ship, Mr. Wilks, Danielle, and Genevieve retrieved every unaccompanied Louisiana newspaper while the guards were either cheering themselves or spacing out passengers to even the weight on the ship. Danielle and Genevieve had no choice but to assume that the papers were local. They passed the folded newsprints to Mr. Wilks to temporarily hide in crates in preparation for destruction. When time allowed, he discreetly slipped them to Aly or Alphonse to destroy in the wood burner.

***

"Grandmommy," said Charles, "no one suspected anything was strange about missing papers or sections?"

"I'm sure they did," said Alette. "But they never suspected us." She shifted in her conversation. "The trip was a cold, long 6 days, but worth it. We docked slightly east of Cincinnati from the Ohio River. If Maman could have hugged Mr. Wilks in public, she would have. She returned to him the borrowed passes through a subdued handshake and teary eyes. A colored man we didn't know days before risked his job and his life to help us escape.

"We each held items that had been abandoned on the ship (trunks, hat boxes, and other cases), appearing as though we were assisting the white people who were headed in the same direction. Dodging guards and blending in with the coils of Negroes and whites at the pier, we finally made it to the end of the dock and further up the road where we were met by three men in button-down overcoats, two colored, one white. They shook hands with Alphonse and smiled. 'Gentlemen,' Alphonse said to the men, 'this is my wife, Danielle Santee, and her family—*my* new family,' and one by one, he introduced us. Alphonse introduced the Negroes as Mr. Lopes and Mr. Eugene. The white man was Mr. Maynard. They removed their hats. 'Everyone,' Mr. Lopes said to us, Welcome to Ohio. Welcome to freedom.' The men were members of a long-standing abolitionist group that received funding to help free enslaved blacks for over ten years. Alphonse had been connected to them through a friend soon after he decided he wanted to marry Danielle. The men had been advisors to Alphonse and even assisted him in establishing an extension of his business and a permanent residency in Ohio. I knew he loved my sister, but I didn't realize the extent of it until that moment.

"We were driven off in a two-horse wagon, down roads surrounded by tall buildings and hard-working people selling things or just trying to get to their destinations. The steel giant locomotives were especially mesmerizing, and I had so many questions to ask once I could articulate them. I had never seen, felt, or smelled anything like it, and I couldn't get enough.

"Whenever I could, I caught moments of the conversation among the adults. We were told to stay away from the docks and police at any cost, that there were people looking to kidnap Blacks and take them down South for a profit. Alphonse knew where we were headed, but before any of us could ask, the men said they were taking us to the home of someone in the organization who houses newly freed colored persons. There, they would groom us into the ways of society, find Danielle and Maman jobs, if they wanted, and me, a school...a real school where I would be encouraged to read and taught to write. Aly could stay there when in town until he was established but would continue to work for Alphonse while Danielle would go to finally live with her husband as they had always wanted. 'Awaiting your arrival,' Mr. Eugene said, 'is Mr. Edmond Soileau.' Neither Maman, my siblings, nor I could breathe.

"Maman held her hand to her heart and said, 'You mean...he's here? On the same soil?'

'He is,' Mr. Maynard said. 'Made it in two days ago. He's extremely anxious to see you, but he has been advised to remain indoors for the time being and rest.'

'The last we were told,' Mr. Lopes said, 'is that he slept almost a full day.'

"He too had traveled on a ship on which he barbered and snuck off the boat, blending in with the crowd on the pier. The men were there to greet him and guide him to the home where we could not wait to reside. Aly pressed his hand on Maman's shoulder in comfort as we traveled north within Hamilton County. Finally, we had reached the home and were greeted by a warm young Negro couple. They introduced themselves as Annie and Paul Fritz. We entered the home, and as the door closed behind us, Mr. Fritz stated to his new house guests, 'Someone has been waiting for you.'"

****

Edmond emerged from one of the bedrooms in a near jog. Lettie broke past everyone, running into his arms, wailing. "Daddy! J manke vou! Reste a mon toujour! Oh, I missed you! Stay with me always!"

"My little Lettie," Edmond cried before looking up at his family, gathered before him at once. Aly and Genevieve raced to hug him, nearly knocking him over. When Aly and Lettie let him loose, Genevieve remained weeping, her arms wrapped tightly around him, patting his back and head to ensure that he was not a figment of her dreams taunting her heart. She pulled away to look at him, studying every feature and body intently, making certain no harm or anything unrecognizable had made its way to his face. Edmond cried uncontrollably, squeezing his eyes tightly before letting his tears fall onto his wife's shoulders. He then kissed her hard. And it was reciprocated. "You have come back to me," said Genevieve. She rubbed his coarse hand onto her cheek and kissed it before sliding over to reveal Danielle, also in tears.

With her arm wrapped around Alphonse's, her husband led her to her father. The father and daughter exchanged stares. They had only imagined what they would say to one another if reunited in flesh, but at this moment, words escaped them. Finally, Danielle recalled and spoke, "I can admit that I did not know you as I thought I did. I am sorry for not knowing all that it took for you to raise your head every day as a man and as a father; for not knowing how much you love us. Aly was right, you *are* a warrior, and I couldn't see that. I am sorry for my words that night and how they made you feel. I pray and I plead that the wounds I caused did not cut so deep that you could not forgive me, Pápa."

"You," Edmond said in the raspy voice that Danielle had missed greatly, "you were forgiven long ago, TiFiy." He stepped closer and allowed his daughter to fall into his arms, where she sobbed in relief. While holding her, Edmond extended his hand to Alphonse, squeezing it in thanks.

Alysaundre noticed that the abolitionists had taken several steps back to witness, with gratification, the family cleave onto one another once more. Soon, Alphonse had joined them in watching the reunion. Aly shook each of their hands but halted once he approached Mr. Maynard. Staring Aly in the eyes, Mr. Maynard slowly extended his hand, allowing Aly to take his time before shaking it.

Danielle was reluctant to leave the home for the evening after finally seeing her father, as was Edmond after learning about her conception with Monsieur Soileau and the loss of a grandchild he never saw growing in the womb. However, Mr. Lopes and Eugene escorted Danielle and Alphonse to his new land.

The rows of trees stood at attention on both sides of the road leading to Alphonse's brick home as if welcoming him and his new bride. Once inside and alone, Alphonse lit the lanterns and candles one by one. Finally able to see Danielle's face, he noticed that she was crying. Even during the ride home, he allowed her to be at one with her thoughts. But in their new dwellings, Alphonse was concerned with her silence and tears.

Looking around at the lavish residence and furnishings and all that was prepared for her arrival, she cried harder at the open bible sitting on a small table below a crucifix, its page revealing a family tree and the name she recognized as her own, thanks to Lettie. And while she could not read the name on the branch next to it, nor the one beneath her own, she knew it belonged to Alphonse and Ruby. "Baby," Alphonse said, gently moving her chin toward his direction. "You want to be back with your family, is that it? Is that the reason for your tears?"

She shook her head, "We are free."

Twenty Two

Lafayette Parish, Louisiana

For a moment, the ticking of the grandfather clock on the main floor of the Soileau mansion calmed the slaves and the family Soileau within the home until sporadic explosions of shotguns and cracked clay shook them from their activities. In the kitchen, Bella helped knead the dough as she and Simone learned to bake a pie from Corrine and Rosezelle. The absence of the shooting caused them to look up at one another with joy. However, their short-lived elation turned to disappointment as the shooting started up again, rattling their nerves. "Simone," pleaded Bella, "why can't you get him to cease shooting practice? He's been out there for hours."

"Papa won't listen to me," said Simone. "He's furious. I don't know that he will return to his normal state until Danielle and the others return."

"And you don't know where they might have gone—where Danielle may have fled?" Simone simply shrugged and shook her head before jolting in surprise at the loud boom.

Demetre shouted in anger before reloading the gun himself, as he did not trust the slaves to do so. Several weeks had passed since he received a letter from a buyer notifying him of a peculiar hogshead received. The buyer stated that "at first glance, it appeared to have a huge bullet hole blasted through it, which one would believe had emptied the sugar." The letter went on to describe how deceptive the lid appeared and questioned the ethics of Soileau & Sons. A second letter from a buyer knew immediately that it was the workings of a fugitive slave. He stated in writing that "if Soileau & Sons could not get a handle on their devilish Negroes, I will be forced to patron a rival company that will see to it that troubles on the plantation do not bleed into the businesses of their clients." And a third in Ohio demanded a new shipment of the product, and a free hogshead full of sugar for the inconvenience.

The Soileau brothers continued to work through the consumer issues. Although each slave was insured, Demetre spitefully created a lawsuit with the shipping company and placed ads in Ohio and every state along the Mississippi River. Only after all ads had been placed did Demetre learn that Edmond had fled as well, and the additional income from his leasing was terminated.

Perhaps the height of Demetre's fury was aimed at Danielle for her ungratefulness and for disregarding his favor toward her. Frustrated that his focus remained on Danielle rather than the hours he had until his daughter returned to school and New Orleans for good, Simone confronted him in the parlor, away from the others.

With bourbon in his hand and a calmer spirit, Demetre looked up at the girl standing over him in a girlishly pink night robe. Her hair, previously in lush spirals, had fallen flat. He offered her a seat in gesture.

"I realize," started Simone sympathetically, "the last number of weeks have not been ideal, but as you know, I am leaving tomorrow and won't be returning."

"And I'll see you off," Demetre said solemnly, looking at his brown beverage and swirling it.

She stared at him. His posture slumped, his appearance, almost dazed. Simone's hurt turned into frustration, "Papa," she said. "I urge you to let this go."

"Why should I?" asked Demetre, "They're my property and I want them back."

"The mere fact that you knew to which I was referring suggests that you're obsessed with what you've lost. I understand that the business is failing, Papa, and I don't want this to be the cause of its demise."

"We have plenty of assets tucked away; your dowry and inheritance being two of them safe from depletion."

Simone's mouth dropped, "Papa, that is not the angle at which I turn. My worry is not of money for *my* future at this moment, but rather the future of this family and the business, especially if you carry forth with this lawsuit."

"Did Emile send you to speak to me? I don't recall you knowing anything about the affairs of Soileau & Sons, nor your knowledge of the lawsuit or the law, for that matter. I must say, you sound very intellectual, my dear."

"You sent me to expand my education, and now you're surprised that I have a mind? There's a lot you don't know about me, Papa. But what I *do* know is that everyone in all of Louisiana knows about the lawsuit; it is in the papers. Rather than being vindictive, perhaps your focus should be on the business rather than the true cause of your angst. You have less concern, if any, over the others who ran away and more over the loss of Danielle."

Demetre looked up from his glass. "Is my little girl giving me business advice—telling me what I *should* do?" he smirked. "'*Should*' is full of uncertainty and naivety. It exposes one's lack of commitment to accomplish something, Simone."

The girl snubbed her father's insult toward her, concentrating on her larger problem. "What's more concerning," she said, "is that you made your choice, Papa, and it's Danielle, just as it's always been. It's Danielle over Soileau & Sons, Danielle over your reputation...Danielle over me...but I've learned to accept it. And did you ever conclude that she had reason to run away?"

Demetre sat up slowly. "You talk as if you knew she was going to flee."

"I didn't know. But if I did, I would make no mention of it. As much as it pains me to say, your emotions toward her have plagued our family, and I fear that it will plague the legacy that my grandfather built. And for that, I'm glad she's gone."

"Do you know her whereabouts? Are you holding the secret in spite?"

"No, but you're consumed with a body who wants no part in the family she served. Wants no part in this life with you."

Demetre stood and walked to the open window, only able to see the darkness of the courtyard and the reflection of him and his daughter. "You know," he started, looking down into his bourbon, "aiding fugitive slaves is a legal offense."

"I have already told you, I have not—"

"You told them how to escape—"

"I did no such thing—"

"Your jealousy has led you to this, Simone?"

"Papa, stop it at once—"

"You admitted that you were glad that she is gone—"

"I am, and if honesty humbles me, I'm a little saddened."

"Child, do you even know what to feel?"

"I'm not a child! And I have every right to have feelings that toggle when it comes to Danielle. And yes, I celebrate that she fled! And if our lives should travel parallel, allowing her to also run into the arms of the one she loves, then I celebrate that too." Simone swallowed hard after she slipped words.

Demetre pivoted, "...the one she loves? Did she escape with a male slave—one from another plantation, perhaps? Did a man help her flee? Tell me!"

Simone swallowed hard again. "I don't know any details of her escape."

"But you know she is in love?"

Simone was disturbed by the eagerness in his eyes to know more. Blood rushed to his face during every second of Simone's silence. She thought about the disregard that he had for her mother as his wife, not just at this moment, but years earlier when all Simone wanted was for her father to look at Etiennette the way he looked at Danielle. All the smiles that should have been Simone's were passed over to his slave. "Yes," Simone answered with conviction. "Her heart belongs to another, and he has offered *his* in return." Demetre was seething, but Simone continued. "She is gone, Father. Let her be. I no longer need a companion, and you have plenty more servants to...help in the house. And as for the others, they have been loyal. Genevieve has served you and Grandfather well, even from the times that she served in his home. Had they been a powerful asset in the fields like the men, or offered in some form, the structure of Soileau & Sons, I could agree to their continued presence on the plantation. But to keep hold of them simply because they add harmony to a family body that you have been accustomed to for so long serves no purpose in any of our lives or livelihoods. Father, let them be."

Refusing to look at his daughter any further, Demetre turned to face the window once more. He waved his hand for her dismissal, but she lingered. When she saw that his bourbon was no longer appetizing to him and that he set the drink down on the desk among the newspapers, slave schedules, and bills, Simone backed away and departed.

The next morning, Simone was absent from the breakfast table but appeared when it was time to bid her family farewell. Bella and Emile had said their goodbyes before loading into the carriage. Etiennette promised to visit soon for an opportunity to bond. Simone's shifty eyes towards her mother's embrace revealed an unwillingness that made Etiennette cast a gaze at Demetre, who did not move to hug his daughter as he did normally. "Goodbye, Father," Simone said in a low voice, hoping his statuesque manner would subside. When it did not, she persisted and embraced him. She nearly cried when receiving stone pats on the back, and when he looked in a different direction. Simone cleared her throat and lifted the hem of her skirt to climb into the carriage with the assistance of Philippe. She wrapped herself in the blanket next to Bella, who comforted her as they rode off to catch their train back to New Orleans, keeping her promise to never return to the Soileau Plantation.

After a month of finding refuge in the Fritz home, Edmond and Genevieve found work in their free land, as a barber and laundress, while Lettie attended a school for colored children. Aly and Alphonse worked alternate weeks along the Ohio and Mississippi rivers before ending for the winter season.

With the help of her brother and husband, Danielle wanted to hear word regarding the well-being of her dear friend, Corrine. But not even the hay man knew of her recent whereabouts. Unsettled, Danielle vowed to somehow obtain news about the woman who had done so much for her.

Because Danielle once received stares and smiles that questioned her likeness in the Soileau & Sons advertising within the store that she and Alphonse frequented, she was advised to stay with her family in the Fritz home while her husband was away, where she learned all that she could about living a free life.

With the savings that Edmond acquired working on ships and his new working status, he had secured land and a home for his family using Alphonse's name until they were sure that advertisements of him and his family's disappearance had been forgotten. Constant glances over the shoulder became occasional for the family, but they learned from the abolitionist organization to blend while remaining alert.

Danielle had recognized her sweet sister, Lettie, again. Her beautiful smile and laughter completed the restoration of joy in her heart when the family gathered at her residence.

Surrounded by opened gifts near the fireplace, Nicholas, Udonis, Genevieve, and family shook their heads at the redundancy of affection between Danielle and Alphonse. With remnants of self-consciousness cloaked around her healed burns, Danielle smiled when she and Alphonse gently rubbed fingertips over the hands of one another as they conversed and cuddled on the sofa, often forgetting they had company. Genevieve quickly found playful ways to distract Edmond from intruding on his daughter and son-in-law. "Let them alone, dear heart. Did you forget that you approved the marriage between the two of them?" Genevieve whispered with a smile.

"I didn't, but my heart did," Edmond sighed, watching his "TiFiy," realizing what it meant to let go. "Come here, Lettie," he said, and requested to hold her until she grew old.

Later, as Danielle and Alphonse tried to teach Edmond, Lettie, and Genevieve carols, Aly sat alone and opened the letter he received two days prior, but had saved to read on Christmas day. The cursive words danced in melodic loops and slants on the parchment paper. His smile deepened as he read the heartfelt words of Trust as laughter filled the room and pleas for Edmond to stop bellowing incorrect lyrics were drowned by Aly's anxiety to respond in writing for the eighth time and to visit her for the fifth.

Looking out of the window in amazement, Danielle experienced peace as the fluffy white snow coated the land on which her two-story home rested. The surrounding trees and the red-bowed reef on her door were dusted with the cold white flakes that blew into the house as she opened the door to step onto the porch. Complaints of the cold from her family shattered around the sitting room, for Danielle to close the door. Alphonse smiled and followed her outside with a blanket. Approaching from behind, he saw the stillness in his wife that was almost picturesque had she not slowly warmed her arms, breathed in deeply with a smile, and closed her hazel eyes. She opened them again when feeling Alphonse wrap a blanket and his arms around the woman and kiss her neck. The two looked out at the snow, grateful to be together. Grateful to feel the same spirit. Danielle closed her eyes again, softly smiling once more, "God is here," she said lightly.

Twenty Three

Winter 1860

The Santee and Soileau families embraced the New Year, welcoming blessings, safety, and good luck. Alphonse and his brothers had been unsuccessful in trying to move their mother to the north as political disagreements bubbled among the states. Besides her stubbornness, Julia Santee feared starting anew, even with the offerings of her sons to help transfer her business of boarding houses.

A month prior, Demetre delivered a beautifully wrapped gift and a note to Etiennette at Evergreen Manor. The envelope's instructions said to open the letter first. However, excited at the presumed idea that Demetre was apologetic and would have her back, she gleefully opened the box which revealed a stone and a letter written with drunken penmanship. It read:

I cannot fix my pen to begin this letter with dear or anything of the sort, as I cannot associate those words with my feelings toward you. And perhaps it is your predictability or your greed that caused me to know that you would disobey the instructions given and reach for an item that you feel would benefit you greater than any words I have to express.

But because I care about your ability to return to your Christmas holiday, let me make this clear and brief. I wish to dissolve this marriage. I am not good for you, and the expiration on your goodness was several seasons ago. But quite possibly, the most wicked act between man and wife has not to do with the biblical sins related to matrimony, but to remain married for convenience, status, or business. Do not bother winding yourself with excitement thinking about what you will gain from our separation. The judge will make his wise decision, undoubtedly. As for Evergreen Manor, it will be sold. You may reside within it until that time.

Lastly, you may have noticed the gift within the box. May it represent the sentiments of our combined hearts. Merry Christmas!

Demetre

The servant retreated from the parlor soon after seeing the gift and moved deeper into the west wing of the house upon hearing Etiennette cry, then scream, and finally shatter a window with the heavy grey stone.

Days of tearful rage and influence from her closest friends caused Etiennette to expose details of their marriage to the judge, which later spilled to lingering journalists. Newspapers soon printed that Demetre Soileau, owner of Soileau & Sons products was in love with his slave and had denounced his wife of 19 years. "To add to the ignominy," one paper wrote, "the slave he loves is the very one printed in newspaper and product advertisements."

While the scandal heightened exposure to the reward offered for Demetre's fugitive slaves, it did nothing to benefit sales for Soileau & Sons. Consumers within the southern states chose to patronize competing sugar companies who purchased from other plantations, causing the Soileau brothers daily monetary loss and the disembodiment of the family structure. Alas, the 60-year business ceased, and assets were sold. First was part of his inheritance, Evergreen Manor. Next cattle, then paintings, and finally, a number of slaves. What small families there were on the plantation, were separated and sold at auction.

Even with financial tussles, Demetre was steadfast in his obsession to obtain Danielle again. He continued to place ads for her recovery in Louisiana and Ohio whenever his finances would allow, gradually lessening the reward as he had lessened his desire for Lettie and Genevieve's return, seeing it as two additional financial burdens. Until one day, he received a letter from a witness claiming to have seen Danielle numerous times.

The letter did not draw his attention immediately, as he had occasionally received several false claims of witnesses having seen her in almost the year that she had been missing. However, this letter, from the wife of a shopkeeper in Ohio, shared details about Danielle that he had not listed in the paper, such as the small birthmark on the back of her neck and the tune that she hummed when in deep thought. The letter revealed that Alette and Genevieve would often accompany her to the store. But perhaps the most startling chaperone was "a gentleman who is said to be her husband and goes by the name of Alphonse."

Demetre could scarcely continue the letter as his fury began to take over. He thought of all the occurrences that had taken place since she vanished and was angered at the humiliation he felt when envisioning Danielle's happiness. Every day, prior to the letter, his stomach dropped at the thought that she was no longer alive, and he mentally planned a proper memorial or burial for her—perhaps the first ever with a headstone in the slave cemetery. And at times, he would stand on the balcony, hoping that her silhouette would appear amid the northern fog of the field.

He was not only incensed by the care that he had for Danielle and her well-being but by the man who was said to be her husband. Simone's admonition to "let Danielle be," floated in his ears, particularly due to a love in Danielle's life. Demetre had never been a man to hope for anything but rather chose to draw his own outcome. In that moment, he hoped out of rage that the man mentioned in the letter as Danielle's husband, was not the same Alphonse that walked upon *his* land inquiring about *his* slave mistress and leaving as the owner of her brother. However, Demetre knew the answer. The encounter with Alphonse replayed in his mind, boiling over until he knocked over chairs and tables, destroying everything on top of them.

Amid the scattered papers, broken glass, and toppled furniture, Demetre, sat on the floor with his hands on his head, panting softly. Jen was too afraid to wait on Demetre, therefore, Thadieus asked his master about his welfare. "Let me clean this up for you," Thadieus said, reaching for broken pieces of the chair.

"Leave it," Demetre mumbled without looking up at him. "Prepare my clothing, horse and carriage. Jeremiah and I are going on a trip."

Twenty Four

The whistling of the locomotive and the tussling of passengers rushing to enter and exit the commuter train at the depot usually gave Demetre a thrill. But as he and his overseer, Jeremiah, had arrived in Ohio stone-faced with too much adrenaline to be exhausted from the long trip, they taxied to the store's address listed in the woman's letter.

A bell above the door jingled as Demetre and Jeremiah entered. A middle-aged woman with auburn hair looked up at the men after closing the curved glass display case. She noticed the high quality of the wool coat and gloves of one of the men and stood with a smile. "Good morning, gentlemen," she said. "May I assist you?"

Jeremiah walked around the store, observing products from tobacco to barrels of apples and other produce. "Mrs. Stanford," Demetre's face was unmoving, his voice unflavored. "Mrs. Georgina Stanford?"

"Yes," she said. Her smile, fading.

"I'm Demetre Soileau. Is your husband available for me to speak with him?"

"Mr. Soileau!" she smiled again with surprise, smoothing her blouse and hoop skirt. "Mr. Stanford is out getting jars of marmalade. Had I known you were coming, I would have asked him to wait and would have had food prepared for you after your long journey."

"When will you expect his return?"

"In a couple of hours. But if this is about your Negress that you're trying to catch, I can tell you more than he can."

"I prefer to speak with and do monetary transactions with men, Mrs. Stanford."

"I understand. That is the way of the land these days, unfortunately," said Mrs. Stanford. She watched Jeremiah pick up a block of soap wrapped with a light blue bow and sniff it. "Is he the marshal?" she wanted to know.

"No," Demetre responded. "He works for me."

"I see. Doing all the dirty work yourselves. Most people have their agents retrieve their slaves. Well, how about I tell you when to return to collect your wench, and I'll see to it that Mr. Stanford is present for me to receive the $350 offered in your advertisement?"

"$250. The ad says $200, sole for Danielle. And you have provided information regarding the one responsible for potentially aiding her, so an additional $50 will be rewarded."

"Very well," Georgina agreed. She pointed to the Soileau & Sons poster in the corner of the store, where hogsheads of sugar with a scooper inside sat before it. "The gal comes in every other Wednesday morning at around 11 o'clock. At the time of my letter, the mother had been accompanying her. And I believe you were offering a reward for her capture as well."

"I *was*, but I've realized that I am only interested in Danielle returning with me." Demetre paused. "And the male that chaperones...describe him," Demetre ordered. His eyes, unblinking and steady on the woman.

She began to describe him, using favorable words, briefly blushing, and ended it with, "That boy's name is Santee. Alphonse Santee."

Demetre clenched his fists and pursed his lips. "You've been most helpful." He motioned to Jeremiah that he was ready to leave.

"It's my pleasure," she said, smiling. "I may allow coloreds into my store, but I tolerate them. My allegiance is to my people, and I'll help in any way I can. See you tomorrow morning."

Demetre and Jeremiah returned to the store early the following morning after Demetre barely rested the night before at the Grand Central Hotel. Mr. Stanford, a husky, bearded man, was there to greet them along with his wife. He mentioned his awareness of the deal they had made and gave permission to continue the transaction.

Demetre nodded at the man, "Thank you," he said. "In spite of how the North feels about the South these days, I am happy to see that there are some people doing their duty within society."

Mrs. Stanford instructed the out-of-town visitors to wait around the back of the building if other customers attempted to intervene or if their presence upon entry caused Danielle to run. Demetre and the overseer did as they were told, waiting beside their rented horse and wagon, Jeremiah, with tightly twisted cloth and small shackles in hand. Georgina watched the door carefully, her heart jittering as customers entered and shopped.

"Excuse me, Mrs. Stanford," a woman said, approaching the counter and blocking Georgina's view of activities. The woman began to ask for Mrs. Stanford's opinion about two different hair products. Mrs. Stanford pushed through her frustration and smiled, offering her experience with each, and tried to look around the woman when she had an opportunity. As the customer lingered in conversation, Danielle entered the store, wearing a dark green bonnet. She was alone. Georgina looked at her husband, who nodded to her. The customer, still conversing, was now discussing her cat and all of its annoyances.

Danielle wasted no time selecting the items to place into her basket as Mr. Stanford quickly rang up two shoppers and sent them on their way, leaving the talkative woman and Danielle, who was approaching the counter. Mrs. Stanford interrupted the talker as Demetre and Jeremiah walked into the store, noticing Danielle, and slipping out of view into the back aisle. "Well, isn't that interesting, Mrs. Love," she grinned, "How about I leave you to shop, and you let Mr. Stanford, or I know if you have additional questions—Mrs. Santee, how are you on this fine day?" Looking perplexed, Mrs. Love turned to retrieve the remaining items on her list.

"I'm well, thank you," she said, unloading the items from her basket and onto the countertop.

"No, Mr. Santee this morning?"

"Not today," she smiled.

"Oh, well, the season must be coming to a close for him soon, is that correct?"

"Why yes," she said. "And I can hardly wait."

"Well, he'll be here before you know it." Georgina watched Mrs. Love take her items to Mr. Stanford, who swiftly calculated the products, totaling $3.00. Mrs. Love retrieved the coins in her purse, conversing while doing so. Georgina continued to speak with Danielle. "I do look forward to your little family expanding."

Danielle smiled politely and briefly looked down. "One day. Maybe. When I'm ready."

Mrs. Stanford totaled the items to $2.00 as Danielle, with money in hand, placed the coins in her hand. Mrs. Stanford placed them in the register as Demetre and Jeremiah neared the front of the store. "And where is your mother this morning?" Georgina asked.

"She is home with my sister, who isn't feeling well. Seems most of the children at her school have come down with sniffles. So, I'm on my way to give her some herbs."

"The poor dear," Mrs. Love intervened. "You know—"

"Have a remarkable day, Mrs. Love," Georgina greeted. Offended, Mrs. Love took up her basket and headed for the door.

Danielle smelled a familiar cologne and straightened, quickly turning around. "I am very disappointed, Danielle," Demetre breathed. Danielle's eyes grew big. Too afraid to scream, her body was frozen as her heart thumped painfully. The door shut behind Mrs. Love before she could hear the commotion of Danielle starting to run and Jeremiah bear-hugging her from behind. Demetre wrestled a gag over her mouth while she fought and jumped, still in the suffocating arms of

Jeremiah. She whaled, later giving in to exhaustion. A river of tears streamed down her face as she locked eyes with a stoic Georgina and was shuffled out of the back door of the store.

Demetre handed Mr. Stanford the reward money and rushed out the door after his slave and overseer. Jeremiah forced Danielle into the carriage, where she bumped her head on the wall of the cabin.

With Jeremiah driving, Demetre sat staring across from Danielle, unhinged by her tears or her attempt to speak to him. He spoke softly, "Have you any idea what transpired since your departure?" Danielle, with tear-filled eyes, stared back. "Your subordination has affected a number of people, and all I have *ever* been was good to you, Danielle. But I am done."

Within the hour, they arrived in front of the courthouse, where passers-by gawked at Jeremiah's use of force, pulling out the distraught young colored woman and pushing her into the building. Demetre was not far behind, staring straight ahead, ignoring the whispers and disagreeable head shakes of the white men and women.

Demetre stood before the judge, gripping Danielle by the arm. Her hair disheveled, and eyes red and puffy, but she pleaded for the judge to turn his heart toward her favor. He said to Demetre, "Your affidavit, Mr. Soileau." Already in hand, Demetre offered it to the judge who adjusted his glasses and read the document granted to him from a Lafayette County judge almost immediately after his three slaves had fled. The judge read the affidavit, occasionally looking up at Danielle, who sobbed. When he reached the line of the description, he took a longer look at the woman and took pity on her. "This is the lady depicted in your advertising?" he asked.

"A trickster, your honor," Demetre answered. "That is what she is. And yes, she *was*. Soileau & Sons is no more." Danielle looked at Demetre upon hearing this news.

The judge folded the paper and handed it back to Demetre. "That's too bad," he said. "And on your plantation, Mr. Soileau, has production of sugar ceased?"

"Not completely. I am able to sell locally. My hope is to grow the business and begin anew."

"With the exception of *this* one and two others that have run away, you still have all of your slaves?"

"No, your honor. I was forced to sell many of them, including my best workers," he looked at Danielle, "Corrine and Philippe." Danielle shook her head and tried to talk. She almost folded as she wept.

"And in all of your troubles, you came back for this *one*. What do you want with her?"

Annoyed by the questions, Demetre responded, "I want what any slaveholder of a fugitive would desire, the return of my rightful property to do with what I will. And I understand that matters in the South differ from those of the North, but I am fully aware of the law and my rights as it relates to the retrieval of what is mine."

"Mr. Soileau, your indignation is brewing and is unacceptable in my courtroom. You will answer under oath as many questions as I allow. Is that understood?"

"Yes."

The judge raised a brow at Demetre's incomplete response.

"Yes, your honor," Demetre said.

As it was the law that Danielle was prohibited from testifying, within a few minutes, the judge found no loophole that would allow her to remain a free woman in Ohio. And he granted Demetre permission to return his possession to the state of Louisiana.

Riding through the plantation on the way to the main house, Danielle saw a difference in the land. The lack of vibrancy, and above all, the shortage of people. There were no children running barefoot in front of the cabins housing the old women who watched them as their parents worked the fields. No singing nor humming, not even rapid chirping from the sparrows in the trees. The memories plummeted back, striking her especially hard when seeing her mother's cabin and dried garden in the distance, her heart mourning to see her and Lettie again. They had driven past her old cabin, which appeared to be ransacked. The door kicked open, still with shrubs and debris from multiple rainstorms and a small hurricane. Unable to speak due to the gag that remained in her mouth, she looked at Demetre and back at her cabin. He said to her, "You didn't think I'd let you stay in your old quarters, did you?"

Danielle brought her hands closer to her body, clanking the chains connected to the shackles on her wrists and ankles. She stretched her stiff neck and back as she had been locked for days in an uncomfortable position alongside the cargo on the main deck of the boat on which they returned. Had it not been for colored crew members who heard her cries, they would not have snuck hardy meals from the saloon intended for white passengers and fed them to her instead of the scraps Demetre ordered to be given to his prisoner.

Under the port-cochere, Jen and Thadieus greeted their master, offering a glass of wine. "Thadieus," he said, "take my luggage. Jen, give Danielle a bath. Her stench is intolerable."

Jen and Thadieus looked further into the carriage and saw Danielle huddled in the corner with her back towards them. Jen hid her disappointment of Danielle's capture and frowzled condition, "Yes, sir." Demetre grabbed her by the arm and slid her out of the carriage and into the house.

"You may take her to the bathing room," Demetre generously offered. "But she may only use the hat tub," he added, unlocking her shackles and allowing her to be escorted by Jen.

Danielle shivered while rubbing her raw wrists and aching jaw as she stood nude in the small tub receiving a cold sponge bath. When Jen would look her in the face, she rolled her eyes and shook her head in disgust. Danielle sucked air through her teeth as Jen used the water can to rinse Danielle of the talcum soap which trickled onto the open wounds on her ankles.

"A'int got the perfumed kind you're probably used to," Jen hissed. "The mistress took *that* with her when she and Master Demetre dissolved their marriage."

"When?" whispered Danielle

"Soon after you left. A lot happened when you and your mammy decided to run, not caring about the grief that would come our way. But that's what you've always done—whatever you wanted for your gain." Jen waited for an apology, but when none came, she handed Danielle a towel to dry herself. Danielle snatched it and stepped out of the tub, angered at Jen's accusations that the downfall of Soileau & Sons was solely her doing. Jen continued, "And now look at you. Look at all of us. Master may not be able to keep up the plantation much longer. Heard him say he's moving into the New Orleans house. And what do you suppose he'll do with us?"

The women hushed at the sound of the door creaking open and Demetre entering the bathing room. He leaned on the threshold with his arms crossed, watching Danielle dry herself and Jen helping her into a nightgown. "Jen," said Demetre, "leave." Jen hesitated as she looked at Danielle, who gaped coldly at Demetre. "I said, go." He reiterated. Jen bowed her head and scurried out of the room. Demetre continued. "You will wear this at all times," he pulled out a bronze-colored slave badge with a leather band looped around it, and roughly tied it to her neck. Still standing behind her, he placed his hands on her shoulders and breathed on her neck. "You have forgotten to whom you belong, but perhaps this will remind you. I know everything, Danielle." He yanked her head back by her hair. "I know of Alphonse and his audacity to traipse onto my land and look me in the face with an agenda to take you from me." Demetre loosened his grip. "But I know his family. I am familiar with how they maintain a livelihood. I know where they live."

"Please, Monsieur," Danielle pleaded. "They did nothing. *I've* been disobedient."

"You've been more than disobedient," he said, lifting the bottom of her gown. He paused and threw it down, "And now you stand before me, a former runaway, tainted. I never expected this behavior from you, Danielle. Oh, the privileges you were given." Demetre moved in front of her. He grabbed her by her cheeks and squeezed, gritting his teeth and bringing his lips towards hers before pushing away her face.

Weary of all that Demetre had done to her, Danielle was depleted of vigilance. "Oui, Monsieur, I was tainted with the belief that I meant something to you, and I hushed all who told me otherwise. I thought that if I did everything you wanted, perhaps you would not only see me as the property you chose to bed at your command."

"Close your mouth, Danielle."

"I've been foolish to think that I was special to you. My ignorance caused me to believe that you were capable of loving someone other than yourself."

"I said shut your mouth, Danielle."

"It is my duty to be true to you, and it was always my intent, despite your ownership of me. However, when the heart you damage belongs to that of my family, my loyalty to them supersedes. You promised that you would never remove any of my family from this place unless it was their freedom that you granted. And none of it proved to be true."

"My goodness. I have spoiled you into thinking that you are *my* master. Stand down, girl."

"And the cruelty endured in this house that hastened my way with great force, even times of which you did not know or cared *not* to know. But somewhere within the hell that surrounded me was a light, and I chose to follow him. You can pull me out of a general store on free land, and drag me across rivers, but it remains that I unapologetically ran from you and into the arms of my husband, whom I love."

Demetre smiled. His smile turned into laughter. "You are still a girl."

"Issues of my girlhood seem to only appear at your convenience."

"A walking fairy tale is what you are. Well, if your 'husband' comes searching for you, I have something for him. Enough of this." He snatched Danielle by her sore wrists and dragged her through the dark hallway of vacant oil paintings and busts from international travels to the servant's stairway and into Rosezelle's old room, locking her in.

For two days, Danielle tried to escape the 8 by 10-foot room with a bed and a metal toilette pail that Jen emptied when she was allowed to bring bread and water. Although the small round window was locked and too high for Danielle to climb out of, she made numerous failed attempts to break the glass. Jen offered no information about the length of time Danielle would have to reside in the room because she was unsure of it herself and was ordered to avoid verbal interaction. Jen left, closing the door behind her, but forgot to lock it. She listened for retreating footsteps headed in the direction of the main hallway and heard the servant's stairway door close. She quickly slipped on a pair of Rosezelle's battered shoes that she found under the bed and ran out of the room down the narrow path that smelled of sawdust, which engulfed the humid air. She chose the path leading to a guest room where she found clothing in the bureau and quickly slipped back into the stairway that guided her to the parlor, as it was closest to the kitchen, where she was hoping to grab food. And as she started to push open the door, she heard Jen's hushed voice nearby speaking to Thadieus.

Jen whispered, "Mr. Demetre says he wants to move us to New Orleans a few days earlier than planned and is selling what's left of the field hands." Thadieus grunted. "He cannot compete with other sugar plantations and can't keep up with the cost to run this one. The sale of the equipment has already begun."

Thadieus asked, "Did you hear what he will do there?"

"Not certain how he will make his living, but he has a friend who is part-owner of a railroad company and owes Mr. Demetre a favor. I just heard he will be working for the company."

"Is he bringing Danielle with us?"

"I hope not," barked Jen. "But I can't see him selling her either,"

"Well, I think he's gone mad just like Madame," Thadieus recalled. "I saw him just staring at the wallpaper in some of the rooms as if he were looking or listening for something. And I was not allowed into the sitting room on the second floor, yet I saw Mr. Jeremiah walk out of it, and also Joel."

"Joel from the field?"

"Yeah. Sounded like they were repairing something. And from the smell of things, they were. Smelled of plaster."

Jen recalled Demetre's strange behavior as well, "But I just thought it was because he was so angry at Danielle and with everything he had gone through, really since the death of his and Danielle's child."

"Perhaps, but—" Danielle's foot slipped a little on the grainy concrete within the stairway.

"We'll talk later," whispered Thadieus as he raced to the west wing of the house to continue packing Demetre's items for New Orleans.

Jen waited for another sound but moved on to pack books from the library when she heard nothing more. Danielle then slipped out of the stairway and into the kitchen, where she gathered dried meats and bread in a scarf. She moved stealthily out of the kitchen and to the panel in the parlor that would return her to the servant's stairway.

"Traveling through walls, I see," said Demetre's deep, cold voice. Danielle and Demetre gaped at each other in an attempt to see which move the other was about to make. Demetre dropped the handful of bills of sale and charged towards Danielle, who tried to run through the parlor and out to the verandah but was grabbed by the waist from behind and tackled to the floor. While Demetre wrestled with the woman on the floor, trying to stop her from screaming, he reached for a marble vase that had fallen to the carpet and hit Danielle over the head with it, causing her to blackout.

As she stirred into consciousness, Danielle moaned, feeling the pounding of her head. When trying to touch it, she discovered that her arms and wrists were bound and that she had been placed in a round-about chair surrounded by the smell of fresh plaster. Unable to stand, she realized that she was bound by her ankles and legs. She breathed heavily, trying to establish her location, but could only make out that she was in a partially opened corner of a wall. The fourth wall was still being constructed. *But by whom?* she wondered. She tried to loosen herself unsuccessfully and rocked within the chair. Demetre entered the room and frowned when seeing that Danielle regained conscious-ness. He locked the double doors behind him. The furniture in the sec-ond-story sitting room was covered in white sheets like an audience of ghosts.

"Monsieur!" Danielle yelled. "Please, let me go. Why are you doing this to me?"

"You have shown me the utmost betrayal that I simply cannot for-give."

"Monsieur!"

"What a mess you've made of me, Danielle. I cared for you deeply."

"And I, you, but—"

"But you chose to run from me after I told you that you were mine, and I would take care of you as long as you were under my possession."

"Monsieur, I couldn't stay after everything that happened that night with the babe—"

"And was it even my seed?"

"Yes! And she was beautiful, with pretty pink lips, your nose, and your birthmark. Her name was Ruby—"

"You fooled me into believing that you were loyal to me," he said with a shaky voice, "That you loved me as your master—"

"But—"

"All the while, you loved Alphonse, who suddenly appeared, and was able to charm me into selling Alysaundre, and you pretended as if you didn't know him! Well, he is going to know how torture feels, without me giving him the slightest touch." Demetre turned to retrieve a wall frame and a slim door with a missing knob.

"Help me, please, someone!" Danielle hollered. "Oh, cher Dieu! Oh, dear God! Please let me see my Maman and my Pápa again! S'il te plaît, laisse quelqu'un entendre mon cri, oh mon Dieu. Please let someone hear my cry, oh my God!"

"No one is here. I sent the remaining field hands to be auctioned, and Thadieus and Jen were sent to New Orleans with Jeremiah," Demetre shared. What slaves he did not sell, were seized by the banks as collateral. Demetre erected the wooden door.

Danielle sobbed uncontrollably, "Don't leave me to die like this, Monsieur!"

"What does it matter? Because you 'have love'."

As Demetre was about to hammer in a square nail, Danielle began to sing through her tears, the song that made him love her. Demetre rested his head on the frame and closed his eyes. He squeezed them shut, yet tears fell. "Pas plus. No more, Danielle." She continued to sing, "Arrête ça, Danielle. Stop it, now." Demetre swiftly removed the frame and placed a handkerchief around her mouth, her tears soaking the cloth as she stared into his eyes. Without thinking twice, Demetre grabbed the leg of a broken chair, hitting her on top of the head, into unconsciousness.

All was dark and all was quiet when Danielle awoke. The wall had been completed, and she could barely breathe. With the gag still in her mouth, she yelled out when hearing a sound, only to discover that it was an animal scurrying on the roof. Careful not to deplete her energy and oxygen, she rocked the chair as best as she could, hoping to knock down the frame or plastered wooden boards. Over the hours, her prayers turned into pleas of rescue, and over the days—orisons of surrender, until finally, her tired, dehydrated body ceased to live no more.

***

Alette gazed at the window as drips of rain fell from the leaves onto fresh puddles. "I felt her presence the day that I suspected she had died," said Alette. "It felt cool and strangely jubilant and peaceful. The day was sunny and beautiful. The air, crisp with a few brilliant clouds. I remember standing outside and being angry that the world continued on for everyone else, that the only pause was between my family and me.

"When my sister never returned from the general store, I had *tremendous* guilt, thinking that had I not gotten sick, she would not have traveled alone to the store to get something for my illness. My mother said it was not my fault. But over the years, I carried the burden although her heart never mended over time, but grew weaker. She had tried to stay strong for so long for each member of our family, but Danielle's presumed kidnapping or death was the final blow. Maman passed before I reached my 20th birthday, and my Pápa lost his best friend.

"When Danielle disappeared, it was difficult to console Pápa, for he only cried alone, but would express his confusion and lack of fairness in front of us, but more so to God. 'I had just gotten her back,' I overheard him say. Pápa kept busy at his own business, Dani Edmonds Barber Shop, and teaching young Negro men the trade of barbering. From the treatment of customers to the precision of each shave.

"Alysaundre and Alphonse searched everywhere for her and asked their fellow rivermen to be their eyes and ears. They even traveled back to the plantation in search of her, looking from top to bottom. Of course, they never thought to tear down a wall. They were not allowed to search registered documents in trace of Demetre and only had their feet and word-of-mouth to rely upon.

"Alphonse used that anger and torment of not being able to find Danielle by helping to free and reunite others. His nautical knowledge and experience became instrumental to the Underground and various abolitionist groups. Still working under his business, he treated each case as if it were his own. And he never stopped searching for her, even during and after he and Aly came home from serving in the Union Navy during the war. He went on to advocate for the rights of colored folks and building wealth opportunities among our segregated people.

"Alphonse remained family to us all, joining us for Sunday dinners when he could and rarely missing Christmas and Easter holiday visits. He and Aly remained best friends and business partners for life, helping him master the skill of sea and river navigation. To me, Alphonse will always be my brother, my angel.

"Daddy gave him permission to move on from Danielle, but he never did. While he had admirers, he never married nor had children, just as he thought he never wanted to begin with. But he was indescribably magnetized to Danielle, as if by an unseen presence with the power to produce a greater purpose than simply companionship. He once said, 'What a privilege it was for our ripples to touch in the ocean. What a blessing it was to fall in love for the first and final time'." Alette was silent as a small, reminiscing smile came across her face. She made a low, short hum. "Well," she said, "they're together now...

"Aly was forced to see life for what it is—fleeting. He learned that he could either fight against it or grab a huge basket and collect all the treasures it offers. He remained in contact with Trust, sending letters and visiting when he could. Until finally, he married her before the war, with his buddy, Chat present. She was good to him and *for* him, challenging and softening him when he needed. But above all, loving him endlessly as he had reciprocated to her. They had 3 boys and 1 girl. He was always strict with his children about their studies. He was firm about literacy and told them that they would be lost in the world without it. Aly said that he never wanted to rely on the words of others—he wanted to read them for himself. I suppose it gave him a sense of control that he had never owned for most of his life, and he did not want his children to taste the same experience. He left a legacy of creating generations that do not take education for granted. While things weren't always easy for him after the war, no one would ever know it by the smile he kept on his face.

"As for me, I became an instructor, teaching at a colored school for the deaf." She began to speak in sign language, "During girlhood, I was under the tutelage of Nicholas Santee and shared my time in regular classes as well. But it was in Mr. Nicholas' school, where I met my deskmate and future husband, Reginald Dubois. Our union and children made Pápa so happy that he had a chance to see at least one of his little girls get married.

"Pápa's mind was a marvelous one, crafted decades before its time. He used to say that once the mind goes, you have nothing, and he ensured that ours remained strong, no matter what we witnessed or endured. There were whispers on the plantation about whether Pápa was my biological father since Demetre's father, Pierre Soileau Sr., had once had his way with my mother. It turns out whips were not the only way to torture the enslaved. Lingering questions about blood relation can tug at a person's spirit for a lifetime, or so Etiennette had hoped for me. My family had never spoken about it in my presence when I was young, but Pápa always knew that I was his and he was mine. And he confirmed it when he casually mentioned it while I watched him repair his wagon. He said, 'Don't you keep lookin' at me with questions circling around my head. Your Maman was pregnant with you weeks before...it happened. And that is all that needs to be said about the matter.'

"To me, he was my peace of Heaven—my reminder of God's existence in a world where His presence seemed to be sprinkled sparingly. Pápa left us 13 years after I married Reginald. No one will ever fill that place in my heart where God exhaled the name, Pápa Edmond."

A reporter asked, "Do you know what became of the Soileau family?"

Alette's face hardened. "Just as she promised, Simone never returned to the plantation. Corrine was sent to be her maid and traveled everywhere with her, even to the Caribbean when she and Simone fled the United States during the war, along with Simone's cousins and Emile. Even Jeffrey made the 4-year escape and avoided each round of the draft by bribing his doctor to produce a note saying that he was not physically fit to be in battle. He soon fled to Nassau. He regained any lost American assets during the war by trading in Grand Bahama Island and returning to the U.S. as soon as the war ended, with enough money to reclaim land and other assets.

"When freedom came in the U.S., Simone returned and she begged Corrine to stay with her, but Corrine kindly told her that despite belief, colored folks were not created to help non-kin live out their lives, 'just as we are not meant to love your families more than our own.' She said that she needed to find everyone she was expected to forget each time she was sold, including Philippe, who had to fight alongside his new master in the war and wait upon him.

"Philippe saved his master's life on numerous occasions but was never acknowledged for doing so. He ran and was helped by black river men, who led him to Alysaundre, who later helped him find Corrine, who became his wife. Corrine never found any of her sisters, except one who was her sister by divine placement. Me.

"Simone's relationship with Demetre never improved. However, he kept his word of holding her dowry and inheritance. The time apart gave Simone and Matthieu an opportunity to miss one another. After Simone completed her education, she and Matthieu married despite orders from his family who, unsuccessfully scrubbed clean any association with Demetre and Etiennette Soileau. The Soileau name was a brief embarrassment to Simone and Matthieu's marriage, but they pushed through. They maintained financial wealth through Matthieu's work with his family business and even had two children. As any good daughter would, Simone still spoke to her mother, despite the strain within their relationship, but handled her at a distance.

"When looting soldiers ransacked Etiennette's home in northern Louisiana, she and her servants were able to fight them off, killing two of the Union soldiers. But I suppose from that experience, she figured her hidden inheritance didn't solve everything and she missed the presence of a man. Ignoring Simone's warnings, she eventually met one whom she thought was rich and of higher esteem and status than he presented. She became the mistress of the man falsely said to be a widower, thus ruining her 'good' name. She died alone, a decade later, after falling down the stairs in her home and breaking her neck.

"Demetre founded a trading company for a year before being drafted. He would have paid the commutation fee as Matthieu and Emile did, but his loan fell through. When a bomb destroyed his legs, they needed to be amputated below the knee. He had a lot of time to think about his life and the ones he demolished. He slowly began to lose his mind and would often call for Danielle in his sleep. Jen and Thadieus continued to work for him even after they were freed. They proved their loyalty daily by accepting the verbal abuse and being hit with objects. They cared for him when pneumonia and infection took his life in the summer of 1866.

"Upon learning of his death and the passing of Etiennette, I didn't celebrate, nor did I mourn. While I don't know if anyone in this room is associated with the Soileaus in any capacity, I will still say my peace, as no consequences will be greater than the punishment I have already endured, and I have watched my tongue long enough. Early on, I wanted their suffering to continue, and naively did I hope that perhaps they would review the accounts of their ways. But in all of their torment and destruction of families, they were not the ones to believe they did anything wrong, and their hearts would not be positively transformed if God were to give them longer life in pain, for Death had scraped its boots outside their door once before. I will say, some servants have forgiven them. But as I sit here, able to see the effects of evil and still breathe it and hear it in my mind, and feel it through my veins, I can only say that I welcome the Lord's intervention in my heart; however, I have not yet lightened my burden.

"I tell my sister's story openly to share the experiences of bondage and the perseverance that came of it, and will continue to live on in our descendants. I understand that her story may not be mentioned in your paper, simply because we, as a country, are selective in whom we choose to honor and what we choose to acknowledge. Either way, I am not here to persuade anyone to take pity on those of us who lived through those heinous times. Nor is it my responsibility to convince anyone that slavery really occurred, although it has been carved into many of our family trees as evidence. However, I tell this story so that you and everyone who has lined up to see the body of a human in the wall will know that she will be laid to rest with dignity in a beautiful, gated tomb next to her family. I share this story for others to understand that she was a young woman who loved, sang, and lived. And her name was Danielle."

Acknowledgements

Song of Redemption was almost never published and was sure to be another piece of oral history to later soften into a whisper before becoming darkened silence. This book was a product of defiance against those who were against its crafting and subject matter. I would like to thank several people who encouraged me to confront with pen and paper, both the richness of the lives captured within this work and the heavy issues that frightened me.

To my mother, Akilah, who has been the caregiver and friend to so many wonderful people, young and old, and the gateway to my encounters with them. Thank you for introducing me to those who graciously shared stories of their lives from sharecroppers, holocaust survivors, and construction workers who discovered the body of a slave in a Louisiana mansion. Thank you for believing in my craft since the age of seven and for boasting to your friends at every opportunity.

To my husband Joey, who has always shied away from the idea of visiting plantations but accompanied me during research and trips to Louisiana. Thank you for listening to my verbal gymnastics regarding my late-night findings, and for taking an interest in the many written drafts.

My loud, hilarious, messy reminders of God's blessings—my Jacia and Jayce, you are all things beautiful. While writing this book, there were times when I needed to hold you a little tighter and was grateful to be able to do what so many of our ancestors were not always allowed to act upon, which was simply to raise and mother their babies. Thank you for allowing Mommy to stare at you in wonderment as you played. Thank you for letting me kiss all over your glorious, perfect faces. I love you.

My love of storytelling, history, antiques, and genealogy has landed me into a world of literary magic because of you, Carole (Granny). Thank you for sharing with me our family legacy in all of its grit, perseverance, and fascination. My strong appreciation for their strength is due to your stories about them and all that I have researched about their lives. I could not help but pay homage to them by sprinkling our family surnames throughout the book. I take nothing for granted, yet I owe everything to all who came before me, including you and mom.

To my best friend Nekiya, whose immeasurable support has always made me feel so blessed that our friendship was paired divinely. Thank you for always believing in me, even years ago during the birth of *Song of Redemption.*

It is with the utmost humility that I thank every professor who has advised me and librarian in Charlotte, and Louisiana who has helped me pull every reference book if they felt that it was what I needed to complete *Song of Redemption.*

Thank you all. My mason jar of gratitude is filled to the brim.

About the Author

Malika J. Stevely is an award-winning author of historical fiction, essays, and African American and women's literature. A graduate of California State University–Fullerton, she holds multiple degrees in English & Comparative Literature and Communications. A former newspaper reporter, she has published numerous articles and conducted interviews with civil rights and literary icons.

Her work has received five-star recognition and has been honored as both a recipient and a finalist of U.S. and international literary awards.

She resides in North Carolina with her husband and children, with whom she enjoys singing show tunes at the top of her lungs. *Song of Redemption* is her debut novel.

www.malikajstevely.com
Facebook: @malikajstevelywriter
Instagram: @malikajstevelyauthor
Author photograph: Lowaunz Farrow

9 798218 548162